10.99

Before Night Falls

MaryAnn Minatra

HARVEST HOUSE PUBLISHERS
Eugene, Oregon 97402

Cover by Left Coast Design, Portland, Oregon

BEFORE NIGHT FALLS
Copyright © 1996 by Harvest House Publishers
Eugene, Oregon 97402

Library of Congress Cataloging-in-Publication Data
Minatra, MaryAnn
      Before night falls / MaryAnn Minatra.
         p.   cm. — (Legacy of honor ; 1)
       ISBN 1-56507-432-7 (alk. paper)
    1. Germany—History—1933–1945—Fiction. 2. Married people—Germany—Fiction.
    3. Americans—Germany—Fiction. I. Title. II. Series: Minatra, MaryAnn, 1959–
    Legacy of honor , 1.
    PS3563.I4634B44 1996
    813'.54—dc20
                                        96-10713
                                            CIP

Printed in the United States of America.

96 97 98 99 00 01 02 / BC / 10 9 8 7 6 5 4 3 2 1

*The Legacy of Honor series is dedicated
to the memory of those common men and women
who showed uncommon moral courage
in the dark Nazi years.*

"There are stars whose radiance is visible on earth though they have long been extinct. There are people whose brilliance continue to light the world though they are no longer among the living. These lights are particularly bright when the night is dark. They light the way...."

—Hannah Senesh
Hungarian Jew, 1921–1944

Berlin 1930s

German Words

Auf Wiedersehen: Good bye
Bitte: Please
Danke: Thank you
Frau: Mrs.
Fraulein: Miss
Gute Nacht: Good evening
Guten Tag: Good day
Guten Morgen: Good morning
Herr: Mr.

Ja: Yes
Jagerschnitzel: Veal steak
  with mushrooms
Nein: No
Ruhig: Quiet
Schnell: Hurry
Schokolade: Chocolate
Strasse: Street
Wehrmacht: German army

Cast of Characters

BERLIN

Farbers
I.E.: exmilitary man, wealthy industrialist
Irwin: oldest son of I.E. Farber
Eric: Middle son of I.E. Farber
Maximillian: youngest son of I.E. Farber

Morgans
Josef: doctor and friend of Max Farber
Emilie: Dr. Morgan's Niece, American

Muellers
Heinz: Farber estate caretaker
Marta: Heinz' wife
Walther: the eldest son
Maria: daughter
Wilhelm: youngest son

Heydrichs
Reinhard: Farber family friend and neighbor
Lena: Reinhard's wife
Elaina: Reinhard's sister

NUREMBERG

Rabbi Bergmann: Retired rabbi in Nuremberg
Natalie: Rabbi's granddaughter
Helga Weisner: Bergmann housekeeper
Handel: Nuremberg cafe owner, Wilhelm's employer

Prologue

Israel, 1970

Jerusalem. One of the ancient, international cities of the earth, its stones a silent witness to the passage of emperors and conquerors, armies, slaves, zealots, and prophets—and a young carpenter-king. History had appointed this place to receive the tears and toil, laughter and agony of a millennium.

It was a sunny morning, the sky an intense blue like a mirror suspended over the placid waters of the Mediterranean, a margin of gauzy clouds to the north. In the east rose a crenelated skyline of modern highrises, flat-roofed Arab dwellings, onion-domed mosques gleaming dull bronze and ocher in the sunshine, slender minarets, and spires of Christian churches. Low, undulating hills of olive trees glistened darkly from a soft, early morning rain. Indeed, it was a beautiful, fragrant morning at Yad Veshem. The directors were very pleased—a gray and rainy morning would have added greater sobriety to the already somber ceremony. Yet today was a celebration too, light over darkness, good over evil, triumph and tragedy inextricably entwined. Today was a day to proclaim courage. Yes, the day was fitting.

The complex of buildings known as Yad Vashem had been started in 1953, 8 years after the rampage against the Jews of Europe had ended. It included a synagogue designed after those humble worship places that had been obliterated in Eastern Europe, a research center, and a museum with the names of the largest concentration camps etched on its walls. It was a place to honor the millions of innocents who had perished. And now another memorial.

"The Righteous Ones of the Nations of the World," non-Jews who had defied personal fear and terrible retribution to show compassion to and to rescue Jews, were remembered here now. Most had made the ultimate sacrifice in the flame of Nazism, a roll call of courage from the countries of Europe. A carob tree, sturdy and surviving, had been planted in the name of each honored one. There were well over a hundred along the path. Today, another tree had been set in the earth.

The prime minister herself had come to this ceremony. She had presented the medal with the Talmudic inscription to the frail little French woman standing nervously beside her.

"'Whoever saves a single soul, it is as if he has saved the whole world,'" she read in a deep voice amplified in the clear air.

The French woman fingered the medal, tears pooling in her eyes as she remembered years past.

"Why did you, Madame? Why did you help the Jews when you could have lived your own life safely?" the translator asked.

"I would not look away," she said slowly. "I could not..."

"You could have saved one," the translator insisted gently. "To save only one—there would have been far less risk."

"Save only one?" She shook her head and smiled faintly. "No. Only once could they take my life. So there was no greater risk to me for one or one dozen."

Soon the ceremony was over. The crowd quietly dispersed down the sloping walk to the parking lot. Two workers, leaning on their shovels, waited until the last guest had departed to tidy up the planting. They watched Prime Minister Meir walk energetically to her long black car, surrounded by government officials and ten serious-faced soldiers. Then it was quiet.

They firmed the deep red soil around the tree. The young man called Shimon looked up, over the sunlit hills toward Jerusalem.

"Think they'll ever find all of them . . . or most of them . . . to honor?" he mused.

"Huh?"

"The Righteous Gentiles. There must be thousands of good men and women we haven't heard of yet. Think how many trees we may plant!"

The older man snorted. "I hope they're out there. Millions of poor dead Jews and only a few who stood up for them. Hope to Jehovah there are more out there somewhere."

"I've heard they are even considering some Nazis—you know, who really weren't Nazis deep down, who tried to help the Jews in little ways."

"Fairy tales," the man countered. "Go look at the museum if you aren't sure how the Nazis felt about the Jews. Like you crush a bug under your shovel without a thought—that's how they were. Gone. Poof!"

The younger man shook his head. "No, no, not all of them. There were some . . . there had to be! You wait, Isaac, someday we'll be planting a tree to honor a German, a Nazi!"

"You are crazy, and personally I would not come to work on such a day as that!"

Shimon shrugged. "Well, my kids know there was a ceremony today. They'll be eager to hear about the gentile when I get home tonight. Mary has them keep a notebook about them."

Isaac shook his head and retreated down the path toward the buildings, but Shimon remained. He knocked the dirt from his shovel absently. His mind was on the ceremony just over. He could still see the little French woman and hear her voice, *I could not look away . . . I could not.* Today was such a day that Shimon liked working at the memorial. The courageous ones restored his faith in man. Even with a homeland now . . . He shook his head and sighed deeply. Times were still hard in this promised land. Yet his coworker's pessimism did not infect him. There were rescuers from every country, even Germany. There had to be good men and women who had not been filled with Adolf Hitler's venom.

As certain as the hills he had grown to love, he knew they were out there. *Yad Vashem.* "A name and a place."

1
Legacy of Honor

Berlin, 1916

Max decided he hadn't had such a nice afternoon in a very long time. Even if this was his twelfth birthday, he hadn't expected to have a fine time at all. The day had started with little promise. His two older brothers had given him their token gifts in a rather bored, disinterested fashion: a compass from Irwin, a knife from Eric. Then they had ignored him, preoccupied with their own pursuits for the day and their friend Reinhard. Frau Mueller, the housekeeper, had made him an elaborate breakfast of his favorite foods including streusel. She had given him an affectionate hug, then hurried off to her chores. The grand house was deeply quiet and still. It had not been a very impressive birthday celebration for the son of one of Germany's wealthiest families— but there was a war on. Perhaps birthdays were counted as frivolous luxuries in wartime, even for the wealthy.

The 12-year-old walked to the front door, opened it, and sat down on the broad steps that led to the sweeping circular drive. *If father were here...* Father would have taken him riding or something. Max didn't care about the gifts his father would have given him. Just to have him home— as busy as he would be. To have his father's arm around his shoulders, even fleetingly. Father would smile at him, tousle his hair, make him feel... *But father was at war.*

Max frowned, his head leaning on his hand. He absently picked at a fresh scab on his knee. It had taken only one swift shove from 15-year-old Irwin to send the slim 11-year-old sprawling. A scratched knee. He hadn't fared too badly this time.

Max didn't want to think about his mother. Thinking of her would make him cry, and surely one of his brothers would happen along to tease him. And he didn't feel like fighting—not on his birthday certainly. But if mother *had* been here things would have been different. Surely Irwin wouldn't be so mean, or Eric so teasing, and father, well, father was so preoccupied and busy.

Mother smelling of roses—he could still remember her favorite perfume. It had only been four years. Of course he could still remember her.

"Maxi, my little son." She would smile and pull him close. A sputtering motor drew Max from his memories. A car was coming down the drive. He stood up and shaded his eyes against the sun. Father? His face broke into a broad grin when he recognized the little coupe. Even in his thinness and his large sad-and-sober eyes, Max Farber was a handsome boy. Thick blond hair framed a deeply tanned face and blue eyes.

The car stopped and Max hurried down the steps.

"There's a boy! A sturdy lad, ja!" This was followed by a deep laugh.

"Dr. Josef!" The boy impulsively grabbed the man's hand. He didn't usually display such affection.

"Didn't think I'd forget, did you, Max?"

Max dropped the hand and retreated a step, suddenly shy and embarrassed. "No, I mean, I didn't think you knew. I didn't expect . . . you know . . ." He shrugged and looked down the gravel drive. The doctor cleared his throat loudly. "Well come on, boy, the fish are waitin' for us! Go tell Frau Mueller to put something together for us to munch on."

The River Spree ran north of the Farber estate. It was only a jog from the property and one of Max's favorite haunts. Huge trees shaded the bank and were perfect for climbing. The river was perfect for swimming, casual angling, sailing homemade boats—or dreaming. The boy and doctor were gone until dusk found them trudging up the lawns, dusty and tired, as the sun was gliding away. It had been a long, sunny, wonderful afternoon for Max.

"Stay for dinner?" he asked eagerly.

The doctor winced to hear the obvious longing in the young voice. "Sorry, Max. I have a train to meet. My brother and his family are due in."

"Your brother who lives in America?"

"Ja, that's the very one."

"Any kids?" he asked just a little wistfully.

"My niece is around five, I believe."

Max frowned, *Too young. Even a girl might make a nice playmate for a change.* The boy sighed. "Oh well," he said, kicking at the ground. "Irwin says Americans are uncouth and strange. He says they are culturally inferior."

"Irwin says that?" the doctor chuckled.

Max nodded vigorously. "He and Reinhard say that; they agree."

"Reinhard? I thought Reinhard was your friend."

"He is ... sometimes. He likes to be with Irwin. Says Irwin is tougher. You know."

The doctor stroked his beard, his brown eyes dilating in anger. "That scar along your jaw. How did that happen? It must have been while I was away in Vienna."

"It was nothing," Max said, kicking at the turf, "an accident."

"Oh? An accident courtesy of your brother or Reinhard?"

"Reinhard, Irwin, and I were playing soccer. I fell; Reinhard said it was an accident. I have to believe him—he's my friend—and Irwin backed him up."

"I see."

"Anyway, Irwin doesn't like to be disagreed with—can get your ears boxed if you do. Father says that's the Farber way, strength and force. Irwin has it, and Eric tries, but I don't." He lowered his voice as he looked up at the man with eyes that were anxious. "But I have to have the Farber something, don't I, Doctor?"

The doctor loved this boy. He had never got past wishing he was his own son. He caressed the boy's shoulder and leaned over confidentially. "Honor, integrity, kindness, Max. You have all three. In generous measure. That makes up for strength and force. I have to go now Max. Ah! I almost forgot! If my head weren't sewed on I'd surely lose it!"

Max smiled.

"Twelve years old today, hmm? Fully 12 years? Not 11.9?"

Max's smile widened. "Of course. You know it."

The doctor reached into his car. "Here's a little something for you, Max. One of my favorites."

Max took the package. "Danke."

The doctor nodded. "Go ahead, open it."

Max tore off the paper. Of course, a book. They shared a love of reading. A red book with gold lettering and gold-edged paper. A book you handled carefully.

"This is one of your favorites?" Max asked as he opened the cover. The doctor nodded again, smiling, and rocked back on his heels very pleased.

"Then it shall be one of my favorites," Max said solemnly.

" *The Scarlet Pimpernel* by Baroness Orczy. Difficult for most boys your age, but not if they have a sharp mind like yours. It's about courage," the doctor said as he climbed into his auto, "that's another thing you have, Maximillian Farber. Enjoy the book. We'll talk it over when I'm out next time. Auf Wiedersehen, my boy!"

Max returned to the stone steps and watched the car. It slowed at the big black gates and the boy waved energetically. He hugged the book to his chest, but he didn't open the volume yet. He would wait for the delicious privacy of his bedroom.

"Honor, integrity, kindness, courage," he murmured.

In his 12-year-old mind he wasn't exactly certain what each word meant, but he was determined to find out. And prove his best friend right.

1918

It had been a very long, hot, dry summer in Berlin. Lightning, in brilliant incandescent flashes, split the night sky nearly every evening. In this capital city, which was constrained by the cultural and economic hardships of war, the citizens often sat on their front steps to watch this free entertainment. It seemed to many that some cosmic battle was being waged in the heavenlies, as if the great conflict south of the Rhine, now in its death agonies, had surged up into the sky.

On the Farber estate, some 25 miles east of that German city, Dr. Josef Morgan paced in one of the upstairs bedrooms of the grand house. He glanced at the curtains that didn't even flutter with a moth's wings and wished again for rain—rain that you could smell and hear in the preamble music, and could certainly imagine. But the heavy clouds remained aloof and unyielding. He sighed deeply and clicked open his pocket watch. Fifteen minutes past ten. He went to the open window and looked down. Nothing. No motor lights or hurried steps. Only the dark shape of his own car. He had sent for the father, but the father had not come. He didn't have much confidence he would. A man on a battlefield was not always easy to reach. Still, he held a small stirring of hope.

He returned to the chair by the bed. The bedroom door opened and a woman entered. She passed him a cup of tea, which he accepted without a word or meeting her eyes. This had been a nightly ritual for almost three weeks and there was no need for words between them. She gave the figure in the big four-poster bed one swift glance. She could detect no change—in any aspect—toward life or death. Like the physician, she could not see how life could remain so tenuously held. Then the doctor was alone again. He moved closer to the bed, picked up the thin wrist, and took the shallow pulse. He leaned forward.

"Max, I've known you were strong, and you're proving it, lad. Keep on now, don't... don't give up."

The eyes flickered open only a moment before they closed. Dr. Morgan sponged the dry, cracked lips. With his professional eye, he studied the thin body and gaunt face. He calculated the boy was now under a hundred pounds. Max had been in the prime of his growing when struck ill. The doctor wondered just how this would affect the boy's stamina and development when he recovered. He *must* recover... There was a discreet knock at the door. The doctor frowned. What need was there of knocking? Eric Farber entered the room with obvious hesitation, his eyes seeking the doctor and avoiding his brother's bed. Dr. Morgan scowled as the boy approached.

"What is it, Eric?" he asked curtly.

Eric finally looked at his sleeping brother.

"How is he tonight?"

Morgan softened. "The same, he's about the same, Eric."

The boy licked his lips nervously. "He's... so thin!"

"Ja."

"Does he ever wake up and talk?"

The doctor nodded. "He was awake this morning, told me he was terribly hot."

"I, I wish I had known."

"Why?"

"I . . . don't know. Maybe I could have spoken to him."

"And what would you have said to your brother, Eric?"

The boy did not miss the man's suspicious tone. He looked to him. "I don't know exactly." He shifted nervously. "You know . . . my mother died from tuberculosis."

"Ja, I know that."

Eric cleared his throat. How small and pale his little brother was! "I don't want Max to die," he said haltingly. "I really don't."

The doctor reached out to give Eric's shoulder a pat. Oh, how all the Farber boys needed attention and affection, even the calloused Irwin.

"Well, remember what you are feeling now, Eric, when Max is up and about and you're thinking of teasing him."

Eric colored. Nothing much in this household got past the doctor's practiced scrutiny.

"Yes, sir. You think then that Max will—"

"Of course I do. Max is strong though he appears to be little more than a skeleton with a wisp of life in him."

"But my mother," Eric persisted.

"The main difference between your mother's case and Max's is that her disease was well advanced before it was detected. Not so with your brother." He drew a deep breath. "He has the resiliency of youth."

"Yes, sir. Well . . ."

When Eric was gone, Morgan returned to the bedside. He did not expect any other visitors to this sick room tonight. He settled in for the hours until one of the servants would come to take his place. This vigil was another nightly routine they kept. He would think about these Farber sons awhile to help himself stay awake.

Irwin. At 17, he was much like his grandfather, the first I.E. Farber, founder of the family business. Stern and proud, he had been a military man in his youth, well decorated in the Franco-Prussian War. He had been one the aristocrats who were so respected and revered in German culture. He begat only one son, Max's father, Irwin Eric, who took up the dual passions for business and military service. He did not have the autocratic stamp of his father, however, that cold aloofness so carefully cultivated. Max's father, for all his faults, the doctor conceded, was a kind, generous, warm man—when he was home. Morgan suspected Farber was continuing a legacy that he supposed would be enough for his three sons. To see them occasionally, to meet their physical needs—it was all he seemed to know how to do. The grandfather would have gloried to see himself appear in another generation in the third Irwin Farber.

Josef's thoughts drifted to when he'd first met the wealthy family years ago. *How many now?* It had been the summer when Frau Farber had died. He had been brought in for consultation in what proved the final months of her life. From then on, he'd been the family's physician. Though so often absent, Josef could sense Herr Farber's implicit trust in him. Irwin had been a lad of 11 then, Eric, 9, Max, 8. The doctor had quickly evaluated the family. Three neglected-yet-cared-for boys, left largely to household staff and tutors. Irwin had been a bully as long as Morgan had known them. He was the oldest, tallest, strongest, and unashamed to wield his power. He had spoken to Morgan in a haughty tone their first meeting, reminding the medical man that his grandfather had been a decorated war veteran. "I am the heir," he had boasted.

The doctor had grinned good-naturedly. "Just be sure you're worthy of it, lad."

Irwin's face had darkened in a terrible scowl.

Eric Farber. The doctor stroked his beard in thought. He knew Eric fell under Irwin's intimidating shadow, was always eager to please, and avoided a conflict. He couldn't know how this tendency in Eric would be exploited in the age ahead. Yet there were rare times Eric feebly defended his youngest brother or objected to Irwin's mischief. In the end, most often, Irwin ruled. *Eric needs backbone*, Josef diagnosed.

Then his eyes rested on the boy sleeping fitfully in the big bed, a frail specter amongst a vastness of coverlet. He picked up the thin arm, tracing the blue veins that were like fine spider webs under the skin. "Max," he whispered.

He had loved Max from the first, taken him to heart as the son he had never had. Their initial meeting had been outside Frau Farber's bedroom. Max had been hunched on the floor staring listlessly at the carpet. He had stood immediately at the doctor's approach, the red-rimmed eyes testifying to the boy's fears for his mother. But the doctor hadn't understood the bruises on the arms—not yet then.

"I'm Max Farber," the boy said clearly.

Morgan was momentarily taken back by the confident tone. But then, this was the son of one of Germany's most noted families. Of course.

"I'm Dr. Morgan, Max."

"Just help my mother," he returned with calm bluntness.

"I will certainly try."

He looked back at the young man now struggling to survive. He was the fulfillment of his mother and the best of his father. Sensitive, honest, brave. *A boy to be proud of*, the doctor smiled wryly, thinking of the grandfather Farber with his walrus mustache, chest decorated with medals, and imposing stature in the family portrait gallery below.

Josef knew Max defied his older brother in a quiet, almost casual way. Max would speak the truth calmly—and pay the price in bruises and cuts. 'You are wrong, Irwin. You shouldn't do that.'

'Have you ever told your father of Irwin's bullying, Max? Because if you haven't I will!' Josef had asked once.

Max's eyes had widened. 'Father knows. He says I must learn to stand up for myself. And I will!'

Josef shook his head sadly at the memory. The doctor closed his eyes and was soon dozing. The door opened and he awoke. It was the groundskeeper. He came forward quietly but strangely confident and the doctor stood up stiffly.

"Yes, Heinz?"

"I asked Hannah if I could take her place tonight, sitting up with the boy, and she said if it were all right with you, I could. I would like to very much, doctor."

"Well, a . . ." The doctor adjusted his tie and vest. He didn't like being caught napping. His voice was gruff, "I suppose it will be all right. You cannot fall asleep however, Heinz. If the boy wakes, he'll need care."

The man nodded and smiled. "Ja, ja, I know. I won't sleep— brought the book to read to Max for awhile." He shoved a thick Bible toward the doctor who moved back as if Heinz had pushed a sword at him. "Yes, well, a . . . here are your instructions. Very important you understand."

Heinz patted the man's arm. "We'll be fine."

"I'm just down the hall if you need anything. Come at once for me if there's a change."

"Yes, sir, I will. You're Max's good doctor."

The doctor hesitated at the foot of the bed. He hated to leave. Finally he relaxed. "I've lost a few patients over the years, Heinz," he nodded, "but of them all, I don't want to lose this one."

Another comforting pat from the groundskeeper.

"Life and death aren't really in your hands, Dr. Morgan. Now you go get some rest; Heinz will watch."

The physician retreated, just a little piqued at the laborer's words.

Heinz Mueller did not take the chair. He stood gazing at the boy for several minutes. His eyes closed and his lips moved silently. Then he was pacing the floor, his hands clutched tightly together. For he knew there was no one but himself and his wife to pray for the young Farber son. He smiled and nodded as if he heard a comforting voice just over his shoulder. Two hours later he went to the chair and began to read from the well-worn book.

It would soon be sunrise—it was very early. The staff was not yet stirring when a tall figure bounded quickly up the steps. The man flipped off the military cape and hat and softly entered the bedroom. He was only mildly surprised to find the caretaker at his son's bedside. Heinz smiled and nodded as he left the room.

Herr Farber came to the bedside. He had looked on death and dying enough that Max's condition did not shock him. But what he did not expect was how much his sleeping son looked like his wife. He began to cry as he knelt at the bedside.

"Maxie, Maximillian...son..."

The man was sobbing and trying to form a prayer as he never had done before. "Take me, not my son, take me."

Max stirred, feeling the hard grip on his hand. His eyes opened. "Sir?"

"Guten Tag, Max."

"You're home?"

Farber nodded. "Yes, Max, I'm home. Now you must get better."

"The war...is...over?"

"Don't try to talk, Max, you're too weak. The war is not over, but I am home."

"Oh."

"Max."

"Sir?"

"I love you, son."

Max Farber smiled weakly.

Down the hallway the doctor was waking. He rolled over to face the window, to judge the hour. The curtains moved in a sudden, light breeze and he thought he heard leaves falling. He leaned up on his elbow. A slow, distant, soft sound.

It was raining.

1920

It was the first lawn party the Heydrich estate had held since the armistice had been signed 18 months earlier. The German population had not felt very festive since that November morning when the French and German generals had met in the wagon coach in Compiegne forest to settle the peace. The fighting was over, leaving silent guns and littered battlefields. Sons and fathers could come home. Peace after four years of war. The economy and the government were in disarray. The war had taken more than just a blood toll; it would take years to rebuild from the ruins. Despair and dissolution gripped the veterans and populace. All that sacrifice . . . for what prize? They were proud, the drive to conquer like a passion in their very blood. The Treaty of Versailles, like a vulture circling a corpse, came swiftly behind the defeat. Now their humiliation flamed to anger and indignation. In a decade that smoldering flame would come to life again with a heat unparalleled in German history.

But for now, parties were few and attended with little enthusiasm.

Frau Heydrich was weary of such pessimism and gloom. Her husband had come home from the conflict, whole and well. And it was time to end these tiresome debates, sullen moods, senseless threats of revenge. "Look at France," she declared stoutly. It had borne the weight of the four years of fighting; it was scorched and ravaged. The Fatherland remained, and all that was beautiful in it. So, over the protests of her family, she held a party on the lawn of their vast estate for no other reason than to celebrate the advent of spring in Germany. From the smiles, the laughter, the air of geniality among the milling crowd, it was clear to see Frau Heydrich's decision was received with relief and favor.

Like the neighboring Farber estate, the River Spree flowed at the edge of the back gardens and lawn. Up the sloping grass to the house, tables and chairs had been arranged with colorful umbrellas. The holiday picnic of fine food, old friends, and a string quartet that played unobtrusively in the shade of a tree recreated a festive atmosphere reminiscent of more prosperous times. Extra boats had been rented for young people to glide along the silver-sheened river. Half-a-dozen skiffs were moored, another six were sailing carelessly in the warm sunshine.

In one boat, a young man was rowing with ease, his oars dipping into the cool water quietly and rhythmically. He watched his efforts—he did not want the young lady half reclined in the stern to think his skill awkward. But it really didn't matter if he jerked and wobbled uncontrollably the entire voyage—or even pitched them both in the Spree. The young girl would hardly have noticed. She was in the boat with the most handsome boy at the party—or perhaps all of Berlin—so decreed local adolescent opinion. It was excusable if she felt a little pride at being with 16-year-old Max Farber. She suspected, no, she knew that most of the other girls were envying her.

She liked to watch the way the muscles in Max's forearms pushed against his linen shirt. Dressed in cream pants and cream shirt, like the other boys, she thought he looked marvelous. He was wearing a straw hat that shaded his face. She could not see his eyes, only his mouth and chin, unless he looked up to speak. She sighed in raptured contentment.

"Having a good time, Elaina?" he asked just a little absently.

She nodded, not trusting that she could keep the adoration she felt out of her voice.

"Eric told me about the scandal you caused in church Sunday," she smiled.

Max nodded and grinned. "You know, I really didn't mean to cause a scandal. I was just tired of the old biddy! She had poked Eric and I a few times for whispering. You know, I could practically feel her eyes burning the back of my neck. And she was supposed to be worshiping!" He laughed again as he thought of the day.

He and Eric were in church; Irwin was off on a business trip with their father in Munich. Max was restless and bored, so he started thinking of the race he and Eric had wagered against each other. They had whispered fiercely about it as the hymns drew to a close, and the rector began his hour-long recitation. Frau Hoffman's strict observation of the two Farber heirs sitting just in front of her enraged her. No one else had noticed the boys' irreverence, but she did. With a finger as sharp and firm as a dagger she had jabbed them both in the shoulders, then necks, finally pulling Max's ear when she determined he was the worst offender of the two. She leaned forward and whispered fiercely, "You are not behaving as a Farber should, young man!" Those around her stirred uneasily and looked embarrassed. Even the cleric had glanced up from his text with an annoyed look. Eric turned red, then refocused on the minister. Max turned red as well, his youthful anger boiling. For 20 minutes he held himself rigidly still. He was thinking.

Then he drew out a paper and pencil, resting them on a hymnal on his knee. He was a rather poor artist, but a fairly good hand at caricature. The head came first with its limp, greasy-looking crown of hair. He drew in a monocle over a bulging, porcine-looking eye set in a flaccid face. It was clear to all in his row and the one behind, who was the subject of this little sketch. A quickly subdued titter went through the row behind him. He chewed his pencil in rapt study. *Women should never wear a monocle*, he decided, *very unfeminine*. Next came the torso. Now the entire back row and Max's own, were staring fascinated. The sermon was some dim oratory quite irrelevant to this unfolding drama.

Frau Hoffman was purple with suppressed rage. Her breathing was labored and a vein in her ample neck was bulging. She was whispering to herself through gritted teeth that she must endure this insolence until the service was over. *Then! Oh, then, it would be a fine spectacle to see!* And Max Farber would be upbraided and the incident chuckled at over dinner by the parishioners.

But Max must finish his drawing. It would not do for a Farber to leave anything incomplete. Carefully, with an exaggerated flourish, he drew the large protruding backside. Eric was shaking with laughter; the back row was looking to their hymnals with acute interest and suspicious trembling. And Frau Hoffman forgot entirely that she was in Berlin's largest protestant church with hundreds to see her sudden explosion. She stood up, the monocle swinging vigorously from its chain, her considerable girth violently energized as she brought her hymnal down on Max Farber's head. It didn't make the society page—but it was spoken of in many Berlin homes for days.

"Ah, what a morning that was," Max announced.

"Will she tell your father?" Elaina asked.

Max shrugged. "She said she would. Irwin will have something to say about it too, you know. He'll say I've soiled the family name or something."

Max rested his oars as he looked back to the land, his face shaded with unhappiness. Max's reasoning over the incident was typically simple—both he and Frau Hoffman had gotten what they deserved. It should be laughed over then forgotten.

Elaina was regretting she'd brought up the subject. She spoke up quickly.

"Do you like school, Max? Reinhard says you don't."

"I don't know. It's all right, I suppose. We have so much military drill and I get kind of tired of that. I do like the literature class and sports."

"Is that all?"

He studied her a moment. *Should I trust her?*

"I like music class. I like it when the professor lets me stay after school and play."

"You play beautifully, Max. You could be a concert pianist when you grow up!"

He shook his head and looked back to the water.

"I don't think so."

"Why not?"

He sighed. "I'm a Farber. Farber's go into the military, then the family business. They've been doing that for a couple of generations."

"And you don't want to?"

The finely chiseled face was thoughtful. His looks were beyond the years of a carefree, 16-year-old boy.

"No," he admitted slowly, "but then, I don't know what I would rather do."

He watched the other boats. He could see Eric racing against another boy. "I do have one idea of something I'd like to do," he said smiling.

"What?"

He turned the little craft and pulled with long strokes until they rounded a bend in the river. They were out of sight of the house and other boats. They were alone.

"I'd like to kiss you, Elaina," he said leaning toward her.

Sunshine and beauty, optimism and hope—they were a beautiful picture there on the river. Germany did have a noble future in fine young men and women—if she cared to take it up.

Elaina laughed. "You are an odd boy sometimes, Max," she said as she moved forward.

"Why?"

"Because you ask if you may kiss when most don't."

He frowned a moment, a little crease between the full, blond brows. "Well, I wouldn't want to if the girl weren't willing. I've not kissed a girl before; I'd like you to be the first."

Elaina was very happy. To kiss the young Farber heir! It was a simple, innocent kiss that they both enjoyed, tasting a new and exciting pleasure.

It was late afternoon, the lawns patterned in purple and gold, when Max and Elaina returned to the party. They could see the crowd of young people gathered behind the summer house. Max could hear his brother's voice before he saw him. It was raised in a belligerent tone that Max recognized all too well. When they stepped around the building holding hands, a dozen young people stood lounging about, sensing the coming drama in this sedate, afternoon party. Max took in the scene quickly. There was some problem between Irwin and a younger boy. No one was objecting to Irwin's rough manner. Elaina's brother, Reinhard, was smiling.

Eric appeared suddenly, quietly, beside Max. He spoke in a low whisper, "Irwin has been in this mood all afternoon. He—"

"With Irwin it isn't a mood," Max interrupted tiredly.

"Frau Heydrich will be upset if there's trouble," Eric said nervously as Irwin began to shove the boy. The brothers exchanged a look—they both knew about shoving.

"Go find Father," Max said quietly, wanting to move away with Elaina, to find something cool to drink.

"He's talking with some men. . . . He wouldn't want to be bothered," Eric pressed.

Max sighed.

The boy called Rudi was pale and nervous. The skinny youth could see he had little chance against the older, heavier Irwin Farber. Max stood on the perimeter, but Irwin didn't give him a glance.

"I said apologize to Miss Braun! I won't tell you again!" Irwin shouted.

"I did nothing wrong, Irwin Farber. You need to mind your own business!" Rudi answered with obvious trembling.

The little group tensed.

"You did nothing except speak to my girl," Irwin replied angrily.

"I don't think she's your girl."

"I'm going to wipe your face in the dirt, then you'll apologize to me and Miss—"

"Irwin, wait."

Irwin swung around, his eyes blazing. "Go back to your rowing, Max."

"Leave him alone, Irwin. Forget it," Max returned calmly. "Rudi's not messing with Sybil. Frau Heydrich won't like a fight, you know."

"It's none of your business, Max," Irwin said hoarsely.

Max did not want to fight.

"Your quarrel with Rudi isn't my business," he said with deliberate slowness, "but you'll fight me before you take him on. You're being a bully, not a Farber."

One of the girls gasped; the boys were grinning. This could be a good fight between the Farber boys.

Irwin lunged at his brother.

"Go, Max!" someone shouted.

"Take him down Max!"

Max's first punch landed squarely on his brother's nose. Red droplets showered both their fine shirts. Irwin staggered.

"Now let's stop, Irwin," Max pleaded.

But Irwin Farber was more passionate than skilled. He felt the anger like a tide inside himself. He roared as he sank his fists into Max's stomach. It sent Max backwards, his head striking the foundation of the summer house in an acutely painful thud. Vaguely he could hear screams, as if he were at the end of a tunnel. He wondered if it was Elaina. Irwin came at him, kicking and clawing, just as Max found his knees. Only then did Max fully realize how incensed his older brother was. They wrestled in the dirt until Max found the strength to push him off. Irwin was standing and panting, blood streaming from his nose.

Max stood up, wobbling. He could barely focus on his brother, everything was spinning. Irwin was not finished. One final punch sent Max sprawling backwards again.

"That's for breaking my nose!" Irwin yelled.

The blow had landed just above Max's eye, Irwin's ring slicing flesh to bone. Now the boys standing in the circle jumped forward collectively, to restrain the older Farber. But he shook them off.

"Don't get in my affairs again, little brother!" Irwin hissed.

"Irwin! Maximillian!" Herr Farber stood shaking, white with anger. "How dare you behave as such hooligans! Go to the house immediately!"

The father didn't seem to notice that his youngest son was staggering.

"Uh, Farber," Herr Heydrich interrupted carefully, "I think we need to call a doctor for them both."

Max gave Elaina a weak smile as she passed him her dainty handkerchief which quickly grew scarlet under his hand.

"Oh, Max, I'm so sorry."

"I'm all right, don't worry. Thanks for . . ." He winked as his father led him away.

"Did I break it?" Max asked the doctor who was applying the final stitches. Max was stretched out on his bed.

"Hmm? Hold still."

"Did I break—"

"Your head? No, just this gash that I can't guarantee won't scar." "No, I meant did I break Irwin's nose?"

"It is intact. There. Let's try to sit up."

"I feel so . . . weak."

"You've lost some blood. Drink this and we may avoid your first faint."

"This tastes awful! Did Irwin have to drink it?"

Dr. Morgan stroked his chin, and smiled. "I doubled his dose."

Max laughed as he swung his legs over the side of the bed. He sat in his shorts and undershirt, tanned and muscled. The doctor shook his head. "I worried about you even after I knew you would survive the TB two years ago, Max. I thought sure it would stunt or weaken you, but look, that is hardly the case. You're as tall as Irwin, and broader. I guess you gave him a run for his money, ja?"

Max shrugged. "It's all the running and weights we do at school. You know, last week I did 50 push-ups in one minute!"

The doctor nodded as he began packing his instruments.

"You're doing very well at school, Max."

"I guess. I don't know what Father really thinks. My grades aren't that good . . . but he doesn't say much."

"He's saying much to Irwin down the hall. I suspect he'll come in here when he's finished. What will you tell him?"

"The truth. I'll tell him what happened. Then," Max picked at the covers, "then I'll take what comes."

"Hmm . . ."

Max felt his head gingerly. The doctor stepped closer to take a final look at the cut above Max's left eye. "Perhaps this is like a badge, Max, a reminder of when you stood up to your brother. I think he may be less likely to harass you now."

Max raised his eyes slowly. "I didn't want to fight him, Dr. Josef. But, you know, that first punch felt so good!"

The physician smothered a smile. "I need to be going now. I want you to take some nourishment then go on to bed. Take it easy for a few days. No running or push-ups."

"You know what else I did today for the first time?" Max's eyes were eager. The doctor was glad—this is the way the boy should look, not burdened and troubled.

"What?"

"I kissed Elaina Heydrich."

"Ah . . . and did you like it very much?"

" 'Bout as much as that first punch," he grinned.

The doctor reached out and his hand rested briefly on the blond head. Then their eyes met and they smiled.

A benediction for the years and miles they would travel together.

2
A Boy Becomes a Man

Berlin, 1921

A chilly autumn evening, cloudless and still—the first night the coal fires would be needed. A Friday night in Berlin, alive with moving cabs and trams and pedestrians strolling along the Kurfursten-damm testified Berliners were out to the theaters, beer halls, cafes regardless of economy. The opera house drew a crowd in furs, jewels and, tuxedos to the premier of a Richard Wagner opera. A lecture drew another small, humbly dressed crowd of 100 to the second floor of the university library where a man spoke for three hours on the merits of communism. The French embassy on Wilhelmstrasse was brightly lit with a party for visiting diplomats. A huge evening wedding at Kaiser Wilhelm Memorial Church was in full progress: a high-ranking naval officer was the groom so it was a grand event. From cellar to attic, in smoky backrooms and ballrooms, from palace to tavern, clandestine to honest—it was a busy night in the capital city.

In one of the districts of Berlin some blocks from the city's heart, on a street unknown to the upper echelon of the city, a man was about to effect history. Not of Berlin alone. Or Germany. Or Europe. Only the whole world. But, of course, no one in the room around him even suspected this. He did. A noisy, cheap beer hall, with a violent, uncertain, somewhat illiterate crowd was a strange place for history to turn. An ordinary night, no accompanying signs or proclamations. Yet history

30

was made over the din of lusty yells, curses, laughter, and frothy steins of dark German beer.

Across the street, down a few doors, sat a small, unpretentious building. The front plate-glass window was darkened, yet in the backroom a light burned yellow and warm. A man was bent over a young girl as he set her broken arm. Her large gray eyes were fastened on him, occasionally smiling faintly at his words. His voice was low and gentle as he spoke to her.

"We are about finished, Greta, then we'll be ready for that cup of chocolate I'm warming, ja?"

She nodded. Her mother sat beside the examining table stroking her little daughter. The father paced the small room, his clothes testifying he had only come recently from work. Dr. Morgan glanced up.

"And how is work, Thomas? Still that double shift?"

"Ja, ja, the same. Long hours. And the men around me very unhappy with everything. The government, the kaiser, the church, and, of course, the treaty. Very restless, very agitated. I hear it is the same all over. Many German workers are angry. And what do we get from Hindenburg? Nothing but more promises. Bah!"

Josef was snipping gauze, not looking up. "Are you a communist, Thomas?"

"Me? Ha! No thank you. I want no revolution. Germany will straighten herself out sooner or later. Let's just hope it will be sooner. It's hard to feed a family of four on a handful of marks a week and coal costing another handful."

The room was quiet as Dr. Morgan finished and lifted Greta up.

"There you are my little one, wrapped up like a Christmas package. How does it feel?"

"All right, Dr. Josef."

"If she would stay out of trees and play like the other girls, this wouldn't have happened," her mother said with a smile.

"My Greta, the monkey," her father said as he tousled her head.

"Ah, trees are made for climbing," Morgan said confidentially to her, "but you must be very careful. Choose only stout limbs. Now—"

Shouts from the street filtered to the backroom.

"What's going on?" the woman asked nervously.

Morgan shrugged. "Now, let's have our chocolate, hmm Greta?"

Greta's father slipped through the door to the darkened front room of the clinic. He stood watching the excitement across the street. A sleek black Mercedes stood in front of the lively beer hall, incongruous in the shabby street of poverty. The man returned frowning and shaking his head.

"What is it, Thomas? What's going on?" his wife asked.

"Only the Nazis and one of their meetings," he chuckled. "You must say this for them at least, they are a very noisy group. A person couldn't fall asleep in one of their meetings, but they're too rowdy to last very long."

"Ja," the doctor agreed. "They are an interesting lot."

"Know much about them, Doctor?"

"No, Thomas. I avoid politics. I treat sick bodies, not minds." They laughed together.

"We are very grateful to you, Dr. Morgan," the woman said softly. "We can pay, well would half—"

"Ja, Doctor, you know, like I was saying . . ."

"Now there, you pay what you can and bring the rest later. Now get Greta home and to bed."

He led them to the front door and unlocked it.

"Be careful on these streets."

The clinic was silent again. Josef locked the door and returned to the examining room. He held the few coins in his hand and smiled. He stretched, yawned, and sat down with his chocolate. He was very tired; it had been a long day—but satisfying. He enjoyed these days in this clinic. He looked around the room with affection and pride. His rest was broken by the shrill ring of the telephone. He hauled himself up tiredly. He only had two maternity cases, hopefully this call was about neither.

"Ja? Oh, Max! What's happened? . . . Ja? He's still unconscious? How long ago did it happen? . . . His breathing? Keep him covered. I'm on my way."

He hung up and opened his black bag. He quickly placed a few things from the glass cabinets in it, his mind already at work on the case. He grabbed his coat and hat. An insistent pounding on the clinic door stopped him; his tiredness had vanished with the rush of anxious energy. He must hurry to the Farber estate, 30 minutes away. He opened the door.

The street was full of indistinguishable shouting and cursing men running in and out of the beer hall. He frowned, glad he was leaving the city. There would be victims of drunken brawls to patch up here. Two men stood in the darkened doorway.

"You are Dr. Morgan?" one asked crisply.

"Ja, I am Morgan."

The man jerked his head toward the building across the street. "You are needed."

The doctor locked the door and calmly stepped past them. Now he could see them better in the lights from across the street. Two men, perhaps in their twenties, wearing brown pants and shirts with a black crooked cross on their arm bands. He could see they bristled with confidence. *Probably factory workers or common clerks suddenly proud and austere in their importance*, he thought.

"As you can see, gentlemen," the doctor lifted his bag, "I was just on my way out to a call. You will have to fetch another physician."

"Nein, my doctor, you must come with us."

"Nein, my young friends. I have a serious case—a man may be dying! I cannot tarry."

He moved toward the car, but the youths blocked him. A shout came from the doorway to the beer hall.

"Werner! Schnell! He's bleeding like a pig."

Dr. Morgan glanced toward the establishment with unveiled disgust. "Come with us, Doctor." They took his arms, their grips firm. He could not challenge their youth or strength.

"You shall hear from the authorities about this . . . this abduction! Depend on it!" Josef fumed.

The young men looked at each other and grinned. Across the street, Josef jerked against their escort. "Let go, I will go in."

Morgan would not have believed so many men could fill the beer hall. He was shocked. *No wonder the noise had penetrated his shop. There must be several hundred men pressed into the tavern's main room.* He looked around, taking in the spilt beer, and the smell of sweat, the strong lights, the overturned chairs—and every man, it seemed, shouting. At the front of the room hung a blood-red banner, the black crooked cross stark against it.

"What is going on here?" he asked the men. But the brownshirts were mute as they parted the crowd roughly and led him past a makeshift stage where a handful of men were arguing hotly. They knocked on a side door which opened immediately. The doctor took in the small room quickly. Apparently its original use was as an office for the establishment. Morgan wondered if these eight men watching him had found sympathy in the owner or had merely commandeered the room—as they had him. He felt a fresh wave of irritation. A man lay prostrate on the table, a cloth held to his shoulder by another man. The six other men were scattered about the room, silent on his entrance. The doctor suspected he was being led into a little enclave of conspiracy— one of temperamental Berlin's less-than-noble pastimes.

A man at his shoulder prodded him forward, his voice cheerful and loud. "Herr Doctor! Thank you for coming so quickly!"

The doctor gave the man quick scrutiny. *Large, beefy-faced, small eyes, receding brown hair. There's something familiar about him*, the doctor pondered. The man could see the recognition in the physician's eyes and was pleased. His chest managed a small swell. "I am Herman Göring, Herr Doctor," he said with a stiff little Prussian bow.

Of course. He had seen his photograph many times. *A German hero, a flying ace from the great war.*

"I did not come here willingly, Herr Göring," Morgan replied stiffly, yet he approached his patient on the table. *A badly bruised eye, lacerated knuckles of the left hand, and a deep gash on the right shoulder*, he noted. He adjusted his glasses and peered closer. *Yes, a very deep wound, most likely from a knife.* So, he was treating the results of a drunken brawl after all, while Herr Farber lay dying. He opened his bag and wordlessly began his work. After a moment, talk resumed between the men, quiet, low, confidential, yet filled with excitement.

"To win by only one vote! A close call!"

"Ja, but the majority, that is what matters."

"He's still out there threatening . . ."

"Ha! Let him threaten!"

Dr. Morgan looked up as he threaded his needle. He noticed one man who stood slightly away from the others, his feet widely planted apart and his arms folded over his chest. Morgan stared a moment at the silent man's mustache. Was he . . . serious about it? *A stubby, severe abbreviation of a real mustache*, he decided, *as if the man had been sniffing boot blacking. I won't take a recommendation for this man's barber, certainly.* Morgan somehow knew this man had not spoken. The man's dark eyes locked with the doctor's.

"You do your work well, Herr Doctor," he said.

Morgan noticed the Austrian accent. He bent back over his task. "I was on my way out on a important case when your men escorted me over here. I can only hope my other patient will not die by this delay."

He glanced up to note this man's reaction. He was smiling.

Göring's voice was jovial. "Herr Doctor, we are most grateful, but you were needed here, obviously. This is an important night, ja a night etched in history!"

Göring looked toward the dark-haired man for approval.

"Ja," the man nodded slowly, "a night of victory for Germany and all true Germans."

The doctor looked up again, a little intrigued. *What could this handful of men be boasting about in their rowdy Nazi gathering?*

"Oh? What has happened?"

They all smiled. Göring stepped forward, eager to enlighten the medical man. "Our fuehrer has received the majority to rule our party. A great night, ja?"

Josef Morgan was puzzled. This "fuehrer" term was unfamiliar.

"Our fuehrer?" he asked slowly.

Göring's round face was flushed red with boyish excitement.

"Our fuehrer," he pointed to the dark-haired man in the cheap, dark suit. "Doctor, this is Adolf Hitler!"

Every man grew still, waiting for Morgan's reaction.

Morgan's voice was steady. "I see." He returned to his patient.

"And what do you think of the National Socialist German Worker's Party, Herr Doctor?" the newly elected leader asked with a trace of amusement.

"I know very little about it, Herr Hitler—except you are noisy." It was tense, then the men laughed. Göring gave him a hearty slap on the back. Morgan frowned inside, he had not meant to compliment them.

The door burst open; a man was shouting and pointing toward Hitler. The group of men surged forward to protect him.

"You have not heard the end of this, nor the end of me, Hitler!"

Morgan finished. He looked to Hitler but the man was looking past him, his eyes fixed and hard. *Almost hypnotic,* thought Morgan.

Hitler's voice was controlled and steely. "And you have not heard the last of me," he returned proudly.

•   •   •

Morgan's little coupe was unaccustomed to the speed the doctor demanded of it. Josef grinned wryly in the darkness; he would not be surprised if the auto didn't give a wheezened sigh of death when the ignition was turned off. But it would get him to the Farber estate—that was all that mattered now. Hopefully they had summoned another doctor when he did not arrive. It had been two hours since Max had called him. Two hours ... much could happen with a serious head injury like the boy had described.

It was Irwin who opened the door to the grand house.

"You were called over two hours ago, Dr. Morgan."

"I am fully aware of that, Irwin Farber. Now take me to your father."

"Such incompetence on your part may have killed my father," he continued acidly.

"Irwin," came a voice behind them on the stairs. Seventeen-year-old Max stood watching his brother. His own face was pale, his eyes piercing. "Please come up, Dr. Josef," Max finally said.

The examination did not take long: shallow breathing, weak and erratic pulse. Morgan suspected there was brain swelling. Irwin Eric Farber had slipped into a coma. The great magnate of German industry and military tradition was dying from a hunting accident at the age of 55.

Morgan stepped back from the bed. His weariness returned. The three Farber sons were staring at him, and he vaguely wondered what was in their minds.

"I am sorry. I do not think he will last the night."

Eric slipped from the room without a word. Morgan watched Max, whose eyes lingered on his father.

"He isn't suffering, is he?" Irwin asked with unexpected gentleness.

"No, I don't think so."

Max knelt by the side of the bed and Morgan could see the exhaustion clearly etched on the young face. He leaned over to kiss his father's forehead ... too late to say goodbye. . . .

• • •

Irwin stood before the library fire, and in its glow the doctor could see the profile. *Is he truly grieving*? he wondered. *The face and posture look so much like the grandfather in the portrait down the hall.* Max sat across from him, his eyes downcast, his shoulders sagging.

"I should go find Eric and try to talk to him. He was . . . with father when it happened. . . . He'll be feeling . . . responsible somehow."

"I'll talk with him as well. He shouldn't feel responsible."

Silent minutes passed. "Tell me, Max, how things are going for you in Vienna," the doctor pressed with kindness.

"It has been a good semester. I'm grateful . . . to Father, that he let me go there. He didn't really want me to." Max studied his hands. "We both knew I'd come back here to the business . . . of course."

"The last time I spoke with your father he told me you were made captain of the ski team in the youth club. He was proud of your success."

"Ja, I was to go to Oslo for the competition next month."

"And go you should. Your father would have wanted you to, Max." Irwin swung away from the fireplace toward them.

"He plays soccer all summer and skis all winter. When he's at home he's banging away at the piano like some amateur composer. Last winter he was climbing in the Alps. He even talked father into letting him take flying lessons. It's time you grow up, Max, and stop all this playing."

"Irwin, I don't think—" the doctor began, but Irwin waved him silent.

"The university in Vienna is a waste of your time and Farber money, Max. It's full of artists and loafs and professors spouting revolution. Father indulged you. Farber men have always gone to Humboldt University. It is time you came home and settled into the business. I cannot run it alone."

Morgan and Max looked at the man across the room, shocked at his words and bitter tone.

"That's right. You must know how things are now, Max, with father . . . gone. Eric understands. Farber company will come to me in the largest share. You and Eric will be equal partners with the rest. You look surprised . . . the testament will explain it all."

The doctor stood up. He had heard quite enough arrogance for one night. "The only thing that should be surprising, Irwin, is your total lack of tact to bring these things up on this night. You can hardly think it would have pleased your father."

"The testament shall prove my words. And you, Doctor, will no longer be the Farber family physician." Irwin turned and left the room.

Alone with Max, Morgan waited for the boy to speak. His heart broke for all that awaited the young man. He had watched this boy grow from a timid lad to an energetic, confident young man. He had defied his upbringing. Now, though, tonight, the boy was hurting. Josef's arm went around the firm shoulder.

"Max? Are you all right?"

Tears pooled in the blue eyes as he nodded.

"I'm going to miss my father," he whispered hoarsely.

3
No Small Concerns

Berlin, 1929

Stadtbahn train terminal was the busiest of Berlin's many stations. Like the source of a giant, sprawling artery, it delivered travelers of business and pleasure to other parts of Europe: Prague and Vienna to the east, Geneva to the south, Paris and Brussels to the west, Danzig to the north. On any given day, particularly at noon or just after seven P.M., an observer might find a fairly representative assembly of European tongues and tribes. And like all travelers, men, women, and children were alternately fatigued or exhilarated by their journey and wrapped up in the particulars of their personal destinations.

A Mercedes was parked near the platform of the terminal. The driver, with his hat pulled over his face, appeared to be dozing in the mid-morning sunshine. On the passenger side, a white-haired man was reading the *Voissische Zeitung*, Berlin's leading newspaper. A young male wire haired terrier sat at attention between them. His head swiveled comically as he attempted to follow the interesting scene in front of him. The dozing man rested a hand on the dog's back, and the animal responded with an occasional eager kiss under the hat. A commotion on the platform stirred the older man from his reading. He leaned forward. A group of reporters and

photographers and a sizable crowd of men and women who carried no
luggage were gathering.

"What's going on?" the man underneath the hat murmured.

"I can't tell. Only a lot of newspaper types. Must be waiting for
someone to arrive."

"Hmm . . ."

The older man returned to his paper. "What do you make of this
thing in New York? What are they calling it? Black Tuesday. Funny the
epitaphs Americans think of. Anyway, this drop in their stock market?"

"In all truth, Josef, I know very little about the stock market."

Morgan snorted with a laugh. "And here you are a German businessman! And a leading German businessman at that!"

Max Farber pushed back his hat and yawned. "My dear doctor, the
business leader in the family is Irwin. He could give you the details
about this stock market thing very efficiently." Max stretched. "Now
me? I can tell you what the ski conditions are in St. Moritz. I can tell
you what opera is playing in Prague or Vienna."

"And what they're catching off Gibraltar?" the doctor supplied.
Max nodded and smiled. "Precisely."

The doctor stroked the dog. "Percy was a gift from Fraulein Shaeffer, you said?"

Max shook his head with half closed eyes. "Fraulein Schiller.
Fraulein Shaeffer is ancient history."

"Ah . . . it is difficult for me to keep your female companions straight."

"Ja, it taxes me at times, also. So, you think my Sir Percy is a fine-
looking fellow?" He rubbed the dog's ears and the animal closed his
eyes in bliss.

"Ja, he appears intelligent."

"He'd better be. I intend that he conduct himself in the European
capitals as a businessman's companion should."

The doctor ruffled the canine's ears absently, and Percy's tongue
lolled in ecstacy. "Does this gift from Fraulein Schiller signify anything?" the old man asked with betraying innocence.

"No more than she knows I like dogs and admired Percy's parents."

"Max, I think a wife at your side seeing the capitals of Europe would be
more fitting and profitable for you."

Max leaned toward his pet. "It's the Frau Farber hunt, Percy. Growl
at him."

Josef's voice carried a trace of exasperation. "You'd make a wonderful father, Max. I'd like to have some tots around—it would be good for us both."

Max tapped the steering wheel in staccato emphasis.

"To be a wonderful father you should be a wonderful or, at the very least, tolerable husband. I do not think, rather, I am not sure I could be that, Josef." His tone lightened as a warning. "So I remain a bachelor, but hardly lacking for the virtues of the fairer sex."

"Max—" the doctor began, a little frown creasing his face."

Look the train's in. Who's the celebrity? Maybe Marlene Dietrich? I'd like to see her! Probably someone political—maybe the corporal."

Josef Morgan laughed, "Careful, Max. I understand calling Adolf Hitler the corporal can offend these Nazi fellows."

"Surely we're not afraid of him and his thugs," Max yawned. "They'll spend themselves out soon enough."

"I don't know about that. They're very popular—everywhere you look is that infernal swastika! Rather a crude symbol I think."

"I don't know much about them, except a few of their ideas seem plausible. The Allies are strangling Germany with the war reparations. How can we pay for the Great War when our people are starving?"

"True, but these Nazis have no apparent respect."

Max laughed again. "I don't know if that's possible Josef, not with their leader a former jail inmate. Look! Who? Ah! It's Max Schmeling!"

The German boxer alighted from the train to cheers and the flash of camera bulbs. He held his beefy paws high. With one more victory, the fighter would head to the United States for the world heavyweight championship.

"Wouldn't the Nazis love to have him in their ranks!" Max laughed. "Look at the size of those fists!" Max pulled his hat back over his face, "I appreciate you bringing me to the station, Josef. Sorry about the delay."

"It's fine, I had only to listen to Frau's complaint of her back. Do you know what she thinks now?"

"She's blaming the French?"

"Ja, they occupy the Ruhr and she says she can feel their unsavory presence in her lumbar regions!"

Josef Morgan watched the crowd around the prizefighter move him like a tide and out of view. He was frowning, but not due to the scene just witnessed. He was thinking of his young friend beside him. There was this nagging concern, completely unconnected with a physical problem or his bachelor state. Indeed, Max was the image of health and vitality. No, and the doctor was troubled and uncertain how to broach the subject. Perhaps it was better left unsaid; it was none of his business really. He tugged at his vest buttons while he thought. *Wouldn't it be like Max—who knew nothing of medicine—telling him he'd misdiagnosed a patient?*

"You promise you'll join me in a month? No backing out at the last moment?" Max asked.

Morgan smiled. "Ja, I'll come. It will be good to feel the sunshine of Gibraltar against the wet and cold of Berlin."

"My sentiments exactly."

Josef tapped his knee, readjusted his tie, refolded his paper, his mind still debating.

"I was in Frankfurt a few days ago and saw a new Farber plant going up. What will be produced there?" he asked.

"A new plant in Frankfurt? Hmm...I don't know. It's probably some new expansion brainchild of Irwin's."

"And you know nothing about it," the doctor returned pointedly.

Max straightened, pushing back his hat. He turned and faced the man squarely. He knew the doctor had something on his mind.

"I don't know about the plant. Why?"

"Max, do you remember the day I went with you to the lawyer's office for the reading of your father's will?"

Max nodded.

"Your father divided control of Farber trust equally among his three sons—much to the surprise of the eldest. You were to have an active role in Farber. That is what he wanted. You could bring balance to Irwin's drive and Eric's uncertainty. You could work for the good of the company—indeed, the good of Germany. Now, you've told me Eric has gone for the military and Irwin is trying to buy out his control."

"Ja, that is true. He wanted my control also. I haven't sold it to him, Josef."

"I know that, Max, but do you know what is going on?"

"I know enough," Max returned a little stiffly.

The doctor turned away frustrated, not even sure why he should care.

"Irwin still needs my approval on the board. I . . . I know in general what goes on. I know Irwin is determined to make I.E. Farber the biggest industry in Europe. He's out to rival Krupp Steel Works. He's ambitious, Josef, I'm not. Is that wrong?"

"Nein. . . ."

"What is it, Josef? What is bothering you?"

"You have so much potential, Max, and it seems to me you . . ."

"Ja?"

"You ski and you deep-sea fish and you go to all the right Berlin parties. You leave your responsibility to that, that secretary of yours, Karl Beck! I don't trust him."

"What is wrong with Beck? He's been with me since I started with the company."

"Haven't you said he does all your paperwork and you just sign your name?"

Max felt himself redden. The doctor had never talked to him this way. Accusation? Criticism? His voice was tight with irritation.

"Josef, you know I didn't choose this. I went with the company to please father. Before he died we talked, and I said I would go with the company. I . . . loved him. But what I do now is my own life. I choose now! I work at Farber, and I do what I want the rest of the time. Call me a coward if you like."

"Max, Max, I did not mean to sound critical, to sound like Irwin. I do not think you are a coward, not at all." He drew a deep breath. "Are you . . . happy, Max?"

"I am comfortable, Josef, and happy."

A train, shrieking and hissing curved into sight.

"That will be my train. I'm sorry, Josef, I didn't mean to get angry."

Josef laid a hand on his arm. "No, no, it is my fault. I meddle too much."

Max and Josef left the car and Max pulled his bags from the back seat. "We are like two old fussing bachelors Josef," he smiled. He slipped the leash on the dog who strained the rope taut with eagerness. "Settle down, my good man. I told you you're going along. No tricks now."

They joined the crowd on the platform, amid the shouts and confusion—porters frenzied with their work, the low rumble of the engine like a harnessed beast about to stampede, children laughing, and the noise of a dozen goodbyes. Homburgs and feathered hats, expensive wool, silk, and fur, well-worn tweed and fashions from three winters past—for this brief time at Stadtbahn, Berlin in its finery and poverty had mingled.

"Max! Max Farber!"

He swung around. A young, tall, blond man in a naval uniform was hurrying up to him. It was Reinhard Heydrich. Orbiting in different social circles, they had not seen each other in several years. A woman, in fur up to her chin, stood beside him. She didn't notice the white-haired man; she noticed Maximillian Farber.

"Max! So good to see you!" Reinhard said as they shook hands warmly.

"It has been a long time, Reinhard. Since your wed—"

Max stopped and reddened, realizing this woman at Reinhard's side was not Frau Heydrich. Reinhard winked and smiled confidentially at Max.

"You remember Dr. Morgan, Reinhard," Max introduced.

The tall officer's smile was a little stiff as he looked down at the medical man. His eyes took in the unfashionable clothes, the slight stoop. "I don't remember," he murmured.

"Ah, well . . ." Josef smiled as he pulled his beard. "I remember you, Herr Heydrich. I treated you once when you were very young. I think it was colic. A terrible case. Your mother was most distraught."

Max looked away to Percy who sat beside him.

Heydrich turned back to Max. "So, Max, off on business or pleasure?"

"Pleasure. To Madrid for a few days, then on to Gibraltar for fishing."

Heydrich slapped his back. "Ah, the bachelor industrialist!" he laughed. "Off to a playground while poor Irwin slaves away to make those Farber millions."

Max shifted his luggage, glancing at the train, not wanting to meet eyes with Josef.

"And this is who you travel with?" Heydrich indicated Percy with the slightest dip of his chin. The sarcasm was in his voice as it had been in boyhood, Max remembered. For a fleeting moment he expected his older brother to step from behind Heydrich's back and add his customary abuse. Max's tone was a light drawl.

"Ja, Sir Percy comes with me. A confidant but he carries only his own tail," Max smiled.

Heydrich's teeth gleamed white in his smooth face. "You always were the loner, Max. You see I prefer a more . . . comfortable confidante. A dog would never do for me."

The woman's smile revealed her own perfect white teeth.

"And you are doing well in the navy?" Max asked cheerfully.

"For now." Reinhard gave a sidelong glance to the smiling woman. "Until something better comes along. . . ."

An old man with shuffling steps and rasping breath brushed past them, stumbling into Heydrich.

"Careful there, old man," the young man said testily.

Morgan reached out to steady the stranger. "There, there, are you all right, my friend?"

"Ja, danke, danke," he replied as he climbed aboard the train.

"He is a Jew," said a voice behind them. They all turned. Three men stood watching the old man. "He should not be on the train," he continued to inform them.

"He is a German citizen," the doctor countered with blunt composure.

The youths gave each other looks, shrugged, and sauntered off into the crowd. Morgan looked back to Max, to say something in the uncomfortable silence.

"You know, there is only room for those of true German blood in the new Germany," Heydrich addressed the doctor, dusting off his lapels some imaginary soil.

"A new Germany?" Max asked smiling. "Are you a member of the Nazi party, Reinhard?"

"Ja, Max." His chin went up. "You are not?"

"Nein, should I be?"

"Of course. It is the future, Max. I'm surprised Irwin hasn't convinced you. It is strength."

"Irwin is a member?" Max asked with real surprise. Again, he imagined the doctor's burning look. Strength . . . that prize quality Farbers should possess.

"You have not read Hitler's *Mein Kampf*, Maximillian?"

Max shook his head.

Reinhard smiled and gave him a playful shove. "Max, stop loafing and look around. The Nazi party will make Germany great one day." He slipped his hand into his deep coat pocket. "Here." He handed Max a book. "Here is my personal copy. Read it while you play in Spain."

Max turned the book over in his hands. He opened the cover; it had been signed by the author.

Josef tugged at his vest again. He had not expected this arrogant officer to plead his case so well.

"It's just that the Nazis one sees on the streets are like those three— a little on the thuggish side," Max said finally, feeling like he had as a boy. Defensive again.... "That is what repels me."

"Well, I hadn't thought of Irwin or myself as thugs. But I say, Max, you come up with another type. You could be the gentleman, polite and proper." He bowed to Max.

It was spoken with a smile, but Max could feel the cut. Just like their growing-up days, nothing much had really changed.

"I must be going, Max. It was good to see you. When you return to Berlin, look me up and we'll go over the book. I can help you with your... education." Another leering wink.

The woman's voice was like a purr, "Reinhard, I would guess Herr Farber is well educated."

"Auf Wiedersehen, Max."

"Auf Wiedersehen, Reinhard."

Max exhaled loudly as Reinhard and his companion moved away.

"I liked him better in diapers," Josef remarked.

Max had temporarily forgotten the old man. He relaxed and laughed, optimistic again. His arm went around the doctor's thin shoulders."You will join me in two weeks?"

"Ja."

Max boarded the train, smiling and waving.

Josef watched until the train was lost in the Berlin suburbs, a thin, solitary whistle stretching like a languid banner behind it. He could see Max's young face in his mind and his energetic wave and smile that gave him a boyish look despite his 25 years. He thought of the woman who had stood at Heydrich's side and given Max a bold and unembarrassed look that none of them had missed. Josef frowned when he thought of the stumbling old man. A new Germany...

"The old one is good enough...with all her wrinkles, danke," he murmured to himself.

And he remembered the proud Heydrich's words: "You could be a different type of Nazi. . . ." He looked back to the empty tracks.

Josef Morgan suddenly felt lonely. He had never been a praying man, and he didn't know why he should start now—but something...Suddenly he felt he should offer up a petition for that old man who had been carried away by the train.

4
While Kings Were Sleeping

Berlin, January, 1933

A torchlight parade that began at dusk and looked like it would last well past midnight was under way on Berlin's principal government thoroughfare, the Wilhelmstrasse. Beginning as a human current at Tiergarten, marchers surged under the triumphal arch of Brandenburg Gate. Thousands of cheering, frenzied Germans lined the sidewalks. It was a night of revelry unparalleled in the city's history. The cold night air of January was seemingly unnoticed by the crowds.

From a balcony of the Chancellery, a diminutively built, dark-haired man stood with an ecstatic face, his hand jerking in puppetlike rhythm in a stiff-arm salute. He would boast this night was but a prelude to a thousand-year reign of victory. With uncanny insight and genius, his boasts often came true.

With every nation preoccupied and disinterested—and a very sharp memory of the last great conflict, the neighbors of the earth did not want to look too closely at Berlin.

And the shadow darkened.

Washington, D.C.

Across the Atlantic, in another capital, a young man knocked gently on a closed bedroom door of the White house. It was 5:45 A.M., but he knew the man inside was an early riser. He waited a moment, then entered. The president still sat in his royal-blue-striped robe and faded slippers, a cup of coffee in one hand, a freshly lit cigarette in the other. His thin hair was tousled, and he had not put on his glasses yet. The younger man, knowing his boss rather well, did not expect a rebuke for the early intrusion—he was here on business of utmost importance.

The secretary himself had gone to bed at midnight, only to be up again at four. His lean faced was lined from agitation and restlessness. There was no good morning greeting between the two men. He approached the table where the man in the wheelchair sat, his notes gripped tightly in his hand.

"He did it," he said in the polished, efficient bluntness he'd perfected in his years of service to the president.

Franklin Roosevelt yawned. "You look sour, Harry. You're not surprised; we're not surprised. We'd be idiots if we didn't see this coming."

Harry nodded, but his eyes were glowing with an inner anger.

"Sure, but even though it has I... I'm still pretty floored by it. I just don't get it. How can the German people be so dense? This guy's a modern Genghis Khan!"

Roosevelt's laugh was deep and rich. Depend on young Harry to give him a good laugh on a morning when the world should be sober.

"He's promised them the world, Harry, that's how he's getting by with it. Genghis Khan. Now there's something I'd love to use in my chat speech tonight." He smiled and drew deeply on his cigarette, as if he pulled nourishment from it. "You've called everybody?"

"They're on their way."

"Then call Jacob and tell him to put my breakfast on the table on the double."

"Yes, sir."

Roosevelt turned his chair toward the bathroom.

"Who did you talk to in Berlin?"

"Shirer with United News Service, and Ambassador Poncet called here. They all sounded pretty depressed. The Germans are having this big parade down the middle of the city." He shook his head with disgust.

"An all-night party like something right out of the middle ages! They watched it from the window in the embassy."

Roosevelt stopped before the bathroom door. "Send up more coffee."

"Yes, sir."

Roosevelt stroked his chin in thought. "An all-night party for Genghis Khan and company. Well, I can imagine there are a few Germans who aren't celebrating."

Harry sighed. "Yes, sir."

They looked at each other, speaking together: "The Jews."

Moscow, 1933

Many Russians would whisper that the dictator was as hard and cold as the frozen Volga River in the heart of a Russian winter—and a Russian winter was nothing to trifle with. And most people would prefer facing it rather than the stern-faced Joseph Stalin. Most peasants and aristocrats would make this whisper fully knowing it could bring death. Very swift, very efficient. Stalin was building the Soviet Union to a great nation, powerful and dominating, perhaps like no other on earth. There was no denying this fact, from the peasant huts to the palace salons. Yes, a mighty kingdom born from the vast land—and birthed on a foundation of blood and bones.

Though it was morning, light was slow in creeping across the frozen empire. The German foreign minister to Russia, Ribbentrop, brought the news personally to the Kremlin. He came without invitation—his elation over the events in Berlin the night before had strengthened his timid nerves. Normally he avoided the truculent, unpredictable Soviet leader, preferring to deal with his subordinates, but this morning he must appear personally. "*Indeed, this first morning of the glorious Third Reich!*" he whispered to himself.

Comrade Stalin was not pleased. He had not slept well, and he did not care to begin his day with the fussy German minister. He was prudent in his own blunt fashion, yet kept Ribbentrop waiting a full two hours. His apologies were brusque as the minister entered the room.

Germany's representative was furious, but held his tongue. He turned from a short, stiff bow to Stalin to address the bespectacled interpreter. "I have come this morning to inform Comrade Stalin that

Germany has a new chancellor! Adolf Hitler has been appointed by President Von Hindenburg. It is a great hour for Germany, and I have come to say we will continue most cordial and amenable relations with our Soviet friends."

The interpreter relayed the words, then returned Stalin's reply.

"I am aware of the events in Berlin, Herr Ribbentrop. You need not have bothered me this morning." Stalin lit a cigarette, watching the German through a thin veil of acrid smoke.

Ribbentrop stiffened. Of all the European leaders, this Russian-peasant-turned-dictator, wearing a khaki military tunic and high leather boots, was really the most insufferable and arrogant. There was nothing noble in his pockmarked face. *He looks like an escaped convict*, the minister thought. Ribbentrop drew a deep breath.

"You knew?"

"Of course," Stalin, via the interpreter, returned smoothly.

Stalin's own secretaries, counselors, and ministers had conferred with him regarding Hitler's ascension. Of course, he had watched the rise with mild interest. He was fully convinced the German patriotic fervor, called Nazism, was not very different than contemptible capitalism.

In the meeting, he spoke to his advisors patiently, like a father to his children: "Nazism is merely a different mask over the same face. You will see."

"Adolf Hitler is not a man to be trusted," the Russian ambassador to Germany said haughtily.

Stalin's dark eyes narrowed. "I trust no one, comrade—not even myself."

The room became tensely still. Then, abruptly, Stalin laughed. "We do not need to fret or worry over this puny Austrian. His smooth words will amuse us, I'm certain, but we will not be fooled. It is not easy to fool comrade Stalin!"

"They say he fancies himself a dragon from German mythology," someone offered with a nervous titter.

Again Stalin chuckled, his hands laced across his middle.

"And the bear always devours the dragon."

And so the world would watch.

Ribbentrop cleared his throat, fumbling with his expensive watch chain. "Well, I see. As I was saying, Germany is eager to continue friendly relations with your vast country. The fuehrer wishes particularly to improve trade between our countries for the economic good of both."

Stalin merely stared.

"I know Chancellor Hitler is eager to meet you," the foreign minister continued nervously.

The Russian snuffed out the half smoked cigarette and stood, clearly signifying the termination of the interview.

"*When* he is invited to Moscow," Stalin said with a smile nearly concealed under the heavy curtain of dark mustache. He turned, his black boots clicking on the marble floor, punctuating his words.

Ribbentrop cursed under his breath and vowed he would not be present when the two great dictators finally met.

Paris

Even the most powerful man in the land was not above an irksome thing like a toothache. And for Albert Lebrun, the most palatable, most preferred, most promising remedy was a good glass of brandy. He put on his slippers and robe, then padded softly down the stairs of the family quarters. He did not want to rouse his secretary, valet, or servant who would surely press a different relief on him.

Though it approached midnight, he could see a light still burned under the library door. He paused to listen and smiled. His grandson and two friends were still up. He pulled the doors open sharply and lowered his eyebrows.

"I could hear you scoundrels all the way upstairs!"

The three jumped to their feet, shocked and nervous. This man with the rumpled pajamas and hair was the president of the Third Republic of France!

"Grandfather!"

"Sir!"

He glowered at them a moment longer then laughed. They sighed with relief as he waved them back to their chairs.

"You will be excused only if you tell me about the mademoiselles you were obviously discussing."

Seventeen-year-old Michael Lebrun blushed slightly and shook his head. "We weren't talking about mademoiselles, grandfather."

"Oh?" The older man moved to the sideboard, drew out a crystal tumbler, and poured himself a deep well of the toothache medication.

"Young men, late at night, a private conversation, and it wasn't about attractive young women?"

"No, sir," Michael insisted.

"Rene, is my grandson telling the truth?"

"Yes, sir, absolutely."

"Phillipe?"

"Yes, sir, Michael tells you the truth. Young attractive women was the topic an hour ago."

The four laughed as the president selected a chair. He yawned and took a generous drink.

"So, what is the topic this hour, boys?"

"The Nazis and their new chancellor," Rene answered.

"Well I would have enjoyed the previous hour's topic far better," Lebrun said, winking at the students.

"What do you think of Adolf Hitler, sir?" young Rene ventured eagerly.

The leader smiled briefly. "Have I not heard Michael say that you are editor of the college paper, Rene?"

Rene nodded. "But this is strictly off the record, sir."

"I personally have never trusted that line, Rene. More accurate, off the public record I think, hmm?"

"Yes, sir, exactly."

"Adolf Hitler over delightful coeds," Lebrun shrugged. "I will tell you what I think of Germany's new leader. I think he is smart and ambitious. He will try to rebuild Germany."

Michael leaned forward. "You say rebuild, sir. Do you also mean rearm?"

"Of course not! I said Hitler is smart. He knows the Versailles Treaty forbids him from rearming. He would not be so foolish to ignore that. I meant rebuild economically."

"Even with the war payments to us?" Michael pressed.

"Germany is wealthy, Michael. She has deep, deep pockets no matter how loudly she whines to the contrary. What she did to our land in the war will be paid for to the last sou."

Rene spoke up. "There is some rumor that the Nazis want to rebuild their army and navy—"

"Rumors, as you admit, Rene," he smiled with a hint of condescension. "Would not the president of France know otherwise?"

The young man looked embarrassed. "Yes, sir."

"I would think that a rebuilt Germany as a neighbor would be of some concern to us, sir," Michael submitted.

Lebrun stretched lazily. "Germany is an energetic nation without question. They want to change their status since their humiliating defeat 14 years ago. I have no quarrel with that. Any proud man has the right to better himself, don't you think?"

"But what if Hitler and his Nazis get too ambitious?"

"Too ambitious, Michael?"

The grandson squirmed in his seat as if he'd been reprimanded.

"The Nazis aggressive when they are bordered by the greatest nation with the largest army on the continent? With our Maginot line a defense as has never been seen in Europe?" The president leaned forward, his gray eyes snapping, his blood well warmed. The toothache was completely forgotten.

Michael considered the old man's words in silence a moment.

"What are you thinking now, Michael? Now speak up! I have critics in parliament, too, remember."

"I don't mean to be critical. But I was wondering . . . France has the strengths you mentioned. But we also have so many problems here, too, in the government and economy, I just wonder if we would really take the time or care to deal with the Nazis if they did dare something?"

Lebrun dismissed the concern with a wave of his hand.

"I admit Hitler has an impressive oratory style, from what I've heard of the man. He's an actor and his audience is quite impressed. A few years and he will likely fade from the stage. The German people are more practical than theatrical. With his boast, he does not concern France."

Michael and Rene gave the old man an obligatory nod. Only then was Phillipe, the youngest of the group, noticed for his silence. He had stood with his back to the group, staring moodily into the fireplace.

"You have been so quiet, Phillipe," Lebrun pointed out.

The dark-haired youth turned and shrugged, avoiding the older man's eyes. "You have nothing to add to this discussion?" Lebrun pressed.

"You say France does not have any concerns regarding this Hitler fellow. I respectfully disagree, sir."

"Oh?"

"There is concern in Germany certainly. The Jews are very concerned."

Lebrun shifted uncomfortably. He had forgotten his grandson's friend was Jewish.

"Perhaps the chancellor has a streak of anti-Semitism, but I really think that it will hardly affect his governing. It is a personal thing, hardly—"

"No, sir," Phillipe returned, stepping forward.

Michael and Rene nearly jumped in their chairs. Phillipe had interrupted the president!

The old man was startled and speechless. Now a light burned in the young man's eyes, brighter than Lebrun's earlier.

"It is far more than a streak, sir. Adolf Hitler despises the Jews. He calls them vermin and maggots. He thinks they have caused all of Germany's problems. He has made no secret of this."

Lebrun was silent.

"Where have you heard this, Phillipe?" Rene asked.

"Have you read the book that he wrote, sir, called *Mein Kampf?*"

"No, Phillipe, I have not read it," Lebrun replied testily.

"My uncle was in Germany last October. He says the book is everywhere—the fastest-selling book in Germany. My uncle brought back a copy. I have read it and it gives Hitler's plans."

Lebrun yawned. "Phillipe, any man can write in a passion his thoughts at that time, and later feel differently."

The young student shook his head vehemently.

"Not this man. You say he wants to rebuild Germany. Yes, he does admit that, but to build it greater than it has ever been in history—superior to every nation on earth. He writes in this book that Germany must have more 'lebensraum,' that is living space. Every frontier must expand. He will accomplish this by force and that means war. He says Germans are the master race and will trample over all the weak and any that oppose him. He will be absolute lord and dictator. He says that France is a mortal enemy, and Germany will eventually reckon with her. He says all of this in his book. And I . . . I think the Germans are reading this eagerly."

The room was awkwardly silent. Rene and Michael looked at the floor. The French president could feel the dull throb of the rotten tooth. He had wanted a good, stimulating, provocative discussion with a youth that was no longer his. He had pretended irritation when he had entered the library, but now—now he was irritated. The Jewish boy was too emotional. Perhaps he was not the best friend for Michael. Michael should run with boys who thought of girls and not politics and affairs that they did not understand. He would speak to him about it in the morning.

Phillipe was not quite finished; his face was flushed.

"I say this, President Lebrun, not as a Jew, I say, to you that, that I would appeal to you to read Hitler's book. He is a dangerous neighbor for France, I think."

The president stood, his voice imperious.

"Rene, you and Michael have asked my opinion and I have given it. Some in France still consider it worthwhile. What Adolf Hitler says and does in Germany does not matter in Paris. It does not matter at all. We have the army and the Maginot line, and he may boast all he cares to. University boys would do well to spend more time on their studies!"

The words sounded weak and feeble; the boys were very embarrassed.

So much would change in six short years—was changing even now in the infant hours of the Third Reich. The old man would forget entirely the late-night conversation. But the three young men never would.

If only the old man had listened to the wisdom of youth. . . .

Chartwell, England

Clementine Churchill rarely came into this deeply masculine, inner sanctuary of her husband, not because she wasn't welcome or didn't enjoy his company—it was the permeating odor of his cigars. It seemed to her like a pungent varnish over everything in the room. But on a very cold January morning, with the gardens of Chartwell frozen, gray, and lifeless, she entered cheerfully and determined, like a breeze of spring. She wanted to speak to her husband about the party they were to attend that evening. She was loathe to remind him, yet she wanted to extract a promise from him that he would go in a most congenial and cordial attitude—and no sly remarks to those around him about the hostess's haircolor or decorating style or politics. She smiled. *So brilliant and so childlike at times is this husband of mine. Sometimes he's like a grumpy old dog on a leash*, she thought lovingly.

She entered with one sharp rap, not waiting for his command. He stood with his back to the door, still in his dressing gown. She had seen this resolute stance many times before. She knew he was deep in thought—almost brooding. A half-smoked cigar was smoldering on the desk, sending up as much smoke as a bonfire, it seemed to Lady Churchill. He heard her approach and masked his surprise, still staring out the frosted French doors.

"Blasted fog has followed us from London," he rumbled.

She came up to him, slipping an arm through his.

"Perhaps it will burn off in a few hours and you can finish your landscape." Painting always put Winston in his most agreeable mood.

Still he said nothing, not turning, sullenly considering something out there in the folds of fog. Finally he spoke, his small porcine eyes moving over her face.

"What has made you risk my den, Clemmie dear?"

"Only to wish you a good morning."

His lower lip worked out in a few jerks, then they both laughed. He placed a pudgy finger on her cheek.

"You are a terrible liar Mrs. Churchill."

She smiled, deciding on taking an indirect tack. "I heard the phone awhile ago. Who called this early?"

"Desmond. He called because he knew I'd want to know . . ." He shook his head almost angrily. "I wanted to know? Can't help but knowing. . . ."

"Knowing what, Winston?"

"Germany has a new chancellor this morning," he snapped.

"Did Hindenburg die?"

"No! He is alive enough to be thoroughly stupid and corrupted and bullied! Which of the three or all three, I don't know! He's appointed *him*!"

Of course Clementine Churchill knew who *he* was. He was the subject of so much of her husband's recent writings—the person he penned warnings about. The writings that had his own country calling him an alarmist, a warmonger, a "croaking Jeremiah."

He swung away from the window, his pacing energetic and rapid despite his portly build.

"Imagine, Clementine! Imagine! A tramp from Vienna, a corporal from the Great War, a pitiful artist, a jailbird... a complete derelict is now in power in Germany! I can't understand it.... What is our prime minister thinking of?"

"Perhaps Prime Minister MacDonald isn't really thinking right now," Winston's wife ventured almost timidly.

Churchill's voice came in punctuated bites. "England can't afford—the continent can't afford—for the prime minister to be caught napping! He is closing his eyes and ears to the disturbing symptoms in Europe. Such a demeanor will only encourage Hitler to greater boldness! In his speech two days ago, MacDonald actually made inferences that Germany should be allowed to rearm, to be equal with France!" He picked up the cigar, drilling it through the air for emphasis. "I can't understand why our government is taking this posture. I can't, Clemmie. Heaven help us if Great Britain is going to be an accomplice to this madness!" His voice slowed to a growl. "And there's the United States simply gaping at what's going on."

The statesman, the orator speaking to England's deaf ears, had condensed his concerns for the world of 1933 into a dozen sentences for his wife. Clementine tried to calm him, derail his thoughts.

"I came in to remind you of Cynthia's party tonight. I didn't want you to forget and accuse me of not telling you till the very last hour."

"Cynthia's party? Oh, Clemmie, please, not tonight."

"Winston, now—"

"That woman always tries to corner me and get a row up. She does it for the benefit of her guests, like I'm some sort of party performer! She wants to talk politics or religion, and I can't promise I'll keep my temper with her. She's a horse-faced, horse-breathed gossip. She riles me, Clemmie, she really does. Don't make me go," he finished in a small voice.

"I'll stay with you. I'll interrupt, I'll do whatever, but we must go."

He sank wearily into a deep leather chair.

"If she brings up the new German chancellor, if she says he's going to do great things for Germany, I can promise you I will offer her a cigar quite forcefully!"

Clementine Churchill laughed. She loved the pudgy man with bull-dog jowls and eloquent ferocity. And Winston smiled. He loved to hear her laugh.

"Winston, I know you're right about Adolf Hitler being a real menace to the continent. But perhaps, perhaps the German people will come to their senses and he'll be stopped before he really starts."

His face clouded then as he stared at the floor. He wagged his head stubbornly.

"A madman, Clemmie, a madman is loose in Europe! Let us hope the good people, the ones not blinded will raise their hands. They must be out there!"

While the shadow in Germany lengthened and darkened, flames of light kindled—trembling at first, then steady, steady . . .

5
Lights

Ann Arbor, Michigan, 1933

The young man walked back to his dorm room deep in thought. Only when he had taken a wrong turn and half-waded into a three-foot-high snowdrift did he realize how distracted he was. He looked up then, shading his eyes against the glare of snow that blanketed the university campus. Across the way he could see dozens of students skating on the flooded football field and he smiled to himself. It reminded him of home—a Michigan winter was not so terribly different from the Swedish one he grew up with.

He was tall, slender, fair-haired—true to his Nordic stock. Many coeds found his accented English charming. Most found him good natured, kind, and a little on the dreamy side. He had come to America to study for a degree in architecture. Confident of this, he would then return home to the banking career his paternal grandfather insisted upon. He viewed these years as his final years of real personal freedom. With typical, youthful intensity, he intended to make the most of his time. He would work in the Swedish pavilion at the Chicago World's Fair come summer, and he planned an auto trip to Mexico after that.

"Raoul!"

He turned. A pretty blonde, her arms laden with books, came smiling up to him.

"I called you three times. Now what great project is on your brain's drafting board that you couldn't hear me?"

Raoul laughed and scooped up her books into his empty arms.

"No project."

"Oh, come now, don't be modest. Dr. Slusser declares you are his best and brightest pupil."

"Dr. Slusser is a very kind man."

"Were you planning a New York City skyscraper or perhaps the new Wallenberg bank in Stockholm!"

His laugh deepened. "We don't own a bank Jenny, I've told you that. But my latest project is a swimming pool and summer house."

"A swimming pool?"

Raoul nodded. "Yes, here in February the university president is thinking of swimming pools and asked me to plan one."

"Ah, so Raoul Wallenberg is all tied up with a swimming pool!"

"Actually, I...I wasn't thinking of that."

She leaned forward conspiratorily, "Something of a more...personal nature?"

Raoul smiled. He did like this teasing young American. They continued down the snowy path.

"Have you ever heard of Adolf Hitler, Jenny?"

"Let's see...he's the premier of the Soviet Union?"

"No, that's Joseph Stalin. Hitler is the leader of the Nazi party and became the chancellor of Germany last month."

"I was close," she shrugged.

"My grandfather wrote me about Hitler and his Nazi party. He wrote they are..." He looked up into the blue sky, lost in thought, and Jenny realized the young man was talking more to himself than to her.

"They are very aggressive. They broach no opposition, no debate. They become rather violent and act as if they are their own law—which is no law."

"They're a political party. How are they different from our republican and democratic parties?"

Raoul shook his head. "I don't think they are similar at all."

"So why, Mr. Wallenberg, across the ocean, a continent away, not even in your homeland, are you so deeply in thought about this group that you didn't even hear the voice of an attractive coed?"

Raoul stopped, looking at her blankly, missing her tease.

"They're against the Jews. They make all these threats against them. Why? I wonder. Jews are a very small percent of Germany's population—of all of Europe's in fact."

"Are you Jewish, Raoul?"

"One sixteenth," he answered with obvious pride. "I don't practice Judaism, but it is in my family line. But it isn't that, Jenny, not because of my blood. It . . ."

"It's what?"

"It doesn't matter to me if it is Jews or Catholics or anybody! The Nazis have no right to bully a group of people like that. It's wrong. Adolf Hitler sounds like a man full of hate. And that can't be very good for the German nation."

He glanced up at the ice skaters. Their laughter reached him in the clear winter air. "Big changes are coming . . . and I'm learning about building, about drawing, about design, about pools! My grandfather expects me to go into finance when I return home." He shook his head, a strange sadness creeping into his voice, "What does all that matter, I wonder? I want my life to count. . . . I want to do something important."

The young woman followed his gaze—but could not see the vision he was seeing.

France

The people of LaChambron, a small village in south-central France, were proud of their energetic, compassionate minister, Andre Trocme and his equally capable, selfless wife, Magda. Trocme was known for the challenging, direct, uncompromising sermons he delivered from the plain wooden pulpit nearly every Sunday. Trocme was quietly unafraid of his denominational superiors or public opinion. He was quite willing to denounce ungodliness in whatever form he saw it. The villagers could depend on Trocme to stay up all night praying over their sick, to lend the last sou in his pocket, to sweat beside them at harvest—and to stand and proclaim the truth.

Trocme knew from local gossip and the newspaper that his country was beset by political unrest and intrigue. It was troubling in a distant sort of a way since LaChambron was so remote and rural. Trocme was not very interested in the events in Paris, neither were his parishioners. Their's was a simple, unsophisticated life.

It was the middle of February when Andre Trocme, sitting before his fire reading a two-week-old newspaper, learned that Adolf Hitler had become chancellor of Germany. Trocme had read bits about the man before. A fellow pastor friend in Heidelberg, Germany, had written him with a brief mention of the Nazi party's efforts to unite Germany, to revive her from the economic morass she had slipped into since the Great War. Trocme raised his eyes from the paper to the bright orange flames. Hadn't he read that the Nazis were violent anti-Semetics? Yes, he was sure he had heard that. Now the party's leader was the authority in Germany. What could that mean for the German people, for the German Jew?

He stared into the flames, deep in thought. He considered waking Magda so that they might pray, but . . . When the knock at the door came an hour later for help for a villager, Trocme tossed the paper into the fire. His mind was instantly on this immediate crisis and the new German leader was forgotten.

Haarlem, Holland

At forty-one her waist had thickened, her abundant brown hair was woven with gray, her face and hands mottled and wrinkled. Her beauty though, was beyond her face, a beauty despite her years—a beauty blossomed from the kindness so deeply rooted in her. But Corrie ten Boom had never thought herself a beauty, even in her youth.

Cheerful, giving, loving. They were words that came quickly to the tongues of her Dutch neighbors when she was spoken of. She was a spinster, still living in the home of her growing-up years, working beside her father in his watchshop. She had a deep laugh, stout arms and legs—and dignity and resourcefulness. The test her life had been prepared for was fast approaching.

She heard the news in the marketsquare as she piled cabbages and beets into her basket. She paid, called a friendly greeting to Mrs. VanDamme who was sweeping her porch stoop, and climbed on her green bicycle. Age or gender didn't prevent Corrie from bicycling all over the city and nearby countryside. Her neighbors smiled when they saw the portly woman peddle past. As she rode, she thought of the shopper's words. *Adolf Hitler was the new German chancellor. Great and swift changes were coming to the Third Reich he had promised.* Corrie had heard vague words about him before. She especially remembered his hatred of Jews.

She tried to think of something else, but the thoughts of Germany persisted. There on the stretch of deserted cobbled road, Corrie ventured to pray aloud.

"Speak, oh my Lord, I will listen. . . ."

By the time she had reached the Beje, she still didn't know why she was thinking of the developments in the far-off land. She entered the kitchen where her sister Betsie was preparing dinner.

"Oh, these cabbages look fine, thank you, Corrie.... Corrie, is something wrong?"

As close as she was to her sister, Corrie felt unable to explain her feelings. She pulled off her hat and coat as she headed for the narrow stairs. "No, no, I'm fine. I'll be down shortly, Betsie."

Alone in her bedroom, Corrie sat down on the edge of her bed. Her eyes fell on the thick black Bible, and she remembered what she had read in her devotions that morning: Proverbs, chapter 14, verse 34. She turned to it again. When she came to the verse, she began to understand.

Righteousness exalteth a nation, but sin is a reproach to any people.'

Now she knew why she couldn't dismiss Adolf Hitler and his German followers from her mind.

She had heard; she slipped to her knees.

Czechoslovakia

It had been a very wet, very cold winter in the village. Most people were at home, close to their fires. The muddy, ice-crusted streets were nearly deserted save for the wanderings of a thin hound, a staggering drunk, and a shrill wind. Inside the tavern was very different—an antitheses to the world just outside the plain, wooden, double doors. The tavern pulsed with light, odor, warmth, and an alloy of human sounds: laughter, cursing, a song sung off-key, glasses slid along the tables. The main room was crowded and vaulted with a thick layer of cigar, cigarette, and pipe smoke. Men and a dozen women talked and drank together while the moon rose in frigid blackness.

In one group, a tall, blond man was obviously the center. He was well liked, suave—even in this rustic setting—and with a liberal amount of charm that the women found very attractive. It was obvious Herr Schindler was a man "moving up, going places," and so many people wanted to be part of his personal orbit. A man of many hearty appetites—who worked as energetically as he played—he was generous to his friends clear down to the seams in his pockets. He was always confident he could procure more money or resources when he needed it. He was laughing, joking, and consuming a vast amount of alcohol. That was not unusual, for Oskar Schindler was known for his ability to hold his liquor, and also his daring motorcycle racing. A married man of only six weeks, his drinking companions knew he was finding marriage confining. His young bride had stayed home.

From a table across the room, a swaying, red-faced young man stood. "A toast to Adolf Hitler...chan...chanc'lor of Germany!"

Most everyone toasted, less for the tribute and more for the comraderie of lifting the glass. Schindler's glass went up, then he drained it.

A man across the table pointed to the lapel pin on Schindler's jacket.

"You've already joined 'em, eh, Oskar?"

Schindler shrugged and fingered the black enamel swastika.

"Business is business, Hans. I'm always on the lookout for opportunities."

Another drinker spoke up with a sour voice.

"I think Herr Hitler acts like he thinks he's God!"

"Perhaps he is," Oskar smiled. "All the more reason to be on his side."

The table of cronies laughed. With so many drinks imbibed, it was easy to accept such irreverence.

"Some say he's determined to punish Jews."

"Who?" Oskar asked.

"Hitler."

Oskar toyed with his glass absently, he had not heard this.

"He has no call to, he said blandly."

"And just how is the factory these days?" someone else asked.

"Tolerable," Schindler answered. He leaned back on the wooden stool and stretched. "But I'll be leaving here one of these days. Better times are just around the corner, I can feel it."

"Good times, Oskar? Is that on your motorcycle or with the Nazis?"

"With my own wits, Hans, my own wits."

"So you'll be leaving us? And . . . Frau Schindler perhaps?"

Oskar reddened. He was saved from commenting by the opening of the tavern door. A dark-haired woman entered. Her eyes searched the crowd, squinting in the fog of smoke until she found him. Oskar stood up, quickly tossing coins on the table. He gave his friends a quick wink, and parted the crowd to reach the woman's side. They kissed, then slipped out the door.

The men at the table did not indulge in their customary suggestive comments of the obvious. Though they were Oskar's friends, the village men were united in their sympathy for the new Mrs. Schindler.

Berlin, Germany

While his face might not be always recognized on the street, like Hermann Göring or Max Schmeling's, the young Lutheran pastor's name was becoming increasingly known. His countrymen were proud, for Dietrich Bonhoeffer was gaining international recognition as a promising theologian and thinker. It was a hollow pride, as Bonhoeffer himself knew, since so many embraced Nazism instead of the truths he declared.

"We're late, Ed, can't you go a little faster?" he asked his friend at the wheel of the car.

"Faster? No, just calm down, Dietrich. We are only five minutes from the broadcasting house."

"And I'm supposed to go on in six minutes."

Bonhoeffer looked over his notes, his fingers tapping nervously. "The Concept of Leadership." An unoffensive, almost evasive title. He smiled.

"Nervous?" Ed asked.

"No, no . . . well, not much."

They chuckled together. Ed glanced at him. *With his blond hair, tall, broad-shouldered frame, the 29-year-old pastor looked more like a businessman or military type or the perfect Aryan that Adolf Hitler exulted.* He kept that thought to himself, knowing his friend's passionate feelings. Passionate and intense about whatever he did—that was Dietrich Bonhoeffer.

But the pastor seemed to sense the thoughts of the driver.

"Still having doubts about my speech, Ed?"

"I'm convinced of your sincerity, Dietrich, you know that."

Dietrich stared straight ahead, his voice still easy.

"But unconvinced about the truths regarding the Nazis?"

Ed sighed. "We've been over this before, Dietrich. I'll grant you that Adolf Hitler is loud and flamboyant. But, Dietrich, you can't ignore the injustice of the Versailles Treaty. Hitler says he'll bring Germany out of that shame and create jobs—restore . . . restore honor."

Dietrich snorted with contempt. "Honor?" He shook his head vigorously. "No, Ed. There is nothing honorable about the anti-Semitism or the military lusting! It's a shameful assault on decency. Our countrymen think they are following a great light, yet they're stumbling in the darkness!"

"Here we are," Ed said, as he parked the car. As Bonhoeffer prepared to dash from the car, Ed spoke up. "Ah, Dietrich, you are going to stick to your notes, aren't you? I mean, you aren't going to say—"

Dietrich laid a hand on his friends arm. "Stop worrying. You've read my paper. I moderated my tone considerably, but I will tell the truth."

"Well, all right. Good luck, Dietrich!"

As the two hurried into the building, Dietrich smiled. *Luck had nothing to do with it.*

He was well over five minutes into his speech, his voice strong, appealing, dynamic. Ed was nodding encouragingly behind the glass. The pastor was discussing the "need" of a fuehrer.

"To what point is leading and being led healthy and genuine? When does it become pathological and extreme? It is only after a man has answered these questions clearly in his own mind that he can grasp something of the essence of leadership."

Bonhoeffer talked for another 30 seconds before realizing the small red light on top of his microphone had stopped glowing. He looked around confused, stumbling over his words, like a man pulled from his dream. Ed was frowning and gesturing. Two men stood beside him, each wearing a swastika arm band. Dietrich burst through the door.

"What happened? What's the problem?" Dietrich asked hurriedly, thinking he could still finish his talk with an apology to the audience.

The two men, joined by the sweating station manager, were unsmiling.

"They cut you off, Dietrich," Ed said stiffly.

"What? Why?"

"Your speech was seditious, Herr Bonhoeffer."

"Seditious? What in the world are you talking about?"

"Lies about Nazism."

"I never used the word Nazism. If you were truly listening . . ."

"We were listening, Herr Bonhoeffer, very carefully. Your speech was blasphemy."

"Blasphemy?" Dietrich felt color rising in his face. "You want to talk about blasphemy—"

"Dietrich, a . . ." Ed began nervously.

"You had no right to cut off my speech," Dietrich returned hotly.

"What are rights, Herr Bonhoeffer?" the Nazi asked with a reptilian smile.

Dietrich swung around to the nervous station manager.

"Are you going to allow this? This is censorship!"

The man glanced at the Nazis and looked away. The room was silent. "Gentlemen, you are besmirching the name of the good German people with this action. Truth cannot be silenced."

"You would do well to be silent, Herr Bonhoeffer. It would be healthier for you. Goodnight."

On the sidewalk, Dietrich felt suddenly drained and sickened. Ed had turned pale. "I'm sorry, Dietrich," he said softly.

Bonhoeffer shook his head, staring at the ground.

"I'm sorry for you, Dietrich, I'm sorry . . . for all of us."

Dietrich looked up, eyeing his friend with a raised eyebrow.

"Have you jumped out of the whirlwind, Ed?"

"Ja. They aren't right, Dietrich."

"They won't silence me. God help me, they won't!"

And the lights began to shine.

6
They Have Eyes... But Do They See?

Vermont, 1933

Two figures, well wrapped against the cold, walked down the snowy road toward the farmhouse on the hill. The sky was flat white, cloudless, sunless, without horizon. It was very quiet on this road bordered by woods of maple, spruce, and pine. They could see the light from a lower window of the farmhouse: a brush of color, vivid and warm. They both anticipated the hot drinks they knew would be waiting in that humble sanctuary from the cold.

The man walking was 59, and his step was still vigorous. His hair was changing from iron gray to white, like the trim beard and mustache on his face. His clothes, while neat and clean, were unmistakably unfashionable and well-worn. He looked as European as his betraying heavy accent. Beside him walked the young woman he had loved for many years, though the paths of their lives crossed infrequently. He regretted that. Still, he was immeasurably grateful for the two months they had had together. They had been months of novelty—even with this thing called the "Depression," he was impressed on his first visit to America. Germany—Berlin in particular—was very distant, very different.

Comparing and contrasting the two countries gave him much to think about.

The tall, 22-year-old woman had enjoyed the time with the older man. Between college and a new job in the spring, their time together had been a pleasure. There had been so much to show him, and she enjoyed his almost childlike reactions and laughed over his attempts at English. She accompanied him as his translator—the poor doctor would have been lost at the medical conference in Philadelphia without her help.

"I will miss you, Uncle Josef," the young woman said in the stillness.

He smiled at her. She reminded him of his younger sister that he had loved, who had died years ago when serving as a nurse in the Great War.

"I have enjoyed my time in America immensely, Emilie. You and your father have made that so. Without you beside me, I would have been a poor dumkoft!"

She laughed. "I have been happy to be with you. I know father has enjoyed it, too."

"I am concerned over your father," he said slowly. "I don't want to alarm you, but he has changed."

Emilie Morgan sighed. "I know. Since that winter three years ago, he has been . . . He misses her, Uncle Josef. I miss her!"

The older man nodded. "Ja. Your mother was a special woman, one to miss. She gave a spark to my brother, and that spark is gone. But it is more than that."

Emilie knew what he was talking about—there was some undefinable trouble.

"He is unhappy beyond his loss, Emilie. Something else weighs on him. I can see it. I think it is connected to his work."

"Since he left the German diplomatic corp, and mother's death, I think his ambition, his drive is gone," Emilie reasoned.

Josef nodded. "He will answer my questions only vaguely. Last night after you went to bed, we stayed up talking."

"Did he tell you what was bothering him?"

"Nein. But he did get very excited, very agitated when we talked of the events in our homeland and Adolf Hitler becoming chancellor. He doesn't think Hitler is good for Germany, not in the least."

Emilie Morgan lived with only a meager, passing interest in her parents' homeland, the country where she was born and had lived her first three years. She remembered Germany from the occasional, brief visits her family had made. Though her German was as perfect as her uncle's, she felt more American than German. Germany and German ways were like old family photos, part of the past but not relevant to her own life."

"What do you think of the Nazis, Uncle Josef?"

"They are better than communists! Communists want revolution!"

"Didn't I hear father say that the Nazis recently outlawed the Communist Party?"

"Ja, ja, it was in the papers a few weeks ago."

"That would be like President Roosevelt outlawing republicans!" she laughed. "It wouldn't ever happen."

"You and your father must remember that your government is a democracy. The Weimar Republic tried democratic reforms after the war. From chaos came greater chaos. Now Hitler boasts he can restore order to Germany. I, for one, think he should be allowed to try."

"Father says Hitler sounds very cynical and brutish."

Josef nodded. "He said the same thing last night. Every politician likes to sound like a hero, a conqueror."

"Then Hitler is full of bluffing and boasts?"

Josef laughed, his arm going around her shoulders.

"You sound very much like your father."

"Oh, I don't know very much on my own, I admit. I haven't followed things like Father has. He also says Hitler sounds too militaristic."

"Ja, I know. But remember, you and your father have not lived in Germany for many years. I have seen the riots in the streets and the lines for bread. German money has been burned for fuel. I've treated the battered from the fights between social democrats and the communists. Perhaps order will come with this new power. I would welcome it. As to Adolf Hitler himself, I met him briefly 12 years ago. I was not impressed with him or his companions, but over the last few years I have moderated a bit. He says he can unify Germany. He has rough edges, but I expect he will modify, too. He'll calm down. If he is nothing more than a bluffer and boaster, then our people will see it and off he'll go! Now enough of that. Look there, Emilie!"

A pair of cardinals, the husband in his suit of flaming Christmas red, the wife in her dull brown, alighted on a snowy branch. Their heads came close together as if in an animated, domestic debate. The old man smiled broadly—he had come to love these American birds. "I will think of this fellow and his wife when I'm back in the city. I will imagine him on the windowsill of my little apartment against the gray of Berlin."

"I wish I had my camera," murmured Emilie.

"My niece behind the camera! You'll continue your photography when you and your father return to Washington?"

"Of course. This new job will not take all my time. I will keep my lens ready for a good assignment!"

"You are very talented, Emilie. I am proud of you."

She smiled. "Thank you, Uncle Josef."

"I leave for Germany tomorrow," he sighed. "This is our last walk together for a time. I have been to your country now, perhaps you will come back to Germany, Emilie. I could act as host for you, ja?"

The young woman smiled. She couldn't imagine having plans to return to Germany.

He leaned toward her, raising a gray eyebrow with significance. "There is no young man you should be telling me about?"

Emilie laughed—he had only asked her this a dozen times in the past two months. "No one."

"American men are blind, ja?"

"Uncle Josef . . ."

"You have not seen the right one, ja? Well, don't be in a hurry, that is good."

"You never married, Uncle Josef? Was there never . . . ?"

The old man paused. "Years ago, but . . . she loved another. And I . . . I had my work. It has been a good life, though."

"I can't imagine someone choosing another man over you."

He smiled and shook his head. For a moment, the long past sadness filled his eyes.

They walked along silently a few moments more.

"And what will the right man for you be like, Emilie? Describe him. If I come across him in Germany—"

"You'll notify me by telegram immediately?" she teased.

"Immediately!"

"Well, let's see . . . dark hair or fair, doesn't matter—but handsome of course!"

"Of course. Like this Gary Cooper in the motion picture we saw last night?"

"Ummm, he would do. But he must also be . . ." She looked at the Vermont hills painted white, the late afternoon deepening the white sky to a smoky gray. "A man of integrity, kindness, and courage. And, of course, dashing and exciting!"

She laughed aloud at her own description.

Josef Morgan nodded with mock seriousness.

"I will keep my eyes open for him!"

Together they climbed the last hill.

Nuremberg, Germany

While Nuremberg could not celebrate the advent of Adolf Hitler with the pageantry and brilliance of Berlin, the southern city was no less caught up in the Nazi fervor flooding Germany during the early days of 1933. Nuremberg was a favored Nazi rally site. In two short years, the Nazis would compose their stringent racial laws for the land and give the city the dubious honor of calling them "the Nuremberg Laws." For now, though, the city hosted parades and parties largely composed of middle-class Nazi members. Yet the whole city seemed to participate, if only vicariously, imitating with grim perfection the pagan rituals of centuries past. And those who clearly saw the truth of Nazism and were revolted, stood in dim doorways or behind curtains and watched in astonishment. *What is happening? Have our neighbors gone mad?* they wondered.

The streets were loud and crowded. University students joined the raucous crowd of swastika lovers with enthusiasm. It was an accepted excuse for not studying.

Two young men and two young women sat at a sidewalk cafe, drinking beer and watching the street. Sometimes they laughed, and made negative comments on Nazis in general and Adolf Hitler in particular. But mostly they watched in silence, in something akin to awe, not wanting to admit even to each other the tiny knot of anxiety they felt over the scene.

Twenty-five-year old Wilhelm Mueller sat at the cafe table drinking from his stein, his arm draped loosely around the back of the chair of a young blonde woman. He drank, laughed, told most of the jokes, but watched the street with casual intensity. He had already had a few encounters with roving street gangs of young Nazis. Mueller knew their violence, and he knew the limits to his own temper. Seemingly lazy and relaxed, Wilhelm Mueller rarely felt relaxed these days—he felt more like a tightly coiled spring.

"Wilhelm, I've heard the university is considering, and I quote, 'relieving Jewish professors of their teaching responsibilities.' What will Walther do?" the blonde woman asked.

"Nazis use the most shady language I've ever heard," the other young woman laughed. "Relieving of teaching responsibilities. Why don't they just say kicked out?"

"Nazis don't know any other language, Hannah," Wilhelm smiled, but he didn't feel like smiling. He didn't like to think of the disappointment of his older brother.

"Walther's already heard something about that. He says he'll move back to Berlin," he continued.

"Berlin? That's worse than here! Could he expect to get a job teaching in Berlin?" the other man, Peter, asked.

Wilhelm shifted uncomfortably. "He says he'd teach someplace rural, live with our folks."

"You going with him, Wilhelm?" the blonde girl asked, leaning toward him.

"If I leave Nuremberg, it will be when I'm ready. No Nazi will run me off!"

They laughed then lapsed into silence as a singing group of older men paraded past carrying a huge poster of Adolf Hitler. Wilhelm leaned across the table, his voice now amused.

"Now, will someone please explain this to me? I just can't figure it out. We've all heard Adolf ranting that Germans are the perfect master race. He describes them as strong, blond, blue-eyed, tall, athletic, suave, on and on. Then look at him! Puny, dark-haired, big nose, beady eyes, squat!"

The youths were laughing again. "He could pass for a Russian Jew!" Hannah said.

"Look at the guys around him," Peter took up, "Goebbels is skinny and pale and crippled!"

"Oh, well Göring, then, he must be their ideal!" Hannah interrupted. "Dirigible Göring!"

They were laughing uncontrollably now, the street scene forgotten, the tables of customers around them ignored.

"Ahem . . ."

It took a full minute for Handel, the proprietor, to get the youths' attention. He stood tall and imposing beside the table, frowning. He cleared his throat again.

They were silent, wiping their tears, and trying to assume a serious attitude.

Wilhelm turned to him. "Ja? Is there a problem?"

The man crossed his thick arms with a flourish. He wore the red and black arm band.

"You are being far too loud."

Peter spoke up, "Oh, all right, we'll quiet down."

"We just got carried away, you know. This is a big night to celebrate, to have fun," Wilhelm added with a straight face.

"I heard the fun you were having, young man." Handel leaned forward, glancing about, then lowered his voice. "I heard your joke of Goebbels and Göring and the chancellor."

"We meant nothing by it. It was just a joke. We will be quieter, sir," Hannah said nervously.

"Is it wrong to laugh in Germany now? Illegal to tease? I don't remember anyone having a problem with calling old Hindenberg a walrus face!" Wilhelm retorted crisply.

"Wilhelm—"

Handel leaned forward, his eyes piercing into the young man.

"Listen, I am German—"

Wilhelm stiffened, his voice hissing, "As I am fully German!"

"Ja, and you are Jewish, too."

"Ja."

"I am trying to tell your stubborn ears, you must be more careful, more prudent in your words when sitting in a cafe telling jokes about our leaders. I can account for myself, I cannot for those in the tables nearby. They may call attention to you when the next group of revelers comes down the street. I would not like to see anything happen in my respectable establishment. Do you understand?"

"You . . . you are a Nazi. Why are you saying this?" Peter whispered hoarsely.

Handel straightened, looking to make certain he was not overheard.

"I wear the band; I am a member. Finish your drinks, then move on, bitte."

He left them. Wilhelm's face was red, and no one spoke. No one felt like joking. Finally Peter stood, pulling Hannah with him.

"Let's go to my place. I have a new jazz record."

Wilhelm stood slowly, his voice low. "Nazis don't like jazz remember?"

The young people smiled, placing their coins on the table. At the sidewalk curb, Wilhelm Mueller turned. The proprietor stood drying glasses with his apron—watching them without a smile. Their eyes locked. The man nodded quickly to the young Jew.

Berlin

Elaina Heydrich was as convinced as she had been 13 years ago: Her escort was still the most handsome, most enjoyable man she had ever known. They had been friends since he wore knee breeches and she ribbons, and they were still friends. That is, as much as he would let you be a friend. Elaina Heydrich had always felt a reserve about Max, a holding back despite his friendliness—as if he couldn't—or wouldn't—open up. She suspected that was why, despite the fact both their families had expected it years ago, he had never asked her to marry. Still, there had been many exchanged kisses, well-charged with passion, since that first one on the river so many afternoons ago. She would never forget that one.

She glanced at Max Farber's profile in the darkened Mercedes beside her. She would like to have molded herself closer to the man, but, instinctively, she knew she shouldn't. He would withdraw; it had happened before. She sensed a conflicting mood in Max this night, a medley of emotions—his good nature versus a pensiveness. If she intruded too quickly, too closely, he would grow guarded. She glanced out the window and wondered for the thousandth time if she loved this man.

Max was dressed as impeccably as Elaina was in his dinner jacket, polished shoes, and the aura of French cologne. An expensive overcoat rested across the seat. He passed the celebrations on the streets of the capital with little emotion, seeing them indifferently. He was not thinking of Adolf Hitler; he was thinking of the conversation he'd had only an hour earlier with his two older brothers. In Irwin's office at I.E. Farber on the

Unter Den Linden, the three men had argued. *Well, mostly only Irwin and me,* Max reflected, *Eric had sat on the edge of the desk inserting only an occasional bland comment.*

Irwin had been both jubilant over the Nazi victory and querulous with his family.

"You've held back long enough, Max. Today's events clearly shows the Nazi party is on the road to power. We are the way of the future for Germany. You must join in! It would be embarrassing for the company to have a leading businessman not a part ... It's like you're in some adolescent rebellion against the family and government!"

Eric glanced up at Max, meeting his eyes and shrugging. Twenty-nine-year old Max straightened and exhaled loudly.

"Don't you have a party to go to, Irwin? It's getting late."

"You haven't heard a word I've said."

Max smiled benignly. "Quite the contrary, Irwin. I've heard every word ... several times."

"Then what is it? Why are you opposing me in joining the Nazi party? A solidified I.E. Farber will find a place of real significance in the Third Reich!"

Max was silent. Often he felt waiting out Irwin's storms was the best strategy.

"It's the old doctor, isn't it? He's poisoned you against us."

"Josef?" Max shook his head. "Actually, he thinks favorably toward the Nazis in some respects. Still, I won't hear you slander Dr. Morgan, Irwin, so stop. I am thinking on my own."

"Like the way you conduct your life, is that it, Max? Be different; anything to oppose me. You dabble in I.E. Farber just enough to know what we produce, then you go off to the Alps to ski!"

Max's voice was sharp. "Do you have any complaint with the travel or work that I've done for the company, Irwin?"

The oldest brother toyed with his pen set. "No."

"Can't you fellows leave this off? I have a date, and I happen to be very hungry," Eric complained.

"For the date?" Max asked roguishly. The two laughed, then broke off when Irwin did not join in.

Max retrieved his coat and hat. "Look, Irwin, it is very simple. Eric joined because he wanted to; you joined because you wanted to. I'll join when, and if, I want to. Don't bother me with this discussion again. Goodnight, fellows."

"Look at the banner!"

Max was pulled from his thoughts by Elaina's exclamation. They could see the huge, blood-red banner that hung from the Brandenburg Gate.

"The city is glitzed up tonight. I'd say the Nazis know how to throw a party," Max remarked.

"You don't feel quite the same elation the crowds do, though," Elaina replied pointedly.

"Elation? No . . . but like I said, it makes for a great party. I bet Reinhard's pretty swelled up tonight."

Elaina laughed. "Yes, very much so. He invited us to a party at Goebbles, but I told him we already had plans."

Max slowed and pulled to the curb. "The Adlon Hotel . . ." he murmured.

"Max? What's wrong?"

"Nothing. Only . . . suddenly I don't feel like going to the bash at the Adlon. Let's go to the 'Blue Moon' jazz club. They have great food, too!"

His blue eyes sparkled with mischievous fun. Elaina had drawn back in mock alarm. "Oh, Max, really—"

"Come on, Elaina, I promise you'll enjoy it."

Anywhere with Max, I'll enjoy, she mused.

"Max, jazz is greatly frowned upon by the party."

"Why?"

"Well, because jazz is a product of the Negro culture."

A retort leapt to his tongue, but he suppressed it. He clenched the steering wheel tightly. "No one is going to tell me what music to like or dislike." He touched the string of pearls at her throat. "What if they decide pearls are too decadent?"

Elaina felt a small stirring of alarm. Max was talking so . . .

He smiled suddenly. "I'm sorry. I didn't mean—"

"Max, you know I support the Nazi Party. We've talked about this before. What is it?"

"I just don't have the political interest in all this. Nazism complicates my life. I don't want it complicated. I like things the way they are." He shrugged and turned away.

The woman knew the wall of reserve was rising. She leaned toward him, "Never mind, Max. I'll go wherever you want to go." She hoped he could hear the unmistakable invitation in her voice.

He cleared his throat, returning to his typical calm.

"I'm sorry, Elaina but I have a hard time following a guy whose name could have been Schicklgruber!"

There was a moment of silence in the car, before they both burst out laughing.

"Max! What are you talking about? Whose name?"

"Our chancellor's. His father's name for years was Schicklgruber."

"Oh, Max, surely not!"

"It's true. Can you imagine 'Heil Schicklgruber!'"

Elaina was laughing hard though she knew she shouldn't.

"Reinhard never told me that."

"He wouldn't, but I'm sure he knows. Hitler doesn't like it mentioned, and will probably pass a law about it soon."

Max slipped his arm around her supple shoulders.

"What will it be, fraulein? The Adlon or the forbidden jazz club? You decide."

"The forbidden 'Blue Moon,' sounds so . . ."

He kissed her. "Let's dance until dawn, Elaina!"

The Farber Estate

A man dressed in the garments of a country house laborer left his quarters on the estate, wandered through the barren patch of ground that was the kitchen garden, and stood at the edge of the lawn. He looked up at the big house. It was dark in every eyeless window; it seemed cold and severe to him.

Heinz Mueller knew this house from garret to cellar. He had been a servant here all his adult years. His father had done the work before him and trained him. This place was his world.

No Farber son was in residence this January night. The three sons, very rarely together, seldom came to their country estate. They lived in town now. The big parties, the guests, and the hunting holidays were in the past—dusty memories like the family portraits in the hall. Heinz grew sad, sometimes, when he realized that since the death of Frau Farber, those times were forever gone.

He heard steps behind him and knew it was his wife.

"What are you doing outside in the cold old man?" she asked affectionately, slipping her hand into his hand in his pocket.

He smiled. "I . . . just came out."

"To stare at an empty house, ja?"

"I thought I heard something."

"A car?" She looked into the darkness and stepped closer to her husband. He was not too old to try to scare her a little.

"Nein, not a car."

She noted his serious tone. "You are thinking of Wilhelm?"

He shook his head. "Not Wilhelm tonight."

She pulled the sweater closer to her throat.

"Well, come back to the house. It's too cold to be standing out in the dark. You probably heard the wind."

"The wind . . ." he echoed absently.

Her smile faded as she looked up at him. Heinz got like this on rare occasion—remote, like he was hearing someone far-off speaking to him in a language only he could understand.

"Love, what is it?" she asked softly.

He squeezed her hand. "Don't be afraid, Marta. I'm all right. You go back in; I'll be in shortly."

She knew from his voice, typically so gentle and patient, that she should obey.

Left alone, Heinz continued staring at the house. But he was facing Berlin. He had heard the report of Hitler's ascension on the radio he listened to with Marta. It made him . . . he couldn't find the word in his limited vocabulary to express it. . . . An hour after the broadcast, he had felt he must go outside. He heard . . . he wasn't certain what he had heard.

He was not afraid for himself. Or Marta. Or the children. He didn't know to be afraid for them yet.

He could not feel the cold. He knew Marta had gone inside, but he knew he was not alone. He had known that since he was a boy of 15 in Vienna. That summer . . . remembering was like a breeze blowing away the fog that shrouded the dawn, and he knew why he was standing here.

"Commune with me, commune with me," he croaked in a raspy old voice only the angels could appreciate. "Between the wings of the cherubim, commune with me, Lord!"

He closed his eyes. He knew it was not his youngest son he was to pray for this ordinary night. Tonight, Heinz Mueller knew his country had become the prodigal.

7
He Alone Sees the Heart

Berlin, February 1933

It was obvious to the most casual observer that since the Nazis had come into "official" power only a month earlier great and dramatic changes were taking place in every area of German life—including the most mundane such as street repair. Chancellor Hitler had vaulted ambitions for the capitol city. It must reflect the superior intellect, culture, and strength of the German people. Berlin would be a model city of the Third Reich, renowned in Europe for its broad avenues and imposing classical buildings. Hitler's own Chancellery was to be redesigned with the clear purpose of intimidating foreign visitors. Buildings were going up; buildings were coming down. There was no argument—certainly no complaint—that the Nazis had improved the economy and employment in Berlin.

A tall man, hatless, dressed in dark pants and a rich leather jacket was walking along the Wilhelmstrasse. He walked slowly and leisurely, one hand in his pocket, the other holding a leash. His face was full of curious interest in the construction sights. A terrier, looking as alert and interested as his master, kept the leash taut. Max Farber had been gone only three weeks yet so many changes were evident. It was amazing, really, that so much was

81

being accomplished so quickly. *No slow grinding bureaucracy for the Nazis*, he reflected. He stopped at an intersection that was being widened, and listened to the low rumble of machinery in the winter morning air. *Such plans, such progress at such speed, the man realized in a flash, must have come from a determined mind months, perhaps years ago. Nazi thoroughness. The chancellor had been waiting and preparing for his rise to the throne.*

Max felt like walking this morning. The day was clear, sunny, unseasonably warm, and mild enough to pass for a day in October. The laborers along the streets worked in their shirtsleeves. Max had left his townhouse with the idea of reporting in at I.E. Farber Company on Unter den Linden. His Mercedes, still loaded with skis and luggage, was parked at the curb of his home on Tiergartenstrasse. He considered it a moment. Even with the dissected streets, it was only a five minute drive from home to office. He frowned; he was in no hurry, he would walk. And he would take Percy, who would relish the busy scenes, and ignore the comments he was sure to receive at the I.E. Farber offices. Max did not care.

Apart from Kurfurstendamm, these three avenues: Unter den Linden, Tiergartenstrasse, and Wilhelmstrasse comprised the pulsing heart of Berlin. All principal government buildings, businesses, military headquarters, elegant restaurants, and fashionable townhouses were planted along these routes. Max lived on the perimeter.

A detour brought Max and Percy to the Berlin State Opera House. It too, was undergoing cosmetic surgery. Max paused at the fence to watch. Percy could smell rodents in the wind and quivered with excitement. Max was interested in the workmen who were sweating and struggling—working for their living in a way that he did not. Though he couldn't have explained it and brushed it aside with a chuckle, he admired these hard-working men.

Max was such a man to draw the eye, alone or in a crowd. One of the laborers on the edge of the construction sight paused, watching the young man. Of course people stopped all through the day to observe the progress—that was not unusual. But this man, looking like a foreigner in his expensively cut clothes and manicured dog, looked more than just casually attentive. The laborer steered the muddy wheelbarrow toward the fence. Percy whined in excitement.

"Percy," Max said firmly but not unkindly. The animal quieted.

"Guten Morgen," Max said cheerfully.

"Mornin', sir," the laborer replied with a swift touch to his cloth cap.

A crease appeared between Max's eyes. An older man showing him deference. He didn't like that. It was the clothes and his obvious wealth. He liked meeting all sorts of people in his travels, and regretted the prejudice sometimes shown because of his wealth. He smiled at the man.

"Nice warm weather this morning," Max offered.

The laborer blew out relieved smoke. "Ja." He sized up Max again, then gave a quick glance to the nearest government building. The huge red-and-black banner hung limp.

"Do you suppose Dr. Goebbels will announce that the Nazis are responsible for it?" the laborer asked with a gap-toothed grin. Max was laughing at the man's bold tease.

Dr. Goebbels was the energetic propaganda minister for the new reich and the echoing voice of Adolf Hitler. The laborer was nodding at his own cleverness—and his accurate guess that this man was no humorless Nazi.

"Fine-lookin' dog, there."

"Danke. Tell me, what's your project here? Expansion or repair?"

So for ten minutes, the working man leaned on the fence post talking with Max as if they were tavern buddies.

"You visitin' Berlin?" the man asked.

Max shook his head. "Nein, I've lived here most of my life."

"Ah . . . so where do ya suppose the money for all this sprucin' up is coming from?" the man asked, nodding toward the building.

"I don't know, but that's a very good question," Max admitted.

"We had Hindenberg tellin' us the treasury was about dried up, and now this new fella steps in and things are flowin' along smoother than mother's milk." He scratched his head. "Things are changin' all 'round. Makes you wonder."

The older man turned his cataract-clouded eyes on Max, giving another quick appraisal of his clothes and his friendly face.

"You work in Berlin?" he asked, a little shocked at his own bluntness. Now he'd have a tale for Emma over the table tonight. He'd talked with aristocracy or something!

Max smiled at the man's hesitation. He bent down for a moment to stroke Percy. "I work up the street . . . sort of at a desk job."

"Ah . . ." the laborer murmured.

Max stood. "Well, I shouldn't be keeping you from your work any longer. I wouldn't want the boss to get short with you. I've enjoyed our talk."

The man's laugh was raspy as he lit a fresh cigarette.

"No harm—I'm the foreman of this section."

"You?" Max burst out, then he blushed. *This man in the cheap greasy pants and frayed shirt was a supervisor?*

"It's the truth," the man laughed again.

"You work alongside your men, then?" Max asked thoughtfully.

"Sure. Ain't no better way. Just 'cause I'm a boss isn't going to make me a slacker. You get lazy and flabby like that. No thanks."

Now it was Max's turn to size this man up. *Flabby? Not much chance. I can almost count his ribs through the thin shirt.* The man read Max's thoughts. "Nothing but lean meat here—no fat."

Max met his eyes and they laughed together.

The man's eyes narrowed as he looked over the work scene.

"Now tomorrow, sir. Things would have been different if you'd stopped to chat." His voice, Max noticed, had been dropped to a softer tone.

"Oh?"

"Today's the last day for me as foreman. Get to go back to the pits tomorrow."

"The pits?"

"Like them there. Do all the heaviest, dirtiest stuff. The digging, moving the rocks . . . the pits."

Max was shocked. This man had to be approaching 60!

"What happened?"

The man was silent for a full minute, and Max decided he hadn't heard—or the answer was too personal to speak of. Slowly the foreman turned, glancing quickly to Max. He squatted down to pet Percy through the fence. "New boss. He came by two days ago and said my work was fine—but it didn't look good for a communist to be a foreman. See, I was a member when I was a young man. Hadn't paid my dues in years 'cause they got too rowdy for me. But the new boss seen it in my records. Said he'd keep me on as a worker, though. I've been working for this company 15 years. 'Course I kinda think these Nazi fellows may make communists look like a bunch of Sunday school tots!" he laughed bitterly. "Yeah, you have a fine-lookin' dog. About a year old?"

"Yes, about . . ." Max replied slowly.

"I'd like a dog like this, but the wife always sneezes around them, so we keep a bird." He laughed again and shook his head.

"Do you have any children?" Max asked, not smiling.

"Two girls."

"I'd imagine this job change will affect your pay."

The smile of tobacco-stained teeth widened. "A bit, yeah. Well, I best be gettin' back or they'll cut me off early."

"I admire your . . . good humor," Max said suddenly.

Now it was the foreman's turn to color. This was an odd one! Not at all like the usual fare that merely slowed at the fence then passed on. This young man, with his fine tailored clothes and friendly ways, was different.

Max fumbled in his pocket and handed the man a fold of marks.

"I think you should take your wife out to dinner tonight, you know, with a new job starting tomorrow," Max shrugged.

The worker was staring with his mouth open. This wealthy Berliner was acting like an embarrassed schoolboy!

"I can't take this, sir," he said finally.

"I wish you would, for your wife you know. . . ."

Their eyes locked.

"Well, I . . ."

"I'm going to be late myself," Max said as he searched his shirt pocket. He handed the man a creamy-white, gilt-edged card. "If you ever need a job, come over. I have . . . connections. Well, auf Wiedersehen! Percy, let's go."

The construction man looked at the card with as much amazement as he had looked at the money in his hand. Printed on it was "I.E. Farber Company, Unter den Linden." He turned it over—it had only one word scratched across it—*Max.*

• • •

"Sir! Excuse me, sir!"

Max was smiling as he stopped before the elevator and took Percy off his leash. He had passed the front reception desk with a friendly wave to the woman sitting alertly behind it. The receptionist treated this green-and-black tiled floor space of I.E. Farber Company as her strictly surveilled dominion, and kept it as sterile as a surgeon's tray, as tidy as a chapel, and as guarded as a military bunker. She came up to Max briskly and authoritatively.

"Sir, dogs are not allowed at I.E. Farber."

Max feigned a puzzled look. "You mean . . . Percy?"

"This dog. Please remove him at once."

"Oh, oh, this dog! His name is Sir Percy Blackney. Handsome chap, don't you think?"

"Sir—"

"You must be new here. You see," Max leaned forward, "I know all the secretaries in the colossus Farber Company. Frankfurt, Munich, Vienna, Warsaw: I know them all!"

"Sir, I am asking you to leave. He is not even leashed according to the new city ordinance!"

"New city ordinance? Hmm . . . no, *he* isn't leashed." He winked.

The woman stepped back, suddenly fussing with the back of her neck.

"*He* doesn't need a leash. A perfect gentleman, Percy."

Percy sat next to Max's left leg, obviously aware that he was the subject of this controversy. He sat statue still, not even panting.

"There, you see, no need to worry. Well, Guten Tag!"

"But, but, sir, now really. My boss will not approve of this!"

She glanced around nervously.

"Your boss? You mean Herr Irwin Farber?" Max leaned forward again, and this time the middle-aged woman caught the full force of the cologne he was wearing. *Or perhaps it was aftershave.* She avoided his blue eyes. "Is this Farber really the tyrant I've heard he is?"

"Oh, no, I mean, I really wouldn't know, sir. He isn't my boss, directly. Herr Schiller manages all the secretaries for the company. And I'm certain he would be displeased—"

"Of course, of course. What about the other brothers . . . oh, I am terrible with names. . . ."

"There is Herr Eric Farber and Herr Maximillian Farber."

"Maximillian Farber. Ja, that is the one." He consulted a card. "Ja, that is the one I am to see this morning."

"Oh, he's not here. I've worked here six weeks and I've never seen him."

"Never seen him? How very odd! Why do you suppose you haven't seen him? I would think no one could get past you!"

She flashed him an appreciative smile. "He is the youngest, and I'm told he is rather irresponsible and flighty. Doesn't work much, just plays. He's a bachelor and always traveling." She was warming to her subject, the desk forgotten, the room free from her vigil. "I am also told he is very charming and handsome and . . ." Her eyes suddenly widened.

"Ja? A handsome fellow you say? Well, I'm relieved. I wouldn't want to transact business with an ugly man!"

The elevator opened and customers and employees poured out in a chatty torrent.

"Why, Max, hello! How was Zurich?"

"The skiing was great!"

The man waved and was gone. Max turned back to the receptionist who had retreated, scarlet-faced, to her post.

Max winked and stepped into the elevator.

Alone in the elevator, Max squatted to ruffle Percy's ears.

"There you are, Percy. Did you hear? Flighty and irresponsible. How do you put up with me, old man, hmm?"

Max passed through the outer offices on the way to his, with greetings for everyone.

"Zurich was perfect. . . . No torn up streets. . . ."

"How's the new baby?" he asked one of the secretaries.

"Percy enjoyed the slopes, too. Only fell once. Agile fellow . . . has a Swiss girlfriend now, too. . . ."

"Dinner tonight, Anna? . . . What company policy?"

The secretaries and minor employees agreed with the sentiment expressed by the sentry on the first floor. Max Farber was very different from his two older brothers—especially the ambitious, stern man who commanded them all from one floor up. Everyone smiled when Max breezed in. He was cheerful, often bringing gifts from a foreign city. He was generous and easygoing, in contrast to Irwin Farber who had the ambition and determination to push the business to an impressive international reputation.

Max stepped into his office with a sigh as he tossed off his jacket. It was, as offices go, a large and well appointed room. One large mahogany desk, deep leather chairs, bookshelves, and a window that gave a spectacular view of Berlin's prettiest street. He sunk into the chair while Percy took the opposite chair and was soon snoring. Exemplary behavior had exhausted him.

There was no individual stamp on this office, nothing that showed it was Max's except the lettering on the door and the monogrammed pen set from Elaina Heydrich on the desk. No trophies or photos or oil paintings. Elaina had complained about it once when she had visited him there.

"Max, I'm sorry, but your office is so, so . . ."

"Boring?"

"Yes. It's so impersonal."

"What does it matter? I spend very little time here."

"I understand, but certainly when you are here you need some color, some personality!"

"I come here to get my work done, that's all."

"Dear Max . . ."

Four neat stacks of papers and files were arranged and waiting for him. Karl Beck, his secretary, was abnormally efficient, Max had long ago decided. He eyed the files, letters, and memos, drew a deep breath, and began. He worked steadily for two hours, letting the coffee grow cold that was brought to him. He dictated one report to the office secretary, then asked, "Where is Karl this morning?"

"I believe he's in a production meeting sir. He didn't know you were coming in this morning."

Max smiled at the veiled statement. No one was ever quite sure when the young industrialist would show up for his responsibilities. "Please send Karl in when he comes."

"Yes, sir."

I.E. Farber Company had become in its 83-year lifespan one of Germany's most successful industries. With a dose of gambler's luck, it had weathered the major and minor convulsions that had seized Germany in the past 50 years: a world war, a worldwide economic depression, a government in disorder, and now a new government proposing radical reforms.

Max's great grandfather had begun the company with his wife's dowry money and a strong desire to help German farmers with improved tools and implements. Within 20 years, Farber was producing the finest farming equipment in Germany. Their success spread. When Max's grandfather assumed control, farmers as far south as Spain and as far north as Russia were turning the land with Farber tools. Driven by consuming ambition, the first I.E. Farber decided to expand into the chemical industries. With autocratic zeal, he put Farber scientists to work, and soon Farber was producing synthetic gasoline from coal. That had vaulted Farber Company into great favor with the government. Max's father had continued the expansion. It didn't seem like the mammoth company could grow any bigger; Irwin, Eric, and Max only had to harness the beast. But Irwin had ambitions as strong as his ancestors, and the Nazi government would accommodate him.

When Max had turned 20, he had gone to work in the Berlin office, working long hours as he learned the trade. Irwin had assumed a rigid paternal mantle over both Eric and Max. No one could have teased, taunted, or implied Maximillian Farber was irresponsible, flighty, or lazy. He had worked hard, his youthful energy and quick mind grasping the inner workings of the huge company. Then, as he turned 22, Max presented his request to Irwin. He would become Farber Company's traveling representative. Irwin grudgingly admitted that his little brother did have the social graces that he so obviously lacked. Irwin's appraisals at parties and business meetings had shown that Max was charming and diplomatic. For the good of the company, Irwin agreed to this position for his brother. It was mutually pleasing: they worked toward the same goal, but in different orbits and rarely saw each other. Max took his assignments, then traveled and filed his reports. Irwin searched hard and brought up any complaints against his work. Max took the grievances with unruffled good humor; Irwin was Irwin.

Some obscure notes from his secretary, Karl, held Max's attention. They were very limited, and Max was a little surprised, Karl was usually very thorough. Percy sat up eagerly when a knock on the door came.

"Come in," Max commanded.

"Guten Morgen, Max. Welcome home."

"Guten Morgen, Karl, danke."

"Percy, you scoundrel, come here, boy."

Max leaned back in the chair, watching his secretary wrestle with the dog.

Karl Beck had become Max's secretary from Max's first day, eight years before. They had started work at I.E. Farber together—one a wealthy heir, the other the son of a bricklayer from Wedding, one of Berlin's poorer districts. Irwin Farber had plucked the young man from poverty and placed him as his brother's aide. Max had accepted the choice with typical equanimity. He would enjoy learning the trade with a young man his own age. Their different backgrounds and social strata so clearly represented in the way they dressed was of no consequence to him. If Max had ever noticed Karl's early awkward diffidence, he had not shown it. Like Max, Karl had learned quickly and worked hard. The secretary could be testy and petulant, but Max brushed this aside and found him completely dependable.

Their age was the only similarity between them. Where Max was tall, broad, and blond, Karl was tall and lanky, with black hair that he brushed severely back from his forehead. He was always pale, giving intensity to his dark eyes—eyes that seemed to Max to be continually measuring his surroundings. After two years, the clothes of the bricklayer's son changed. He became fastidious in his dress—almost dapper. It was not uncommon to overhear Karl Beck boasting of the cost of his newest tie to office subordinates gathered around the coffeepot. Max had heard snatches of office gossip, that Karl was teased about his fine rags and that the women found him attractive but too remote and moody.

In private conversations, the sir was dropped and Karl called Max by his given name. It was a mutual business friendship that Max valued. In the early years, Karl had accompanied Max on the traveling assignments, but then Max had decided the best arrangement was for Karl to remain in Berlin to be his liaison with Irwin and the home office. Karl did the hundreds of mundane tasks that Max would have found terribly boring. Karl often signed memos and letters with Max's scrawl when Max was out of town. On those matters that required Max's involvement as a controlling partner, Karl often gave a summary of the information. After a quick signature or verbal assent over the phone, Max was moving happily to something else.

"Percy's getting fat," Karl observed.

"Too many Swiss pastries," Max laughed.

Karl stood in his habitual hunched posture, his hand jerking to his pocket for a cigarette. His eyes met Max's as he instantly remembered his employer's intolerance. His hand stuffed into his pocket, he slouched into the chair Percy had vacated. He was very relaxed with the young German industrialist.

"And a few Swiss pastries for you, Max?" Karl asked with a thin smile.

Max shook his head with a shocked expression.

"You know this trip was strictly business."

"Ah . . ."

"Percy found a lady, though. Made an undignified scene when we left, but I think he's over her."

Karl pointed to the desk. "You've gone through the work?"

"Ja."

They then discussed the recent business trip and the papers Max had just gone through.

"I've only one question."

"Your brother wants to see you before you leave. What is your question, Max?"

Max frowned. "Why does he want to see me?"

"Herr Farber did not tell me."

"That doesn't bode well. This memo here—it's uncharacteristically brief for you."

He waited. Karl's eyes narrowed. "Merely notes from a recent meeting, Max."

"A meeting," Max perused the paper, "between Irwin and Reinhard Heydrich and a Herr Himmler that I've never heard of, concerning business possibilities."

"That is correct."

"Why is Reinhard, a naval officer, coming to Farber about business possibilities? Does he want Irwin to give him a job?"

"Herr Heydrich has a job. He is no longer with the navy."

Max's eyebrows went up.

"Heydrich is working in the new intelligence branch of the government here in Berlin."

"Is that to suggest there was no intelligence in the Nazi government before Reinhard went to work?"

Karl Beck knew Max well enough to know this was a joke. He gave his customary thin smile, but didn't laugh. Max was chuckling before he saw the man's face, then he broke off awkwardly.

"I see. . . . What business proposals did he discuss?"

"Herr Farber has some ideas for expansion of Farber Company."

"Expansion . . . with the government?"

"That is correct."

"You're getting evasive in your old age, Karl. Your laundry list would give me more details than this note."

"Not really, Max."

"What is Irwin's expansion idea?"

"Of course, he plans to tell you. It is a confidential matter—"

"I have a cryptic memo here on it, Karl."

Karl Beck's face did not display the enjoyment he was feeling over yet another confirmation that he knew so much more than this young heir.

"Diversity. Working closer with the government on goods and services they might need. And the government offering a working relationship to Farber before anyone else, including Krupp Steel. Herr Farber is interested in that."

"I see," Max repeated. "I.E. Farber is not making enough in farm equipment and chemicals?" Max commented as he swiveled toward the window.

Karl waited, finally asking, "Is that all, Max?"

Max turned. It was rare to see a contemplative look on Max Farber's face, and Karl was surprised.

"Have you joined the Nazi Party, Karl?"

"Ja."

"That will be all for today, Karl. Danke."

Since acquiring Percy, Max had fallen into the habit of talking with him. He expected someday to get caught and be embarrassed, but Percy was such a good listener . . . so faithful. Percy came and placed his front paws on Max's knees. "You smell a rat in the wind, Percy, hmm? . . . Let's go up and see Irwin. No growling, young man."

• • •

The Farber magnate sat hunched behind his massive desk, his pen flying smoothly. He did not look up when the door opened. Irwin Farber's body had begun a premature casting of age: sagging face, yellowing eyes, thickening midsection. Max wondered if he was trying to look like the Nazi boss, Herman Göring. His close-cropped hair was graying, and gave a bulletlike similarity to his head. His skin was perpetually ruddy, but not with the healthy color Max had. Irwin looked so much like his paternal grandfather that Max was always a little surprised when he saw him. He had not forgotten those boyhood days when he had hurried past the grim oil painting in the portrait gallery. He used to feel like the old man was about to lean out of the gold-leaf frame to grab him.

Max slipped into a chair. "You need a secretary like mine if your paperwork resembles the Alps, Irwin."

Irwin looked up. "I do my own work." His eyes squinted on Percy. "Maximillian, can you not be parted from that animal?"

"Nein, we're inseparable," Max shrugged.

"Well, I will separate him if he does anything in this office."

"His kidneys are under control, Irwin, don't worry. Why did you need to see me?"

Irwin leaned back in the chair. "Thursday night there is to be a meeting at Herman Göring's home for leading Berlin businessmen. I have to be in Dusseldorf so I can't go. Eric . . ." he shook his head. "You have to go to represent Farber. It's an important meeting. I understand the chancellor may even put in an appearance."

Max knew his brother was expecting a refusal.

Max yawned. "Sure. Write down the time and address."

"You'll go?"

"Of course. It'll be interesting. I'd like to see the Nazi big boys. And I won't have to cook that night—or did they want me to bring something?"

Irwin's voice was sharp, yet controlled. "Max, this is business. Can you possibly understand that?"

"I can." He turned to Percy, "Your tux back from the cleaners yet?"

The signal vein twitching in Irwin's left temple alerted Max that the flippancy had gone too far. Irwin was crushing a paper.

"They know you are not a registered party member. But if I hear one word that you've been a buffoon—"

"We're too old for threats, Irwin. You know how your wife Katrina worries over your blood pressure. Now, what about this meeting between Heydrich, Himmler, and Farber Company?"

Irwin was still grinding his teeth. His voice was clipped.

"Nothing until it's further developed, so don't worry about it."

"I'm not worried," Max returned calmly, "but I'd like to know."

Irwin stood, tossing down a pen. "When I have detailed plans, you'll be brought in. I'll expect an in-depth report Friday morning of the meeting at Göring's."

Max stood tiredly. He scanned Irwin's face for something, for some...tenderness...something besides this belligerence that was always between them. Irwin was staring at him impassively.

"All right," Max sighed, "auf Wiedersehen, Irwin. Come along, Percy."

●　●　●

Irwin Farber felt distracted after his interview with his brother. For a moment, there at the end, when Max had stood and slowly faced him, he had thought of his mother. Strange how a long-ago memory, irrelevant to his life now, could come suddenly to mind. He saw himself at eight years old when Max had playfully pushed him in the fish pond. Irwin had reacted with a mean-spirited shove on the little boy's chest. Frau Farber's gentle smile had faded and she had scolded him. Max, he knew, more than Eric, more than himself, looked like their mother with his blond hair and vivid blue eyes. Young Irwin had sensed his mother favored her blue-eyed boy above the others, and Irwin could not forgive her that.

It was a cold, calloused heart that beat in the chest of Irwin Farber. Still, still, when he had seen the quick flash of hurt in Max's face, he had felt an unexpected sorrow, like the sting of rebuke from his long dead mother. He should not be so hard on Max. They were brothers....

The phone jangled rudely on his desk. He talked for five minutes, and by then, the warming feelings were gone. Irwin Farber held his passions fiercely, and they were not easily changed. *Max should grow up,* Irwin thought. *Heidrich had mentioned with laughter that the youngest Farber was gaining a reputation as a boy never grown up and always in the company of a terrier!* Irwin rubbed his jaw with some inner pain. *And there had been Max's questions, prying...*

Max must not blunder into things he was too dense to understand. Irwin reached for the intercom. He would summon this secretary who made Alps-sized work into neat little piles.

• • •

The man stood at his third-story office window, hands shoved in his pockets, scowling, a cigarette hanging limply from his lips. He watched as his boss left the building and climbed into a waiting car. He knew Elaina Heydrich was at the wheel. He wondered vaguely if Percy sat between them or in the backseat. He had seen Max's broad smile just before he entered the car. *Almost always smiling—that was Max Farber. Young, handsome, and one of the wealthiest men in Germany*, Karl thought bitterly.

He traveled to all the important capitals and enjoyed the playgrounds of Europe. He skied, fished, yachted—any sport, any recreation he fancied. Life was a holiday for Max Farber. And women... they fawned over him, pursued him! Max had everything. Karl's scowl deepened, what did he have in honest comparison?

• • •

A light was burning in the upstairs window on Tiergartenstrasse, a muted, amber glow through the rain-streaked glass. Max lay on a burgundy-colored sofa in his study, staring up at the sculptured ceiling. Hearing the rain, he thought of the construction man. *The rain would make his job more difficult the next day. Working patiently for his family and making his little Nazi jokes.* Max had taken a liking to him.

The nagging headache that had plagued him all day had drained him. He didn't seem to notice that his headaches always seemed to come after an exchange with Irwin. He smiled wryly: a throbbing headache and his friend, physician, and housemate, Josef Morgan, was snoring indelicately in an overstuffed chair across the room. When the snore reached a certain treble, Percy sat up, his head cocked in bewilderment. Max watched him and laughed softly. Dr. Morgan was exhausted from a long day at his clinic on Friedrichstrasse.

Max glanced around the room. This was home and this study was his favorite room. Even Elaina had smiled and said this room was Max.

"It could use a little tidying up though, Max."

"Tidying up? I couldn't find anything then!" he'd replied.

Books, including all his favorites since boyhood, *Ivanhoe*, *Treasure Island*, *Scottish Chiefs*, *David Copperfield*, and *The Adventures of Sherlock Holmes* lined the shelves. Skis were propped in the corner, along with fishing rods, crumpled hats, and boots. Models of boats, paintings

of boats, shells from a Mediterranean beach, maps, microscopes, a telescope, a radio half completed were scattered about the room. A few
dirty cups and saucers, newspapers, a stale sandwich, a trash can over-
flowing with paper airplanes he had made for Percy to chase—the clut-
ter of a bachelor filled the room. There was no military paraphernalia,
no swords, knives, or guns. Max enjoyed this room.

He stood, stretched, and sauntered to a bookcase. Dr. Morgan, who
was out for the night, wouldn't be a companion for Max. *It was just as
well*, Max reasoned. He wasn't sure he felt like talking much anyway.
His friend would want to know about his morning at work. He would
have to tell him about Irwin, then Josef would shake his head and mut-
ter. If he mentioned Karl, the older man would likely boil over. He'd
never liked Irwin's choice for Max's secretary. "The man was too
brooding and secretive," he told Max. Max would smile and soothe him,
after all, a man had to trust his secretary.

At the shelf he stopped and, for a moment, if Josef had been awake,
he would have suddenly seen the face of a 12-year-old boy, thoughtful
and hurting. Max was looking at his photos: faraway places, Josef and
Max on a fishing trip in Spain, Eric at his graduation, Elaina in front of
the Eiffel Tower. A wedding photograph of his parents, happy and confident. He reached for a glass paperweight. It had sat on his mother's
writing desk, a gift from his father. It was a sprig of edelweiss preserved
in glass. Gathering dust and cobwebs was Elaina's first gift to him—a
tennis racket now warped and useless. She had given it to him on his
thirteenth birthday. He had scratched their initials into its wooden
throat. "You are a sentimental man," Josef had once accused him with a
smile. And Max had agreed.

He picked up a scratched, blue top his father had given him so many
years ago. It made him think of the playground he'd passed in the Tiergarten
that afternoon when he and Elaina were strolling after their lunch. Children
laughing from the swings, mothers pushing prams, he had lingered a moment to watch. Then he felt Elaina's eyes upon him. He knew what she was
thinking, but neither spoke. Children . . . he enjoyed hearing their laughter.

He held the wooden top and frowned. He would have no children
of his own. He didn't trust that he could be a decent father because of
too much pain in the past. With Percy watching him and Josef across the
room asleep, Max Farber felt a choking loneliness as heavy as the slant-
ing rain outside.

8
The Dark Side
of the Moon

Berlin, February 1933

T he chancellor of Germany was in a testy, peevish mood. Outside his office the sun was blazing brightly, but inside his throne room men sat with darkened minds and scowling faces that matched the fuehrer's temper. There would be no levity or exulting in this meeting. This morning Adolf Hitler was restless with frustration. He was too close to total power in Germany to allow any mistakes or give ground to any real or perceived threat to his ascension. His cabinet of loyalists must fully understand this, so he paced and orated for over an hour.

He had chosen Göring to represent the Nazi party in the German parliament, the Reichstag. It had been a pivotal but incomplete success. Now Adolf Hitler was convinced his position as chancellor would topple unless all opposition was smashed—and smashed swiftly. And the opposition, to Adolf Hitler, seemed largely encompassed in the Reichstag. All members were not loyal Nazis; many were passionately the opposite. But Hitler would allow no threats to the new order, even by the established Reichstag. But how to crush it?

The enclave had debated the possibilities for two hours as the chancellor stalked around the room with a smoldering look. His dark hair hung limply over his pale, sweating forehead and into his left eye, but he didn't seem to notice. And no one was about to tell him he looked like an unkempt stage actor.

Göring offered half a dozen impractical suggestions, and the six men at the table had argued against his childish ideas. His face had grown red under the morning application of rouge.

"You will not leave this room," Hitler roared, "until an acceptable solution comes forth. I will not tolerate spies and traitors in the Reichstag! I will not tolerate communists! I will not!"

Propaganda minister Joseph Goebbels was the calmest and spoke the least. A few of the men had wondered if Hitler's favorite wasn't daydreaming as he drew figures and doodles on the paper in front of him. That proved he was Hitler's pampered pet—no one else would scribble and dream in front of the fuehrer! But the dark eyes of Goebbels were snapping in his thin, pasty-white face. He cleared his throat loudly and dramatically. Every eye turned to him.

"Herr Göring, there is an underground passage recently constructed under your palace for a new central heating system. Your people have told you this, of course."

Göring's eyes narrowed on this man he dwarfed in size. "Of course!"

Goebbels' smile was thin and patronizing, "Of course, ja. Then you are also aware that the underground passage connects the basement in your building to the Reichstag."

It was tensely silent as all eyes swung to the fat Göring. Hitler stood rigid and unsmiling.

Göring flushed as he shifted in his chair. Even in this new government, the architects were jealous, suspicious, and paranoid.

"I did not know! I did not know!" He sounded like a petulant child.

"Is this a lesson in building structure, Herr Goebbels?" Reinhard Heydrich asked. He was eager to be involved in this conversation that had the fuehrer's attention, and he personally believed it was wiser to cultivate Göring's trust than Goebbels'.

"No lessons in construction, Herr Heydrich. But it is profitable to know these things. Our fuehrer is quite right, as always, on his assessment of these political concerns. The communists and their kind do possess a threat, but the Reichstag is an institution the Nazis no longer need." His voice became high with excitement, as it always did, and he cringed inside since he knew he was mimicked behind his back—even by these peers.

"The Reichstag can no longer threaten us if there is no Reichstag!" he finished triumphantly.

He swept the room with his eyes to make certain he had their complete attention. Göring was gaping and sputtering.

"No Reichstag! What are you talking about?"

"Burn the Reichstag," Goebbels shrugged with false calmness. "From the ashes will rise a new order! The one-thousand-year-Reich!"

"But how?" Heydrich whispered, as if enemy ears were pressed to the door.

Goebbels pushed his paper forward. "Down the passage. Twelve trusted men with gasoline and self-igniting chemicals. In and out in less than 30 minutes. It's childishly simple."

Hitler's face was radiant. "We will declare that the communists did it to begin their revolution! I will go to President Hindenberg afterwards and demand that the constitution be suspended for the protection of the people and the state!"

Everyone at the table was nodding. Goebbels had struck an ingenious plan.

"With this master stroke we eliminate the threat *and* individual and civil rights," Goebbels added. "The communists will be rounded-up and arrested."

"They will be more than arrested," Hitler barked, then his voice softened as he gazed at Goebbels. "Brilliant plan! When?"

"Tomorrow night, February 28," the propagandist smiled. "Tomorrow night a bonfire Berlin and all of Germany will not forget!"

• • •

Max did not like to admit he was nervous, but he was. Josef stood watching the final preparations with mixed emotions. He was amused and a little concerned. He wasn't sure Max was ready for this sudden immersion into Nazi politics, but then the paternal-like pride swelled at the appearance of the vigorous young man knotting his tie at the hall mirror. Max would be fine and full of stories in the morning. Elaina had dropped in, appearing casual. *She said she had come to help—as if Max were incapable of adequately grooming himself*, Josef frowned to himself. Her true motives for the sudden appearance were as obvious as

Max's nervousness. She had come for a little final coaching, and Josef could see she was just a little nervous herself.

"If you get stuck alone with Göring, try talking about hunting. He's a real hunting enthusiast according to Reinhard."

"Elaina, I know very little about hunting," Max replied with a smile.

"Well, all right.... If you get cornered by Goebbels, I'm not sure... Reinhard says he's rather unpredictable. He—"

"Which fork is the salad fork, Josef? The inside one or the outer?"

Josef shrugged, and the two men exchanged a wink.

"Just seem enthusiastic to whatever Göring says," Elaina continued.

"Elaina, what should I do if I don't have a napkin and I dribble? Do you think a stain would show on this tie?" he teased.

"Oh, Max, really!"

Max was laughing as he placed his arm around her.

"*You* aren't nervous are you, Elaina?"

"No, I just... well, I do wish Reinhard was in town to be with you."

The arm withdrew quickly and stiffly. Josef watched from the staircase where he leaned. He knew his young friend well. He saw the amusement leave the clear blue eyes though the smile lingered. He expected Elaina would miss the tone that had chilled almost imperceptibly.

"You think I need a nursemaid, Elaina?"

"Max..." She glanced around seeing Josef regarding her with a tolerant smile. "I know you haven't been around these men and their types very often and it may seem strange to you," she said hurriedly. "You know what I meant Max."

Max was pulled against his will into memories of years ago when he had been left in the care of Irwin and Reinhard. He shook his head, attempting a laugh.

"What should I do if I come face-to-face with Chancellor Hitler? Any suggestions?"

The young woman laughed nervously. "I've yet to meet him, Max. I can't advise you; *I* would probably fall over in a faint! He has such eyes!"

Max peered closely. He had never seen the cool, controlled Elaina act so adolescent. Josef came up and slapped his back.

"Better get going, Max, or you'll be late."

"I wanted to walk, the night is so clear. You can see—"

"Max! You can't possibly think of appearing on foot!" Elaina said, horrified.

"Oh."

He gathered up his hat and coat. "Well, what's your verdict, Sir Blackney?"

Percy lay stretched out on the stair landing, his head on his paws. At his name, he sat up, eager and expectant.

"Do you think I look all right? One for yes, two for no."

Percy gave one quick bark, his tail whipping the floor for approval.

"There, you see, Elaina. What have I been saying? He's brilliant! I'd imagine Herr Göring might appreciate it if I brought him along. I think I have an old bow tie upstairs—"

"Max . . ."

"No? Really, Elaina. You know how things can get boring at a party, and I'm sure Göring wants this to be a success. I'm still working with Percy on a salute. Think how that would go over!"

Josef was chuckling, but Elaina's smile was tight.

"Max, you cannot go thinking this is a party. It's a business meeting."

Max's smile dropped. "Of course, yes, well, come on down old man, and give me a send off," he said to Percy.

Percy vaulted down the stairs to place his front paws on Max's chest. Max ruffled his ears, his face serious.

"Hmm? Ja, if I see Frau Göring's poodle, I'll try to get her a—her paw prints. Be a good boy."

"I'll get you some smelling salts if you think you'll need them, Max," Josef spoke up poker-faced.

Elaina colored.

"Thanks, Josef. I think I can keep my wits. Well, I'm off!"

Elaina slipped her arm through his as they headed down to the Mercedes parked at the curb.

"I'm sorry, Max."

"For what?" He turned and the lamplight from the street caught glints of light in his hair. He was close and smiling at her. She felt her pulse quicken.

"I have confidence in you, Max, I really do. I know you will represent Farber Company perfectly. I just know I'd be nervous if it were me."

"I understand," he said as he kissed her cheek.

"Will you call me when you get home?"

"If it isn't too late."

He climbed in the car. "If they have any of those little finger sandwiches cut in swastikas shall I wrap one up in a napkin for you?"

She laughed in spite of herself and waved him away. Her smile faded as soon as the car was out of sight. *Dear, handsome Max, so boyish, still holding my heart all these years.... Tonight... tonight could be so important for us both.*

● ● ●

The young man in the plain wool jacket shifted uncomfortably in the passenger seat. His companion at the wheel detected the mood and grinned.

"It's paid for," he laughed, knowing his friend's thoughts about the car.

Wilhelm Mueller shrugged irritably. "Then spend some money on a new muffler, Herschel. I feel like I'm going down Berlin's main street sitting on a farm wagon full of rotten cabbages!"

Herschel Grynszpan guffawed and slapped the wheel.

Indeed the old car did look out of place along the sophisticated Kurfurstendamm as a sleek Mercedes passed by. Wilhelm felt like every pedestrian on the sidewalk and every driver on the road was staring at them in disgust. It was not exactly the most polished entrance into Germany's capital. Though he had grown up just 25 miles from the city, Wilhelm had not been in Berlin in over 10 years. He knew he was gawking through the dirty windscreen, but the city was so changed... so Nazified! Swastika banners hung from most government buildings and many were neatly posted in shop and restaurant windows. He shook his head, "And I thought Nuremberg and Munich were bad," he muttered.

Again Herschel understood without amplification.

"Nazis are like breedin' rabbits! They're everywhere! They're really more like fleas and ticks... You watch, they'll drain Berlin to the dust one of these days!"

"Not Berlin, she'll stand for a thousand years," Wilhelm spoke curtly, remembering the unpleasant times he had experienced here.

"A thousand years? You sound like the fuehrer!" Herschel mimicked the leader, "'I will lead you in a thousand-year Reich!'"

"I said Berlin, not Adolf and his gang. They'll be gone one of these days . . . soon hopefully."

"Yeah, and I'd like to be the one to put each Nazi away," Herschel said with passion.

Grynszpan swung the car onto Wilhelmstrasse, between the line of government buildings. He rolled down the window as he slowed the car and stuck out his hand in the imitation of a gun.

"SS Headquarters, bang. . . . That's the new Propaganda Ministry, there. Can you imagine needin' a big place like that to crank out lies."

"A big building for breeding big lies," Wilhelm shrugged.

The car crossed Unter den Linden and passed the floodlit Brandenburg Gate. *It looks impressive enough to stand a thousand years*, Wilhelm mused, although he had always found the monument gaudy.

Herschel nodded. "That's Dr. Goebbels' place." He pointed his finger and exhaled a loud bang.

Wilhelm noticed a couple on the sidewalk pause to stare at the decrepit auto. "Cut it out, Herschel. Roll up the window."

Herschel laughed, "Then I can't shoot the Nazis, Wilhelm! Bang, bang!"

Wilhelm frowned, freshly irritated that he had agreed to this trip to Berlin with the embarrassing Herschel Grynszpan. The young Jew was part of the university crowd in Nuremberg, but Wilhelm had never felt very close to him. He was too intense and unpredictable. Still, Wilhelm's crowd of young people accepted him, though he was only 18, and they were in their early-to-mid-twenties. Herschel seemed to know a little bit about everything with his fertile, active brain. He could spout off on most subjects with more than just superficial, boasting knowledge. He could talk for hours about the Nazi party, their history, their ascension, their doctrine, and its major players. His friends quickly noticed he seemed to know people in every walk of life. If a bit of information—legal or illegal—was needed, Herschel knew how to obtain it. His eccentricities and uncertainties made Wilhelm Mueller uneasy.

The car came nearly to a stop in front of the Reichstag building, the seat of power. "Think he's in there?" Herschel asked, without a trace of his usual humor.

"Who?" Wilhelm yawned.

"Hitler."

"I don't know. Who cares? He's probably in bed asleep—"

Herschel's hands tightened on the steering wheel. "If he came out now, right down those steps—even with his bodyguard—even with ape-man Göring—I'd drive up there, up the steps, and run over him! I would!" Wilhelm glanced at the darkened gates. He had no doubt the boast was a real one.

"Yeah, well let me out before you try it. I don't like the idea of becoming Swiss cheese by Nazi machine guns. Let's go get a beer."

Herschel whipped around with blazing eyes.

"You mean you wouldn't kill him if you had the chance?"

"Well...no, Herschel, I wouldn't."

"Then you are crazy and stupid, Wilhelm Mueller," he spat viciously. "He and his vermin are after you!"

"Not me personally, Herschel, now turn the car around."

"Yes, you idiot, you! You are Jewish and he hates all of us!"

"My parents are Jewish but—"

"Then you are a Jew, whether you like it or not!"

"I don't even practice their religion," Wilhelm countered testily.

"That does not matter! You are a circumcised Jew! Hitler hates *every* Jew in Germany, whether they are like you and don't care or like a rabbi or a boy in Torah school!"

"Cool down, Herschel."

The driver turned the car in a wide arc on the avenue. Wilhelm would breath easier when they were on some nondescript Berlin side street.

"Well, I'd kill him without a thought," Herschel restated calmly.

"Yeah . . ." And for the hundredth time, Wilhelm wished he had stayed in Nuremberg and away from the hot-headed, bound-for-trouble Herschel Grynszpan.

"I want to see Göring's place, then we'll go get that beer," Herschel said. "Then where to?"

"My folks," Wilhelm said reluctantly, "we'll spend the night there."

Visiting his parents always made Wilhelm a little anxious because he could never predict how the visit would go. And with the strange Herschel in tow . . .

A thin whistle escaped from Wilhelm's lips. The street in front of Göring's residence was lined with cars. The young man had never seen so many limousines and Mercedes' in one place.

"Must be a big party; turn around, Herschel," he commanded.

"Are you kiddin'? You afraid of these guys? I'm drivin' right past the front door to get a good look."

They could see men hurrying up the stairs to the house, light filling nearly every window in the black February chill.

"I bet there's a hundred Nazis in there," Herschel hissed.

"Not that many. But look, only men—no ladies."

"A lady wouldn't go with a Nazi. . . . Wonder what they're up to in there?"

Herschel stopped opposite the front door. They could see a butler standing in the open doorway. A man stepped from a Mercedes near them, adjusting his tie and smoothing his hair though it looked perfectly combed to Wilhelm. *He's nervous*, Wilhelm decided. He leaned to get a closer look. The man looked too young and boyish for a Nazi chieftain. He glanced their way, his attention drawn by the sputtering engine. Herschel lowered the window again. He didn't hold out his hand, but spoke boldly for Göring's guest to hear.

"Bang! Bang!" he laughed.

Wilhelm watched the man's face. Clearly puzzled, there was something familiar about him. Blond hair, tall and broad . . . The man hurried up the steps.

"Let's go *now*, Herschel. I've had enough sightseeing for one night," Wilhelm said tiredly.

The driver nodded and chuckled again.

● ● ●

As host, Hermann Göring knew the true purpose of this gathering of German business leaders. Adolf Hitler had told him precisely whom to invite and what to say to them. The jovial and loyal Göring had accepted the directions with enthusiasm. He frowned, but said nothing when the chancellor strongly urged that no alcohol be served at the meeting. Göring, second in leadership in the Nazi regime, wisely kept his opinion of the lack of alcoholic beverages to himself. So the invited men stood a little awkwardly in Göring's large dining room, balancing cups of coffee in their hands, and vaguely wondered just how puritanical these Nazi leaders really were.

Göring moved about the room with bubbling exuberance, furthering his reputation as a slightly ponderous, overgrown boy who suddenly found himself in the heady shadow of immense power. Still, those few who knew him well knew a man of hardness and determination lurked underneath the jocular exterior. While his guests wore traditional black suits, Göring had chosen a drab-olive military uniform lavishly covered in medals from the Great War. He gestured with a ribboned baton, and jewels flashed on his pudgy fingers. He was as flamboyant as his boss was precise, unassuming, and severe.

Göring greeted each man personally, pumping his arm.

"This is Maximillian Farber," an aide whispered loudly to Göring.

"Herr Farber, so delighted you could come!"

"Danke, Herr Göring."

Max waited as the eyes swept over him.

"You were captain of the Berlin ski team in 1929 when the Swiss cup was won, ja?"

Max smiled. "Yes."

Göring rocked forward on his toes, an idiosyncrasy he'd developed. He considered something on the ceiling. "I've always admired athletes. I've tried skiing, of course, but my balance has always been difficult. . . ." He then waved Max aside as he greeted another guest.

Max felt his nervousness dissolve as he moved away from his exultant host and into the crowd. He was envisioning the Nazi Reichmarshal on skis as he accepted a cup of coffee from a passing waiter. While Max typically found business meetings boring and avoided them, this one was different. Sauntering casually through the crowd, greeting a few familiar faces, he quickly assessed the mood of uncertainty and tension among the business leaders. What was going to be required of them by this new, fast-moving government? Some had come from duty and fear, others from eager support, and still others from unconcealed curiosity. Young Farber conceded he belonged to the latter group. He recalled Elaina's anxiety. She had articulated her concerns, "Say the right thing, Max, this is a business meeting." It was obvious she had little faith in him. He frowned, and watched Göring leave the room.

He placed himself near a window that looked out on Herr Göring's now frosted garden. He leaned against the wide windowsill, almost blending in with the heavy, wine-colored drapes. The room was filled to capacity; the men stood tense and nervous, waiting. Fifteen minutes elapsed, then 25. Still Göring did not return. *What was the point of this delay*? Max wondered. He watched with amusement as men looked to their Swiss watches and frowned. Their conversations took on a low grumbling sound. They had better things to do than loiter in Herr Göring's dining room. Max yawned as he thought about his tennis date at his athletic club the next day. He'd stay another five minutes then slip from the crowd. No one would notice him gone. Irwin would just have to fuss.

Then he heard the word Farber in some group slightly forward and to the left of him. He peered around someone's shoulder. A knot of six gray-headed and balding men stood awkwardly holding their empty coffee cups. Max, staying behind another group, edged along the windowsill. They could not see him.

"Well you know ... ja ... but Irwin isn't here. . . ."

"Didn't you see him when he came in? It was the young Maximillian. Ja, I'd heard that, too. I hear he can be very inane. . . . Ja, that makes him popular for the party circuit. . . ."

"Why would Irwin send . . ."

"Oh, he's probably left by now. . . ."

"Ja, I've seen him around town in that convertible with an Airedale in the seat beside him!"

"What does Reinhard think of him as a brother-in-law?"

"Ja, money helps. . . . Ha, ha . . ."

"He's nowhere around, so stop worrying. Young Farber is a nice, congenial sort. Problem is, he has never grown up. . . ."

Max's face was flaming, his mouth suddenly very dry. He turned abruptly, his head slightly lowered. He brushed through the crowd; now was the time to leave. He stopped near the door Göring had exited. He had to get out of this room! . . . But then the door swung open and Göring appeared, his barrel-chest expanded to capacity, his eyes flashing, his mouth smiling broadly. A shorter, thinner man came into the room briskly behind Göring. He looked around the room quickly, and a slight smile trembled on his thin lips. Max stopped abruptly and backed into a line of men.

The chancellor of Germany had joined the meeting.

• • •

It was a wooden table, old and scarred, and the green-painted legs were chipped. The top was covered with a red-checked oilcloth. There was a finer table, polished and draped in linen in a nearby room, but this old kitchen table had witnessed the full life of the Mueller family—the meals; projects of paper, clay, and paint, wood and nails; bread dough being fashioned with child hands; games; and schoolwork. The Bible often lay open upon it. Unvarnished and ugly, to Marta Mueller the table was like an altar. She had poured out so many tears and prayers over it—and so often for this youngest son she loved so deeply. What was he thinking of as he sat staring at the cup in his hands? If only she knew . . .

Across the red-checked cloth, sat the father. Marta studied their profiles. The gray hair receding and thin on the old man, the full brown hair falling over the forehead of the younger. Heinz Mueller was staring at his hands. Yes, it was easy for anyone to see they were father and son, separated by generations, but also separated by much more.

"More chocolate, Wilhelm?" Marta asked.

He looked up and didn't smile, but his voice was gentle to her. "No thank you, Mother." He had hardly touched what was in his cup.

His wife's voice roused Heinz from his thoughts. He looked up at her, nodded at something unspoken between them, then to his son. Rarely did he look at this young man without thinking of the old Bible patriarch, Abraham, who had been blessed with a son in his old age. His son had been born when he was nearly 50. A joy to be a father again when most men his age were preoccupied with retirement and failing health.

"Where is Maria tonight?" Wilhelm asked, disappointed that he hadn't seen his sister. "I haven't had a letter from her in a few weeks."

"She is well. She and the other youth leaders have taken the children's choir to Vienna."

"I remember now, she told me about it in her last letter."

"*We* don't get many letters. . . . Everything we know comes from Walther," Marta said gently, as she joined her men at the table.

"I'm pretty busy. . . . I work on Saturdays now, at the Nuremberg Bicycle Club, so Sunday is my only day off."

She shook her head. "Tell me again."

"Monday, Wednesday, and Friday I work at the *Nuremberg Tribune*. I clean faculty offices in the university's education department on Tuesdays. At night I wait tables at Handel's Cafe. Thursday, I work at a Jewish newspaper," he finished hurriedly.

Marta nodded. "Ja, you are busy, son." She patted his hand and he smiled then. He knew what was in her mind and in his father's—such a schedule would surely keep him out of trouble.

"You work on a Zionist newspaper, *Jacob's Ladder,* Ja, Walther has told us. What exactly do you do, Wilhelm?" Heinz asked.

"I'm their photographer. I also do some writing and odd jobs. It has a small circulation so they can't pay me much."

"A boy who cares little for religion works on a Zionist paper?" Heinz commented with a smile. He sipped his chocolate as he watched his son.

"I work with them because they needed someone. They've become my friends and—"

"How is it you have Jewish friends when you regard Judaism with such disdain?" Heinz interrupted.

"Father, I've never said that, and you know it."

A silence descended over the small kitchen.

Wilhelm drew a deep breath, and his voice was patient.

"My friends and I, we don't always agree on everything, but they accept me as I am."

Heinz nodded. "A young man who is searching and who has not yet found . . ."

Wilhelm looked away and studied the ceiling.

"Heinz," Marta placed a hand on his arm.

"When I was your age, Wilhelm, your mother and I were married. I was doing what I loved, which was to manage the lawns and gardens of the Farber estate. I wanted to make this a beautiful place for Herr Farber and his family. I—"

"You have toiled over this place for years Father, and look—they don't even appreciate it! The sons don't even live here or care that you've grown stooped!"

The father smiled.

"I'm sorry," Wilhelm said softly.

"What you have said, perhaps, is true. Still, it has been a good life for your mother and me. And I thought for Walther and Maria and you, Wilhelm."

"Father, look—"

"What I was saying was that I cannot remember not having my faith, Wilhelm. I have told you this before. I did not go through the questions and searching that you are when I was a young man. I . . ." He spread his hands in appeal. "I want to understand you, son, but I'm an old man, I . . ."

"Father, I am not like you as you admit. I do have questions about life. It's not as simple for me as it was for you. Sometimes I wish I were more like Walther, but I'm not. He's predictable and dependable, and you can't expect me to be like that."

Marta broke in, "You are a good son, Wilhelm."

Wilhelm shifted in his chair and tried to think of something to say.

Heinz cleared his throat. "This Zionist group, are they radical?"

"Our newspaper reports on the news of the Jewish community of Nuremberg and of Jewish concerns across Germany. We report without censorship, which is becoming a rare thing in our country."

"I would think such a newspaper could draw the attention of our new government."

"We are not afraid of that!" Wilhelm replied quickly and firmly. The parents exchanged a look.

"Your work is dangerous then?" Marta asked with a little alarm. She had been beginning to feel secure about her son's jobs and relationships.

"I'm not afraid, Mother, but I am careful. Don't worry."

"I am proud of your many talents, son," Heinz began.

Wilhelm gave him a wry smile. "But you wish I had stayed enrolled in the university."

Heinz shook his head. "We have been over that before, Wilhelm. I don't hold it against you."

"Well, it was the best decision for me. I don't have the brains Walther does."

"You are a good writer," Marta said smiling, "when you write."

"I only want to say to you now, that in all you are involved in, be certain your convictions are well placed," Heinz added.

"Ahem . . ."

Herschel Grynszpan, dressed in pajama bottoms, stood leaning in the doorway. He gave a gaping yawn, then smiled as his eyes focused.

"Oh! A little family confab? Over the friends your son brings home, huh?"

"No, just a family discussion," Wilhelm replied. He reddened, and his parents looked uncomfortable.

"Well don't mind me, I just need the—"

"Down the hall, turn left," Wilhelm said irritably.

Herschel nodded and disappeared. Wilhelm looked back at his cup. This visit was going the way of all the others, strained and miserable. He saw their looks and could divine their thoughts. They had smelled the beer on Herschel upon their arrival an hour earlier. Herschel was too hearty and strange for the rural couple.

"This Herschel, he belongs to the group of Jews that are your friends?" Marta asked softly.

Wilhelm nodded. "He comes around. . . . I don't know him that well."

"Why did you come to Berlin?" Heinz asked.

"The Jewish newspaper here wanted to talk with me . . . about different things of mutual concern. Herschel has a car and offered to give me a lift."

"I see."

Marta stood up, her voice falsely cheerful.

"I think it's time we all went to bed for a good rest. You must have a hearty appetite for blintzes in the morning!"

"We were going to leave pretty early, Mother, to get back in time for work."

Marta's smile dropped. "You cannot stay for breakfast?"

He saw her disappointment and responded. "We'll stay. I've already bragged to Herschel about your blintzes."

"You could come with Walther next time he comes. Maria will be very disappointed she missed you."

"I'll try. I miss Maria, too."

Wilhelm started to rise, but his father caught his hand.

"I do not mean to embarrass you or make you uncomfortable, but it would please me if I could . . ." He stopped and withdrew his hand.

Wilhelm watched him and his face softened. His friends had always teased him about the age of his father because he looked closer to being his grandfather than father. Walther had accepted the teasing with a shrug, but Wilhelm had always had his fists poised. The gray head would soon be completely white.

"Ja, Father," he smiled faintly. "It's like our tradition of having blintzes in the morning."

The old man nodded and smiled. "Ja, food for the body; food for the soul."

Marta smiled too, though her eyes brimmed with tears.

Wilhelm sat down and his father's hand touched his son's head. "Lord, this old man thanks you for this son . . ."

● ● ●

It was as simple as Goebbels had promised. The SA Stormtroopers' leader was more than willing to undertake the proposed arson. It would be an honor to fulfill any request of the fuehrer's cabinet. He hadn't even raised an eyebrow or mentally questioned this controversial task—to burn the almost-hallowed Reichstag. And, of course, he had been impressed with the need for utmost secrecy. Only the designers of the plan and the dozen arsonists were to be privy to the plan. One slip of tongue by any of them . . . yes, the leader understood perfectly. He would choose the men personally; they could be trusted.

It was eight o'clock when the Stormtroopers passed through the darkened tunnel connecting the palace with the Reichstag. A few were thinking about the task, ignite a mammoth building of three stories, hundreds of rooms, many passages. Others had thoughts of the tale this would make when they were old men. The men worked swiftly with only the light of a few flashlights, spreading gasoline and chemicals on preselected areas. They started the fire. Then they were running back down the tunnel. They stripped hurriedly, changing clothes. The gasoline cans and soiled clothes were placed in a truck going one direction, and the arsonists in another. Their leader checked his watch. Goebbels had been wrong in his estimate of how long it would take. It had taken exactly one-and-a-half hours. There was still time to go to a tavern on the Kurfurstendamm. There they could appear innocent, sip their beers, and look at the Berlin skyline to proudly watch their success.

● ● ●

Max was amazed. He had never heard anything like this before and had certainly never witnessed anything like it. He suspected that, at times, his mouth had fallen open in surprise. Adolf Hitler had been talking for over two hours. He had entered the room in the bombastic wake of Göring and stood quietly, stiffly, for a full minute. He was sizing up the crowd, looking as if he could enter their very souls with his eyes. Then he began speaking, and Max was transfixed. The man had more energy than could possibly be imagined. He stood still with his arms gesturing—chopping the air, placed on his hips, now clawing out to his audience. While he stood, his feet were planted widely apart, defiantly. Then he paced, jerked his head, pointed at them, clenched a fist at them. When he would momentarily stop, Max was close enough to see that Hitler's eyes were twitching spastically, his face glistening with sweat. Max's eyes grew wide; he could hardly concentrate on the words from the man. But he knew the fuehrer had covered topics such as foreign policy, economics, liberalism, and, of course, the evil communists. It was a violent ranting.

"...a nation adequately armed will break the shackles of Versailles!" Hitler pronounced.

Max did not pause, then, to wonder what the phrase "adequately armed" meant. Then Hitler stopped. He was wiping his brow. The room was perfectly still. The audience of men had stood unmoving throughout the tirade. Hitler's voice became calm.

"I am very grateful to you for coming tonight. You have honored Germany. You are men of vision and power, and we have a glorious future together! Our Third Reich will triumph for a thousand years—and you will be part of that glory! You!" His eyes narrowed on the men closest to him—and then rested on Max Farber.

It was not difficult to notice Max in this group of balding, paunched men. Max stood tall, straight, young, blond. The fuehrer's eyes warmed. *Now! This was the kind of German who typified the master Aryan race. This kind of man! Flawless!* Hitler thought. The chancellor's head jerked around to the hovering Göring. They whispered only a moment.

"There you see young Maximillian Farber! You all know his family. His grandfather served with distinction in the Prussian war, and his father, I.E. Farber, was highly decorated in the Great War. Here stands his youngest son, at this meeting because he, like his ancestors, is a man of great honor. You are the future, young Farber! You are Germany! You will provide sons which will be the pride of the Fatherland! With such men as this, as all of you, Germany will always be great!"

● ● ●

After the fuehrer had publicly recognized Max, he turned sharply and left the room through the door he had entered by. Göring took Hitler's place, rocking forward on his toes as he explained to this assembly of men they were indeed privileged—and must help finance the growing Nazi party. His pleadings lasted only 15 minutes, then he nodded goodnight to them.

The crowd of men came as close to undignified as they could, as they pushed to the front doors. Some were openly grumbling at this two-hour monologue they had taken standing—and with nothing stiffer than coffee to fortify them! Others were gloating—they had been in the same room with Adolf Hitler!

Max stepped out into the crisp night air, drawing a deep breath. His thoughts were tangled; he wanted to slip into his car, drive into the blackness of the night, and think. He was surprised when a voice hailed him as he was coming down the steps.

"Max! Max Farber!"

He turned. It was Edourde Shulte, a banker and an old friend of his father's.

"Ed." They shook hands warmly. "It's been years! How are you, sir?"

"Fine Max, just fine. Ja, it has been years. You were a skinny lad when I saw you last, but fine-enough-looking that you gave my girls racing pulses!"

Max was laughing.

"It was quite an evening," Shulte said, nodding back toward the house where men were still flowing out.

Max nodded, not wanting to offer much comment.

Shulte wisely lowered his voice and leaned toward Max.

"If I had known so much mysticism and paganism was going to be spouted at me, I'd have stayed home! Mary said I should."

"You . . . you wish you hadn't come, sir?"

"They are gangsters, Max, all of them! I suspected it before I came. Tonight it has been confirmed."

By now they had reached Max's car. Max ran his hand across the sleek black car door, his face frowning. Shulte rested a friendly hand on his shoulder.

"Heady stuff for you tonight, eh, Max?" His voice was kind, not teasing.

Max looked at him. "You knew my father . . . very well, Edourde."

"Ja, I did, Max. He was a fine man and a good friend."

"If he had been alive, he would have been in that room tonight— and not his youngest son. He would . . ." Max ran an unsteady hand through his hair, watching the cars as they left. All the important men of Germany . . . and he had been one of them. Göring had remembered him; the fuehrer had singled him out. Max wondered if the little group he had overheard talking about him had suffered their own embarrassment.

"Max?" Ed queried.

"I think my father would be supporting the Nazi regime. He'd say they could move Germany forward out of the shame of the last war."

The older man was looking at the street and nodding slowly.

"Perhaps, perhaps . . . but I think he would stay apart from the Nazi goals. Adolf Hitler is a vulgar, unstable, little man who could be very dangerous."

Because he had little interest, Max had heard only snatches of some of the speeches Hitler had made over the radio. This had been his first personal experience. He had seen a slight, dark man whose oratory was dramatic—almost hypnotizing. Could he be nothing more than an actor?

"Do you really think he is dangerous, sir? The only danger I saw tonight was that he could work himself into a heart attack as my friend Josef would say."

Shulte sighed. "Frankly, Max, I think I'm like a lot of men in Germany—like a lot of men in that room tonight. I'm not sure what to think. Why is it I feel like someone is trying to stuff a honey-covered rotten egg down my throat?"

Max laughed as Shulte again patted him on his back.

"Whatever you do concerning the Nazi party, Max, be careful. This much I do know: They do not like opposition." He glanced up at the sky. "Look at that star!"

Max nodded, looking at the bright half-moon and the star hanging below it. "Venus."

Shulte shook his head. "Looking at it makes me feel kind of puny. It helps me remember who is really in control! Well, it was good to see you again. Gute Nacht!"

Max stood watching until the banker was out of sight. He slid into his own car deep in thought as he drove away.

It was nearly three in the morning before Max arrived at home. It was a short drive from Göring's home to his own. But at the Unter den Linden, he had been halted by a tide of cars and pedestrians. Everyone was hurrying in the cold night toward the Reichstag. It was burning, throwing orange and blood-red flames against the sky. Huge plumes of gray smoke and people shouting filled the air. The fire brigade could do little as the structure was consumed. Max pulled his car as close as he could and watched. A part of German history and a Berlin landmark was crumbling into ashes. He sat alone in the car and watched, deep in thought again.

• • •

"I'm going to party headquarters at ten. I'm joining the Nazi party," Max said bluntly the next morning. They had talked about the fire already. He had given Josef a description of the meeting at Göring's. He didn't bother to say anything about what he had overheard—or how he had been singled out by Hitler.

Josef continued to stir his coffee placidly, thinking of Irwin Farber and Elaina Heydrich who supported the new government.

"Just like that? Are you sure about this, Max?"

"Have you changed your opinion of the Nazi party, Josef? You said they have rough edges but that we should give them a chance," Max asked.

"I know, I know . . . it's hard to explain, Max."

"Please try, Josef. As my friend, tell me what concerns you."

The doctor sighed. "Max, there are times when I am with a patient and I get a sense of what the problem is before I have all the facts tested. It doesn't happen all the time—call it instinct or intuition. I don't know what the future is for this Nazi government, who of us does? But I am concerned with these fiery speeches Hitler makes nearly every night on the radio. And people seem almost in a fever about what he says. I see these black-booted young men on the streets with their arm bands and hard, proud faces. And I wonder . . . Ah, Max I'm just an old man. . . ."

"I'm joining the Nazi party, Josef. I'm not going to be a Nazi like those men in the black boots or like Reinhard Heydrich! I will carry a card, nothing more, nothing less." He ran his hand through his hair, knowing that Josef would not like what he was going to say. "It will please Elaina; it will pacify Irwin. I think it will uncomplicate my life."

"I am not so confident it won't have quite the opposite effect, Max."

"I think it would be what my father would want me to do," Max said softly.

Josef didn't speak as he gazed into his coffee cup. Still trying to please the father....

• • •

Harsh winter winds vanished under milder, warmer breezes as spring came to Germany. The ice-crusted Rhine and Danube Rivers melted, beeches and oaks trembled in new leaf. The barley fields stood slender, green and a foot high. The little town between Nuremberg and Munich had seen the hurried activity of laborers just outside of town all winter. The cold had not slowed them in the least. After a week of friendly inquiry, the townsfolk learned the Nazi party had ordered this vast construction project. Some were honored for the distinction of being chosen by the new government for this large project; others remained curious and uncertain. So, when the geraniums were blooming blood-red in the gardens of Dachau, the gates of the new camp swung open. It was ready for occupancy.

9
Wilhelm's Journey

Spring, 1934

Wilhelm was late. It was Tuesday, five minutes till five. He was supposed to be at the cafe at 4:30. He did not want to lose this job, for the hefty Handel was a generous employer. Not waiting for a ride from his friends, he hopped onto his ancient bicycle. The rims scratched in protest as he sped across the winding, cobbled streets of Nuremberg. He must concentrate on how to avoid the end-of-the-day traffic clogging the narrow streets. *What was a shorter route?* he said to himself as he mentally plotted his course.

He knew he looked foolish and impoverished on the battered bike, and hoped none of the university girls he knew would see him. He was halfway to Handel's Cafe, his white shirt already sticking to his back, when he turned the corner and abruptly came to a stop. The street was blocked a hundred yards in front of him. He pushed the bike to the sidewalk and waited, trying to appear casual though his heart suddenly began to pound. He glanced around quickly—two-story apartments, a cafe, a bookstore, a music store, a grocery. An unpretentious, typical German street—except a group of young Nazis had gathered at the corner and partially blocked the street. Wilhelm counted the Nazis—at least

118

eight of them. The groceryman was sweeping in front of his shop, but Wilhelm could see that he watched the scene also. He could also see a few faces in the apartment windows hiding behind the curtains, watching. The Nazis' backs were to him, but he could hear their tone and their laughter. He had seen groups like this almost daily in the city in spontaneous or organized marches. *They flaunted their power and were arrogant*, Wilhelm fumed. *They acted like they owned the city. Bullies*! He chewed his lip.

Now he could see as the Nazis shifted position. They had circled a . . . a rabbi! Wilhelm gripped the handles of his bike. A rabbi—a man of at least 60 years. His view was blocked again. Wilhelm turned to the shop window as if he were suddenly very interested in the instruments on display. He was staring, but he didn't really see them. His mind was racing. *I should turn the bike around and take the long way. Handel will scold, perhaps even fire me. But it's better than this trouble that is not mine.*

He finally focused, and in the glass he saw that the groceryman on the sidewalk opposite was no longer watching the scene; he was watching Wilhelm. The young man swung around. A man of 40, heavy and balding, the grocer wore a spotless white apron stretched across his middle and was still staring at him. Wilhelm looked back to the group. He could see that all but three of the group were leaving, surging forward with lusty songs of triumph. The rabbi was on the street, his beard in the dust. One of the Nazis was still kicking him. Wilhelm carefully leaned the bike against the wall, slowly, as if the thing were priceless and unscratched.

"I wouldn't," called the man across the street quietly.

"You wouldn't? I will!" Wilhelm countered testily.

Wilhelm walked forward quickly. Only three soldiers remained. They were his age.

"Beating an old man? Need help?" he asked with a trace of a smile. The three were surprised. They looked at Wilhelm and then each other.

Wilhelm quickly checked out the rabbi who was still bent over: white hair, his face bruised, and the lips that were split and bleeding freely. *It could be my father*, Wilhelm thought.

"You belong to the party?" one Nazi asked quickly.

Wilhelm shook his head slowly.

"Then you're a Jew lover," one of the Nazis spat and stepped forward menacingly.

"I *am* a Jew," Wilhelm said softly as he sprang forward.

Vaguely he could hear a scream as he knocked the first Nazi down with a powerful blow to the nose. The two others were on him instantly, clawing, and kicking. He fought hard and got in good hits until he was pinned by one of them.

One of the Nazis gripped his shirt front.

"What is your name, punk? Tell me now!"

"Wilhelm Mueller," he slurred, too confused to make up a name. Wilhelm doubled over as the man pummeled him in the stomach and face. One of the Nazis pulled his head back by his hair as another worked him over.

Wilhelm could feel himself spinning into unconsciousness. He thought of his brother Walther, who would be worried when he didn't show up at their apartment that night. *If only I could work my arms free.* He struggled but it was useless. He could feel the warm blood dripping from his face down to his neck. They would beat him senseless, then finish the old man. He hadn't helped the rabbi. Blackness, and no more pain...

Has it been hours or mere minutes? Wilhelm lay on his side, crumpled, and staring into the smooth cobbles. Then his eyes focused. The rabbi was still on his knees, but there was another man beside him. Not young smooth hands, not the brown sleeves and black-and-red bands. *Where*? He pulled his head up, feeling like he was going to be sick. The shopkeeper was helping the old man up.

"Here, they have gone. Steady...I will help you into my shop. You can have some tea....They have gone. Can you stand?"

The rabbi nodded. The merchant then stooped over Wilhelm. Their eyes met just a moment, then Wilhelm felt himself pulled up by the beefy arms. "I...I think I'm going to be sick..." But instead he drew in deep breaths.

"Come along to my shop. You will be all right," the merchant urged.

There was a searing pain in his ribs where he had been kicked. One eye was already sealed shut, blood was streaming from a gash at his hairline, and his knuckles were cut raw. He felt weak, but he could stand. The street was strangely quiet. It felt like hours had passed. He looked down at his smashed watch: 5:15. He looked at the rabbi who was now crying. Wilhelm staggered up to him.

"You're all right, sir. They've gone. This man will help you get home."

"Did...where...did they get...my...?" he rasped.

Wilhelm gripped his shoulders. "What?"

"He's hallucinating, probably going into shock," the grocer said calmly as he took the old man's arm.

"No, no . . ." the rabbi shook his head. "My...granddaughter...Did they ..."

Then Wilhelm remembered the scream. Someone had screamed when they began to beat him. He swung around and his eyes found her in the shadow of a doorway. Still dizzy and weak, he stepped toward her. "They've gone. Don't be afraid."

Still she waited. He reached out his hand. "Come on. It's over. Your grandfather needs you now."

She stepped out onto the street, a young girl clutching an instrument case to her chest. She could not be over 14 or 15 Wilhelm guessed. She was very pale; the terror still shaded her eyes. Wordlessly she stepped past him and into the arms of her grandfather.

"I was...so . . ." she wept.

The old man stroked her hair, crooning softly to her.

"You did as I told you, Natalie. You hid. You did not come to me. They did not see you. Blessed is the daughter who obeys."

Still she clung to him and cried, but the old man had regained his composure with the finding of the girl. He searched for Wilhelm quickly with his watery blue eyes. "And blessed are you, young man."

Wilhelm bent stiffly to dust off his pants. His clothes were filthy and blood-stained. He looked up and down the street and wondered how many had stood as silent witnesses—only the grocer had responded.

"Come to my shop, all of you. We must look to your cuts."

Wilhelm shook his head and turned to his bike.

"I am Rabbi Bergmann, and this is my beloved granddaughter, Natalie. We live on Elenstrasse. Please come to us tomorrow, that we may thank you properly."

"You don't need to do that," Wilhelm replied hoarsely as he looked away.

"Bitte."

Just like my father, Wilhelm smiled crookedly.

"You need to get home or in the shop. They could always come back to finish their noble work." The shopkeeper's words were clipped.

The rabbi nodded and, still holding the girl, followed the grocer. Wilhelm could not ride. He should just leave the bike, it was worthless anyway. He felt very tired; he would leave the bike. He turned back.

He looked to the trio now entering the shop. The girl finally looked up at him. She suddenly reminded him of his sister, Maria. . . . He was swept by anger.

"You won't come in? Your cuts need—" the grocer implored again. Wilhelm shook his head. "Thanks, but I'm late for work."

• • •

"It may need stitches, but that's the best I can do," Walther Mueller said quietly as he stepped back from the table where his younger brother sat.

Wilhelm shrugged, fingering the place gingerly. "The other night after the movie I overheard Johanna say that the scar on some movie star's chin made him look very dashing. Maybe this will gain me some points with her."

He slipped off the table and padded to the kitchen for something to drink. Walther went to the threadbare couch, sat down, and watched him.

"You're interested in Johanna Wagner? Since when?"

"Since . . . since I finally noticed how pretty she is," Wilhelm smiled.

Walther frowned. "I guess I don't need to remind you she's a Gentile."

Wilhelm sank into a chair with a groan. He felt like every muscle had been stretched, every bone cracked.

"No, you really don't need to remind me, Walther. Oh, there's no place on my body that doesn't hurt. . . ." He could feel his brother's eyes on him in the dim room.

Walther leaned forward, and Wilhelm knew what was coming. He had that lecturing look on his face.

"Wilhelm, you . . ." He shook his head and looked away.

"I what? Go ahead, say it. If you don't you'll be moody all night, and it's your turn to make dinner."

"Wilhelm, you need to be more careful. You need to see how things are in Germany. Not ignore them or pretend—"

"You think I don't know how things are in Germany!" Wilhelm flared. "Walther these punks go around beating up old men and frightening little girls! And no one but a turnip peddler comes out to help! You don't think I see what Germany is coming to? Now you're reminding me that I can't court a pretty girl because she's not Jewish—but I'm not really either—my parents are!"

"Don't get so excited, Wil, you've lost so much blood. . . . Look, it's just that I feel . . . well—"

"Don't feel responsible for me, big brother. It's not your job. I'm 26 years old."

Wilhelm closed his eyes, suddenly feeling drained. *How could I not know what was going on in Germany*? He could see the eyes of the young girl in his mind: the stark terror, the helplessness in seeing her grandfather bloodied. *Of course I know. What is the Jewish paper I work for already saying and had been saying for months*?

"The old rabbi wants me to come by his place tomorrow. Think I should?"

"Ja, that would be nice for him," Walther replied.

Wilhelm was growing sleepy. "I guess I will. . . . He reminded me of Papa. Walther, the girl could have been Maria. . . . Why is this madness happening?"

"I don't know, Wilhelm, I don't know. . . . What did Handel say about you being so late?"

"He said, 'Don't let this happen again,' then he told me to go home and get patched up."

Walther was staring at the floor. Wilhelm could barely see his face. "What's—did you get a notice, Walther?"

Wilhelm thought he could not hurt more than he had when he looked into the eyes of the young girl. But now, to see his sensitive brother suddenly sad and bowed. . . .

Walther's voice was very slow and tired, as if he had suddenly aged. "The dean came to me personally—at least it wasn't with a letter. He came . . . he had tears in his eyes, Wilhelm. He said he had no choice. . . . He said I was his best professor, but . . ."

"But there can be no Jewish teachers at the University of Nuremberg!" Wilhelm nearly shouted as he stood. He staggered to the window.

Walther shook his head. "I shouldn't have told you . . . not tonight."

"Ha! You think I wouldn't notice!"

Wilhelm leaned his head against the pane, his voice a hoarse whisper: "What is happening?"

"Wilhelm, I will go back to Berlin and find a job—"

Wilhelm swung around, "Who is pretending now?"

"I can find a job in a country school where it won't matter. Papa said so. Anna and I were going to marry in the summer. Now . . ." he shrugged hopelessly.

Wilhelm had felt rage when he saw the old rabbi bent into the dust. He felt the same rage surge up from his stomach now. He had always protected Walther, even though he was three years younger. When Walther's calm reasoning and patience had failed in schoolyard battles, Wilhelm had been there with eager fists. No one could call the slender, quiet Walther Mueller names and not feel the wrath of his younger brother.

He turned to look at the man hunched over with his head in his hands, *turned out of the profession he loved, separated from the woman he loved* . . . Wilhelm turned away shaking his head. There was nothing he could do. His fists had not saved the old rabbi, and they couldn't save his brother now.

• • •

Four men and two women made up the entire staff of Nuremberg's only Jewish newspaper, *Jacob's Ladder*. They were gathered in the basement of a funeral home that was the latest offices for their paper. They had had to move three times in the last nine months due to the harassment by Nazi gangs. They were hiding—and Wilhelm didn't like it. Printing the truth was beginning to exact a terrible price. They were gathered at the table, each frowning and somber, as Wilhelm explained the reason for his battered face. He had not wanted to venture out of the apartment with his face so bruised because it was embarrassing. But life still goes on, jobs still had to be attended to since there was rent to pay. He would have to swallow his pride and face the humiliation that he had not fared better in the contest of fists.

The room was silent for nearly a minute before anyone spoke.

"The problem is, Wilhelm, you are too impulsive. You cannot attack a Nazi gang by yourself. You were woefully outnumbered. You should have seen that."

"Wilhelm saw an old man, a rabbi, being beaten, Simon! You don't think of numbers then. You do what you must. Wilhelm has great courage," a young woman interjected hotly.

"Misplaced courage becomes foolishness," Simon returned as he lit a cigarette.

"What would you have done, Simon?" Wilhelm asked tightly.

"I would have turned my bicycle around and gone to work."

"*What?*"

"Simon! You can't be serious!"

"I am very serious. Wilhelm was outnumbered; there was nothing he could do. He admitted he didn't rescue the old man. He just got beat up for his efforts. I'm telling you, the only way to strike at Nazis is in numbers or in a planned fashion—when you have some real chance of success. Jumping into a battle like Wilhelm did does no good for anyone. And now these thugs will be looking for him so they can finish their work. He gained nothing."

Daniel, the editor, stood up, stretching. "I'm going out for coffee. When you young minds have finished with this, I'll come back down and work on the paper."

"But tell us what you think, Daniel, as our resident gray beard."

He took a patriarchal pose, stroking his chin.

"Well, for myself, I agree with Simon's logic and reasoning. The facts cannot be disputed as he so bluntly pointed out. Wilhelm was beaten for trying to rescue Rabbi Bergmann. Very logical, Simon."

The group of young people were shocked. Simon was smirking through a veil of cigarette smoke.

"However! If I were Rabbi Bergmann, then, without question, Wilhelm was right. We write in our paper each week that Germany is losing her soul to Nazism. Then I tell you, young Wilhelm has been beaten and redeemed a piece of Germany's soul back. If more men were as such, well my young friends, Herr Hitler would be back in Vienna sweeping streets!" He placed his hand on Wilhelm's shoulder affectionately, then he left the room.

Gretl squeezed Wilhelm's hand under the table. Finally, Simon spoke as if the former discussion had not taken place. He scanned each face.

"This is the best time to bring this up. I trust all of you, and Daniel is too old to be involved."

"Involved in what?"

"Involved in a group of us who are taking matters into our hands against these Nazi thugs instead of waiting for the civil authorities to do anything."

"The police force is largely comprised of Nazis now."

Simon stood. "Exactly. What happened to Wilhelm and to the rabbi is going to keep happening. But we don't have to stand around like a bunch of Jewish babies waiting for it to happen to us. If this evil has come to Nuremberg, so be it!

"What do you suggest, Simon?"

"I suggest you come to our meeting tomorrow night. Nine-thirty at the tavern on Herrenstrasse. Don't write the address down; don't say anything to anyone. And don't tell anyone—don't tell anyone your plans. Don't bring a friend that you think might be interested. Watch yourself as you come; make sure you don't pick up any shadows."

Gretl giggled. "This sounds like one of those French espionage films."

Simon's face was hard. "This isn't pretend, Gretl. This is serious. Don't bother to come if you aren't—this isn't for the weak and nervous. If you're content to let the Nazis steal and destroy and beat up our people, don't come."

●　●　●

Wilhelm could not determine which he felt a larger measure of— embarrassment or anger. Or a perfect alloy of both. The rickety bicycle he usually rode was gone, no longer proclaiming him blocks in advance over the old streets of Nuremberg—now it was his own face. Usually mild and friendly, now it was often suspicious and tense. Today, it was distorted with purple bruises and cuts that people noticed. It was obvious he had been worked over with human hands—kneaded like bread dough. Some people stared openly, others turned away. A bandaged head, a black eye, a split lip—these were common in the city now. At least as long as Jews and those who did not embrace Nazism were openly defiant. But Nuremberg was fast becoming Nazified in every quarter. Disagreement and opposition would soon be forced underground until it was completely wiped out. But even Wilhelm, feeling frustrated and depressed, could not ignore the beautiful spring morning. As he walked, he saw the ancient German city for what it had been—a university town of history, culture, and dignity. A city of Gothic beauty, narrow houses with gabled roofs, winding streets, and ornate stone bridges. *I wonder what it will be like when the convulsions that grip it are over? Will I still be here*? . . . He didn't want to think about it. He didn't want to think of Walther leaving or Simon's words. So he thought about his destination and questioned, again, the wisdom of it.

It took him a full 30 minutes to cross the city from his own apartment to the address the old rabbi had given him. He was clearly surprised as he turned on the street. He had expected a cheap apartment block much like his own. These two-story houses, pressed side-by-side, with their steep roofs were clearly prosperous middle class. A wealthy Jew still in the city? Did *Jacob's Ladder* know of him? He climbed the steps and prepared to ring the bell—then he paused. Somewhere inside someone was playing the violin—and playing it well, though Wilhelm admittedly knew very little about such skill. He buzzed and waited, feeling nervous. *Well, just a moment to say hello and see how the old fellow is faring, then I'll be off*, he said to himself.

The door swung open. A thick, deep-bosomed woman regarded him with searching eyes.

"Guten Tag," Wilhelm offered.

She nodded.

"I came . . . is this the home of Rabbi Bergmann?"

"Ja."

"I came to see him for a moment."

Then recognition flooded her face as she interpreted the battered young face. She grabbed his hand, pulling him almost off his feet and into the foyer. Wilhelm was shocked. She looked like she was going to embrace him!

"Ja, you! The young man who helped Rabbi Bergmann yesterday. God bless you, oh, God bless you!"

Wilhelm turned scarlet as she pumped his hand.

"Is he home?"

"Ja, ja! But you see, when Natalie plays he allows no interruptions. He calls it his balm of Gilead, you see."

Wilhelm didn't see.

"And, of course, today, with what happened to the poor man yesterday . . ." Her eyes scanned the ceiling. "He needs all the balm he can get. Natalie has been playing for almost an hour."

"Well, I'll just come back later," Wilhelm said, and took a step back.

She seized his hand. "Oh my heavens, no! Rabbi Bergmann can be fierce when he needs to be, which is rare, thankfully. He would scold me down to my eye teeth if he knew I'd let you slip away. You just come along!"

She pulled him down the richly carpeted hall. They paused before a double paneled door and she placed a thick finger to her lips.

It was the most beautiful room Wilhelm had ever seen. He had never found much beauty or warmth in the richly appointed rooms of the Farber estate when he had glimpsed them as a boy. This room, it . . . Suddenly, quite unexpectedly, this room calmed him. He felt as if his body was giving a large, collective sigh. The anger he felt was draining away, leaving him tired and weak. He sank into the plush chair the woman showed him before she disappeared.

It was a room of book-lined walls and oil paintings and fresh flowers. At the end of the room was a bank of tall, narrow windows. The rabbi sat in a chair near the windows, his profile to Wilhelm. The old man had closed his eyes, but he was smiling. Near him stood the young girl, half-turned to her grandfather and the windows. Neither had heard or seen him enter.

Wilhelm could see her slender fingers as they held the violin, as they pushed the bow back and forth. He felt himself mesmerized by them. Even the gold patina of the violin was beautiful against the creamy whiteness of her face. Her thick, dark hair that hung to the middle of her back was braided and tied with a blue satin bow.

This music is so soothing, so calming, he thought. He had never heard music like this before; he typically preferred much louder, racier fare. *This* . . . His eyes were getting heavy, so he pushed himself up in the chair. Then he closed his eyes, forgetting what he had come here for. Within one more measure, Wilhelm Mueller was asleep.

• • •

They were all smiling at him when he awoke. Even the woman had returned. The girl almost laughed as he jumped awake. *How long? Long enough for someone to have set a small mahogany table before me laid with a tea service*! They had drawn up chairs across from him. *How embarrassing to have strangers watch you sleep*, Wilhelm thought and felt distinctly irritated with himself. He ran a hand swiftly across his chin to see if he had drooled as Walther always teased him of doing. His voice was shaky, "I certainly hope I didn't snore."

The rabbi leaned back and laughed deeply. The girl smiled at him before she dropped her eyes to her lap.

"I apologize for watching you sleep, young man, but you looked so comfortable . . . and at peace. Well, we didn't have the heart to wake you."

"Too many late nights, I suppose." He wasn't about to explain how this room had affected him.

The rabbi reached across the table to shake hands. "It was good of you to come, Wilhelm Mueller. Our prayers have been answered."

Wilhelm shifted uncomfortably. "Well, I . . . I wanted to see that you were all right."

The rabbi passed fingers along his own bruises, nodding and smiling. "It would appear we attended the same matinee, nu?"

Wilhelm nodded and smiled.

The rabbi turned to the young girl, "This is my granddaughter, Natalie."

The young people nodded briefly at each other.

"Will you serve us, Natalie dear?"

"Ja, Grandfather."

Both men were silent as she poured. As he accepted his cup, Wilhelm could not help but look at her hands closely. They were beautiful hands. *How come I have looked at women before, but never really noticed their hands*? he asked himself.

"And what did you think of Natalie's playing?"

"Oh, Grandfather," the girl blushed.

"Was it not the very music of heaven? How could you keep from drifting away from the tether of this world to the next, eh?"

"Ja, it was very nice," Wilhelm agreed.

Wilhelm sipped his tea and waited, feeling awkward, while the old man's eyes appraised him.

"So, tell us about yourself, Wilhelm," the rabbi asked gently.

Wilhelm cleared his throat. "Well, I...I live across the city, near the university, with my older brother. He's a—" Wilhelm stopped and studied his cup a moment. He attempted a calm tone.

"He was a professor of languages, the youngest in the school's history. He was probably the best they had over there. I work at the school as a custodian, and as a waiter at a cafe. I put in some time at the *Nuremberg Tribune* when I can." He frowned into his cup again. It had not sounded very impressive to him, either.

Bergmann's face was impassive as he slowly nodded.

"And why is your brother no longer the university's youngest professor, may I inquire?"

Wilhelm did not really want to talk about this. He exhaled as if in pain, "Because he is a Jew."

They locked eyes. Then the girl extended a plate of pastries to Wilhelm. He wasn't hungry but he reached for one.

"And what will he do now that he no longer can teach at the university?"

"He's going back home. My parents live near Berlin. He hopes to find a job. He was hoping to be married this summer."

He could not keep the bitterness from his voice.

"Well, it is most unfortunate that he has lost his position, but he should not despair. I'm certain that by this summer he will be able to marry and return to his teaching."

Wilhelm felt he might choke. "Sir?" His voice was incredulous. The rabbi smiled patiently.

"I understand what you are thinking. It is because you are young and full of the future; I am old and see the past. But measures against Jews are as much a part of who we are as a people as our laws are. Every generation, every country has seen persecution. You should know this, I'm sure your father taught you this." Wilhelm did not want to be unduly blunt, but he felt he must set the old rabbi straight from the beginning.

"Yes, my parents have taught me the history of the Jews. But you see, their faith is not mine."

He expected an outburst from the religious man sitting across from him. He glanced at the girl. She looked shocked then her eyes returned decorously to her lap.

"I see, ja, I see," the rabbi said with a smile, and Wilhelm relaxed. "As I say, tell your brother this storm shall pass. We Germans are a people of reason and dignity. What is happening now is simply an aberration from that. Reason and dignity will remain when this Nazi chaff has blown away.... Now, another pastry?"

"No thanks."

The rabbi was licking his fingertips in ecstasy. "Hilda's creations are sinfully delicious!"

Wilhelm laughed in spite of himself, and was surprised to hear the clear laughter of the rabbi's granddaughter.

"Sinfully delicious? Well, this is enough sin for me today. I'd better be going. I only meant to drop in to make sure you and your granddaughter got home safely."

"We are very grateful to you, Wilhelm, most grateful."

They stood and shook hands.

"Well, thanks for the refreshments and," he turned to Natalie, "the concert. It was very nice."

"You will join us for dinner tomorrow after synagogue?" the rabbi asked. "I am retired, but we go faithfully. Dinner is at two."

"Thank you. I don't know....Well, goodbye."

Outside on the steps, Wilhelm ran his hand over his very tender, raw face. "Aberrations," the rabbi had said. Well, his aberrations hurt. He shook his head in frustration. *Reason and dignity...*

● ● ●

Rabbi Bergmann would have been horrified if he'd known it was his myopic attitude of the Nazis that finalized Wilhelm Mueller's decision to join the local Jewish resistance group. First, the beating he and the rabbi had received, then Walther's humiliating experience. Even the Zionist newspaper could not stir up the people. There could be no giving in, no giving up—no matter what the odds. *They were German citizens just as much as any dogmatic Nazi!* Wilhelm finalized in his mind. Discussions with friends of the injustice of the violations were academic. Walther could retreat; he would choose to fight. He had enough in his mind to spur him, but strangely it was the frightened face of the rabbi's granddaughter that rose most often in his mind. *What had she done in her sheltered, virginal world to see such violence?* It was this that propelled Wilhelm Mueller to the meeting Simon had spoken of.

It was beginning to rain as Wilhelm made his way down across the city. He had paused half a dozen times to look into a store window to see if anyone had followed him. It did seem a little melodramatic to think someone was following him in the shadows, maybe only a few steps behind him. Then he remembered that the men who had beaten him had his name. But in their euphoria perhaps they had forgotten it. . . .

He skipped down the steps that led to the tavern. No one glanced up as he entered. He stopped at the bar long enough to drain off a stein of beer. He was early. He paid, then casually headed for the men's room. Instead, he opened a door that led down narrow, dark, musty stairs. At the bottom was another door. He could see a light from the crack underneath. He paused. A voice was raised, high, thin, excited. He recognized it immediately. *Of course Herschel Grynzspan was here. And full of himself.* Wilhelm frowned.

He had hopes of entering in unnoticed, but Herschel's sharp eyes had seen the movement. He hardly paused in his flow of words. "There, you see! Wilhelm Mueller! Look at his face! This is what we are talking about. Nazi apes did that. He was alone against half a dozen!"

Wilhelm sank into a chair, irritated. Apparently his beating was already common knowledge—and was being enhanced as well. And here was Herschel pointing him out in a voice that seemed to be amplified by a megaphone. But then, as he gazed around at the assembly of nearly 20 young people, he realized he knew most of them. Simon nodded unsmilingly from a position near the front. There was Gretl across the room, smiling at him. He smiled back, but groaned inside. Gretl with her obvious attention for him. She was a nice girl, and Wilhelm had no desire to hurt her.

The meeting lasted over three hours. Many plans against the Nazis had been presented and debated.

In the end, after the tavern upstairs had locked its doors, the group made two specific decisions. They would call themselves the "Widerstand," the Resistance. And they chose their first retaliation. They would burn the office of the university-sponsored Nazi newspaper.

Wilhelm went home that night feeling very satisfied. He could tolerate working with Herschel Grynzspan. He belonged to something now. He was no longer drifting and uncertain—he had a purpose.

10
The Beginning of the End

Berlin, Fall 1934

Irwin Farber had been entertaining government officials all evening in his private dining room at the prestigious Herrenclub. Now, as the enclave broke up after four hours of feasting, drinking, and revelry, the eldest Farber looked a little red-faced and dissipated. The room was quiet after the men, with overhearty goodbyes had left. Irwin remained at the head of the long dining table. He didn't seem to see the cluttered table or the oil painting of a nude which hung on the wall in front of him. He didn't seem to notice the stagnant air from a dozen cigars. For Irwin Farber it had been a successful gathering, never mind the hefty expense that would come directly from his own pocket. He sat, relaxed, fingers laced across his middle. He was not thinking of his wife and children at home. He was thinking of his young mistress who was waiting for him.

There was a light knock on the paneled door near his side. It drew him from his thoughts.

"Come in!" he barked.

Karl Beck, Max's personal secretary, stepped in, closing the door softly, but waiting at the threshold. Irwin glanced at him, then pulled a bottle toward him for one last drink.

The secretary did not attempt to disguise his disgust at the scene. It didn't matter that this was his true and final boss. The stench in the room assaulted him like a blow in the face, and the painting and table littered with food repulsed him. But he stood statue still, watching Irwin Farber through half closed eyes.

Farber pitched back the last drink. "I wouldn't bother you at home—and after hours—but I leave for Austria early in the morning."

"It was not a particular bother, Herr Farber," Karl answered with his typical trace of arrogance.

Irwin studied him openly. He had grown to dislike the fastidious, almost effeminate, young man. Yet he trusted him implicitly; they were allies of sorts. But deep down, Irwin Farber suspected that the loyalty went only as far as the man's greed was satisfied.

"Where is my brother?" Irwin asked roughly.

Karl knew exactly which brother he was speaking of, but deliberately misunderstood.

"Eric has been posted to the garrison at Stuttgarte, I believe."

"I do not refer to Eric," Irwin snapped.

"Max is in Paris."

"Paris . . ." Irwin smoothed the linen in front of him, his forehead drawn in deep crevices.

"Your meeting went well, Herr Farber?"

His head jerked up. "Ja, very well. Many important plans were laid tonight. Great progress for Farber Company is ensured. I will apprise you of them when I return next week."

Karl nodded obediently—wondering what kind of holiday this tenacious, moody man could provide for his family.

"When is Max to return from his playground?"

"I believe he said he would be back Friday. He wanted to be here for the opening of the new opera house."

"Well, before he returns I wanted to impress upon you, Herr Beck, the importance—indeed the profound importance—of our strict communications. I want you to continue editing Max's memo's as I instruct." He leaned forward, his eyes beady and intense. "I don't want Max to know anything of this meeting. Nothing. No accidental line in a memo like last time. Keep him busy with the usual, trivial affairs that are his responsibility. To him, Farber Company is running predictably, and I don't want anything to pique his interest—nothing for him to bother about or question."

"I understand, Herr Farber."

"Good." Irwin rose heavily, straightening his tie. "Then you also understand, Herr Beck, your diligence and faithfulness in this matter will be rewarded as certainly as the success of our plans that were made tonight."

"I understand perfectly, Herr Farber."

"That is all."

Beck's step was light as he left the prestigious Herrenclub. Keep Max Farber in the proverbial dark. What assignment could be easier?

● ● ●

A string quartet was playing some Wagner composition in the background because Richard Wagner's work was the preferred music of the Nazi government. This was part of the decree Joseph Goebbels had made as he established cultural standards in all the arts for the Third Reich. Obviously this particular quartet had not adjusted to the new standard, and was straining up and down the scales. The people at the large, round table tried not to notice, but looked embarrassed. After all, this was a high-society birthday celebration.

Max was fond of watching people attempt to conceal their discomfort—especially people somber and humorless like his older brother or the conceited Reinhard Heydrich. So Max half-listened to Elaina beside him and absently ate from the plate of veal parmigiana in front of him. He was watching Reinhard across the table. Reinhard was talking and laughing, eating and drinking—and growing visibly agitated. Max knew what it was: the music. It was grating on his nerves. He had spared no expense for his wife's twenty-fifth birthday dinner at the Kaiserhof Hotel. The setting was elegant; the food was perfect. The music was obviously less than perfect. Max glanced at Lena Heydrich. She looked resplendent in her flashing diamonds and silk, and happy with her gathered friends. If she noticed the discordant music, she did not reveal it.

There were eight couples around the table and Max knew all of them. Irwin and his wife, Katrina, sat near Reinhard. Max noted that even Irwin seemed relaxed this evening—perhaps it was because of the wine bottle he kept close to his glass. Max allowed his thoughts to wander away from the clang of silverware and conversation. *Irwin drank too much.* Max smiled to himself. What could he do or say? Any comment would not be welcomed. He looked at his sister-in-law. *Had she noticed? How could Irwin drink Schnapps at the office all day and keep a clear head to make all those decisions?* A few drinks gave Max a dizzy head and a roaring headache afterwards.

"What did you think of the fuehrer's speech last night, Max?"

"Hmm?"

It was Rolfe Oberg, Lena's brother. Stabbing at his veal, he repeated the question.

"Ah, well, that is a considerable question, Rolfe," Max replied as he dabbed at his mouth. No one but Rolfe would hear his reply. He could get by with saying anything—except he knew Rolfe was a fanatical Nazi. "I thought the speech was nicely vociferous and protracted."

Rolfe nodded energetically. "My thoughts, too. I especially liked his taunts to Great Britain."

"Ja, very garrulous."

Rolfe turned to the person sitting on his other side. For all of Max Farber's silliness, he used too many big words.

Max returned to his veal, smiling. Elaina leaned toward him, whispering in his ear.

"Max, behave yourself."

Max chuckled, pleased at her perfumed nearness. He had felt a little distracted by her loveliness all night. When she leaned away, he looked up to find Reinhard's pale eyes upon him: hard, cold, unsmiling, probing. Max did not flinch or look away. Finally Reinhard turned to his wife.

The quartet had started on a new piece as the white-jacketed waiters brought another course of the meal. Max motioned one of them closer. "Please ask the quartet if they would play a piece by Mendelssohn or Hindemith."

The waiter bowed and moved away.

"Delicious veal," Elaina commented.

"Excellent," Max agreed. "Josef tried to make veal parmigiana once. I could've sworn he'd smothered one of my old fishing boots in tomato sauce!"

Elaina was laughing when the waiter returned. He bent down between the two. "The quartet leader apologizes Herr Farber, but they cannot play the composition you suggested."

Max was genuinely surprised. "What? Why not?" I'd think any quartet would—"

"Sir, it is the composers of the music. They are forbidden."

"Forbidden?" Max's voice came out louder than he had intended.

A few conversations at the table paused; Elaina stopped eating. The waiter lowered his voice. "The composers are Jewish. Reich musicians..." He shrugged and left.

"Forbidden?" Max repeated with moderation.

Elaina felt the looks. "Max . . ."

"Is something wrong, Max?" It was Reinhard Heydrich's voice, direct, pleasant.

The table had quieted. "No, nothing wrong, Reinhard, danke."

"You don't like the food?" Reinhard smiled.

Max laughed shortly. "No, no the food is fine. It's great. I merely made a request of the quartet."

"And?"

Max felt rising annoyance. Reinhard was obviously pressing him. Typical—no reason to be surprised.

"And I find it amazing that this quartet cannot play any Mendelssohn or Hindemith. I think if they could, we would all enjoy it." Max returned to his plate.

"Mendelssohn and Hindemith are Jews," Reinhard continued, still smiling. "The works of Jews are now banned in the great Third Reich, Max."

"So I have just learned, Reinhard," Max answered amiably.

The table had grown very still; no one was talking, few were eating. Eyes were turned nervously to the table, or to the two men having the exchange. *I could win a million dollars now if I bet on what Irwin's face looks like*, Max thought. He knew Elaina had stiffened in the chair beside him.

Reinhard had leaned back in his chair, his head slightly tilted, his tone amused. "You do not approve of Herr Goebbels' decisions about music?"

So Reinhard wanted to corner me. Max smiled and, to those at the table, looked supremely relaxed. He saw Lena Heydrich's hand rest lightly on her husband's arm. *Spoiling the party, Reinhard*? Max mused silently. *That's far worse than the unskilled quartet.*

"I make no secret that I enjoy fine music, Reinhard. And a string quartet is one of my favorites. This group you've hired is talented. I enjoy fine music by whomever the composer is. It is the music itself that counts. Is it good or does it sound like a couple of cats fighting? The composer matters very little when you hear a beautiful, creative work."

"Even Jewish?"

"Even Jewish. I will put a question to you, Reinhard. If I went over to the quartet here and gave them two pieces of music to play, could you tell which one was written by the French composer or which one the Italian wrote? Which was a Catholic or protestant or atheist? Could you tell by the notes that flowed from their instruments?"

Reinhard was silent. The room was tomblike.

"If you liked one piece above the other, wouldn't that be all that mattered?" Max continued calmly.

Those who dared, riveted their eyes on Reinhard Heydrich. Silly or not, Max was making sense.

"It would matter if my government made laws concerning it. You are a part of the Nazi party now, Max. I would think you could understand this."

"Well, Reinhard, on fashioning a stronger Germany, on a healthier economy, that I can understand. On music, a delight or a horror to the ears, that I don't understand. I know what I like and that's what matters."

The birthday guests were fidgeting. Frau Heydrich was scarlet. She didn't know if she should be angry with her contentious husband or the foppish Max Farber.

"Gentlemen," she called to the quartet, "a little Viennese waltz if you please. Music for these two music lovers!"

Nervous laughter at the table erupted as the guests exhaled with relief. All present knew the fiery temper of Reinhard Heydrich. They also knew Max Farber had sealed his future with the Heydrich family.

• • •

"So, what did you tell him?"

Elaina Heydrich looked up at her brother in front of the cold fireplace, standing tall with his hands behind him. For a moment Reinhard's blond paleness made her think of marble. He was made of stone, perfect and polished like the fuehrer wanted. But his blue eyes were alive, snapping with simmering anger. *I've never seen Father look this way—and certainly never Mother. Where did this look come from?*

"Well?" His voice cut sharply through her analysis.

"I told him I had a headache," she replied simply.

Lena Heydrich sat at the end of the sofa. She looked nothing like the happy woman she'd been only a few hours ago. She looked nervous.

"Well, I will modify my nouns for your feminine ears and say that yes, Maximillian Farber is a headache for the Heydrich family—besides an embarrassment to his own."

"Reinhard, please . . ." Emilie pleaded quietly.

"Please what, sister? Please not state the true and obvious?"

She leaned back into the sofa. She was very tired yet unwilling to be scolded like a truant schoolgirl by her brother. She was her own woman, living alone, making her own decisions, and doing well. She did not like this family meeting—but she could not dismiss it. The truth was, the independent Elaina was just a little intimidated by her confident brother. And it was not comforting to know he was no idiot. He knew his power as well as she.

"Now is the time, Elaina, tonight, to come to a final understanding about Herr Max Farber." His tone broached no argument.

"What kind of understanding, Reinhard?"

Reinhard flared instantly, "You know very well! Enough of this relationship you have with him! The man is an imbecile, a buffoon! A boy that refuses to grow up!" He was pacing now. "It has been this way from the very beginning, since our family knew their family. Max has always been different, defiant in his own stupid way—nothing like Irwin or Eric." He shook his head vigorously. "I won't tolerate this any longer, Elaina. I hear the teasing remarks from people about what it would be like to have Max Farber as a brother-in-law. Then I look out my window and see him speeding down the Unter den Linden in his coupe with that Airedale in the seat beside him."

"Percy is a magnificent terrier," Elaina stated calmly.

Reinhard didn't seem to hear her. "When he joined the Nazi party I thought at last he had grown up, had found his senses! I hoped it would put some steel in his spine and give him purpose. Yet I hear nothing but inane speeches about beautiful music and string quartets!"

"You did badger him tonight, Reinhard," Elaina ventured with sudden spirit. "We could all see he didn't want to speak."

"I wanted to show his stupidity. I wanted you to see, Elaina, that you cannot marry a man like that!"

"Max has not asked me to marry him—"

"I don't even want you around him anymore, to be seen with him!...Defending Jews! He won't be much use to the party if he continues this way."

"Please calm down," Lena soothed.

"Can you imagine how embarrassed Irwin was tonight?" Reinhard growled.

Elaina straightened. "Reinhard, you've known Max as long as I have. But I know him better. He is a kind, generous, gentle man. I agree he isn't ambitious or...he's...he's Max."

"You think you can reform him?" her brother sneered.

She had thought of that, but she didn't want to admit it.

"Women can't reform men, Elaina. They shouldn't even try. Men are men with all their flaws and all their strengths. As far as I can see Max Farber has no strength. He is completely unfit as a husband."

"Elaina, he is an embarrassment with his odd ideas," Lena interrupted. "You know he's always saying these unexpected things like he did tonight."

"He does have a sense of humor, even if it is a little overdeveloped," Elaina protested softly.

Reinhard snorted derisively. "I would be willing to overlook his oddities, his overdeveloped sense of humor as you put it. I could put up with that. I could manage him. But tonight proves among other things that Max is not loyal to the party."

"Reinhard—" Elaina began.

But he loomed over her. "No! You will have a strong man—a man of determination. A man who follows the party with all of his being because he knows it to be the destiny of Germany."

Lena attempted a touch of calmness. "Reinhard is right, of course. Max is pleasant in his own simple way, but wouldn't make a good husband. You know that in your heart, Elaine. Once you're free of him, you will find a good man, fully deserving of your love."

Reinhard snorted again, and Lena flinched as if he had struck her.

"Elaina, you will tell him. You will tell him tomorrow," Reinhard said icily.

Elaina stood suddenly. She had had enough—enough of her brother and his wife. "I am *not* a girl of 16 that you can order around. I will tell him if I choose. . . ."

"And if you do not choose correctly, Elaina Heydrich, then you will choose to no longer be part of this family."

He bowed and swept from the room.

Later that night, like a young girl with troubled dreams, Elaina stood looking out her bedroom window. The lights of Berlin glittered like gems; everything seemed so peaceful—everything she did not feel. They were right—and a part of her hated them for it.

For years she and Max had been friends, confidants. A boy and a girl, then a man and a woman. It had been easy to like Max.

During his university years they had drifted apart, moved in different social circles. After he had come to Farber Company their relationship had resumed. It was a comfortable thing; they liked many of the same things. He was a perfect—indeed, impeccable-theater escort. He was affable and popular at parties, and very handsome and virile.

She knew they had an unspoken understanding. Someday they would come together as man and wife, it was only a matter of time. Lately she had noted that Max's ardor had increased, like a slow-burning flame leaping to life. She had not been afraid or threatened by it. She waited; she knew he would get around to asking her to marry him.

Now . . . Ja, they were right. Though he has a pedigree more sterling than mine, though his German heritage was of honor and respect, he did not seem to fit in with his family's tradition. Everyone could see that. He hasn't really grown up. You can see it in his expensive toys and travels. It's endearing, but it's frightening, too. I want a husband, not a son. I want a man who moves things, who shapes things.

Germany was changing, coming out of the dark and it was terribly exciting. Elaina wanted to be a part of it. She wanted Max to be a part of it. But she knew deep down, as well as her blunt brother did, that Max would be left behind if he did not quickly change. He would be left with his quick smile and his fishing rod . . . and Percy.

Lena had said, "You know that in your heart, Elaina." True again. But what Lena did not know, nor Reinhard, was the full heart of the woman who stood gazing out into the night. In that heart, born years ago, was an undying love for Max Farber.

It was the largest protestant church in Berlin and had been the Farber family church for a century or more. This fall evening it was filled to capacity and quietly elegant with the hundreds of long white tapers that were lit along the stone walls. But the crowd had come less to worship than to see and hear the man that filled the pulpit. To some, sitting in the front rows, there was a little disappointment at the sight of the slight, gray-headed man in the plain wool suit who rose to speak. They had expected someone more commanding in presence. This man looked like an unpretentious shopkeeper. He was Martin Neimoeller, a hero of the Great War, now author of the bestselling autobiography, *From U Boat to Pulpit*. Their disappointment soon fled. He was a vibrant, interesting speaker. He held his audience captive for two hours by speaking of his war experience, openly discussing his conversion to Christianity, elaborating on the sufficiency of Christ—and his agreement with the impressive Nazi agenda. Max and Josef Morgan who sat in the middle of the church listened as eagerly as those around them.

Then it was over and Max and Josef were walking home in the cold, crisp evening. "Let's go fishing for a few days Max. Let's go to the Elbe. I had a patient come in who has a cousin up there and he says the fish are really biting."

"All right." He glanced at the older man out of the corner of his eye. Morgan's tone suggested he was suddenly in a cross mood. Earlier he'd been fine. "I just need to see Elaina before we go."

"Call her," Morgan answered in a clipped tone.

"She . . . I have tried to call her. She hasn't returned my calls since two nights ago—the night of the party."

"Miffed, huh?"

"I don't know. I mean, I'm not sure why she would be. Unless it was over the thing between Reinhard and me and Jewish composers. I tried to smooth that out." Max gazed into the night sky.

"Well, as a physician, I can tell you a woman's body is a lot more complex than a man's. Same thing with their emotions. She may be upset with you but won't be able to tell you why."

"Oh that's comforting," Max chuckled.

"I think it could take a lifetime to understand a woman," Josef continued.

Max fixed his eye on a planet in the heavens: brilliant, shining in smooth, vaulted blue. It was comforting, suspended in the night sky— Jupiter.

"Well, it seems to me if you loved her you wouldn't mind taking a lifetime to understand her. You know, like an adventure."

Now Morgan laughed. How like Max this reasoning sounded.

"Uh huh, well, what if she wanted you to understand her all on the first day and wasn't willing to go through the adventure? What then?"

"She'd just have to be patient with me. If she loved me deeply, as I loved her, she would. If not, well," he shrugged, "I'd be in trouble then."

They stopped at a corner, but Morgan didn't turn to face him.

"So are we talking about a hypothetical woman or Elaina Heydrich the Miffed?"

Max smiled. "What did you think of Herr Neimoeller?"

Morgan's protest died in his mouth, and his smile instantly faded.

"I liked it better when he stuck to his personal experience and his faith—that was all very interesting. He's a fine speaker."

"But . . ."

"But I don't particularly like him inserting politics from the pulpit. You'd think God would prefer His servant to talk about Him and not Adolf Hitler!"

"Ja, you make a good point, Dr. Morgan."

They reached the steps of their house. Max looked up and saw Percy sitting in the windowseat on the second floor—waiting for him with a huge canine grin. Morgan followed his gaze.

"She likes Percy all right?"

Max was startled. He turned to look at his old friend who was smiling slightly. "You know me well, Morgan."

"From your backside to your tonsils, ja."

They both laughed till Max sobered. "She likes Percy. I admit I've never really asked her about our relationship."

"I know you've known each other for years, but does she understand you, Maximillian? Do you understand her? You might want to make certain, really certain you both are starting from the same place. Starting off at different places, well, could cause a collision."

"I think she understands me," Max replied, fingering the wedding ring he now carried in his pocket.

"And you her?"

• • •

He was one among hundreds in the vast room of the Chancellery. His appointment was exactly at noon. He was unsmiling and inwardly nervous as he stood stiffly in the spotless new uniform. He had come to say the oath—then the room would empty and refill with more of his contemporaries. This had been going on for hours before he came, and would continue for hours after he left. He kept his eyes rigidly forward even when the group of officers passed with the fuehrer in their midst. All he could see were heads and backs in front of him and the banners that hung from the vaulted ceiling. It took less than 30 seconds to say the words the general gave them. A solemn chorus filled the room.

"I swear by God this sacred oath that I shall render unconditional obedience to Adolf Hitler, the fuehrer of the German Reich, supreme commander of all armed forces, and I shall at all times be prepared as a brave soldier to give my life to this oath."

He left the room having only caught a glimpse of the top of the fuehrer's head. Eric Farber had heard about the controversy before he had entered the room. Everyone had heard it, and many were complaining in a very muffled, under-the-breath way. The military was no longer swearing allegiance to the German constitution as it had for decades of its glorious history. Now their allegiance was to one man. Eric had felt a slight inward warning at this pledge, but he ignored it, as so many others obviously did. Allegiance to Adolf Hitler must be synonymous to allegiance to Germany: All for the good of the Fatherland.

A Farber must continue the rich military traditions—whatever the cost.

• • •

Of all the Farber sons, Eric Farber looked most like his father, the second I.E. Farber. Taller than Irwin and not as broad as Max, he had a serious face that lacked the frowns and hardened creases of Irwin. As a young boy, Eric had wanted to be a doctor—something that would have greatly surprised Josef. But Eric had learned quickly that Farber men went into the family business. Like Max, he quickly found he was disinterested and unsuited for it. That left only one other suitable option for a Farber—the military. So he joined with high hopes that he had at last found his place. The decision had greatly pleased Irwin. He swiftly moved to buy Eric's shares of Farber stock. His control was almost complete.

Eric stood waiting on the platform at Stadtbahn. Max had promised to see him off. Eric felt a twinge of pride and affection as Max parted through the crowd on the platform. Max was so pleasant and agreeable. Fleetingly he wondered why they had never been close. Max's face lit up when he spotted Eric and they shook hands warmly.

"Off to the army!" Max enthused.

Eric smiled. "Guten Morgen, Max, thanks for coming to see me off."

"Sure. So are you all ready for Wilmershaven?"

Eric turned slightly, pulling Max away from the crowd. He lowered his voice. "Actually, Max, I'm not going to Wilmershaven. I'm only telling you, so that if anything happens—"

Max stopped. "Anything happened? What are you talking about? You said—"

"I know, I know. That's what I was told to say to friends and family."

He glanced around, suddenly nervous.

"Eric, what's going on?"

"I've decided to try for the airforce, Max—the Luftwaffe. I want to be a pilot. Our bases are filled, so they ship the excess candidates to other places. I'm being sent to train in Russia."

"Russia!"

"Max, not so loud. This is hardly public knowledge."

"But why Russia?"

"The treaty, Max. You know the limits it puts on the army and navy. There's not even any provision for an airforce. So, we train secretly— very few are to know about this."

"Who figured all of this out? I mean, if the foreign press . . ."

"Exactly. We've heard it came directly from Göring, with the fuehrer's approval, of course. It's the only way of getting around the Treaty of Versailles."

Max was silent a moment. "Training for what, Eric?"

The young man shrugged. "Whatever the big guys decide, I guess. I just want to fly. Just keep where I'm at under your hat. As far as you know, Eric Farber is in Wilmershaven."

"Sure," Max said slowly.

Eric could see his brother was troubled.

"So what's new with you, Max? How are things in the Farber empire?"

"Oh you know, typically empirish."

They both laughed, then Max leaned forward. "How long do you think you'll be gone?"

"They say at least eight months."

"Well," Max continued cheerfully, "then I'll tell you now. By the time you get back I hope there is a Frau Farber."

"Elaina?"

"Ja."

"Congratulations, Max. I'm happy for you both."

"Well, actually Eric, I haven't asked her yet. I hope to today."

He pulled the velvet box from his pocket.

Eric held the ring, his face softening. "Mother's ring."

"Ja, you remember the will said I was to have it?" Max reminded, apologetically.

"Well, that's great." The train whistle sounded long and shrill. "That's for me."

"Auf Wierdersehen, Max."

"Be careful up there, Eric."

He waved from the platform, and Max found himself wistful that they had not spent more time together. Russia...

• • •

Since Farber Company was such a large enterprise, it was not surprising that a thriving, highly accurate network of company gossip also existed. Therefore a handful of secretaries on the "upper floors" knew that Maximillian Farber was about to be called on the carpet by his older brother. Since Max was so popular with the Farber subordinates, they looked sympathetically at the young man as he jaunted past them. His smile seemed tragic—a man smiling before the guillotine.

Max stepped into Irwin's office without bothering to knock. He was fully expecting to be reprimanded about the Jewish musician business. Though two days had passed, he knew Irwin had not forgotten, nor likely forgiven him for it. A postponement, but no reprieve. Yet he hardly cared. He was thinking of his luncheon engagement in a few hours with Elaina Heydrich. And he was wondering if it were normal to be this nervous. He was wondering if the setting would be romantic enough for Elaina. He was wondering what she would say. . . .

So whatever the curt summons meant, it wasn't weighing heavily on his mind. There were far more important things than Irwin's typical, unsatisfying bluster. Still, he had asked Karl Beck for an interpretation of the summons. Karl had shrugged and turned away. *He knows*, thought Max. Another time he might have felt a little more apprehensive.

"You called?" Max stood before the massive desk.

"Sit down, Max."

Max sat, waiting.

"Eric left?"

"Saw him off on the 8:30 train."

Irwin toyed with his paper knife.

"Is this about last night?" Max asked pleasantly.

"You embarrassed the Heydrichs," he said bluntly.

"Reinhard Heydrich embarrassed me, but we're grown men, so I think we can get over it."

Irwin's eyes narrowed. "Max, you tend to say very . . . imprudent things in public. Reinhard Heydrich is a powerful man in the government now. You'd be foolish to irritate him."

"I should be afraid of Reinhard?" Max asked with a trace of boyish curiosity.

"You should be wiser with what you say!" Irwin snapped.

"It was a dinner party, Irwin, not a party rally. I thought it was a relaxed and—"

"Max!" Irwin stood up impatiently. "You've always resented my advice—even now! I caution you—"

"I am not afraid of Reinhard Heydrich! I'm going to say what I think. I meant what I said the other night. It's utter foolishness to not allow fine music compositions to be played because of their composers' religion. Such decisions will make Germany a laughingstock in the eyes of the world. Does Herr Goebbels really want that?"

Irwin shook his head fiercely. "You think Goebbels cares about what the world thinks about our music?"

"Perhaps he should. Does the fuehrer and his cabinet want Germany to become a cultural wasteland because she won't tolerate Jewish musicians? We are the country of fine—"

Irwin cut him off sharply. "What is this sympathy for Jewish musicians, Max? What is wrong with German musicians?"

Max laughed. "Mendelssohn and Hindemith are Germans! As German as you or me!"

The elder Farber leaned threateningly across the desk.

"You are in the Nazi party, now! You know our fuehrer's feelings about Jews. Whether you agree or dislike it does not matter in the least. You must understand the way things are now, Max. . . . You disgraced Reinhard and Sabra and Elaina the other night with your arguing."

Max said nothing. *Did I disgrace Elaina? Is that the source of her sudden coldness?*

His silence infuriated Irwin. "You curb your silly tongue or—"

Max stood up red-faced, his fists clenched, "Or what, Irwin Farber?"

Irwin's eyes were bulging with rage. He stepped back.

"We grate on each other. We do not work well close to each other— or even in the same town. *I* control Farber in Berlin. You need to move on."

Max was stunned and couldn't conceal his surprise.

"What do you mean?"

"I drew this up a week ago." He shoved a paper across his desk toward Max, but Max didn't even reach for it. His eyes were still riveted on his brother.

"I . . . I have an appointment. Summarize it."

"There was a board meeting yesterday. I informed the directors of your recent sloppy work on certain matters. It's all lined out in this paper. I recommended that you be replaced. I also suggest that you be given the position of Executive Director of the Farber plant in Bavaria."

Max's mind was spinning too fast to settle on any one thing clearly. *Sloppy work? A board meeting that I knew nothing about? Had Karl told me and I forgot? A small plant in Bavaria? Out of Irwin's reach . . .*

"Of course, the directors are wise men. They agreed with the proposals," Irwin continued cooly.

Max slowly gathered up his jacket and hat.

"You can't do this, Irwin. You bought Eric off; you can't dismiss me like that. You know I have some legal control, also. It is not for sale." He was standing very straight though he felt suddenly weak and tired.

"I've ceased to be afraid of you Irwin. You need to understand that."

"If the board has voted . . ."

Max managed to leave without slamming the office door.

The secretaries were not surprised that young, carefree Max Farber looked a bit pale and his smile seemed shaky.

● ● ●

Max had one hour to vent his anger, so he took Percy for a long, brisk walk in Tiergarten, which was turning leafless with the advance of fall. He was angry with Irwin—but not over his arrogance or his plan to get rid of him. Max wouldn't allow the rejection to sting him like it had since boyhood. He was angry that Irwin had the power to nearly ruin his day. This was an important day—he didn't want anything to cloud it.

An hour later he appeared on Elaina's steps, cheerful and composed. "Mind if Percy comes along?" he asked as he opened the car door for her.

She shook her head wordlessly.

"Where are we going, Max?"

He smiled. "A surprise."

They drove to the Farber country estate. Max's spirit's began to sink with each passing mile—Elaina was quiet and withdrawn. Max glanced at her. She did look lovely, though. As always, she was stylish in her chestnut-colored slacks and tweed jacket. She was the picture of German aristocracy: a finely chiseled face and perfectly coiffed hair. Classic.

Max didn't want to bring up the unpleasantness of the party; he wanted to talk about them, so he sped along, hoping the beautiful countryside would affect her, remind her of better times.

"Here we are!" He pulled into the circular drive in front of the house.

Percy jumped out, eager and yapping. That brought the caretaker, Heinz Mueller, from around the house. He wore overalls, muddy at the knees, and was smiling broadly. It was good to see a Farber on the place.

"Guten Morgen, Herr Faber!"

"Guten Morgen, Heinz. How are you?"

"Fine, sir, just fine."

"And it is nice to see you, Fraulein Heydrich. You look so lovely this morning," the gardener continued with a bow.

Elaina smiled and relaxed. "Danke, Heinz."

Max took Elaina's hand as they followed Heinz around the back of the great house.

"What were you working on, Heinz?" Elaina asked.

"The roses. I'm getting them ready for winter."

"The place looks great. You do fine work, Heinz," Max said.

"And Marta keeps the house ready to open on only a moment's notice," the gardener said with a sly smile.

Max smiled, understanding the old man's thinly veiled suggestion. "And do you have what I asked for ready?"

Again the caretaker bowed. As if by prearranged signal, his cottage door swung open. Marta appeared, hurrying forward, beaming, with a picnic basket in her arms. She presented it to Max.

"Danke, Marta. I'm very grateful. I'm sure it will be delicious." He steered Elaina down the lawn to the riverbank. A boat was tied there, with cushions and blankets in the stern: the old boat of their youth. Now Elaina understood. She groaned inwardly, she knew what was coming. Max's face confirmed it. He was smiling and eager—as she had seen him a hundred times before. Wanting to please her, wanting her acceptance, and wanting her.

"Max," she said softly, looking into his eyes.

"Ready for a little voyage, fair fraulein?"

She looked around for some diversion. Percy was whining as he tried to find the courage to get into the unsteady boat.

"Is he going?" she asked with a slight trace of irritation.

"Not if you don't want him to. Percy, I'll be back. Now, stay." He helped her into the boat and they slipped out into the river, sunshine casting a silver veneer over the water.

"I'll keep us in the sunshine so you'll be warm," Max promised.

He watched Percy on the shoreline, mournful but obedient. His eye's were fastened on Max.

"You know, if I whistled right now, the old fellow would be in the water in a flash," Max said, thinking out loud. "He's a loyal fellow."

Elaina was watching him. Loyalty...Max was so handsome.... She felt herself weaken. As a young girl, she had lived for the sight, for the voice of Max Farber. She had been the envy of so many and now he was ready to marry her.

Max turned and their eyes met. He was glad to see that the guarded look had vanished from her eyes. She was smiling slightly.

"We kissed out here so many years ago," she said.

He nodded. "My first kiss."

"And mine," she replied.

She glanced away from the intensity of his eyes. He began rowing. When he finally anchored, they opened the basket and enjoyed all that Marta had made. Max ventured a few jokes, and soon Elaina was laughing.

She looked out over the water, toward her family home in the distance: the Heydrich home.

"This is a lovely day, Max. It's been very nice—everything you planned. I will always remember and treasure it."

Max looked up sharply from his plate. Her voice suddenly sounded sad, her words final.

"Elaina?"

She would not look up.

"Elaina, I'm sorry about the other night. If I embarrassed you. . . ." Still she was silent, still she would not look up.

"Elaina, I didn't mean to anger Reinhard. I only . . . answered him. Elaina?" He took her hand. It was cold.

"Max, I can't marry you. I . . . can't."

A full minute passed. She squeezed his hand, "That is why you brought me here, isn't it, Max?" she asked gently.

He nodded.

"Max, I don't want to hurt you. I don't. We've been such good friends for so long. I—"

Max's voice sounded hollow. "Reinhard was angry; he made you do this."

"No Max. He didn't make me. He can't do that. But . . . but he did make me see we are too different to . . . to marry."

"Our differences have never mattered in the past, Elaina. As you said, we've been friends."

The boat glided along, with neither speaking. Max watched Percy as he trotted along parallel to the boat. Even Percy looked worried.

"Max, why didn't you ask me to marry you years ago, when we first became of age? I was waiting for you to ask . . . but you never did."

Max hadn't expected this hard question. He leaned across the oars frowning. "I'm not sure. I suppose I didn't want to give up being a bachelor. And I wasn't sure what love would cost."

"Max, I think there is a woman for you and a man for me that would be better for us than we are for each other. I'd hate myself forever if we married and made each other miserable. If we disappointed each other . . ."

The Nazi thing. Joining had not been enough, Max thought bitterly.

"We might not have enough love to carry us through, Max, if times got difficult for us."

Max was staring at the bottom of the boat. He didn't seem to notice Percy's distant whine.

"Oh, Max . . ."

Finally he looked up at her. "Can't I turn back the clock, Elaina?"

She laid her hand on his cheek, tears filling her eyes.

At the shore, Max helped her from the boat. She paused, then leaned against him. His arms went around her.

"Please don't despise me, Max," she whispered.

"I will never feel that way, Elaina."

They walked up the lawn. The afternoon shadows had grown purple and cold. Max stopped and looked back to the river. This is where they had begun, this is where they ended.

● ● ●

Being a medical man of over 40 years, Josef Morgan looked at men and women with a sharp, disciplined eye to detect problems in their bodies. Still, it didn't take much scrutiny to see that his friend was wounded and hurt. It was not a physical ailment—Max still looked strong and vigorous. But from the look in his eyes and the stooped line of his shoulders, a broken heart could be clearly diagnosed.

Max told him everything—everything from Irwin to Elaina.

"Of course she was right. You probably knew that before me. When she was . . . telling me we could only be friends, a part of me agreed. I . . . I knew she was right. But as she was saying it, I felt like she was choking the life out of me."

Josef drew his arm around Max's hunched shoulders.

"There are other women, Max, and one who will really be right for you."

"That's what Elaina said—except I don't feel like looking for anyone else."

"Ah, now, men have been saying that since Adam and Eve had their first squabble when she burned the bacon."

"Not bacon, Josef."

"Lamb, then. Since way back men have wanted to give up, and here we are, in 1934, with our world very well populated. Men don't give up.

You remember when you broke your foot skiing? I could hardly keep you off the slopes before your foot mended."

Max shrugged, staring into the fire, saying nothing. Josef dared not broach the subject of Irwin's tirade. He could not be charitable regarding Irwin.

"Josef, I tell you, I feel tired and old . . . and worthless tonight. Absolutely worthless. I'm 30 years old, and I have nothing. One of the richest men in Germany—and I have nothing. What has my life been for?"

Max shook his head. "Do you have anything in your black bag for this, my friend?"

Josef lowered his head to hide his own tears.

The doctor was just a little concerned. Max was not "bouncing back"' with his usual cheerful optimism. Their quiet evenings were even quieter now. The games of chess were played without the typical rivalry and Josef always won. Max often sat stretched out in his library chair, staring into space. Josef could see that Percy, who sat beside the chair waiting for the hand to ruffle his ears, was worried.

"Max—"

"I'm all right, Josef. Don't worry. I'm just thinking a lot of things out."

So Josef comforted Percy—and waited.

Then, one night after he had gone to bed and drifted into the world of dreams, Max was there at the side of his bed, eagerly waking him up, telling him he was sorry but he couldn't wait til morning. Josef was surprised and relieved. The wait was over.

● ● ●

The Farber Company gossip network was once again furiously active—an unprecedented event had taken place. By quitting time at five, even the receptionist who patrolled the first floor knew about it. Max Farber had summoned his brother to *his* office. The secretaries feigned intense devotion to their work as Irwin passed. No one wanted to meet eyes with the thunder-faced Farber.

Max stood looking out his office window. The red-and-black banners were the only color on the gray mural of the autumn day. Max decided it was a view he was not going to miss. Karl Beck stood behind him, trying to appear relaxed as he leaned against the bookshelves.

Max was subdued—and acting as if he knew something that Karl did not. He was usually talkative and cheerful—not this morning. This morning he had called his secretary without explanation. Waiting for Irwin and watching Max left Karl Beck edgy. Though he knew where his deepest loyalty lay, he didn't care to be caught in the crossfire of a sibling dispute.

Irwin entered the office equally agitated. He gave Karl a swift frown, which was returned, as he came to stand before Max's desk. Max turned, and Irwin nearly caught his breath. Max looked pale, as if he hadn't had much sleep lately. Max glanced at both men before he sat down.

"Please sit down, this won't take long. Rather than explain this twice, I've asked you both to be here. I've given your request a great deal of thought over the past week, Irwin." Max looked down at his hands on the desk. Irwin was watching him, measuring him. "I can't do what you requested. I have no desire or intention of becoming the plant manager in Bavaria. I've carefully reread the company charter and thoroughly understand my control in the company. You can't make a substantial change or implementation without my agreement. That was the way grandfather designed it and that's the way father wanted it, also."

Irwin seemed transfixed by Max's authoritative tone.

"I'm taking a year's leave of absence from the company. I'll decide my future with the company when I return. It will take Karl and I a few days to put things in order."

Now Max stood, his tone and posture, a new look in his eyes, announced he'd allow no debate or interruption from Irwin or his secretary. He was in control.

"Dr. Morgan and I are going to South America, Brazil specifically. Dr. Morgan has a good friend who is a doctor in a small, primitive village. He needs help, supplies, and so on. This is the kind of thing I've been looking for, a place where Farber Company can help." He emphasized his words, expecting an explosion of protest from his brother. "Not making a profit or expanding, just helping. It's called charity. Other big corporations do it, and Farber is behind things in that respect. If you want to publicize it here, that's entirely up to you."

"How much do you propose to take to Brazil?" Irwin asked with surprising calmness.

"It's all written out here." Max handed him a paper. "The board of directors received their copies last night. They—"

"Last night?" Irwin turned red.

"Yes, because we sail at the end of the week, I had to move quickly with this so I went to all their homes last night. All of them seemed receptive to my plans. So, there you are."

Irwin pretended to read. But his mind was racing. South America was far away—better than Bavaria.

"What exactly are you going to do there, Max?" Karl asked.

Now Max gave them his first smile. "That's the exciting part, Karl. I'm not quite sure! I hope to build bridges and things like that. Get my hands dirty, you know. Farber Company started out in farm tools: plows, spades, shovels. We started out simple and in the soil. Maybe the old ways aren't so bad."

"Percy going?" Karl smirked.

Max's smile did not falter, but there was a slight change to his tone. "Of course. Isn't Max Farber known to be inseparable from his Airedale companion?"

Karl shifted uncomfortably, his eyes narrowed on Max.

"Oh, one last thing . . ." Max strolled back to the window, both men held captive. "I'll need monthly reports from you, Karl. Of course it will be your usual quality work, nothing sloppy. I've also outlined the kinds of things I'll need to vote on."

Karl stiffened, his voice cold and defensive. "Has my work been sloppy recently, Herr Farber?"

Max leaned against the windowsill, arms folded, head slightly cocked—almost amused. "Not to me personally, Karl, but Irwin mentioned something about sloppiness last week."

A tense silence settled over the office.

Max cleared his throat. "Now—"

"If your expenses in charity in Brazil exceed your estimates . . ." Irwin finally managed.

Max nodded. "Of course, they will come from my own pocket. . . . That's all, gentlemen."

Irwin stood. Max looked so relaxed now, but his tone . . . Irwin was unaccustomed to it—and unaccustomed to being dismissed.

Left alone, Max slumped into his chair. He was excited. He knew he was doing the right thing. But he was a little disappointed: Neither man had wished him well.

11
Wilhelm's Justice

1935

Like a false lover, many in Germany embraced Nazism for the color, pageantry, and excitement it brought into their otherwise predictable, monotonous lives. What this new "religion" really meant for their country only vaguely mattered. An intoxicating stimulus had entered their lives—and they grew addicted to it. As the addiction strengthened, the people noticed less and less the voices of dissent and disagreement to the new order. The economy, foreign policy, politics, culture, education, and religion finally spoke with one voice. Only one. A tumult and a silence settled over the land.

Three German cities became the primary and resplendent Nazi jewels: Berlin, the seat of governing power; Munich, the political power seat; and Nuremberg, a favored party rally site. Each city regarded itself with distinction and displayed superiority toward its smaller, rural neighbors. All three cities nourished large Nazi party memberships and secret state police forces. Soon the Geheime Staatspolizei, quickly abbreviated to the Gestapo, became notorious for its swift and zealous suppression of defiance and crimes against the state. Crimes against the state became definable as largely whatever the local boss decided. And he had thousands of willing minions to carry out his terror. Though harassed and mistreated, by early 1935 the Jews of the greater Third Reich still walked free. *Midnight was only moments away.*

Nuremberg

The sky over Nuremberg threatened rain with clouds piling up on the horizon like an overturned laundry bag of dirty pillows. It was calm but very cold as Wilhelm jogged across the nearly deserted center square. He had never been late to the Saturday dinners at Rabbi Bergmann's, and he was determined nothing would change that. While they had had no discussions on the matter, he wanted to prove to the elderly man he could be responsible and reliable. He didn't know why it was so important to him.

There was no explaining to his friends—or himself—about this time he was spending with the Bergmanns. He usually preferred visiting his young friends with their animated discussions, their energies, their passions. Why this attachment to an old man and his quiet young daughter? He could confess that the Saturday meal from Hilda's kitchen left him satisfied for days, which was good since the rest of the week was so lean. The conversations with the rabbi, covering a dozen topics, were enjoyable. The old man laughed and Natalie smiled and Wilhelm relaxed and felt comfortable. It was as if that first visit when he'd fallen asleep had set up an atmosphere of tranquility so in contrast to the other six days of his week. Any book he chose, the rabbi lent him from his vast library, and Wilhelm marveled at the rich leather and gilt-edged pages. To be trusted with such an expensive book when he was so obviously poor....

"So, there's a daughter! Ah, now it is explained!" His best friend Peter had said, poking him in the ribs.

Wilhelm laughed. "I told you, she's a kid! Twelve or 14—I don't know," he shrugged.

"Sure, sure, 12 or 14! I bet she's 18 and very pretty. I'm going to tag along and see."

"No you aren't, Peter!" They fell on the floor wrestling. "It's just the food...I like to eat!"

He stood in the hallway, so quiet and clean, shadowy and somber. It reminded him of a synagogue. He smiled—such a comparison would please the rabbi. He stood waiting as he did every Saturday while Hilda went down the hall to announce him. He was amused now by this formal little routine. He checked his appearance in the long oval mirror. *Bet that thing weighs a ton and cost a ton*, Wilhelm speculated. He was forever estimating the rabbi's wealth. He combed his hair with his fingers and smoothed the navy sweater his mother had sent. There was nothing he could do about the scuffed shoes.

Hilda returned briskly, the scent of something delicious trailing behind her. Wilhelm's stomach rumbled loudly and the housekeeper's eyebrows arched. "Ah, the rabbi is still resting. He'll be down shortly; Natalie will receive you in the library."

Wilhelm entered the room and went quickly to the ornate fireplace where a fire crackled and hissed.

"Guten Tag, Natalie."

"Guten Tag, Wilhelm," she returned softly, barely raising her eyes. Suddenly Wilhelm thought of Peter's tease. *Eighteen and pretty.* She was sitting on the sofa, hands folded, looking into the flames. *Glossy, thick, dark hair, smooth, china-like face, deep-brown eyes. She would be pretty in a few years, sure*, Wilhelm noted, surprised.

"So, how is your grandfather?"

"All right." She hesitated a moment, her face clouded. "He was a little troubled after synagogue today. There was a . . . disturbance."

"Oh?"

She smoothed her skirt, never looking at him directly.

"Yes, a gang of . . . young men stood outside, yelling during the last part of the service. It was difficult and upsetting to all of us."

Wilhelm turned away to warm his hands. He could think of nothing to say. The rabbi lived in an illusion, and it angered Wilhelm. Was the young girl also blind? Of course, she was just a child, obviously under the overwhelming influence of her grandfather. Wilhelm frowned and added another log to the fire.

He turned around cheerfully. "Let's have a game of chess while we wait!" He moved toward the expensive board.

"Well, I don't think—"

"Oh, come on. You know how to play. You're probably a shark under all the shyness!"

Natalie blushed a bright red, and Wilhelm laughed. They made their opening moves in silence. Natalie dared to watch his face when he was concentrating on the board. His eyebrows were drawn together—she had never been so close to him. She could look closely now—if she dared. There might not be another chance soon.

"Your move!"

He looked up and found her staring. For a moment he was startled. "Ah, now what are you thinking of, Fraulein Bergmann? Thinking I'm going to be an easy win?"

"I was thinking that you are handsome," she said as she moved her knight.

Now Wilhelm turned red with embarrassment. He was familiar with girls who flirted; he was not accustomed to such directness. He searched his mind for a topic to discuss.

"While your grandfather isn't here, may I ask you a very personal question?"

"Ja," she nodded slowly.

"How is it your grandfather is so wealthy? I've tried to figure this out."

Natalie smiled then, holding back a little laugh. Wilhelm came to a swift decision—*she definitely would be very pretty in a few years*.

"My grandfather was the only child of Alex Bergmann."

"The guy with the statue inside the library?"

"Ja, that was my great-grandfather. He was a banker and an architect. He designed many of the buildings in Nuremberg. When he became wealthy, he built the hospital and orphanage. That is why there is the statue. He left part of his wealth to my grandfather."

"And your parents?"

She sighed. "They, and Grandfather's only other child, my Uncle Alex, died in the influenza epidemic of 1920. I don't remember them of course."

"So your grandparents raised you."

"Ja, my grandmother died eight years ago. She was a very happy woman. . . . We had very good times. When she died, Grandfather retired to raise me. I was born in this house."

"Your move," Wilhelm commented after moving his bishop. "So . . . Nuremberg is all you know, I mean, this house, school, synagogue."

She looked at him quickly, as if she were gauging something.

"Ja. I know it must sound very dull to you."

"Doesn't it to you?" he burst out impulsively. "I mean, I'm sorry, I didn't . . ."

"We have one of the finest private libraries in the city. I have great adventures in my books."

"Books are all right, sure, but . . ." He shrugged.

An embarrassing silence settled between them.

"Checkmate!" There was a slight note of triumph in the young girl's voice.

"What? You can't do that!"

"Why not?"

"Well . . ." Wilhelm scratched his head, "because I didn't think of it first! I knew you were a shark!" He wagged his finger at her. Now she laughed in earnest.

Rabbi Bergmann stood in the doorway, his fatigue and depression slipping away as he watched the young people and heard Natalie's delight. "Ah, Herr Mueller, so good of you to join us! Did I neglect to tell you my granddaughter won the Nuremberg chess championship in the junior division last year? It must have slipped my mind!"

Wilhelm was beginning his third plate of food when he glanced over the elegant table of spotless linen, silver, china, and crystal. *Wouldn't my friends marvel at this*? The rabbi was leaning back contentedly, swirling his wine in a long-stemmed goblet that reflected the afternoon light. Natalie was slowly finishing her ambrosia.

Wilhelm's grin was a little sheepish. "I'm always concerned about hurting Hilda's feelings after she's obviously gone to such effort."

"Such a sensitive young man, Natalie, take note!"

The three laughed. After the meal they adjourned back to the library.

"Another game of chess, Wilhelm?" the rabbi asked slyly.

Wilhelm shook his head. "I've had enough humiliation for one day, danke."

"It is true my granddaughter possesses many talents. Fortunate will be the one who someday finds this treasure!"

"Grandfather, you're embarrassing me."

"There is no need to be embarrassed with the truth, child. A little Bach or Mendelsohnn, Wilhelm?"

"Danke, but I have to be leaving soon. I have an appointment this evening."

"A young man and an evening appointment.... Is this fraulein a good Jewish girl?"

Wilhelm smiled. "Your subtlety reminds me of my mother, Rabbi Bergmann.

The old man chuckled. Natalie watched Wilhelm's face closely without reserve.

"My appointment is with male friends. It's just...work."

Rabbi Bergmann nodded slowly. "Your employer is very generous to give you Saturday evening off. I would think it would be one of his busiest times."

Natalie knew the slight twitching downward of the eyebrows signaled a frown or a change in emotion in their new friend.

"It is. But the place fills up with Nazi students and Gestapo who enjoy Handel's Cafe on Saturday night. He thinks it wiser for me to take my day off then."

"Very thoughtful of Herr Handel."

Wilhelm leaned back and nodded. "Ja, he is very considerate."

"You have told me he is a party member and that he knows you are Jewish."

"He's a member in name only. He has no interest in persecuting Jews. He's very practical, and I'm a good worker for him."

"Yes, I imagine you are. But does working as a waiter employ the full extent of your talents, Wilhelm?"

Wilhelm smiled again. He had learned the rabbi's ways as well as Natalie had memorized his own expressions. The rabbi plodded slowly, indirectly, then at last arrived at his goal.

"Did you play soccer in your youth, Rabbi Bergmann?"

Bergmann laughed heartily. He did enjoy this young man who had come so suddenly into their lives. So brash, confident, friendly...and rebellious.

"I did play soccer many years ago. And my question, Herr Mueller?"

"Well, sir, I don't expect I'll work for Herr Handel forever. I'll find something better. Now, though, it...provides."

The rabbi nodded. "You were a journalism student in the university?"

"Ja."

"So, writing is something that interests you."

Wilhelm answered slowly. "Frankly, sir, I'm not sure where my abilities lay. I like to write; I'm all right at it."

"So how are you using this ability God has given you?"

The young eyebrows contracted. Natalie knew Wilhelm had not especially liked her grandfather's question. But suddenly Wilhelm smiled, and Natalie was unprepared for the answer.

"I am writing each week, Rabbi Bergmann."

Now it was the rabbi's turn to frown. He waited, his lips pursed, his long fingers steepled.

"Yes, sir. I write for the Widerstand. A pamphlet each week. In fact," Wilhelm dug into an inner pocket of his jacket, "here is one of them." He handed the rabbi the cheap yellow paper. With a voice that betrayed him, he spoke confidently of his work, but Natalie could see he was eager for her grandfather's approval. The rabbi pulled at his chin. He did not unfold the paper.

He sighed. "I have heard of Widerstand. All of Nuremberg has."

Wilhelm sat tensely at the edge of his chair, waiting. This new friendship had come to a deciding point. Would this be his last Saturday feast?

The rabbi spoke carefully. "This paper most likely advocates committing acts against the established authorities. It attempts to incite the populace against the government." He pulled his glasses off and began to slowly polish them. "Is this the best way to use your talents, Wilhelm?"

The young man's voice was firm. "Yes, sir, I think it is. The 'established authorities,' as you call them, are wrong. Jews and non-Jews alike should not be held hostage by a gang of bullies and brutes." Still the rabbi was silent. Natalie was spellbound by Wilhelm's boldness.

"Sir, the Nazi hoodlums that disrupted your synagogue today are trying to control Germany. Would you choose them over good Germans of reason, fairness, intellect? No, of course not. Why are we allowing them to take over? Why are we accepting or ignoring the fact that the very worst, the very basest men want to govern us? This is not just against Jews! This is against freedom and honor! It is good against evil!"

Wilhelm's voice had risen; his face flushed. This old man was too smart to come face-to-face with truth and back away from it!

"It will pass, Wilhelm. A time of persecution, but it will pass," the rabbi said finally.

"No, sir, I don't think so. I love Germany too much to think so."

"But Wilhelm . . . Wilhelm there are so many. You and your compatriots are too few. When the purging is over, we will remain. To confront them only invites pain and—" His voice had begun to tremble.

"Sir! You did not confront them that day. You were minding your own business. You didn't possess any threat to them. Would you have had me ignore you that day?"

"I am grateful, Wilhelm, I . . ."

"What if they had attacked Natalie? Would you have wanted me to stand and watch?" Wilhelm stood and pointed at the girl, his eyes blazing now.

"No, no, Wilhelm."

"Think of Natalie as Germany, Rabbi Bergmann."

"Grandfather," Natalie whispered, as she went to put her arms around the man. "Please don't, Wilhelm, please."

"Coffee?" The indomitable Hilda stood glaring at Wilhelm from the doorway.

"Yes, Hilda, danke," Natalie said calmly.

Wilhelm's voice was unsteady. "I . . . have to go now."

"Please stay and have coffee with us, Wilhelm." Natalie's voice bore a trace of unexpected strength. Wilhelm watched the old man compose himself and then he slowly sat down. Rabbi Bergmann was pale.

"I'm sorry sir, I didn't mean to frighten you."

Bergmann smiled weakly. "Of course you didn't. You are young and I am old. Old men frighten easily."

Wilhelm accepted the coffee from Natalie wordlessly. His eyes met hers. Like her grandfather's there was no condemnation or anger in them. He sighed with sudden fatigue. They drank in silence for several minutes.

"I do have to go or I'll be late. You should burn that paper," Wilhelm said pointing to the pamphlet still untouched in the rabbi's lap. "It is considered illegal to own one."

"I will be careful. I want to read it—it is your work."

Wilhelm stared into his cup another minute. Finally, he looked up at Natalie. "Can you skate?"

"Ja."

"They are opening up the pond in the park tomorrow afternoon. You should go; you would enjoy it. Well, thanks for dinner again."

The rabbi reached up for the customary handshake. Wilhelm's throat tightened.

The rabbi's face was as calm and benevolent as ever.

"Until next Saturday, please be careful . . . my son."

Natalie Bergmann was struck by how quiet and lifeless the room seemed after the young man had gone: the steady pulse of the clock, the sputter of the fire—no other sound. She reached for her violin and waited for her grandfather to name his preference. But the old man, with his head resting on his hand, and a faint smile on his lips, was staring out the window.

"Grandfather?"

He seemed not to have heard her. "Natalie, I'd say the young man and I did have our chess game after all."

• • •

It was a perfect day for ice skating: windless, clear, and sunny, yet crisp. Vendors with their little carts of steamy schokolade on the rink's perimeter did a brisk business. At least a hundred skaters took their turns on the ice during the course of the day. Now the afternoon slowly paled, with the sun diluted and the sky an icy flat-blue like the reflection of the ice. It grew colder. The huge municipal buildings that bordered the square were gray and lifeless. The trees were barren masts, colorless, quiet, cold. Around the pond, however, was laughter and splashes of vibrant colors from sweaters, scarves, and coats. When twilight came in just over an hour, the smoky torches would be lit for nighttime skating.

Natalie Bergmann was enjoying herself even though she skated alone. She wore a scarlet wool coat, and her hair was tucked up under an expensive fur hat. She had developed the opinion that her hair piled on her head gave maturity to her face.

"I predict some young boy is going to stumble in his skating when you glide by, my dear," her grandfather said as he wagged a finger at her.

She smiled, and kissed him quickly. Then she lowered her chin into her collar and went back to the ice. *There is only one young boy I want to notice me*, she thought.

Rabbi Bergmann had found a space on a bench beside a heavy-set German mama. They had a lively conversation punctuated with laughter as they traded advice on raising girls. Bergmann relaxed as he watched Natalie weave through the skaters. *A fine suggestion from Herr Mueller*, he admitted. *It is good for Natalie.*

Wilhelm had not seen the Bergmann's when they arrived. He was on the opposite side of the ice among a group of young men and women. They had already been skating for several hours and were now trying to decide where to go to eat. Since most of them were poor, their choices were severely limited. But it had been an enjoyable day, and Wilhelm anticipated a relaxing evening of conversation and a little innocent flirting. Then he saw the scarlet coat.

Wilhelm was very glad to see her. *Had she shown some independence from her grandfather?* Wilhelm wondered. He smiled wryly when he spotted the black-coated man on the bench. Well, at least she has gotten out. Hands in his pockets, he left his friends and glided smoothly out to Natalie.

"Guten Tag, Wilhelm!" she called breathlessly.

He gave her a sweeping bow and attempted a pirouette. He wobbled badly. His friends were pointing, other skaters were laughing—and Rabbi Bergmann was nodding and smiling. Natalie gracefully swerved and sped away. Wilhelm struggled to catch her.

"Hey! Wait!"

"You will make me fall!" she taunted over her shoulder.

Finally he reached her, catching her gloved hand in his.

"I'm the best skater out here! I planned that little move."

She laughed delightedly. "You really expect me to believe that?"

He shook his head. "Nein, not you! You are a smart girl! You know when a fellow is giving you a line. You'll do well when you're older."

"Thank you, Wilhelm."

"So, he let you come skating. That's good. Having fun?"

"Ja, Grandfather is very thoughtful."

"Right, I know that." Wilhelm waved to the old man. The rabbi nodded.

"Any friends here with you?"

Natalie took a deep breath. "No."

"So . . . do you, you know, have any friends?"

"At school, a few, yes. But they could not come today."

Wilhelm watched her skates for a few seconds as they cut perfect curving lines in the ice.

"You're very good. Win any skating awards in the juniors last year?"

"Not last year—I didn't enter. But I won when I was 10 and 12."

"What? Are you serious?"

She was smiling and nodding, delighting in his shock.

"All right, come on and tell me what else. Let's have your resume of honors, Fraulein."

"There is nothing else, Wilhelm, really."

He peered at her disbelieving. "Come on, chess, skating, what else?"

"Well, last year I placed third in the Vienna Spring Festival in violin."

He shook his head. And he thought this girl was practically entombed in her home with a possessive old man!

Natalie slowed to a stop and looked at Wilhelm's waiting group. "She is pretty."

"Who?"

"The girl who is watching and waiting for you."

"Gretl? Oh, she's just a friend. Well, I'd better go. I just wanted to say guten Tag."

"It will be auf Wiedersehen now, Wilhelm," Natalie said with a pretty smile.

"Natalie, was your grandfather very upset about yesterday?"

She was touched by his concern. "No, not that I could see."

"I just wanted him to . . ." he shrugged, "understand. I wanted him to understand the way things are."

Her voice was soft, causing Wilhelm to look at her closely.

"He understands. I . . . understand. Grandfather simply keeps hoping."

"Well, auf Wiedersehen."

"Auf Wiedersehen, Wilhelm."

Wilhelm sailed across the ice to his friends. Natalie went to the opposite side.

Suddenly a squeal of brakes sliced through the crisp winter air. An old green truck pulled up near the ice. Young men in their brown SA Stormtrooper uniforms piled out. One carried a small swastika banner.

There were over 20 of them. Like an abrupt end to music, the skaters and spectators halted where they were, as if frozen. A man climbed to the hood of the truck, hands on hips. Commanding. His face was already pale, and from where he stood, Wilhelm could smell vodka. The Nazi scanned the crowd, pleased he had gained their total attention so easily.

"Now listen! By the authority of the Nuremberg Council this skating pond had been declared off-limits to Jews! Hear Me? No Jews!"

No one, Gentile or Jew, moved.

"We are here to enforce this law!"

Wilhelm's group was nearest the truck. All of them were Jews. Wilhelm snorted loudly. "Law! Ha!"

"Hush, Wilhelm," a friend hissed.

The man on the truck scanned the crowd with an angry scowl.

Some skaters slowly resumed, but others moved uncertainly. How could such a thing be enforced? How could these men determine who was Jewish?

"If you are a Jew get off the ice now!"

Natalie had lost sight of Wilhelm. She skated up to her grandfather. He was speaking to her, but watching the unfolding scene.

"A nice chat with Wilhelm?" he asked.

"Ja, very nice."

"Well, it is growing colder. I think it is time to leave. Here, sit here to take off your skates." He stood between her and the rink, blocking her view.

The man on the Nazi truck jumped down. His gang moved among the crowd, speaking loudly, roughly. Bergmann saw them approach Wilhelm's group. He made sure he was blocking Natalie's view.

"Natalie, please hurry my dear."

"I'm trying Grandfather, but I have a knot in my laces."

Natalie felt little fear for herself or her grandfather. She knew they could hurriedly slip down a nearby side street away from the danger. But after the months of Saturday dinners, she knew something of Wilhelm Mueller's spirit. He would not take this command to leave silently or passively. A cold knot filled her stomach—*he was certainly going to be hurt. Grandfather had said it only the day before: "To confront them only invites pain."*

Wilhelm stood on tiptoe to look over the crowd, making certain Natalie had made it safely across the ice. A wave of hot indignation filled him as he watched her prepare to leave. The young girl's outing had been spoiled because of these bullies.

The Nazis pushed themselves boldly forward to confront Wilhelm and his group of friends. A stiff, expectant silence hung between the two groups. The apparent leader of the SA stood with his feet planted apart, chin jutting forward. Wilhelm thought he had a flabby baby-face despite all his sternness.

"Show us your party identity cards!" the soldier barked at the four young men. The Jews shifted uncomfortably. "Do you *have* party identity cards, hmm?" he sneered.

"No, we do not have cards," Peter said calmly.

"No cards! Did you hear that fellows? Well, well, I wonder why? That must make you communists—or Jews."

"Or intelligent, loyal Germans," Peter returned with a trace of a smile.

The baby-faced Nazi reddened, and his comrades crowded closer to Wilhelm's seven-member group. "Tell us your names! Write them down, Kurt."

Wilhelm stood at the edge of the young people, watching with absorbed fascination as the clouds of vapor puffed from the Nazi's mouth. *Just like a dragon*, he thought.

No one volunteered his name. The girls were quietly edging away. Wilhelm could still feel Gretl clutching the sleeve of his jacket.

"I said, Tell us your names!" The man's eyes blazed and rested on Wilhelm. "You. What are you staring at?"

Wilhelm grinned slowly. "Well, honestly, I was thinking you look like an overweight bulldog. You know, one that lives on cream puffs and dirties the snow. . . . Then I decided you're a dragon, a mythical creature that blows a lot of smoke."

There was a low murmured growl among the Nazis. The leader grabbed Wilhelm by the collar.

"A dragon, eh? Then you will feel my fire, smart mouth!"

The rabbi took his granddaughter's arm when she stood. He could see the Nazi leader drawing closer to Wilhelm. He could also feel his own heart racing and he felt light-headed.

"Natalie, we must go quickly!"

Natalie was staring at the scene across the rink. She could hear the blades cutting the ice as many of the people resumed skating.

"Wilhelm is . . ."

"Natalie, please." He was trying to pull her now.

"Grandfather, we are safe here, but Wilhelm is in danger. We . . ."

"There is nothing we can do. He has brought this trouble upon himself, Natalie. Now, my granddaughter, please, this is no scene for your eyes to witness."

Natalie turned to face him. She could see he was cold and frightened. He was startled to see the tears in her clear blue eyes.

"Natalie?" he whispered. But the girl gently pulled away from his grasp. She turned and took a few steps forward. *I can't leave until I see what happens to our new friend*, she thought. *I can't help him directly, but I can't leave him either. He had been our rescuer once not so very long ago.*

Wilhelm continued smiling even as the Nazi shook him.

"You asked me what I was thinking. Did you want me to lie?"

The Nazi pushed Wilhelm away, sending him sprawling to the ground. Wilhelm jumped up with his fists ready, but Peter was at his side, his hand on his arm. "Too many, Wilhelm. These cowards always bully in groups."

"You and I, fat boy," Wilhelm spat out. "You win, we'll leave. I win, you leave."

Several men in the Nazi group laughed. The leader was smirking.

"I would love the pleasure of grinding you up, swine, but on another day. Today you will leave because we tell you to. We do not care to disrupt this place of fun for the citizens of Nuremberg. And they will not share the ice with Jews. So you will leave in one minute. You can see you would be pitiful against us—even your women would laugh." His eyes ran boldly over the girl by Wilhelm. "They are pretty. We could entertain them for a time while you lick your wounds. . . ."

Raucous laughter greeted this.

"Come on, let's go." Peter pulled at him.

The group turned and moved down the street, but Wilhelm hesitated. The Nazis were waiting, arms crossed, relaxed in their victory.

"The Jewish general just can't take defeat," the leader taunted. "Look at him, eaten up with frustration. His little army deserted him!"

His friends were safely down the street, and Wilhelm had forgotten entirely about the Bergmanns. *Will it always be like this? Never a day when the tables were turned or at least balanced?* He felt the fury that smoldered. *Why hadn't the other Germans on the rink come to stand beside me? They were afraid.* He glanced around at the square. The statue, Justice, stood like a sentinel in front of the Nuremberg court building, a silent witness.

The Nazis were so confident that most of them turned away, laughing. Wilhelm sprang forward, grabbing the Nazi banner that hung loosely in someone's hand. Capturing it, he turned, and darted for the ice. The Nazis roared and shouted, but none of them had skates.

The skaters on the ice stopped and gave him room. He could see many of them were smiling. Natalie's hands were clasped to her mouth, tears freely streaming down her cheeks. Wilhelm spun and raced, and held the Nazi banner high over his head. The Nazis on the shore, stomped and shouted with rage. Wilhelm watched them from the corner of his eye. He knew what their next move would be. They would ring the ice and try to capture him when he came off. He sped to the far side, kneeled, and tore off his skates. The Nazis were running and slipping around the perimeter. He leaped up, running, banner still high, to the side street away from his friends. The Nazis could not capture him.

• • •

The office of the Nuremberg Gestapo chief was very small and now cramped with Nazi youth. Sunlight poured into the window, in dusty shafts, picking up the cigarette smoke as if from a smoldering fire along the walls and floor of the room. The Gestapo chief listened quietly to the story from the furious youth. Each wanted to tell of the crime in his own colorful, verbose way.

"They were Jews! We should have thrown them all into the truck and brought them here!"

"Their day is coming, young friend, we must be patient."

"Be patient!" the moon-faced youth shouted. "He stole our banner! A Jewish swine stole our banner! A disgrace for all Nuremberg to see."

"Oh, I hardly think this little theft is known in all of Nuremberg," the chief soothed. "You must let the Jews think they have a little triumph. What is a banner in their hands when total power is in ours? Now—"

"If we only knew who he was. We've scoured the Jewish hangouts."

"Oh, you can be sure he's underground by now. From what you tell me, the fellow must have a few brains along with his guts. What you should concern yourself with is not your missing banner, but finding the members and the leader of the Widerstand. That is what truly matters. If anything is disgracing Nuremberg, it is them. We are closing in on them. It is only a matter of time."

One member of the group was silent, taking no part in the heated discussion. He was thinking, searching his mind. The brown-haired banner thief had looked so familiar.

The Gestapo chief was wrong—this time. All of Nuremberg did hear of the youth who had grabbed the Nazi banner, danced with it on the ice, then raced away into the winter gloom. Two nights later the citizens were startled to see the same Nazi banner again. They stopped and stared and hurried on. The sight was quietly spread and soon many were crossing the central square to look. Someone had climbed the 30 foot ice-covered Justice statue during the night at obvious risk. There in the sunlight, a vivid splash of red against the gray, the banner was wrapped tightly around the statue's eyes. Wilhelm Mueller passionately hoped this latest statement would speak more eloquently than anything he had written.

12
There Is a Tide, Which Taken at the Flood...

Brazilian village in South America, 1935

The man stood silhouetted on a low hill against the vast turquoise background of the South Atlantic. His hands were in his khaki pants' pockets, his face was turned toward the water. It was an hour or so before sunset. A few children in ragged shorts and thin shirts were playing down on the rocky shoreline with the ball the man had given them. Later they glanced up to the hill and paused, their laughter dying away under the crash of surf. The man was framed in front of the dying gold flames of the sun. He looked so tall and powerful, like a god to them. They couldn't see his face at this distance, but they knew who he was. If there had been any question—which there was not—it would have been confirmed in seconds as a dog dashed past the man's legs in pursuit of a butterfly. One of the children gave a low whistle. The dog stopped and looked down to the water's edge. Then it looked back to the man, tail whipping, tongue lolling, expectant. They saw the tall man jerk his arm out at the dog with some mute command. The dog tore down the hill yapping, leaping over small rocks. He barreled past the laughing children into the water. When they looked up the hill again, the man was sitting, and they could see he was laughing. A happy god had come to their land.

Max thought he would never tire of this stunning view of the ocean from the hill. It had entered his mind before, on other evenings like this, that he could live here forever among these friendly, accepting people, pouring his energy and money into their lives. He could work beside them becoming sweaty and dirty and tired by nightfall, feeling hungry—and satisfied. Or he could go off to other places of crises and needs and begin the work again. Or he could return to Germany.

"I think the only thing I miss," he said aloud to himself, "is the skiing."

He snorted at himself. Only a sport to call him back to his homeland? *That is a little depressing*, he admitted. He leaned back on his elbows. *Surely there are more ties*. He had perhaps a dozen letters in the bungalow that he shared with Josef. A dozen or so letters: some from a few friends, two from Elaina, one brief letter from Eric, and, of course, the impeccable monthly reports from Karl. Max sighed.

"Max. I thought I'd find you here." Max turned and smiled. Josef was huffing a bit as he came up the back side of the hill. He eased himself on the grass, and both men fell silent for several minutes."

"It is awfully pretty here," Josef sighed. Max nodded. Josef pointed to Percy. "As much as that animal stays in the water, I'm surprised he hasn't grown fins!"

Max chuckled. "It's the kids as much as the water, I think."

"Are you trying to say he prefers their company to two crusty old bachelors?" Max laughed again, and Josef smiled.

"Finish the inoculations?" Max asked.

Josef nodded. "All done. I'm going to go out tomorrow and check on a few patients in the morning."

"I'll hitch up a cart and take you."

Josef nodded, pulling at his beard that had gone totally white in the past year. He glanced up at Max now lean and muscled, brown as a hazelnut, shaggy-headed and bearded. He laughed.

"What?"

Josef pointed. "You. The suave, impeccable Max Farber, Berlin's most eligible bachelor!"

After they laughed, Josef sobered. "Max, the mail came in a little while ago. I have a letter from Dr. Hoffman, who took over my practice. His wife wants to go back to Vienna, and he needs to return to his own practice. So . . ."

"So our adventure has come to an end. It's time to go back," Max said slowly.

Josef nodded. "This year has been deeply satisfying for me, Max. I've enjoyed every moment. I wouldn't trade the people we've met, the things we've seen and done for anything. But this is for a younger man—for you. It's time for me to go home."

"Home to cold, dreary Berlin," Max said with a little smile. His arm swept out, as if he could gather in the warm winds and beauty and quiet of this place. "You're leaving this for days of rain and cold and sooty skies and swastikas everywhere!"

"Ja, and Herr Linemann's gouty toe and Frau Zimmermann's latest phobia, and all the others that come to my drafty clinic on Friedrich-strasse."

Max was silent. He sat back up, gazing at the sea. Percy was weaving up the hill. Josef watched him and noted that the young face did look older, a little lined by the eyes. And a sadness that Max could not conceal or disguise with any amount of jesting and jokes was evident. Max sighed deeply.

"Here I . . . I've felt worth something, Josef. These simple, honest people have let me work beside them, accepted me as I am. There's been no politics or intrigue. Back in Berlin all I can see is disagreements with Irwin over any plans I make. I can't see any purpose or value in my life back there, but I'll go back with you." He gave Josef a thin, wry smile. "A good Farber son doesn't run away from his responsibilities."

The two men rose and turned to walk back to the village. Max placed his arm around the doctor, the lightness had returned to his voice.

"You know, I bet I could build Percy a swimming pool in our back garden. What do you think?"

"Max, I think you could do anything you put your mind to."

"I was only joking."

"Max, I feel like there's a change coming for us both when we return. It makes me a little afraid; I'm too old for much change."

"You are not that old."

Josef shrugged. "I can't explain it, but there's something ahead for us both."

"Pleasant, Josef, or not so pleasant?"

Josef paused to look him in the eye. "Both."

Max looked back to the ocean and sighed. "'There is a tide in the affairs of men, which, taken at the flood, leads on to fortune!'"

Joseph finished the Shakespearean quote with a twinkle in his eye: "'Omitted, all the voyage of their life is bound in shallows and in miseries.'"

• • •

He knew it was her from the long blonde plait down her back with the blue ribbon tied at the end. The rabbi's daughter was leaning against the stone rail gazing into the pond. Other couples were strolling also, young and old. She didn't stand out. But Wilhelm immediately knew it was her. He had stopped on the plaza, half turned, then placed himself beside a monument, leaning against it so he could watch her from a distance. *Feeding the ducks like any young girl should be allowed to do on a balmy spring day. But a Jewish girl out alone?* Wilhelm frowned. *Hadn't she learned from the day of ice skating months ago?* He sighed. *How can I think like this? Who wouldn't want to do as he pleased on a day like this? Why shouldn't anyone be able to feed the ducks in pleasure and freedom?* Of course, he understood why not. He walked toward her, hands deep in his pockets. He would just say hello.

She heard his step and turned. For a moment, he saw fear cross her face. Then she smiled, relieved and glad to see him.

"Guten Tag, fraulein." He gave her a little bow.

Her smiled broadened. He was treating her like she was closer to his own age. She returned his greeting with a nod.

"Wilhelm."

It was then, at that moment, with the sun dimpling the water behind them, that they both realized they had never been alone together. The rabbi had always been there with them. Natalie clutched her hands tightly, willing herself to act calm and sophisticated. She didn't want to sound like a girl of 16, all shy or giggly.

"How are you today?" she asked.

"Fine. And you?"

"Fine."

"And your grandfather?"

"Fine, danke."

"He's at home?"

She nodded. Wilhelm cleared his throat, and they both leaned on the rail facing the river. *Well, I said hello*, Wilhelm thought. *Now I should say goodbye and move on. Why subject her to any awkwardness and embarrassment?* Yet when he had watched her from a distance she had looked so lonely and sad. *How often does she get off by herself? Shouldn't she be in a company of girls her own age? Perhaps she wanted to be alone?*

"So, what are you doing today, Natalie?" he asked casually.

She continued gazing at the water. "I went to the library for a few hours, then I've just been walking home slowly. It's so nice out."

Walking home slowly, he nodded.

"And you?"

"Just loafing on my day off."

Minutes passed as they both stared into the water.

"So, did you want to be alone?"

She turned to face him, clearly puzzled.

"Excuse me?"

"Did you want to be by yourself, since, you know, you usually are with your grandfather?"

"I don't know, I . . ." Her eyes moved over his face.

"Look, what I'm saying is, Do you want to do something together, like—"

"Ja, that would be nice, Wilhelm. Danke."

"Good, because it's really better to be out with someone these days."

Her face clouded. *He is only concerned for my safety. Well, of course. Isn't that enough?*

"Please do not feel as if you must escort me just because you ran into me."

"I don't, Natalie," he said smiling.

She relaxed. "All right."

"What do you want to do?"

"Anything."

"Good. We'll go tell your grandfather so he won't worry, then go out to the Zeppelin field where they're having a circus. And we'll go to Zingle's for the best ice cream in Nuremburg. All right?"

She smiled and nodded.

Rabbi Bergmann was inwardly trembling, though he trusted Wilhelm Mueller implicitly. He had liked the young man from the first—

completely apart from his rescue attempt. The three were knit together by the violence they had suffered—an elderly pacifist rabbi, his cloistered young granddaughter, and an impulsive young Jew who spurned his faith. All three had witnessed it, had felt it, but they hadn't responded the same. The rabbi could not help but imagine the two young people out on the streets of the city would be targets to be molested.

"We'll be very careful, Rabbi Bergmann," Wilhelm assured.

"Ja, I know you will, certainly, but . . . there are such dangers. We all know too well that until reason is restored, we must be very, very careful."

Until reason is restored. Wilhelm shifted with irritation, reminding himself he must remain respectful.

"The day of ice skating, you remember, of course, Wilhelm."

"Rabbi, it may be a long time before that reason is restored. You will want Natalie to continue a full life with some adjustments. I am her escort, an adjustment." He bowed.

The rabbi looked at Natalie's expectant face. *How can I deny her?* "When will you return?"

"No later than eight."

"Eight at night!" His lined face paled.

"Please, Grandfather. I'm 16 and eight o'clock is really not late at all."

Hilda stood behind them where only the rabbi could see, with her hands on her broad hips, her eyes alternately threatening and pleading for him to acquiesce.

"Eight o'clock, I promise," Wilhelm pressed with a smile.

The rabbi watched them hurry down the steps, then retreated to his favorite chair to pray.

● ● ●

They sat on a park bench as the sun was setting scarlet and gold behind the spires and towers of Nuremberg. Natalie was dusty and tired and full of sweets—and very happy. She sighed with contentment, and Wilhelm glanced at her from the corner of his eye, grinning. Her hair was windblown, her cheeks pinked.

"I've had a—," she stopped. *To say wonderful would sound gushy and juvenile, though it was true.* "I've had a very nice day, Wilhelm. Danke."

It had been a day of pleasure for them both. The Nazi banners still hung in every street. They had seen the arm bands on many men and women. At the Zeppelin field there had been a Nazi orator at one booth, shouting and posturing to a bored crowd. But no one had bothered them. They could imagine without difficulty that peace and goodwill prevailed in Nuremburg that day.

"I'm glad you enjoyed it," Wilhelm answered. Then he laughed, "You know, I had no idea you were 16."

"You thought?"

"Well, I thought you were younger, about 12 or 14. I'm not good at guessing ages."

"I see . . ." She smoothed her skirt. "I would think you'd have spent your day off with a . . . a girlfriend."

Wilhelm stretched lazily and smiled. "Who said there is a girl-friend?"

"Well, I thought the girl at the rink that day . . ." she shrugged, not looking at him.

"I believe I told you that day that we were just friends. There is no girlfriend at the moment." He tossed a rock into the fountain. *Why should I confide in this young girl*? She still reminded him of his younger sister. "There *was* a girl, but she . . ."

"Yes?"

Wilhelm crossed his arms. "She liked me well enough until she got caught up in the Hitler Maiden Corp." He snorted. "Then she sounded like she could recite *Mein Kampf* by heart. 'Wilhelm,' she said, 'you are a very nice boy, but you are not an Aryan. Germany cannot be made great through Jews, I'm sorry.'

"I said, 'But yesterday I was all right.' She gave me this pitying smile and replied, 'But today I know the truth."

He was reflective a moment. and Natalie heard the bitter tenor in his words.

"Then she said, 'I will miss your kisses. You kiss better than any boy I know.'"

He laughed aloud. "That was a real comfort."

He cocked his head at her. "Do you have a boyfriend?"

"Of course not! I . . . couldn't!" she finished softly.

Wilhelm was instantly sorry he had teased.

"You could have one. You're pretty."

She could feel herself grow warm with his words.

"Your grandfather is pretty protective," he added gently.

She was looking at her shoes. "He is my family, all I have. I love him deeply."

Wilhelm nodded and looked back to the sunset.

"You have not minded spending the day with me?" Natalie asked.

"No. I've had fun. Growing up, my sister and I did a lot together, you know, had fun like this. We were close."

Natalie ignored the comparison between her and his sister.

"Were close?"

"Maria and I don't see each other very much anymore. I'm here, and she's in Berlin. I guess as people grow up, they grow apart."

Natalie regretted her question.

"Your grandfather is like my father in many ways. Have I ever told you that my father is close to your grandfather's age?" Wilhelm questioned.

She shook her head.

"I was a surprise for my parents. Papa calls me his Isaac."

"You are close to your father and mother?"

"Well . . . not exactly. I'm a little too wild. Walther is an easier son to love."

"I'm sure they love you as much, but in a different way."

He shrugged and was silent.

"Your grandfather, well, I don't feel nervous around him—even though I know he sees my flaws."

"Wilhelm, what flaws do you think my grandfather sees?"

Her voice had a mature quality that he could not miss. He turned to look fully in her face, and she returned his look.

"Well, they're the same ones you must see since you've been around me as much as your grandfather has."

She brushed back her hair. "I haven't seen any."

He cocked an eyebrow at her. "No? I'll tell you mine, if you'll tell me yours."

"But we could not tell anyone else," she said with a half-smile.

"Of course not! All right, I'll go first. One, I'm impulsive. And I have a temper. And . . ." Suddenly he dropped his voice. "And I'm 27 years old and I don't know what I want to do with my life—that's a big flaw. Your turn, though I hardly think a rabbi's daughter can have flaws."

Natalie laughed. "I have heard rumors in school that the children of rabbis are often the wildest."

"I've heard those rumors, too, but not you."

"I have flaws. I want to be ... different. I grow weary of being responsible and predictable. Sometimes I wish I weren't Jewish. Grandfather would be so disappointed if he heard me say that.... I get angry, I get envious. There you see—I have many flaws."

Wilhelm peered at her closely. Her face had grown sad in her confession. It was the look he had seen so often in the quiet rooms of her home. He had meant to give her a fun day—an escape from the routine of her days. Now she was sad. Why had he brought up this discussion of flaws? Dummkoft!

"Come on. We have one hour left and I won't lead you a minute late to your doorstep. Let's go get some strudel."

"Wilhelm, how can you be hungry?"

"I'm always hungry," he grinned. He took her hand, pulling her to her feet. And, thoughtlessly, didn't remember to release it.

"You know, I've heard somewhere that even diamonds have flaws," he said cheerfully.

Natalie controlled the tears that came to her eyes and smiled. Impulsively, she leaned forward and kissed him on his cheek.

"There you see!" he smiled broadly. "A flawless kiss!"

He left her at her door just as eight tolls of the great clock reverberated through the city. Wilhelm smiled with pride.

"Thank you for a lovely day, Wilhelm. I . . ." She looked down at her shoes, suddenly shy. He leaned forward. "I will always treasure this day," she continued.

"You sound like it's the last one. We'll do it again sometime." She looked past his shoulder, into the beautiful, quiet twilight. *Now it was Wilhelm who wasn't facing the reality he always accused her grandfather of ignoring. Maybe I have a better sight than either of them*, she thought, knowing in her heart that this was the last summer of peace.

● ● ●

Wilhelm didn't have time to decide which was louder—his panting breath or his running footsteps. Usually he tried to run with some degree of caution and quiet, but tonight was not such a time. Tonight he was running with only the thought of escape and survival. His new pursuers' determination and energy matched his own—equal contenders, even if Wilhelm was terribly outnumbered. He did have time to wish again that Herschel had not come along on this "raid"—or at least that they had split up instead of trying to escape together. Two running men attracted more attention than one: two made more noise, and two were harder to conceal behind a trash can or in a darkened doorway. And having someone with him stirred his sense of responsibility. If things got tough, well, he might be able to only save his own skin. He should feel no guilt over that; it was the grim law of self preservation: work together, but hang separately.

They swerved into a dark alley, Wilhelm mentally acknowledging this would be the first place the pursuers would look. He hurriedly surveyed the end of the alley. They flattened themselves against the damp, cold wall. The night was deceptively quiet, 12 deep strokes of a Nuremberg church clock a few blocks over sounded, and their own pounding hearts seemed to match its intensity. They strained to hear any other sounds—especially carefully placed footsteps.

"We've lost 'em," Wilhelm whispered, leaning close to Herschel's ear.

Herschel shook his head vigorously. They stayed rigidly still another full three minutes.

"I told you. Now—" Wilhelm began. But Herschel clutched at his arm.

"No!...They're out there...hiding, waiting for us to step out."

"Maybe, but I don't think so. We can't stay here forever. I'm freezing. Now I'm going to slip out, then you can come after me. We've got to split up."

"No." Herschel's voice was a hoarse, panicked whisper. "No, Wilhelm."

"Dummkopf!" Wilhelm snapped.

"Ja, ja. I don't want—"

"Ruhig!" Wilhelm hissed.

Footsteps. They pressed themselves tighter into the damp rough wall. A man and woman passed the alley opening.

"All right."

"Nein!" Herschel's fingers dug into Wilhelm's arm. "We can't split up."

Wilhelm knew what the problem was, but gritted his teeth without voicing it.

"We're only three blocks away. You know how to get back to the apartment. Don't worry, just act—"

"Wilhelm, bitte, I . . . please don't . . ."

Wilhelm could feel Herschel trembling. Disgust surged up in him. Herschel was always so vocal in their secret meetings—loud, authoritative, confident. He was always suggesting violence against the Nazis—extreme measures that the group was as yet unwilling to take. Tonight, in the center of danger, he'd proven himself what Wilhelm had always suspected: a cowardly boaster. It was why Wilhelm could barely tolerate their sharing a flat, and why he had avoided "working" with Herschel. But tonight when Fritz had suddenly fallen ill, Herschel had been pressed into the plan. It was Herschel's fear that had alerted the Nazis. So now they were running along the dark, cold, menacing streets of Nuremberg. Wilhelm knew if they were caught the punishment would be far more than simple harassment or humiliation.

Herschel's voice was high and thin. "We can't go back to our place. You saw what they were doing to Peter. They'll beat him until he gives them all of our names. They'll be waiting for us."

Under his jacket Wilhelm could feel sweat plastering his shirt to him like a second skin. He had slipped on ice while running, and now his left elbow made him nearly cry out in pain. He wondered vaguely if he had broken it. He could envision Walther shaking his head. *Another broken bone, Wil? Are you trying to set some record*? His feet were wet up to his ankles from the cold puddles of water he ran through. He was starting to shake, and he knew it wasn't just from the piercing cold. *I can't afford to give into fear as Herschel has. I can't.* He closed his eyes wearily and tried to still his labored breathing.

"Wilhelm? Are you listening? I said we can't go back to the apartment."

Wilhelm's composure snapped. Too many days and nights of living by his nerves had drained him. He grabbed Herschel by the collar.

"Look. You're going to listen to me and do exactly what I say, when I say. We're going to split up. I'll go first. You count to 500, then follow.

Walk slowly and don't panic. Go to the apartment, circle it, and go inside. I'll be there."

"But—"

"Herschel!" Wilhelm spoke as fiercely and loudly as he dared. He was wild-eyed, and sweat was glistening on his face. He shook the young man with an unexpected rush of strength. "The apartment is safe because Peter didn't give us away. Do you hear me? Now I'm going."

Wilhelm pushed him away and jogged softly to the end of the alley. He paused and looked both ways. Then casually and easily he stepped into the street. Herschel was on his own.

• • •

Wilhelm lay tense and rigid, staring up at the ceiling. The room was warm and dark and all he wanted to do was drift off into the oblivion of sleep. But he could not. He had pulled off his wet socks and boots then slumped into the narrow bed, under a rough woolen blanket. He decided he would wait until morning to examine his arm. But it wouldn't let him sleep due to the sharp pain that went from his wrist to his shoulder every time he moved. He could hear Herschel's ragged breathing in the darkness across the room. It had a nasal whine that had kept Wilhelm awake on other nights. Tonight it was more than his injured arm or Herschel's nocturnal music that had stolen his sleep. He turned to look at the shadow Herschel cast against the wall. Wilhelm knew Herschel had fallen into a fear-induced exhaustion almost as soon as he had touched the bed. When he had entered their apartment breathless the two men had not exchanged a word.

Wilhelm slipped his good arm behind his head, exhaling deeply, willing his body to relax. A thousand thoughts competed in his mind— and one picture he did not want to remember—but would never forget. Well, he would deal with it first and get the worst over with. There, in a darkness like a vast movie screen before a show, he went over each moment of the night, of their raid against the Nazis. It had been a simple plan, but, as always, not without its dangers.

The Nazis had erected huge bulletin boards at strategic spots around the city to announce rallies, the fuehrer's latest promise or threat, and the ongoing blasphemy against the Jews of the city: The Jews were responsible for all the economic problems of Germany. They had been part of the hated Treaty of Versailles. Jewish men molested Aryan women. Their religion demanded human sacrifice. They had killed Jesus Christ. They were vermin, a plague on the land. Wilhelm, and so many like him, had grown sickened by the bold, offensive banners that seemed to blemish every corner.

So, it was time to do something about it. It was time to show the Nazis that the Jews of Nuremberg were not going to take these lies and slander without protest. Each night Wilhelm and two others would steal along the streets under the cover of darkness to damage or destroy the bulletin boards. They had found that bituminous paint covered the messages very well.

After three successful nights, something had gone very wrong. The street was deserted near the huge post office building of Nuremberg. The good citizens of the city had long been in bed. This Nazi billboard was seen by hundreds of Germans each day. Wilhelm was determined that they would see a far different advertisement in the morning. With bold red strokes, they wrote, "Where will they stop? Who will they come for next? Nuremberg awaken!"

The Nazi youth had been just as busy as Wilhelm's group, with a blood-lust to find these troublemakers of Germany. After three nights of desecration to their boards, they posted vigils in the shadows of the city to capture the rebellious Jews. They would make an example of them for all of Nuremberg to see—to see and understand the futility of protest.

Wilhelm only had a moment to react after he saw them from the corner of his eye. Peter, bent down and putting their cans in a sack, did not see or hear them at all. Wilhelm had time to leap—only to fall with a heavy thud on the cold sidewalk. Winter had reasserted itself strangely over the city, and a thin layer of ice coated everything. Herschel swung wildly, sending one assailant to the ground. Then he ran.

Wilhelm knew in a split second he was in a fight for his life. This was no schoolyard tussle of egos and emerging muscle, or even a fiery, short-lived match. These men would kill him, so he fought to kill as well. In his mind the thrashing and cursing, the fist meeting bone, the blood chilling on the skin generated such a noise that it would bring other Nazis soon. Then they would be doomed. But now, there were only four Nazis against them; the odds were far better this time. With a powerful swing, Wilhelm sent one of them to the sidewalk unconscious. Herschel had swung himself over a board fence. Peter, Wilhelm could see, was in trouble. Two of the Nazis were savagely beating him. The thin, wiry, academic Peter could not last long under such punishment. Wilhelm shoved off his own attacker and went to help him. Then, in the beam of moonlight, Wilhelm saw the quick flash of metal. He knew in sickening comprehension what was about to happen. At that moment a fist connected soundly with his abdomen and he fell to his knees, doubled over, gasping for breath. He heard only one word. It came from Peter's lips.

"*Nein . . .*"

By the time he could focus, he saw Peter sprawled on the ground, looking strangely relaxed, his eyes open as if he were casually studying the stars. The Nazis seemed to have forgotten Wilhelm. They seemed stunned at their own deed. Wilhelm watched as blood dripped in soundless drops from the knife to the pavement. *Peter,* his best friend. . . . The bile rose in Wilhelm's throat. He slowly stood. Still, with their backs to him, the Nazis did not hear him. They stood with their hands on their hips, considering the situation. Wilhelm felt dizzy, but was cognizant enough to step back quietly. "You were too quick with the Jew, Thomas. You killed him before we could get information from him."

Wilhelm was now half-a-dozen yards behind them, wary and alert—and hurting. He decided when they came after him, he would take one of them with him. The man he had knocked-out was rising groggily. He squinted into the darkness.

"Get him! He's getting away!" he yelled, his voice hoarse.

Wilhelm turned to run. He jumped the fence, found Herschel and hid. They would have been safe except the beam of flashlight fell close and Herschel whimpered. Then they were running again. Knowing this part of Nuremberg better than the Nazis, they were able to elude them.

Wilhelm swung his feet over the bed and, staggering a little, moved into the cubicle that served as a kitchen.

"Wilhelm?" It was Herschel's voice, soft, childlike.

Wilhelm frowned. "What?"

Herschel understood the tone. "Are you all right?"

"My arm is killing me. I'm taking some aspirin."

Wilhelm walked to the window. Herschel watched him a moment. He could see Wilhelm's pale face in the moonlight: Wilhelm was in a terrible mood. "I'm sorry, Wilhelm."

Wilhelm had not expected this from the cocky Grynszpan. He shrugged, and grumbled, "All right."

Wilhelm couldn't see Herschel's face, but he could hear the fear in his voice. "I don't know what happened. I . . ."

"You panicked," Wilhelm offered abruptly.

It was silent. Wilhelm thought of his mother. She had called him stubborn once when Walther had apologized and he had not accepted it. He would never forget her words, *Your heart is small Wilhelm, you must make it bigger. You must forgive as you have been forgiven.*

He sighed in frustration, his voice neither forgiving nor hard.

"Everyone panics at some time. This was . . . your time tonight, I guess." He wished Herschel would go back to sleep.

But Herschel could no more sleep than Wilhelm could. He sat up. Wilhelm could see Herschel's red hair sticking out in a hundred directions as if in emphasis to his rioting emotions. In his thin shirt, he looked like a boy of 13. He turned back to the window and looked out at the night.

"Peter isn't back," Herschel said shakily.

Wilhelm wetted his lips against the sudden dryness. He faced Herschel slowly. "Peter isn't coming back, Herschel. They killed him." Herschel stood up stiffly, his mouth gaping, then he fell limply back to the bed. "Wilhelm . . ."

Wilhelm moved woodenly to the bedside, his hands jammed in his pockets. The room no longer seemed so warm. He sat down beside the weeping young man. He watched him shaking in sobs just a moment before he realized he no longer despised Herschel Grynszpan.

"They killed him before he could tell them anything. I overheard them say that. So, for now, we're still safe. That's why the apartment was all right. Aw, Herschel . . ."

Wilhelm made two cups of strong, hot coffee, indifferent to the knowledge it would keep them awake when they both so desperately needed sleep. They sat on the bed drinking, each wrapped in his own private grief and horrors. Wilhelm closed his eyes, leaning against the wall. *How could one night feel as if I had aged ten years?* But to be honest with himself, it was really more than this one night, it was the last ten months of his life since he had joined Widerstand. *Ten months of excitement and danger, late nights and missed meals. Living like a criminal running from the law*, he smiled to himself. But it quickly faded.

There was no law in Nuremberg, nor in all of Germany for that matter.
Daniel, who had published the now extinct Jewish newspaper, had condensed it to one sentence, "Germany is becoming a prison, where the
criminals are in charge."

Living like a criminal, what would my family think? He had not seen
them in almost a year. After Walther left for home, Wilhelm's letters
took a predictable turn, arriving the first of each month like an expected
holiday. They were newsy letters that told his family very little. Such
faithful and descriptive correspondence eased Wilhelm's slightly ruffled
conscience. All the scrapes and near scrapes he'd been in, the vandalism
and petty larceny, the planned retaliations at the Nazi Trojan horse—he
could envision his father's disapproving face and his mother's calm horror if they knew the truth.

Wilhelm's cause—striking back at the Nazis and waking up the
good people of Germany—was his life and work. He worked every
evening at Handel's for food and rent money. He was living like a
vagabond in a cheap, one-room apartment, and living as an unrepentant
prodigal. And in his own way, Wilhelm liked and thrived on this life. He
used his skills of decisiveness and resourcefulness; he was energetic and
tireless. He felt his work with the Widerstand was important to Germany—quite apart to what it meant to him as a Jew. It was noble work
in its own crude, sometimes brutal way—and he knew his family would
neither understand nor accept it. While this made him feel cut off from
them, he could not abandon his cause.

His life fell into as predictable a routine as the Nuremberg clocks
that tolled the hour. Evenings were spent waiting tables. There he was
polite and efficient, neutral on every topic, quiet—and listening to table
gossip like a miner picking at a vein of gold. The Nazis who frequented
Handel's provided a wealth of information. He had surpassed even Herschel in this delicate art of spying. Nights consisted of planning raids or
stalking Nazis strongholds around the city. The citizens were shocked
and amazed at the anti-Nazi graffiti that sprouted all over—there was
bold rebellion in the camp!

Wilhelm secured the group's affection by single-handedly planning
and organizing a raid on the university Nazis' parade ground. When he
had found out that an impressive drill and parade was planned for the
following morning he went into action. From contacts in the rural districts surrounding Nuremberg, Wilhelm collected four tons of revenge.

Under the cover of a cold, moonless night, Wilhelm and six others, driving borrowed trucks, shaped a gigantic swastika out of piles of manure on the field. It didn't make the *Nuremberg Tribune*, but many in Nuremberg privately chuckled over the incident.

But it was Wilhelm's real gift of writing that gained the respect of his companions. Pamphlets were the earliest, most widespread, and common opposition to the Nazi government, and Wilhelm's were the best. All of Germany's principal cities harbored resistance groups churning out anti-Nazi tracts from hidden presses. These tracts were dropped at significant areas of the city, sometimes dramatically from a church or clock tower into a crowded square below. A blizzard of cheap paper and crooked type protesting injustice and calling the German people from their moral stupor swirled to the ground.

Wilhelm's love of writing was revived. His ability to digest the truths of their cause into a single, stirring page was phenomenal. Hidden under the floorboards where he sat, was his collection of articles he'd authored. Once he had wistfully thought of sending one of the papers home to his parents—to confirm his value and show them he was using his gift. His mother could press it in the scrap album she kept of all his school compositions.

Wilhelm's mind went back to the opening line of the first pamphlet he had written: *Nothing is less honorable of decent people than to allow themselves to be governed by a company of bandits with shallow minds and dark ambitions.*

But Wilhelm never sent his work. It was better that his family knew little of his involvement, and he wasn't certain how they would receive the news.

Wilhelm's thoughts rambled on. *The most dangerous task of all after the ink had dried had been pamphlet distribution.*

Each member of the group was given a location to leave 100 pamphlets. Over the months, Nuremberg had become accustomed to the pale-yellow paper left on train seats, park benches, public restrooms, and library shelves. Their success had emboldened them to distribute their leaflets to outlying towns and villages. One day a week, Wilhelm boarded a train posing as a traveler carrying one suitcase. On the trip, a sympathetic rebel to their cause would exchange his suitcase with Wilhelm's, then they would go back to their respective homes.

Each successful distribution is a small victory to be proud of, Wilhelm mused.

Hours later, Herschel finally dropped off to sleep, and Wilhelm, again, stood before the window. *Yes, each bold raid had been successful, until tonight. Tonight's penalty had been a terrible one. I'll have to tell the others in the morning. Although fear would haunt all of them, they must not give up*! He glanced at Herschel. The young man seemed to be sleeping peacefully. He continued staring out the window, looking over sleeping Nuremberg as if it could comfort him. *What will sunrise bring*?

● ● ●

The meeting was untypically brief. The four young women of the group huddled together and wept. Herschel was mute as Wilhelm crisply outlined what had happened. With Peter gone, their group was now at 14 members. When the silence lengthened, Simon stood and dismissed them.

"We'll meet tomorrow night, above Blomberg's Bakery at 9:30. Use more caution as you come."

"Wait!" Wilhelm's voice was strong. "Wait, please." All eyes rested on him. "I know . . . I know how all of you are feeling. I . . . Herschel and I were there, we saw it. . . . But we can't let this sidetrack us from our purpose! We've gotten leaflets into the hands of hundreds of people. They have to be thinking about what we write about; they have to be considering what the real truth is. We can't stop now! This is our time— not our father's or grandfather's—*our time*. We have to be able to tell our children that we stood, that we didn't lie down—"

A young man's voice was acidic. "None of us have children, Wilhelm. And none of us will have the chance with an enemy like this. They will try to wipe us out. For me, it's time to leave Nuremberg."

"Leave your home?"

"Yes, leave my home. My home has given into insanity. I won't give my life as one dead Jew on the street when it won't change anything. I'm leaving, and if you are smart," he said sweeping the room with his eyes, "you will leave, too."

The room was tomblike, only the young man's receding steps echoed above them.

"Peter would have wanted us to keep on," Wilhelm said tiredly. He waited for someone else to speak. The group shifted nervously, nodding, as they quickly filed out of the frigid basement. Only Herschel, Simon, and Wilhelm remained. Simon's voice was soft.

"I had a phone call this morning, early. They . . ." He tugged at the collar of his frayed shirt. "They took Peter's body and propped it up on the Justice statue. They plan to leave it there for several days." Wilhelm sunk to the chair. He half-expected Herschel to dissolve in hysterics. But the young man remained motionless, rigid, eyes glassy.

Simon shook his head. "You all right, Herschel?"

Herschel nodded, still looking off into space. Simon and Wilhelm exchanged a look.

"You were right about what you said to them," Simon said as he drew out a cigarette. "We'll see tomorrow night how many agreed with you. Ah, Peter . . ." he left off, shaking his head.

"Did the thugs get a good look at you, Wilhelm?"

Wilhelm shook his head. "It was too dark."

Simon ran a weary hand through his thin hair.

"My contacts tell me the Gestapo and brownshirts are stepping things up. The district leader came down. He doesn't like the reputation for rebellion that Nuremberg is getting. They're scouring the city for us. They took Daniel to their headquarters for questioning this morning."

The gentle editor of the *Jacob's Ladder*? Wilhelm felt sick.

Simon squinted at him through a curtain of smoke. "They're closing the net, Wilhelm. They want all of us—but they particularly want the author of the pamphlets. They want the one who tied the banner on the statue. It's only a matter of time, Wilhelm, you know that."

Wilhelm did not speak. He was cold, hungry, tired, in pain—and hunted.

"Don't go back to your apartment. If they get anything out of Daniel, they'll get your name. He knows you were part of this group."

"Ja, ja, but I never told him any names. He wanted to know very little. He wasn't sure he approved of us."

"I'll tell everyone tomorrow night that you'll be laying low for awhile. You should find a new place to stay. And stay away from your old haunts."

"Run and hide," Wilhelm added bitterly.

"You should give up your job at Handel's."

"Without work, you don't eat, Simon, remember? I can't exactly stand on the corner and get paid for my good looks."

"Wilhelm, listen, you know they are as determined to silence us as we are to speak. We all have to prepare for the very real possibility—indeed probability—that we are going to be tracked down."

"The only thing I'm prepared to do is not give in easily. They may kill me, but they'll bleed with me."

"Here." Simon shoved a revolver into Wilhelm's hands. "I carry one, and you should have started a long time ago. The stakes are higher now. We have to play as rough as they do."

"Like the Friday night poker games we had when we were in school?" Wilhelm said, shaking his head. "You were merciless when you cleaned me out. I didn't have food money for a week! You know, I never thought I'd be saying this because I always wanted to grow up and do whatever I wanted—have this great, exciting life. . . . Now I'm looking at the past, and kind of longing for it."

Simon cleared his throat. "We've had some ups and downs over the years, but I'm glad we've had this chance to work together."

They looked at each other and nodded. This might be their last meeting. Simon pulled Wilhelm to the corner of the room, while looking at Herschel who still sat staring into space.

"Is he all right?"

"I don't know. He's clammed up. Last night . . ." *Peter lying on the cold stone. . . .* Wilhelm closed his eyes a moment. "I need some coffee."

"What about him? If he's off, he's dangerous to us."

"I'll babysit him for awhile, I guess." Turning back, Wilhelm said, "Let's go, Herschel."

He turned to Simon. They shook hands.

"Well, good luck, Wilhelm."

"My father and a certain rabbi I know say there isn't anything called luck. Everything is part of a design, they say. So tell me, Simon, am I in the Nazis design or in my own? Who is controlling whom?"

"When you figure it out, Wilhelm, put it down in a pamphlet. I'll be looking for it."

Wilhelm smiled sadly.

"Auf Wiedersehen, Simon."

13
The End of a Beginning

1936

September came golden and mild to Nuremberg that year. The strength of summer had faded. In the emerging Third Reich, September had greater significance than ever before. Shopkeepers, restaurant proprietors, and hotel owners prepared for and welcomed the month with energy and expectation. It would prove to be their most successful month of the year. The Nazi party rally convened September 1, and was a two week orgy of feverish pageantry and paganism. Hundreds of thousands of party leaders and troopers gathered to exalt the party and listen to fiery speeches by their fuehrer and his cabinet. The town was choked in a sea of the SA's brown shirts and the dull green uniform of the German army, marching through the streets, their jackboots echoing like subterranean thunder. It was a rhythm heard every day and late into the night. Torchlight parades through the streets each night added further glamour and excitement. Swastika flags hung from most buildings, as a stamp of requisition. The shops of Jewish merchants were locked and dark. Germany had never seen anything like this before, and the citizens of Nuremberg loved it.

"Here it comes," Herschel said with a nudge to Wilhelm. Wilhelm turned to glance at his companion. Herschel seemed to have stirred from his apathy of the last few months. He looked alert and normal. *Good*, Wilhelm thought. *Being with this strange young man was wearing on my nerves.*

Wilhelm stretched up on his toes. This first glimpse of Adolf Hitler would most likely be his last. He was prepared to be unimpressed; the crowd he was packed in seemed far more a fascination. It was a sobering sight for a Jew or any German man or woman who did not embrace Nazism. Wilhelm had never seen so many people—all of Nuremberg and many more—surged on the streets, cheering and yelling wildly.

"We want our fuehrer! We want our savior!" a woman at Wilhelm's elbow screamed.

Wilhelm and Herschel shared a look of disgust. Then the black, open car came into view. The arms on all sides of the two young Jews jerked up in salute. Wilhelm's mouth fell open. *There is no describing this*! His mind raced. *No one will believe what I'm seeing. This looks like worship*!

The German leader was on his way from Nazi headquarters at the Deutscher Hotel to the Luitpold Hall to deliver his speech. As the car passed the frenzied crowds, the cheers swelled to hysteria. Wilhelm saw a woman across the street toss a bouquet of roses to Hitler's car. Then she lifted her hands and fell into an ungraceful faint. Wilhelm looked back to the car to see what she had seen. Adolf Hitler stood in a plain, worn-looking gabardine trench coat, his right arm was raising somewhat feebly in Nazi salutes. *He is expressionless*, Wilhelm thought, *he looks tired and flabby, common and coarse*. He searched for all the adjectives he would need when he wrote of this later. *Brooding. And yet somehow Hitler was causing this frenzy with his physical presence.* A quick look to Herschel found the man pale and sweating.

"You all right, Herschel?" Wilhelm shouted above the din.

The young man nodded dumbly, his eyes glazed over.

Wilhelm grew nervous. *What if he tore through the crowd shouting and tried to get at Hitler? He told me once that he would welcome a chance to kill a Nazi—especially Hitler—last year in Berlin.* Wilhelm pulled at his sleeve.

"Come on. We'll go listen on the radio."

● ● ●

The propaganda minister's irritating high-pitched voice was a speech teacher's nightmare. It did not, however, keep Goebbels from being chosen to deliver one of the most important speeches on the final night of the rally. He was unable to conceal his gloating over Göring as he strutted about the stage like a bantam rooster. *He would deliver the new laws concerning German Jewry before a crowd of over 100,000.*

One-hundred-and-thirty antiaircraft lights were placed around the perimeter of the huge zeppelin field, sending shafts of light hundreds of feet into the night sky. It created a stunning, almost supernatural effect and could be seen many miles away. Even those people neutral or opposed to the regime had to admit that the Nazis did things in a colossal fashion.

The radio would carry his words across Germany. There would never be a greater night of professional triumph for Goebbels. Then the fuehrer would come to the podium in a blaze of unparalled glory.

It took Goebbels 70 minutes to deliver the new laws. Jews were deprived of German citizenship. They were now "subjects". Marriages between Jews and Aryans were forbidden. Jews could not employ Aryan females under the age of 35. Jews were banned from public office, civil service, journalism, radio, farming, teaching, the theater, films, banking, law, and medicine. Jews could not own businesses. Seventy minutes that changed millions of lives forever.

• • •

The Nazi youth spoke up again, louder now.

"The Jew that grabbed the banner was Wilhelm Mueller. I had a class with him at the university. I recognized him. I've asked around, he is known to hang around with some of the Widerstrand. He was best friends with Peter Zimmerman."

The Nazi chief, exhausted from the week's activities, suddenly sat forward, his eyes alert, his voice crisp.

"You are positive it was Mueller?"

"Yes, sir."

"What class were you in with him?"

"That's easy to remember: journalism. Wilhelm was top of the class. Sharp."

"A Jew . . ." the leader hissed, then continued. "Well, well, this has become most interesting. Our Jewish banner thief was a frustrated writer." He opened a drawer and pulled out some yellow pages. He handed several to the young man. "Take these back to the professor you had. See if he can identify the style. So, it appears your thief and my author may be one and the same—Wilhelm Mueller."

The young leader, feeling redeemed at last, broke into a wide smile.

• • •

Wilhelm stuffed his few clothes into an old leather bag. He grabbed only the books that he could fit in it. *I'll have to leave the rest*, he sighed with regret. The rich-green book he placed in an inner coat pocket. He hefted up the bag, speaking softly. "My life's riches fit in a bag, Handel."

The hefty restauranteur wagged his head knowingly, sadly. Wilhelm came near. "I don't have time to tell you how grateful I am for all you've done: for hiding me out here, work, everything."

Wilhelm winced at the bruises on the big man's face.

"They worked you over pretty good."

"I'll survive. Now you must go, Wilhelm. They will come back. They want to find you very badly. Leave the city. Schnell!"

Wilhelm swallowed hard. "I am. One stop and . . . I'm gone. I don't know where Herschel is, he wandered off. Maybe it's just as well. Anyway, I hope he won't show up here."

"God bless you, my young friend. One day we will meet again when Germany . . . repents." He broke down, weeping, but Wilhelm didn't know how to comfort him.

• • •

The Bergmann house on Elenstrasse was darkened in every window. Still Wilhelm hurried up the steps. He started to ring the bell as he always did, but suddenly he thought of how the sudden shrillness might frighten them if they were huddled in fear behind the door. He rapped on the wood and waited. He could hear a tumult a few streets over. Would it flow down this street? He turned his collar up against the chill and knocked again. Surely they were not asleep. Then some instinct told him they were close.

"It's Wilhelm Mueller!" he called as loudly as he dared. "Wilhelm!"

Still nothing, no light or noise. He turned and began down the steps. He heard the door crack open behind him. He turned and dashed inside.

He drew the bolt back across as Natalie fell into his arms. The hallway was completely dark.

She was crying softly. He held her, stroking the unbraided hair. They didn't speak. Finally, she relaxed against him.

"Are you all right? Are you hurt?" he asked gently, pushing her back.

"I'm not hurt."

"Where is your grandfather and Hilda?"

She had told herself she would not be found weak and crying by him again. But now, what did her little pretending and dreams matter?

"Is he here? Is he home?" Wilhelm pressed with growing dread.

In the darkness, he felt her shake her head.

"Here, come on." He led her to the stairs where they sat. He waited until her breath became even.

"Your hands are as cold as mine," he said lightly. He took them in his, rubbing them together.

"You came, Wilhelm. God sent you to us," she said finally.

His laugh was shaky. "I don't know about that. I just knew I wanted to come and check on you, your grandfather, and Hilda after all that has happened today.... Where is he, Natalie?"

"A friend of Grandfather's called and said a group of elderly Jews had gathered at the synagogue. They wanted Grandfather to come and pray with them. They were . . . afraid. He said he must go and encourage them. Hilda insisted he not go out alone, so she went with him. That was hours ago, Wilhelm."

At synagogue on a night like this? Wilhelm felt his insides tighten.

"Well, if anyone can steer Rabbi Bergmann through a crowd, Hilda can. So we shouldn't worry. I'm sure they will be back soon."

"What is happening out there? Please tell me."

He was silent.

"Wilhelm? Please."

"I . . . I don't want to tell you, Natalie." He drew a ragged breath. "The last rally is over. Hitler and his bullies left after they whipped the crowd into a frenzy. Jewish shops and homes are being broken into and looted. If they find a Jew on the street, he is beaten."

"You'll not leave?" she asked clutching his arm.

"No, of course not. I won't leave." He started to stand. "Let's get a fire going and make some coffee. When your grandfather gets here they'll be cold and—"

"No, Wilhelm, please! No lights. If the Nazis come down the street and know this is a Jewish house . . . Please!"

"All right, all right. Calm down."

The firmness in his voice struck the young girl. Now she stood. "My flaw, Wilhelm, my flaw!" she cried.

"What? What are you talking about?"

"Fear. I didn't tell you that day—I was too embarrassed. I didn't want you to keep thinking of me as a frightened little girl your sister's age . . . who . . . who watches her own grandfather get beaten and does nothing!"

Wilhelm went to her, taking her arms in his hands. "I haven't thought that, Natalie. You were right to stay hidden that day. If they had found you . . . you know what could have happened."

"Still, Wilhelm, I was so afraid. I felt paralyzed. Your voice barely pulled me from it. I can never let that happen again. Yet tonight I watched Hilda and Grandfather leave for the synagogue. They told me I must stay here— alone."

"Again you did right, Natalie. There is courage and there is foolishness. I think we are both learning about that."

Her voice was soft. "Grandfather is wrong, isn't he?"

Wilhelm sighed with sudden weariness. "Ja, he is wrong. I am sorry that he is, but . . ."

She was leaning against him. "I know. This is the beginning of a long, cold night for the Jews of Germany. Grandfather doesn't understand; I do." She pulled away. "You make the fire, I'll make the coffee. They'll be very cold when they come in."

He felt a lump rise in his throat. He had wanted her to understand what the rabbi had shielded her from, but the loss of her innocence, her youth, saddened him beyond words.

• • •

Natalie had fallen asleep on the velvet sofa while they waited for her grandfather. Wilhelm paced between the fireplace and the front windows, watching the street through a slender crack in the heavy drapes. He must be ready if the Nazis came for the wealthiest rabbi in Germany.

He fingered the cold revolver in his pocket and thought of his parents. *What would they think if they could see me now? Pride or shame? I don't know.*

From the months of living on the precipice of danger, Wilhelm's hearing had sharpened. He could hear Natalie's even breathing, glad that she had been able to fall asleep and escape the horror for a time. From the firelight he could see her face clearly. At that moment, Wilhelm realized she really wasn't the young girl he had been thinking she was. *Sixteen. On the brink of young womanhood.* Her blonde hair spilled across the pillow in a current of gold. He had never seen it unbound. He took a step closer as his heartbeat quickened. *Her smooth skin is unblemished. She almost looked porcelain.* Wilhelm reached out and brushed back a strand of hair, and she didn't stir. *Very pretty. Another time, well, if I were younger*, he mused. He stood up abruptly and walked to the window. *No. Not even if we were closer in age. I'm hardly suitable for her hand.* He glanced over to the shadowed hallway at his bag. *All I own, past, present. . . .* He frowned. *What is the future on a night like this?*

She sighed in her sleep. He looked at her again. *Very pretty, no question—and very Aryan-looking—if it comes to that.* Somewhere, from the back of the great house, Wilhelm heard a noise. He tensed and drew out his revolver.

Wilhelm quickly and quietly moved toward the noise. He sighed with relief when he discovered the housekeeper and the old man entering through the back of the house like two thieves. Hilda embraced Wilhelm and the rabbi sunk to the stairs.

"Ah, Herr Mueller, you always appear at the right moment! How precious you are to us," the rabbi said, speaking softly so Natalie wouldn't awaken.

Wilhelm smiled and turned to Hilda. "You got through. Any problems?"

She patted her middle. "I guided the rabbi through that worthless rabble like the great warship Bismarck. A few swings of the hips and they fall away. No one bothered us."

"You are very faithful, Hilda Weisner," the rabbi said softly. "A righteous Gentile, ja."

She shook her head and chuckled as loudly as she dared.

"A German woman with a loud voice, a stern eye, and a pair of granite hips that is all. Now, I'll make coffee." She disappeared down the corridor.

The rabbi looked up and nodded at Wilhelm.

"God in all his great wisdom has seen fit to send my beloved Natalie and I a Gentile and an unbelieving Jew to help us."

Wilhelm leaned against the bannister. Tonight was not the night to get into a long discussion regarding his lack of faith, still he spoke gently. "What I have seen lately in Germany confirms my unbelief, Rabbi Bergmann. A loving God wouldn't allow this to happen—certainly not to His chosen people."

The rabbi stood stiffly. Tears filled his eyes.

"I will not deny, my young friend, that what we are seeing with our natural eyes is very, very tragic. Tonight I saw . . ." He broke off shaking his head. "But it does not deny His existence, Wilhelm, it confirms it. With our spiritual eyes, we can see a battle between good and evil, between the spirits of Satan and the spirit of the living God. He is in control, Wilhelm. He is still on the throne. He *will* win this battle. To belong to God you are on the winning side. Remember that."

Wilhelm scratched his head. "I don't know . . . I'm angry that this is happening. I can't change it, I can't affect it, I'm powerless."

The old man smiled. "Come along, I want to show you something." By the light of a candle they entered the rabbi's study across the hall. He led Wilhelm to the table where a group of silver framed photographs was clustered. He pointed to each one.

"My wife . . . our wedding . . . Natalie as a baby . . . her parents."

Wilhelm reached for one of the photographs.

"Who is this?"

"He was my youngest son, Alexander. He died when he was nineteen."

Wilhelm placed the photograph back on the table.

"You remind me of him, Wilhelm. He was full of energy and ideas, always questioning things. When he became sick with influenza, he was in a poor house across town. He was angry with me and rejected our faith. I was with him when he died. I told him . . . I told him I loved him very much, but I don't know that he heard me. I told myself if I ever met a young man like Alex I would love him as a son. I would not disapprove of him."

"Sir . . ."

"Ah, you're embarrassed of course. Come along."

"Sir, I want you to take this." He gave the old man a folded piece of paper. "It is my parents' address. They live on an estate outside of Berlin. If you ever need help, I mean, they could help you if things got where you had to leave Nuremberg."

"I will not leave my city, Wilhelm. Why I am more German than Hitler himself!"

A trace of impatience filtered into Wilhelm's voice.

"All right, then for Natalie's sake, if she might need a place."

"We will be fine." He led Wilhelm back to the hallway. They both glanced in at Natalie. "Hilda will have our coffee soon."

"I have to go; I can't stay for coffee."

"Why? You can't go out on a night like this, Wilhelm. If you must leave wait till daylight."

Wilhelm shook his head. "I can't. They're looking for me. Under darkness, I have a better chance."

"Who? Why?" The old man was growing louder with alarm. Hilda had joined them, holding the tray, as she listened to the exchange.

"The Nazis. They're after me for things I've done against them, like the pamphlets and other . . . things. They beat up my employer, tore up my old apartment, harassed my friends. So you see I have to leave Nuremberg for a time."

"Where will you go?"

"I'm not sure. I have friends in the country, some in Cologne." He patted the man's shoulder. "Don't worry, I'm the kind of scoundrel that always manages to land on top. I'll be back someday." He turned to Hilda. "Back and ready for another Saturday dinner."

"You are leaving?" Natalie said, as she stood in the doorway.

The rabbi watched their faces. Wilhelm smiled.

"For awhile. Time to change scenery, you know."

The rabbi took in the hair that fell loosely around her shoulders, the face and emerging figure. *Very lovely*. He looked at Wilhelm. His looks at the girl were swift and evasive. *Ah . . .*

"But it is unsafe on the streets," Natalie added.

"I'll be all right. I can run pretty fast if I have to. Well, I better be going."

"You must take some money. Let me go upstairs—" the rabbi began.

"No, sir, I can't do that. I won't take your money."

"Don't be a goyim! What do I have money for but to help those in need? How much do you have in your pockets?"

"I don't know—enough for a train ticket, though."

The rabbi snorted derisively. "To a suburb of Nuremberg perhaps!"

"Sir, I can't take your money. Now, I have to go."

The rabbi grabbed his arm. "Wilhelm, bitte. Bitte, let this old man have the chance to help you."

Wilhelm sighed. The rabbi dug in his pockets. "Here, take at least what is in my pockets." He stuffed a wad of marks into Wilhelm's hands. "There you are, my son. God go with you."

They shook hands. "Your composition, Wilhelm, was very, very good. Use your gift for writing again one of these days."

Wilhelm could not speak. He walked to the door.

"Oh, I almost forgot." He pulled the borrowed book from his jacket. "Thank you for the loan, I enjoyed it."

The rabbi waved it aside. "Keep it until you can bring it back to discuss over dinner, ja?"

Wilhelm smiled. His eyes fell on Natalie who had gone to a hall closet. She came up to him as if they were alone. She was carrying his ice skates. Wilhelm was shocked. She had been there, seen everything when he had thought her safely away. She had taken the risk to reclaim his skates. They looked into each other's eyes. Wilhelm forgot the rabbi.

"You are very brave, Natalie," he whispered.

She smiled. "I will keep these safe for you until you return ... to us."

14
The Color
of a Child's Cap

Berlin, late September 1935

His train arrived in the late afternoon. The sky was flat gray, and a brisk wind kept the many flags and banners taut. He smiled to himself, *Typical Berlin weather as I had expected.* He was one man in a vast crowd at the cavernous train terminal and later, one pedestrian among the many on the busy streets. He kept his collar turned up, his homburg pulled low. He did not want to be recognized—and he wasn't. To keep his identity a secret, he had sent his canine companion home with his friend. Max Farber was home.

As a boy, Max had spent many hours walking on the vast Farber estate. It was a habit and a pleasure that had followed him into adulthood. Even when his travels took him to busy foreign cities, he found time to walk. He favored the slopes and Alpine villages in Switzerland, the garden paths in Paris, the sandy shores in Italy. So while Josef took their luggage and Percy back to the apartment on Tiergartenstrasse, Max started walking. He had been reading German newspapers since they'd entered Austria, and caught snatches of conversations from his fellow travelers about his homeland. He shouldn't have been surprised when he stepped from the train. But he was. A quick glance at Josef, revealed the older man was experiencing the same reaction.

Men in uniform were everywhere, the black of the SS, the brown of the SA, and the dull green of the German army. Max noted them particularly, having limited knowledge of the three organizations. *Could the Nazi government be building the German army back up in violation of the Treaty of Versailles*? he wondered. *Why were foreign powers not protesting this? I haven't read anything of it in the papers.* The swastika seemed to be stamped on placards, flags, or banners in almost every building in the city. He turned to Josef as they loaded the cab.

"I really hope Irwin has invested in a flag and banner company," he said with a sly grin.

But the smile dissolved as he took to the streets. It was more than men in shiny boots and uniforms or the prolific punctuations of red and black that troubled him. He could not define it at first. Large pictures of Adolf Hitler in a commanding pose, one hand on hip, chin thrust out, declared he was their saviour. Huge posters in store windows and on corner sign-boards trumpeted Nazi ambitions for the German man, woman, and child.

"Adolf Hitler will show us the way!"

"Our only hope ... Adolf Hitler!"

"Germans defend yourselves! Don't buy from Jews!"

Max stopped and read each poster carefully. He watched as groups of teenage boys stood spellbound by the boasts. He had seen posters like this before he had left Germany a year earlier, but they had been more of a campaign variety for the Nazi party. This was ... At street corners, Max found a new feature to the city. Red, glass-fronted boxes offered a newspaper, *Der Sturmer*. Max bought a copy and quickly scanned it. He glanced around, stunned. This on the streets of Berlin? He had never seen anything so violent, so pornographic, so anti-Semitic. He stood back and watched men and women buying the paper. He stuffed his copy into the closest trash bin. A man, dressed in a leather trench coat and hat and waiting at the curb, was watching him. Max felt his eyes, clearly suspicious, probing, wondering why had he rejected the paper.

"Heil, Hitler!" the man said, half smiling as he strolled up to Max. The man's right arm raised and stiffened. The salute was more than in vogue, it was the unspoken required greeting. Max was clearly puzzled.

He had heard it on the train, at the crowded station, on the streets. Was it a greeting, slogan, or command?

"Guten Tag," he finally replied with a slight nod, preparing to move on.

The man nodded. "Just as I thought. You are a visitor to our city. I pride myself on recognizing visitors and foreigners to Berlin. Where are you from, sir, if I may ask? With your fine German accent—Munich or Frankfurt perhaps?"

Max had no desire to be unfriendly or continue this conversation. But he could not keep from smiling. "South America actually. Arrived this afternoon."

"Well, I can advise you. 'Heil, Hitler' is the accepted greeting. It pays tribute to our fuehrer."

"Not guten Tag?"

The man stretched a little. "No, not really. That expression is out of date."

"Well, I am miffed! The guidebook said, well... when I paid... for a perfectly worthless guidebook." Max affected a pout. "I certainly hope the tradesmen of Berlin are more honest than those of Brazil."

"Of course, of course. You will enjoy Berlin, I'm confident."

"Since this is your city, please tell me, why all the banners, the posters, the flags? Does it take a thousand of them to tell citizens and visitors alike this is a city under Nazi control? It seems, well, frankly a little gaudy to me. I would think Berliners would be embarrassed. I can see this is a beautiful city under all the swastikas."

The man's eyes swept over Max coldly. "Sir, the flags represent our total power—the future of Germany under our fuehrer's hand."

"I see, well, the swastikas remind be of a crippled spider flattened on a hot plate!" Max smiled.

The man could not conceal his shock. He pulled Max closer.

"I will tell you this, such statements are very imprudent here. Being a visitor, you do not know these things, but you must try to understand. And you obviously don't know that I am a Gestapo officer." He bowed. "I received my position a week ago," he continued proudly. He brushed dust off the arms of the coat that was too heavy for the warm, autumn weather.

"Well, congratulations! Gestapo? What is that precisely?"

"The state's secret police. We are to ferret out all enemies of the state," he paused, still smiling, "both foreign and German."

"Ah, very, very equitable of you. I truly admire a sense of fairness. Nothing worse than a brutal, unscrupulous police force who only bullies one type. I was in Paris recently, they could take lessons from you."

"Well, I . . . well, yes. But I noticed you didn't seem to care for *Der Sturmer*. I noticed that." He raised up on his toes, bringing his head level with Max's shoulder.

"Did you really? That is very observant of you! Did you learn that in your Gestapo training?"

"No, I mean, yes. You didn't like the paper?"

"Blast it, I left my glasses at the Aldon. Nothing but a sloppy, vulgar mess of words to me. Frightful when you have to depend on wire and glass for your vision. Couldn't be a sharp-eyed Gestapo agent like you," Max chuckled.

"No," the man said slowly.

"I feel so fortunate to have run into you, an efficient, bumptious Berliner, to explain these local nuances. Could you tell me about the gate or monument there? Is it the Blomberg Gate? I just don't trust my guidebook any longer!"

The little Gestapo man turned, his arm swinging out.

"This is the Brandenburg Gate, built to honor King Fredrick Wilhelm. The chariot on top is driven by the goddess of peace—I don't believe I got your name," he commented as he turned back toward Max.

But the visitor had disappeared into the crowd.

● ● ●

Max continued walking across the city, deep in thought. Passing Tiergarten, he didn't miss the stark white poster, "No Jews Allowed." The same poster hung on the theater doors, most restaurants, and many shops. He had known of the Nazis' hatred of Jews, but he was stunned to see that it had infected Berlin so thoroughly. *What were the Jews of the city doing about this? What could they do?* Max's mind was racing. *Was this the unpleasant change Josef had sensed they were to face?* He knew his oldest friend would be as sickened by this as he was. He turned east and walked swiftly.

The shop bell was shrill and shattered the silence as Max stepped in. Outside, the wind had risen and with it came the smell of rain. A man stepped from behind a curtain at the back of the cafe. His face broke into a smile instantly.

"Max! I thought I must have poisoned or offended you, it has been so long!"

They shook hands warmly. "Neither, Rudi. I've been away from Berlin this past year. Just got back today."

"Sit down, sit down."

"I'm starved, Rudi. I haven't had Jägerschnitzel in a year!"

"I have some on the stove—five minutes."

Even though it was odd, Max was grateful he was the only customer. Soon Rudi was back with the steaming food. They had gone to the university together, been on the soccer team and the tennis team. Though socially miles apart, they had been friends until Rudi dropped out to marry and manage his father's cafe. As far as Max was concerned, Rudi Schmidtt served some of the best food in Berlin. They talked and laughed over old times until Max finished eating. Max leaned back, patting his stomach. "You've made me a very satisfied man, Rudi. After walking across the city for a couple of hours, seeing the changes, I wasn't sure I'd have much of an appetite."

Rudi nodded, but said nothing.

"How are Magda and the girls?"

"Fine. They would have been here today, but little David is sick."

"You have a son?"

"Ja, ja," a wide smile creased the cafe owner's face. "Seven months old, a beautiful boy."

Max stared into his coffee cup, his voice low. "I envy you, Rudi, you're a rich man."

Rudi stared at Max a moment. *One of the wealthiest men in Germany is sitting in my humble cafe saying I'm richer.*

"How's business these days?"

Rudi laughed hollowly, glancing around the room. "Turning them away, Max, by the droves."

Max waited.

"You remember—Magda is Jewish, Max."

"Yes, I remember. She scorned me for you. Her eyesight improved any?"

Rudi laughed loudly; he did like Max Farber.

"Some of my customers still come, Jewish and Gentile. But the others, they don't want any trouble from the Nazis."

"I didn't see the sign in the window."

"Most everyone on this street is my friend—we've all known each other for years. I've grown up here. They are good people. They don't want to hurt me. About three months ago, a truckload of SA came by and put up a sign, 'True German's don't eat Jewish slop.' That night, someone in the neighborhood came and took the sign down. No one has singled me out, and the SA haven't come back." He sighed deeply. "But I know they will. So, it has slowed business down a little."

Max rubbed his eyes wearily. "I'm sorry, Rudi."

"You know the funny thing is, Max, when the Nazis first came to power, I was for them. Like a lot of folks, I didn't pay much attention to the Jewish stuff. I figured that would go away, no big deal. Then Goebbels and Göring started speaking on the radio and in the paper saying Jews were responsible for all the troubles in Germany—that they were not true citizens. It just got bigger and bigger, and I looked around and saw a lot of folks believing their lies. Magda...she wants to take the children and run away. But I tell her, could it get worse than to not be counted as a citizen of your own homeland?"

Max drained off his coffee and stood.

"It's going to rain and I'm walking, I better go."

"You're walking? I can give you a lift."

"That's all right. I've been on a train for over a day." He stuck out his hand. "The food was great, tell Magda hello for me."

"It was good to see you, Max."

Max looked down at his feet a moment. "Now I'll tell you a funny thing: Rudi, I'm embarrassed to be a member of the Nazi party." He sighed. "I'll be back again."

He went to the door, his hand resting on the knob. In all their carefree university days, Rudi had never seen Max Farber look so sad and worn. "If you need anything, anytime, you know where you can find me."

● ● ●

Two blocks from Rudi's, Max froze in his steps. Darkness had fallen, and the streets were largely deserted of pedestrians. But a truck had pulled up to a curb, and a dozen SS men were loading the open truck with people who filed silently from an apartment house. Men, women, and children huddled and clutching bags. Max noticed a small knot of observers at the opposite corner. He crossed the street, still watching the scene.

"What's going on there?" he asked quietly.

They turned to him with a mixture of fear and suspicion; silently, all but one turned away and entered another building. One older woman remained, clutching her sweater at her throat. Her voice was close to weeping. "They are Jews. The Nazis are taking them away."

Max watched as the last man then child was roughly handed up into the truck. The little girl's hat fell off into the gutter. She reached for it, but the Nazis jerked her forward. Max could hear her protest. The truck rumbled away, and the street was cold, dark, and silent again. The woman turned to Max, strangers knit together by a shared horror. She was trembling. Max still stared down the street.

"What has happened to us? They did nothing! Those are God's chosen! How can we raise our hands against them?" the woman cried softly.

Max finally turned, as if seeing her for the first time.

"You do not believe all the propaganda on the streets?"

Her voice was scornful. "Of course not!"

He nodded thoughtfully. "You give me encouragement, frau."

She looked back to the darkened apartment. "Did you see? They were so silent! Not a word . . . as if they had no voice."

Shaking her head, she retreated to her own apartment. Max could feel the cold through his thin jacket and the exhaustion that was creeping into his bones, yet he felt oddly alert. He walked slowly to the spot where the truck had stopped. He reached down and picked up the red wool hat the child had dropped. Carefully he placed it in his pocket.

The Mercedes sped along from Berlin to the Farber estate under a full moon that made the road look like a ribbon of yellow gold spiraling into the darkness without end. Max had the curious feeling he was being led along the road, though he steered the car and knew the destination. He couldn't explain the reason he was on this road, though he had tried to tell Josef. He could only say he wanted to get out of Berlin, and that he wasn't quite ready to resume his old life in the city. All he could think of was his country estate. Somehow, there, he hoped to find peace from the turmoil he felt churning inside.

"You took a long walk, Max," Josef had said.

Max nodded as he added some clothes to his still packed bags.

"A long walk, ja," he agreed.

Josef looked haggard and rubbed his chin thoughtfully.

"I . . . I'm glad we came back, though . . ."

"Ja?"

"I'm troubled like I think you are, Max. Dr. Hoffman and I met before he left for Vienna. He showed me the patient lists, and we discussed a few cases." Josef turned to stare out the window a minute.

"What else?" Max prodded gently. The two men knew each other so well.

Josef was shaking his head. "He turned away all my Jewish patients. He was rather proud of his attention to duty, as he called it. Nine families turned away." Josef stood. "I'm going to bed. I have a big day tomorrow."

Max smiled. "Trying to find nine Jewish families?"

"Ja. They will need me. They need a doctor like anyone else. I was making progress on many cases and he sends them away with a cheerful good day. Max, I tell you I had no idea this anti-Semitism would be so prevalent in the party. I thought Hitler and his cronies would have been thrown out by now over half the things they've done! Absolutely criminal behavior!"

He switched off the desk light. "I know I had to come back to Berlin, Max. I know what I have to do."

Max sighed, "You know. I'm glad for you, Josef."

The old doctor placed his arm around the young man as he had done a hundred times before.

"Max . . ."

"Don't tell anyone I'm back in town if you can avoid it, Josef. I'd rather be anonymous a little longer. I need more time to think. I have to find out why I've come back, Josef. I'll stay out at the estate until I have some kind of an answer."

Through the black iron gates, down the gravel drive, he parked before the huge, dark, silent mansion. Max Farber had come home. He climbed from the car stiffly, feeling the lack of sleep for the last 20 hours. Percy sensed his master's mood and waited by his leg instead of dashing off. Max pulled his two leather bags from the boot of the car and wandered to the back of the house.

It was so quiet on the Farber estate, and now, at nearly 10 o'clock, the knock on the door caused Marta Mueller to nearly jump from her chair. She and Heinz had been rereading Wilhelm's letter together.

"Herr Farber!" she gasped, squinting into the darkness.

He smiled wearily. "Guten Nacht, Marta."

Heinz came up quickly behind her. "Sir!"

Max sagged against the doorframe, suddenly feeling faint. They took his arms and led him into the room, wordlessly. Marta quickly fetched a cup of tea. Percy curled up on the hearth rug, one eye cocked open with attention.

"Danke, I . . . I didn't realize just how tired I was. It hit me all of a sudden." He looked into their faces. "I'm sorry to show up like this and alarm you."

"You are ill, Herr Farber?" Marta asked.

"Nein, just very tired. I'm going to be out here awhile, Marta. Do you think you could drop the herr and just make it Max?"

She demurred, looking at her husband. "I don't think I could, sir, I mean, I never, I—"

"Then how about Herr Max? A compromise."

"Well, all right, sir."

"You're staying overnight?" Heinz asked with surprise.

"Ja."

"But the house . . . we aren't prepared, sir."

"I'm sure it will be fine, Marta. If you could just unlock it for me, Heinz. I just want to go to bed and sleep for . . ." he glanced into their fire, "a long while."

But he was awake at sunrise the next morning. He lay in the huge four poster bed of his youth, smiling as he smelled coffee wafting up from below. The efficient Marta was at her duties. Then he realized Percy had taken liberty with his exhaustion and enthroned himself on the end of his bed. He nudged the dog with his foot. Percy rose up to come lick his face. Max laughed aloud.

With an arm behind his head, he surveyed the room. He had been born in a room down the hall, and he had known this room all his life. A big, high-ceilinged room, with massive mahogany furniture, lime-colored drapes. All the personal effects like pictures or books had been removed to his Berlin apartment or put in the library below. He picked up his jacket that he'd tossed on the floor only hours ago. Reluctantly he reached into the pocket, hoping it had all been a bad dream. But his fingers instantly met the soft wool. He pulled it out. Percy investigated it with his muzzle. In the morning light he could see it was a deeper shade of red, more like scarlet. Rather ordinary, not expensive. *A child's hat. How was that child this morning*? He closed his eyes against the thought.

His only plans when he and Josef had left Brazil, was to return to Berlin and make a proposal to Irwin. An expansion of Farber Company, but not in chemicals or metals: a return to farm implements as Farber had been decades ago. He would manage this division as well as the division of Farber charity like he had been doing. This had been his plan. It had seemed like a good one, but now he was not certain. The events of the day before seemed to be pulling him . . . where?

He leaned back, the child's hat still in his hand. His eyes fell on the window seat. He yawned, and rolled over on his side. Something . . . a long ago memory. He sat up suddenly, smiling. He had forgotten about it for years! When he was 12 he had decided he needed a secret place to put private, personal things. Irwin and Eric were forever badgering him about his things, and were disrespectful of anything personal. He had gotten the idea from one of the many adventure books he was always reading. A secret place. Carefully he had smuggled a saw and other tools to his room. He had worked feverishly and joyfully. He would have something his brothers didn't know a thing about. No one would know! He would not even tell Dr. Morgan. As an amateur carpenter, he had done remarkable well. Under the cushion of the window seat, he had made a secret compartment in the woodwork.

Max quickly crossed to the window, as excited as he had been as a boy. He hoped more than dust remained from his past. Percy whined at his side. "Let's have a look, boy." He removed the cushion almost reverently. It looked undisturbed. He found the hidden groove and slid back the panel. It was a compartment two feet wide by two feet deep. It contained one white box. Max carried it back to the bed.

A swimming medal he had gotten when he was eight, a hateful letter he had written to Irwin but never sent, a rough drawing of horse, a letter from his father during the war in France, a tortoise shell hairbrush that was his mothers', sheet music from Elaina. He reached for the red leather book at the bottom of the box. Of course he knew what it was. His favorite book from boyhood. He had read it on his birthday every year for years after he had received it. He couldn't remember why he had hidden it away in this box.

The Scarlet Pimpernel. He called for his breakfast to be brought up and propped himself in bed to read. He read all day and finished at sunset. It was the story of a man who had risked his own life to save others. The man could have spent his days watching the persecution from a distance. But he was a man of courage and creativity; a man who appeared as one thing when he was really quite the opposite. The character had appealed to Max the first time he had read the book. Dimly he remembered something Dr. Morgan had said to him when he had presented it to him years ago. *Honor...*

Max stood and walked to the mirror. He stood in his shorts and undershirt, barefoot, hands on hips. He looked himself over. Tall, strong, young, wealthy—and thought benignly foolish by others.

His eyes fell on the scarlet hat on the bed. What had the woman on the street said? *They were so silent... as if they had no voice!*

He smiled, the despair he'd felt lifted. Now he knew.

15
A Capital Girl

Washington, D.C., March, 1936

The driver of the De Soto noticed that the cherry trees were budding along the Potomac. She passed them every day to work, and she had grown to love them over the years—a timeless distinction of the city and a herald of her favorite season of the year. She concentrated on the heavy, late afternoon traffic that surged onto Pennsylvania Avenue and its tributaries, and listened to the chatter of her best friend in the passenger seat.

"Oh, Bess, I hate to go on job interviews! And this one," the driver interrupted, shaking her head. "They say he's so grumpy."

"And I've heard from Mary Clifford, whose cousin's best friend worked for him, that he asks really personal questions. You're braver than I am, Emilie Morgan."

"Next Friday is my last day at work.... I'd really like to get this job."

"Most people don't even get an interview, so that's a good beginning."

"I just wish I weren't so nervous. I feel like I might pass out right there on his desk!"

Bess gave her a roguish look. "Baxter would probably love that. They say he has a thing about legs—very select about his female employees, hires them on shape."

"You're lifting my confidence, dear Bess. . . . Why do you think I have on new silk stockings?"

Bess was applying a fresh veneer of red to her full lips.

"I keep telling you that you shouldn't worry about this job interview. The answer to your problem is so obvious."

Emilie rolled her eyes and sighed. "Marriage."

Bess snapped her compact closed. "A-plus for Miss Morgan. You tie up a fella and your money worries are over!"

"And your new worries begin."

"Ah, but such worries might be pleasant to work out!"

The two young women laughed.

"It isn't as if you haven't had plenty of offers. Ernie would take you even after you've rejected him for years!"

"Your brother is very persistent and very kind, Bess."

Emilie smiled to herself as she imagined a baby in her arms with her face and Ernie's wild red hair and flag-like ears.

"You are too . . ." Bess began.

"Select."

"Exactly." They passed the capitol and Bess jabbed a finger in its direction. "There. You live in the shadow of the capitol and you still want to marry a congressman, right?"

"Senator, Bess, senator. They make it to the White House more often."

Bess gave her friend a playful poke. "Your dream man's out there Em . . . yeah, I can see him. Tie, glasses, briefcase . . . and too boring to care what your legs look like!"

"Ha! He'll care!" Emilie's smile was wry. "I know what's going to happen, Bess. He's going to leave his office on his lunch break and decide to wander over to the Smithsonian, you know, for a little inspiration."

"Passing through the American History Museum."

"Of course. And my last day was the day before and we never meet!"

"Stick with Ernie or Tom, Em."

Emilie smiled and shook her head. "Almost there."

"I'm meeting Jerry at 6:30 at Little China, then we're going to the Metro to see *Wife Versus Secretary*. Are you going to join us?"

"Depends on how long this interview takes. If I'm still standing . . ."

"Maybe we'll be able to celebrate," Bess said, giving her friend's arm a squeeze. "You'll be fine."

"I don't know. . . . Anyway, I doubt I'll make it. I pick Dad up at five o'clock."

"Where's he been?"

"Boston. He has a friend who recently came over from Germany. They're old friends from way back."

"Well, bring him along. Jerry and I don't mind. Your Dad is a swell guy."

"Thanks, Bess. Okay, get ready."

Emilie slowed as cars and trucks went speeding past. She was careful of the trolley just in front of her. "We're coming in!" Emilie laughed as Bess grabbed her purse and pretended to put on her parachute. This was a routine they went through often.

"Jump!"

The door flew open and Bess bolted out with a smile and a wave.

A job interview with the *Washington Post* was highly coveted. Actually, most any job prospect in 1936 America was prized. Emilie Morgan knew that as well as anyone. What jobs were available were often unavailable to women. "They should be home having babies," was the general attitude. So she drew a deep breath as she opened the door to the office of Sam Baxter, manager of *Post* photographers. How proud Dad would be if she could greet him at the station with the news! Especially since she hadn't told him she was being laid off from the Smith. Just outside the door, she smoothed her hair, checked her skirt and stockings, gripped her portfolio tighter, and drew another deep breath as if she were plunging under water. Asking directions, she was directed to Baxter's office.

"I'm Emilie Morgan . . . here for an interview," she said, knocking on the open door.

He gestured for her to sit, without bothering to look her directly in the face. The chair, she noted, was positioned to the left of the desk, instead of in front. She crossed her legs carefully. He barked out the door for coffee, then leaned back, taking in her legs and moving upward.

Emilie was determined not to waver under his boldness. She stared at the gray hair that was swept across his pink dome of a head. She ignored the way his lips jerked forward and sideways during his perusal. *Heavy prickly eyebrows, mottled cheeks, snapping brown eyes. He is comical looking—and very powerful on the Post*, she thought.

He had not said a word to her. He cleared his throat and leaned over his desk, giving it three little taps.

"How old are you?"

"I'm twenty-four."

One tap.

He didn't bother with the resume in front of him.

"Where do you work now?"

"The Smithsonian Institute. I've been a guide there for the past four years. It's a very nice place to work."

"Why you leaving, then?"

"It isn't my choice to leave, sir. I'm being laid off. They're having to cut back because of budget concerns."

One tap.

"Where do you live?"

"Georgetown."

One tap.

"Far drive to the *Post*."

"Not much farther than to the Institute. I don't mind at all."

"Married?"

"No sir."

One tap.

"Single girls always create problems in the workplace. Do you live alone?"

"With my father."

"Yeah? What's he do?"

"He's a retired diplomat, and now he does a little consulting work for a German company."

"Where's your mother?"

Emilie realized she was no longer nervous. Now she was irritated. "She died six years ago."

The coffee was brought to him. He drank and winced.

I hope he scalded his tongue, Emilie thought impudently.

"Why aren't you working in the photography profession now? You come to ask for a job with the *Post* with no experience."

Emilie straightened in her chair. "I'm not working in the photography profession full time now, that is true. But I do freelance work when I can. It's all there in the resume on your desk."

He looked at her directly and grunted.

"Never bother with resumes. Folks lie on 'em half the time."

"Well . . ."

"Where did you go to school?"

"I'm a graduate of Smith College. I have a degree in journalism."

Two taps. He gulped the coffee again. "Why have you come to the *Post* looking for a job?"

"Well . . . I'd like to work on a newspaper as a photographer, and I think the *Post* is the best paper . . ." He was watching her with ferretlike eyes.

"Yes?"

"Certainly the best in Washington, and probably the best paper on the East coast. Far better than the *New York Times*."

Three taps.

He reached for her portfolio. He leaned back. She was relieved to see he spent time on each one, not hurrying through, while muttering and grumbling.

"I was a photographer for my college magazine, and my senior year I covered the convention in Chicago. I—"

"I'm a Republican myself," he announced, not looking up.

"Oh. Last summer I did a photo essay for the Gettysburg Historical Society. Three months ago I did some work for the Institute. . . . That's the booklet I did for them."

Two taps as he closed the portfolio slowly.

She cleared her throat. "Mr. Baxter, I'm a very quick learner. I can grasp the kind of work you want here with little problem, I'm sure. I've lived in the Washington area since I was 12. So, if you will give me an assignment I can fill it before you could tap your pen three times." She smiled, but he did not.

He slid the portfolio across the desk toward her.

"Good work, but I need someone who can race up the capitol steps or dash down to the Navy yard. If I sent you to Foggy Bottom to cover a fire, you'd be attacked. You don't look strong enough—your legs, they aren't stout enough."

Her mouth fell open. "Stout? You want stout legs?"

"Gotta have 'em." He stood up. "'Sides I'm not partial to hiring young girls anyway, especially a single, pretty one. Complicates things. Times are still hard, no matter what President Frankie does. Did you see yesterday's front page photo? Dust bowl in Oklahoma. Hard times, Miss Morgan. I feel I have to hire a man in hard times."

She stood up slowly. "May I ask you a question?"

"You can ask, no promise I'll answer." He smiled thinly.

"Why did you agree to this interview? Why didn't you just toss my application aside?"

His head tilted, as if seeing her for the first time.

"I like to have a pretty girl in once in awhile. This place can be pretty stuffy, know what I mean?" He gave her a wink.

Emilie gathered up her purse and portfolio. But not before she gave his desk one quick tap.

● ● ●

Since it was Friday, Union station was thronged with lobbyists and Congressmen leaving the city, but Emilie had been to the terminal too many times to be intimidated by the press of humanity. She knew exactly where she would find her father. Standing on tiptoe, she scanned the platform near the Boston train. Since she was five minutes late, she knew he would be waiting for her at the pretzel wagon, having a warm pretzel that he loved, and chatting with Joe. She hurried through the crowd, breathless as she came up to the cart. She didn't see the lean figure of her father anywhere.

"Hello, Joe!"

The tall black man, glanced at her from the corner of his eye and continued waiting on his customer. Emilie glanced at her watch and waited. The friendly Joe must not have heard her. She stepped away from the cart, searching the corridor. Had the train come early? Had he taken the taxi all the way out to Georgetown? No, not the economical Thomas Morgan. She chewed her lip, then she noticed Joe was waiting hesitantly at her elbow.

"Joe, is the 5:00 late?"

"Ah, no, Miss Morgan, it done come and gone, Ma'am."

It was then she heard the timbre of his voice. She turned around to look at him. Behind him she could see he had left his cart unattended, something she had never seen him do. But then, who would contend with the over-six-foot pretzel seller?

"Joe? Is something wrong?"

He was wringing his cloth cap and looking at his shoes. Emilie forgot her father or the crowd surging around them. She touched his arm. "Joe?"

His deep brown eyes flooded with tears instantly.

"Ma'am, I's so sorry to be the one . . . to have to tells ya. I done seen Mr. Morgan. He . . . well, they had to carry him off the train 'bout 30 minutes ago, ma'am. I's so sorry, but he done had some kind of attack on the train 'fore they got here."

"An attack?" Emilie was startled at how hollow her voice sounded, as if it came from the far end of a long train tunnel. Someone else was speaking with her voice. Instantly she was seeing the face of her father as he had looked three days ago when they parted. She had stood on tiptoe to straighten his tie, and he had rested his hand on her shoulder.

"You've made the years without your mother livable, Emilie Morgan. Ja, more than livable, a blessing too."

"Miss Morgan? You want to sit down or something? Let me get you something cool to drink."

"An attack?" she repeated faintly. "Where did they take him? Do you know which hospital, Joe?"

His tears cascaded over his cheeks. "I don't think they took him to a hospital, Miss Morgan. Done too late."

• • •

The third floor office looked out on Fourteenth and E streets, from which a steady, muted din of car honks and trolley bells could be heard. It was a small office, unpretentious with half-a-dozen wooden chairs, a table, desk, filing cabinet, and coffeepot. A map of Europe adorned one wall, a United States map on the opposite, and a framed star of David hung over the door. The gold etching on the frosted door did not invite interest: "Bureau of Consumptive Resources and Education." It sounded very Washingtonian in a city of a thousand departments, agencies, and bureaus. Those who passed through the door often chuckled at the purposely misleading moniker.

Since 1933 it had been the "official'" headquarters of the "Rescue of European Jews" division of a Washington Zionist group. At Hitler's ascension, some Jews in America—many were recent refugees—saw with a vision their European contemporaries did not. Nazism was much more than a popular political movement that also embraced anti-Semitism. It was a real threat to every Jew on the European continent. This small band of men and women worked with an intuition and feverish purpose so that in the coming storm they could be counted on to offer help to their Jewish brethren. The group wrote letters to Jewish communities throughout the states with recent news of crimes against the Jews that the local American papers didn't seem to deem newsworthy. They collected money from wealthy Jews. They prepared passports and exit visas. They lobbied senators, congressmen and the president. They worked—sometimes within the confines of legality, sometimes without, to save Jewish men, women, and children from persecution.

The four men sitting around the office were silent as they read the articles in the Washington and New York papers. They were glad to see the *Post* had given the story prominence as the front page leading story: "Hitler Remilitarizes Rhine." The youngest man among them gripped the page closely as he studied the black-and-white photo of the German fuehrer addressing the crowds. He wondered how many Americans reading their morning papers really cared that the German army had just marched into this Rhineland place, thus breaking the treaty that had restrained them for almost 20 years?

Isaac finally tossed the paper down. "All right, I admit it. I'm totally ignorant! I've lived in Brooklyn most of my life, and I have no idea where the boundaries to this Rhineland place are that Hitler just stepped into."

The youngest man stood up and studied the map of Europe.

"Here. You see, it isn't a separate country, it's a province that stretches along the Rhine river and borders Belgium, France, and Germany. It's been demilitarized since 1920. Neither Germany nor France is supposed to occupy it. Versailles made it a neutral place."

"A buffer zone," Isaac offered.

"Exactly. But Germany has always felt it was really theirs and that the Treaty of Versailles had stolen it from them. Whoever claims it gets a real prize, because it's a rich industrial area. Germany has located at least two industries there in the last few years, Krupp Steel Works and

Farber Chemical. Now they've moved the military in on the excuse that the several million Germans living there want to be under the protection of the reich. It's a serious gamble for Herr Hitler."

Even though he was the most recent addition to their group, the other men listened to him with respect. The door opened and another member of their group entered.

"It took me awhile, but I have them." He held up a Paris paper and the *London Times*. "The Brits and Frenchies decided this was front page stuff too, but you're going to choke when you read it."

They hunched together to read.

"France will appeal this German action to the League of Nations." The young man standing at the map slapped it in frustration.

"They could send their army over and finish this up in an hour! The Germans would be running back to Berlin with their tails between their legs!"

"And Adolf would be finished."

"Read Britain's response: 'Occupation of the Rhineland by the German army seriously threatens previous treaties. But we have no reason to suppose that Germany's present action threatens hostilities.' Ha! A polite way of saying go ahead Herr Fuehrer, do what you like."

He read further. "The foreign secretary says 'Adolf Hitler is merely claiming his own backyard.'"

The newest member strode to the window, and glanced toward Pennsylvania Avenue. "Well, if Britain and France are doing nothing, we should expect Mr. Roosevelt won't either."

Stephan, the head of the group, leaned back, searching the ceiling. "I can't help but feel this is a prime opportunity lost. Such may not come again."

"Then Adolf's gamble has paid off," the young man said with a frown.

● ● ●

Sunlight poured in through the tall, paned windows, casting yellow geometrics on the carpet. The young woman sat in a wingback chair across the room from the windows, seemingly fascinated by the patterns. She had sat unmoving like a model in a portrait studio for almost an hour, very composed and quiet. Yes, very quiet like the house itself. She was completely alone in this two-story brick home on one of

Georgetown's fine, old streets. Gracie, the cook, had gone shopping, even though not much was required for only two people. The woman sighed and walked to the windows.

Emilie Morgan stood looking out at the clean-clipped, pocket-sized lawn. The other houses looked as lifeless as her own. No barking dogs, no stalking cats. Alone. Another sigh escaped her. She continued watching for several minutes more then returned to her chair. It might appear she was waiting for someone, but she had no appointment to keep. This morning was a duplicate of every other morning for the past three weeks.

She glanced at the hallway. A hat lay on the cherry-wood table there. *A sign of life*, she noted, *however indirect*. The owner of the hat had absently left it there over an hour ago. *I hope he won't return for it soon.* Even if it gave a voice in the house, she didn't want to face him again—not today anyway.

She could hear the lawyer's crisp, precise voice in her mind.

"I've brought the final papers concerning your father's estate, Miss Morgan."

She perused them, quickly floundering in the legal language.

"I'm sorry, Mr. Crewes, but really . . . I . . . hardly understand a word of this. Couldn't you summarize it for me?"

"Summarize?" he asked with a stiff, shocked tone.

"Well, yes. You know, summarize or simplify."

He tugged at his tie as if it were suddenly strangling him. "Well, I usually don't summarize. . . ."

"Please, just tell me what all this means to me."

"You are the sole heir to the estate of Thomas and Anna Morgan," he returned bluntly.

"All right. I can understand that."

He adjusted his glasses. "Perhaps it would be best to begin this way. Tell me what you know of your father's employment and financial history."

Emilie ran a hand through her hair, trying to collect her thoughts. "Well, my father was a diplomat with the German embassy for years. I'm not sure how long, at least 20. What he did as a young man before that, before he left Germany, I don't remember. We came to the states when I was nine. We lived in New York City for three years, then we came here." She kept her eyes on the lawyer's natty, olive-colored tie. If she looked at this room, measured it with her eyes, it would bring up too many memories. *I won't cry*, she told herself. *I must keep my voice factual and unemotional.*

She shook her head. "I'm sorry. I'm talking about the house and you wanted to know about his career."

"It is perfectly all right, Miss Morgan. This is a convenient time to insert that this house is paid for and, being the sole heir, it belongs to you now. That should be a comfort to you."

She wanted to laugh out loud. An empty house was a cold comfort when grief was like a raw, gaping wound.

She cleared her throat. "My father retired from the diplomatic corp when my mother died six years ago."

Mr. Crewes smoothed the paper on his knee, his thin lips twitching nervously.

"Yes, well, that brings us to another relevant point."

She waited.

"Do you know about your father's retirement, Miss Morgan?"

"Well, I know that's what we lived on until my father began with the Farber Company. I don't know how much he received."

"Miss Morgan, this is most unpleasant. The fact is, your father did not receive any retirement after 1933."

"What do you mean?"

"I had only one conversation with your father on this, about six months ago. He gave me the outline of facts . . . for it distressed him. He was very concerned that you would not be left with any debts if anything happened to him."

She gripped the arms of her chair, calming her voice.

"Why didn't my father receive any pension after years of service, did he tell you that?"

"Very simply, Miss Morgan, your father would not take a vow of loyalty to the Nazi government."

She closed her eyes a moment. *All those years that he had worked so hard, so faithfully, and so tirelessly for his homeland and his adopted country. To be treated this way!*

"Miss Morgan? Are you all right?"

She nodded. "Please go on."

"In late 1933, your father was employed by I.E. Farber Company of Berlin. He was to act as a liaison between Farber and interested business investors in America."

She nodded again, her voice low. "Yes, I remember. He was very happy to be working again. He . . . traveled, came home tired . . ."

The lawyer cleared his throat. By now, Emilie had come to understand his mannerisms. "Yes? What happened then? Did something happen with his pension to Farber?"

"Miss Morgan, please try to understand that your father was a private man and did not want to trouble or alarm you. He expressed that to me quite firmly. Farber Company fired your father well over a year ago."

She straightened in her chair. "What? I've seen him at his desk working, and taking trips and . . ."

The lawyer was shaking his head. "I'm sorry . . ."

The young woman's voice was hoarse. "What have we been living on then? My father wouldn't allow me to use my income on the house or living expenses. I was to save it . . . I . . ."

"Your mother had dowry money they had saved for you. It was . . ." Now the stoic lawyer seemed to stumble on his own emotion. He shook his head to take himself in hand. This was not professional.

"It was important to your father that this money go to you, a gift from them. But it was used to live on when . . ." Mr. Crewes was eager to leave this house in Georgetown.

"I see."

"There was enough to pay for funeral expenses and my retainer. Here is what remains." He pushed a paper quickly across to her. "Now, if you'll just sign here, we're all finished."

She did not miss the relief in his voice. At the door, he turned, apologetic, "Your father was a fine man, Miss Morgan. Good day."

An hour had lapsed under the steady pulse of the mantel clock. Emilie sat rigidly still, trying to absorb all she had learned. Now her father's depression was explained—but too late. She could not help him or try to cheer him. He had died broken and unappreciated. *How could this have happened? Why had his country stabbed him this way?* she wondered bitterly.

Her eyes fell to the newspaper laying on the sofa. She had read through it listlessly earlier in the morning. Now the article came back to her. At the time she had only given it a half-interested glance: "Hitler Remilitarizes Rhine." Germany. She stood up and angrily snatched up the paper. Crying, she ripped it into shreds. She did know enough about her father's feeling to know he would have been very sad to read of this aggression. *It feels good*, Emilie noticed, *to tear and scatter the pieces around the room.* After a time, she felt calmer. She could imagine her father smiling, shaking his head at her.

The thud of the knocker on the front door made her jump. Had Mr. Crewes returned for his hat? She went to the door reluctantly and swung it open. It was not Mr. Crewes.

"Hello," the voice said brightly.

A young man stood on the steps. She estimated he was close to her own age; he was of medium height, had green eyes set in a slender face with a scattering of freckles across the bridge of his nose, and straight brown hair. He was smiling. "You're Emilie Morgan," he stated.

"Yes."

"Helen told you about me; she told you I would call."

"Helen?" she repeated dully.

"Helen Jacobs, you work with her."

"Worked, past tense," she corrected stiffly.

"Oh. Well, she told me she told you about me."

She was shocked at his confidence. *Helen had mentioned it weeks ago—and he expects me to remember. And doesn't even call first. . . .*

"I don't recall specifics, it would have been weeks ago, and I'm sure she would have given me a *name*."

Only then did his eager, confident smile falter slightly.

"Name?"

"*Your* name."

Suddenly he laughed—and Emilie relaxed just a bit.

He stuck out a hand. "I'm Will Cutler, a friend of Helen's."

"She may have mentioned you, but as I said, that was weeks ago. A lot has happened since then."

"I was in the neighborhood, and thought I'd just stop by to say hello. You know, a phone call seemed too impersonal"

"Oh? Well, it's more considerate, really," she interrupted coldly.

"Well, yeah. Helen thought we might, well, have stuff in common." Emilie tightened her grip on the doorknob, ignoring his bright smile.

Helen Jacobs was always trying to match her up with someone—this time she had gone too far.

"Actually, this really isn't a good time for me," Emilie said as she backed up to close the door.

"Oh, yeah?"

"Yes," Emilie returned with a trace of exasperation, "I'm busy."

"Busy." She could see in his eyes he was laughing at her.

She wanted to close the door in the face of this brash Will Cutler.

At that moment a cat dashed past her legs out into the yard. He ran to the maple tree and climbed up. Emilie brushed past the young man.

"Jasper! Jasper Cat, come here!"

Cutler came up beside her, hands in pockets, smiling.

"Fella just wants a little freedom."

She turned and gave him an annoyed look. "He can't ever get down by himself. He sits up there and howls pitifully. *Jasper, come here!*" The cat only looked at his mistress with taunting feline eyes.

"Looks like a power struggle to me."

"It is," Emilie snapped. *Why was this stranger still standing here? Didn't I tell him politely to leave?*

"So how do you usually get him down?"

Emilie's voice softened "I . . . I don't get him down. My father always does."

"How?"

She looked him full in the face, then. "Thank you Mr. Cutler, but I can manage."

"Look, Miss Morgan, I understand. I'll leave—but let me help you get your cat down."

She glanced up at him. He was smiling. *Well, he is just trying to be nice.* "My father always stands on that bench there and puts a piece of food on his shoulder. Jasper takes it and gets on his shoulder. It's kind of a little thing . . . between them."

He began to move the bench. "Go get me something then. Nothing runny if you don't mind. This is a new shirt." He laughed at her startled face.

Emilie watched as the young man climbed on the bench with the piece of cheese on his shoulder. "Come on, puss, come on. That's right, Jasper."

He came across the lawn, smiling broadly, Jasper perched on his shoulder purring contentedly. He handed the cat to Emilie.

"See? Your father and I have that touch," he said cheerfully.

She buried her face in the animal, to staunch her tears. Cutler stepped back, surprised.

"Well, maybe I'll call ... when it's a better time."

She looked up. "Would you like to come in for some lemonade, Mr. Cutler?"

"Only if you don't call me Mr. Cutler. That's for my old man. I'm just Will."

She led him back to the sunny front room, amazed with herself at inviting this unsettling stranger into her home.

The newspaper storm greeted them both. Emilie felt herself redden. It was obvious someone had had a tantrum. She fetched a basket and hastily picked up the pieces. Cutler bent down to help her.

"You know, cats can sure be destructive creatures, yes, sir," he smiled.

Emilie had the distinct feeling he could see right through her, and was, in fact, laughing at her again.

"Yes, I'll get our lemonade."

When she reentered the room with the tray, she found him wandering the room, examining the many black-and-white photographs that covered the walls. She sat down and watched him. *Hmm. He's wearing tan trousers and a light-blue window-pane-checked shirt. Average build. Bess always came to her opinions quickly and bluntly about eligible young men. Bess would say he was neither ugly or handsome.* Emilie wasn't sure. His personality was rather forceful, far more than his looks were.

This room always embarrassed Emilie when she saw strangers examine it for the first time. She felt she must explain, but he spoke before she could, his back still to her.

"Your work? Helen said you were a photographer on the side."

"Yes. My mother insisted on framing my best work. My father kept it on after she died, even though I protested that it made the room look like an art gallery," she finished with a little laugh.

"I think it's all great. You do very good work. I think I like this group best."

She smiled, fighting back all the memories they instantly conjured up. "We spent the summer I was 19 in Pennsylvania among the Amish. I took those pictures. My father said they were the best work I've ever done. It was . . . a wonderful summer."

She looked down at her lap, angry with herself. *Only an hour ago I felt so fragile and wounded. Why am I talking so much to this man?*

Will sat down across from her.

"Thanks," he said accepting the glass. Now quiet returned as sharply as it had earlier. Emilie occupied herself with stroking the cat. She could feel his eyes on her lowered head. He didn't seem to notice the silence.

Finally she couldn't stand it any longer.

"You said Helen Jacobs told you about me. What did she say we have in common?"

"Germany."

She stiffened. "Germany?"

"Yeah. We both were born there, raised here. And I'm an amateur photographer myself. Not nearly as good as this, though."

Emilie stared at her hands. She was typically comfortable around men her own age. Working at the Smith as a guide, she'd had plenty of attempted flirtations and suggestions made to her. But this man . . . he frankly made her nervous. And that made her a little mad.

She was surprised at the sudden abruptness in her voice.

"As I said earlier, I'm kind of busy now."

If he heard her, he was ignoring her. He swept the room.

"Nice place you have here. Classy."

"Thank you." *It's all mine*, she added bitterly to herself.

The cat suddenly stretched and jumped from her lap to Cutler's. Will laughed. "I like a grateful cat. Hey, boy."

She could tell he was boyishly pleased.

The room and the house were so terribly quiet and still. Finally she lifted her eyes to his, and shook her head. "I'm not busy at all. I . . . I feel like I'm dying." Her eyes filled with tears.

His smile dropped instantly, his hand froze on the cat.

"My father died of a heart attack on the train from Boston nearly four weeks ago. Two days before that, I found out I was losing my job at the Institute. My father's attorney just left: I own this house, but I have little money. That's all. I ... really don't know what ... I'm going to do."

Her body shook with sobs as she buried her face in her hands. The stranger was removed from her mind. All she could see was the face of her mother and father, so loving—and gone. Minutes ticked by in the quiet room, then a hand was on her shoulder.

"Here, you need this." He thrust a handkerchief in her hands. "It's clean."

She was startled to find him still sitting across from her. He seemed to read her thoughts, and smiled. "Yeah, I'm still here. Blow before you drip."

She leaned back in her chair, her eyes closed.

"I don't know what's the matter with me. I don't know why I told you all that."

"I'm very sorry about your father. What I said earlier, with the cat, I didn't know . . ."

She was surprised at the sudden gentleness in his tone. She had known him less than an hour—really knew nothing about him at all— yet she instinctively knew he was sincere. He leaned forward to look into her face. "How long has it been since you've been out of this house?"

She looked away. "A few days after the funeral I went out to lunch with a friend. Since then, I ... I've stayed in mostly."

"A few weeks too long then. It's like a tomb in here."

Her eyes widened at his bluntness. She started to protest, to demand he leave immediately, but he stood up before she could speak. He was looking down at her, shaking his head. *He's acting like he knows everything about me, and has known me for years*!

"I'm not against grieving. I know a little about it myself. But you're right when you say you're dying. This is killing you. Your father wouldn't want you to be like this. You need to get out."

"Really, Mr. Cutler—"

"The name is Will. Come on, let's go get something to eat," he reached for her hand.

"No, I don't think I can."

"Sure you can. What are you hungry for? Let's eat at the Capital Coffee house. I can afford it this week. You're the penniless heiress so I'll be forced to pay." He pulled her to her feet.

"I don't think I've ever met anyone quite like you," she said in a gasp.

He grinned. "You haven't."

"You're almost . . . rude."

"Almost rude, yeah, I like the sound of that. Go change—you can't go looking like that. I'll wait, but hurry, I'm hungry."

She was being commanded, and it was very foreign to her. *Why am I allowing this stranger to take such liberties?*

She paused, her hands on her hips. He stood across from her in mock imitation. Finally Emilie Morgan laughed.

"The matinee starts at 2. We'll see Garbo's new flick, *Camille*. No debate on that."

"Do you suppose I can choose what I want from the menu?"

"If I can afford it, sure.

She hesitated again. He *was* overwhelming.

"Come on, Emilie," he said gently. "Time to shake off the funeral rags!"

● ● ●

Emilie Morgan couldn't have imagined that her day could possibly end this way. That morning she had stared up at the ceiling of her bedroom which was as smooth and unrevealing as her future. Now she was sitting in the Capital Coffee house, across from this Will Cutler who was making her laugh for the first time in weeks. It gave her a curious feeling of fright to be talking so much—like an uncorked bottle or undamned river. She usually only talked so openly with Bess whom she had known for years. Sitting there at the table with the little red-checked cloth she felt she had been pushed out of the shadows onto a stage with the drama already in progress.

But he listened, he really listened. He teased her and poked at her attempted reserve as if he were a very old friend or brother. She brushed back her hair and sighed. Will sat with his fingers laced, unashamedly regarding her.

"How do you know Helen Jacobs?" Emilie asked, searching for a topic.

"I met her at a party."

"And she was talking about me?" Emilie asked with a little smile.

"Yes, she said she worked with this gorgeous dame who can rattle on about American history for hours."

Emilie looked down to her lap, blushing and shaking her head.

Cutler was pleased he could make her blush.

He continued. "When I get excited, my accent comes out stronger. German is all my parents speak at home. So when Helen heard it, she said she worked with a girl at the Institute that spoke German also. Said she was smart, no nonsense, and pretty—in that order. Coffee?"

She nodded.

"So you didn't like the movie, huh?"

"It was all right," she shrugged. "Garbo is too sultry and . . . secretive for me. I don't trust her."

"Too secretive . . ."

She leaned back in the leather booth. "Almost like you, Mr. Cutler."

For just an instant she could see she had startled him. Then he smiled. "Me?"

"Yes, I've done all the talking all evening. Very unfeminine. I know only that you're Helen Jacob's friend. You know my life story very nearly. Have I forgotten to tell you when I cut my first teeth?"

"I have no objections to your talking, Miss Morgan. I don't think it's unfeminine at all."

She shook her head slightly and looked across the restaurant.

"It isn't like me to talk so much. You've cast a spell over me," she finished with a little laugh.

He was looking at her too intently. Then he looked away, suddenly disturbed. He busied himself with the remainder of his meal. Emilie was intrigued. *What had he seen that shadowed his face*? She didn't know it was a look she would see cross the amiable Will Cutler's face on other occasions. *Won't I have a story for Bess in the morning! Maybe I'll phone her when I get home.*

He wiped his mouth and lifted his cup in a mock toast.

"Here's to *my* little autobiography. You'll be disappointed."

"I doubt that."

He cleared his throat. She was surprised. *After his brash confidence all afternoon, he was actually acting nervous*!

She smiled. He brightened and leaned forward. "You have a great smile."

"Thank you," she stumbled.

"Well, all right. I'm 25 years old. I was born in Frankfurt, Germany, the oldest of three children. I have two younger sisters. We moved to the United States when I was eight. My father's brother was already here. He said we could have a better life in the states, so we settled in upstate New York. My father is a printer. When he realized people had trouble with our name, Bodelschwing, he decided to change it. He passed a billboard for Cutler tires one day, and the Bodelschwing family became the Cutler family. When I was 12, my mother got TB so we moved out west. When I was 18, I left home. I decided I'd work my way across the states to New York City. I remembered it as a boy and decided I'd find my fortune there." He stopped and gave a wry smile. "There's a lot of stuff in between that you would find boring—or shocking—so I won't go into that. But I finally made it to New York. I stayed there about a year working odd jobs. A friend said he was coming to D.C., and I got interested and came with him. I thought maybe I'd find the good life here. So, here I am."

Emilie stirred her coffee. "And have you found it?"

"I've been here two years, and yeah, I like it all right."

"And your work?"

He smoothed the table linen, then looked up with a smile.

"Ever heard of *The Mount Vernon Voice*?"

She stopped stirring her coffee. "Are you serious?"

He chuckled. "I guess you've heard of it then."

"Of course! Anyone who lives in Washington knows of the *Voice*. I guess it would be right under the *Post* for the greatest job I could get. Are you a photographer for them?"

"Some of my work makes it in. The old man is pretty picky. Mostly I do odd jobs around the place: a little writing, a little ad patch-up, a little marketing." He shrugged.

"You work for Washington McVinty!"

Clearly she was impressed; clearly Will Cutler was pleased.

"Yeah . . ." He poured himself more coffee.

"It was my father's favorite magazine," Emilie enthused. "He said it contained so much of the spirit of democracy that has been diluted in our day. I even think he sent a few copies to my Uncle Josef in Berlin."

Cutler frowned. "I'm surprised it would make it in past Nazi censors . . . from what I hear."

She sighed. "Is McVinty really a bear to work for?"

Cutler nodded. "He's no slacker and doesn't allow any slackers on the staff. He does most of the writing. If there's a senator or congressman who agrees with him he lets him write a guest piece. He's a tyrant, but I enjoy working for him."

"How in the world did you get a job with him?"

He laughed loudly. Emilie reddened. "I only meant, without much experience or . . . or—"

"Or education?"

"Well, I . . ."

"Luck. I've learned the American truism the hard way: It isn't what you know, it's who you know. I met certain people when I came to town and that was that. I guess the old man kind of liked me."

"I've lived here most of my life, and you . . ." She joined in his laughter.

"What can I say, Miss Morgan? You just need natural charm I guess."

She made a face. "And stout legs, Mr. Cutler."

• • •

"So did he try to kiss you at the door?"

Emilie shook her head laughing. "Bess!"

"He's not a senator or a congressman. Does he look like Gary Cooper?"

"No."

"Then I can't imagine why you're interested in him."

"Bess, when did I say, suggest, or imply that I was interested in him in the way you mean?"

Her friend leaned across the luncheon table. "When did you say, suggest, or imply that you weren't?"

"You are impossible, Bess Bennett. I just met him yesterday."

"And are vastly improved. You're even breathing again."

Emilie looked away a moment.

"Em, I'm sorry. You know what I meant."

"I know . . ."

Bess glanced at her watch. "Five minutes, or Crabtree will have my head." She scanned the crowded diner. "Anyone here look like your Mr. Cutler? I need a mental picture."

"He isn't mine. Bess, I won't tell you anything else if you continue to be so ridiculous."

"Tell me what he looks like, quick."

"Brown hair, slender . . . green eyes, I think."

"Knowing how selective you are, and your description is so boring, he must be ugly. But I'll reserve judgment till I see him. Looks are a lot, but not everything."

"Bess, who said anything about you meeting him? Good grief!"

"Are you saying he didn't make a date with you? He's losing points with me fast."

"You're hopeless, absolutely, criminally hopeless. He did not make another date . . . exactly . . . which is fine with me."

"Why?"

Emilie sighed. "He made me talk too much . . . somehow."

"Ah, he's like a priest. Could be bad, could be good—depending what your penance is."

Emilie threw a napkin across the table. "I don't know what Jerry sees in you!"

Bess tossed her curls and ignored her. "So you blabbed a lot. He probably liked it. . . . though I'm not sure why."

"I think you'd better get your ticket. You're going to be late and I'd side entirely with Crabtree this time."

"What did he say at the door if not a marriage proposal or date?"

"He said, 'see ya'."

Bess's mouth dropped open. "He's in the negative column completely, both feet in the grave! I can't believe it! You mean he takes you out to eat and to a movie and leaves you at the door with 'see ya'? Emilie, were you in an old bathrobe with cold cream and slippers? He's about as romantic as Nick with the toothpick is behind the counter! Worse!"

Emilie was laughing. "I don't think he was trying to be romantic, Bess. Just friendly, harmless, and—"

"Comatose!"

"Quit! He was very nice. He rescued Jasper—that should count for something. Besides, Bess, I'm really not interested in romance right now. I'm interested in getting a job. I need a job. . . . Don't start."

"All right, all right. Any prospects?"

"Everybody seems to be laying off people," Emilie moaned, shaking her head. "I've applied for a few secretary positions, yesterday I tried the Library of Congress. Nothing."

Bess heard the tenor in her friend's voice. She knew the time for flippancy and teasing was over.

"So what do you think you'll do?"

"I don't know. I let Gracie go. . . . I hated to do that. . . ."

"How long can you live on what you have in the bank?" Bess asked gently.

Emilie's face clouded. "Maybe six months if I stretch it. . . . I don't know for sure."

"Then you have time to look and find something."

Emilie nodded, her smile tired. "Time is something I have plenty of right now."

● ● ●

Emilie lay stretched across her bed, listlessly flipping through a recent *Vogue*. When she tired of it, feeling a little guilty for such a waste of time, she turned to the latest issue of *National Geographic*. She propped herself up with Jasper curled up in her lap. *Now here is a magazine that inspires me! Imagine . . . an assignment to Africa or Russia! Taking pictures of such beauty in faraway places . . .* She closed her eyes and heard the hawkers in the markets of Marakesh and felt the sand on her legs as she snapped pictures of the ancient Sphinx. *Getting a job photographing Washington would have been more than enough*, she thought, knowing she loved this city. *It's given me my love of American history. It's an exciting place to live with the ever-changing political climates. Now though, I feel stagnant and useless, a player on the sidelines.*

She had had half a dozen interviews besides the *Post*. They had all gone well, and she was qualified for all of them. But no one was hiring. The democrats and republicans could agree that the economic depression was lessening considerably from a few years earlier, but the effects were still in evidence. She glanced out the window. Rain was coming down in thunderous sheets. She would try again tomorrow. *Perhaps I'll end up as a salesclerk at the Five and Dime, or a waitress at a blue-plate diner.* "And the blue collars will try to pinch, and the white collars will propose, Jasper," she laughed out loud.

Stroking the cat, she suddenly thought of Will Cutler. Though he had stepped out of her life, he had not wandered far from her mind. Four days had passed since he had delivered her to her Georgetown door with a 'see ya.' *Was that just a casual, token goodbye or was it a vague promise? Well, I really shouldn't care* . . . She leaned back, hugging her knees, trying to come to some judgment on why she was distinctly disappointed that he hadn't called. She thought over each moment of their time together. Suddenly she jumped from her bed and hurried down the hall to her father's bedroom. The curtains were open, the bed was made, and everything was in order . . . She had unpacked his suitcase and placed the silver-rimmed glasses on his bedside table. The room looked like it was waiting for the owner to return, take up his slippers, the book, the glasses. She wasn't ready to pack his things or give away his clothes. Not yet. The feel of his ties, and socks, his comb, the smell of his aftershave, was a painful pleasure. She walked to the dresser and picked up the framed picture of her mother smiling and waving for the camera with the Alps in the background. *Mother, how I wish you were here to tell me what to do.* She felt the sting of tears in her eyes. She turned around and went to the table for the stack of magazines there. She was surprised she hadn't thought of this the night she had met Mr. Cutler. She picked up the stack of *Mount Vernon Voice's* and hurried back to her room. Settling back on her bed, she began her search through them, noting the name of Will Cutler in the small staff box, seeing the photos he had taken and the articles he had written. *All are very good.*

The phone jangled beside her, sending Jasper in a flying leap to the floor. She picked it up distractedly, expecting Bess.

"Hello, Emilie, it's Will."

Well, that's very friendly after four days, as if we were chums from way back: "It's Will."

"Will?" she asked cooly.

A short pause. "Will Cutler."

"Oh, hello."

"Did I interrupt something?"

"No. Actually, I was looking through some old issues of the *Voice*."

"Fine taste. How's the job hunt going?"

"Not very well."

"Then you can come with me tomorrow. I have an assignment to take some pictures around the capitol. I thought we could have lunch on the mall or something."

Emilie leaned back, twisting the cord around her finger. Was he asking or telling her?

"Well . . . I don't know. You know, if it's still raining . . ."

"About 10:00?"

She couldn't help but laugh. "I bet you're the kind that was always able to charm your teacher out of that paddling you so richly deserved."

"I was at the top of my class. I'd really like you to come Emilie."

● ● ●

"A lovely day for taking pictures—good light," Emilie said as Will loaded his camera with film. He sat on a bench while Emilie strolled in front of him, looking out over the sparkling Potomac. Hearing the happiness in her voice, he looked up. She wore a white dress trimmed in navy, a little white hat, and her purse and shoes were navy. *Very sharp and out of your league, Cutler*, he told himself. *And very lovely*. He returned to his camera, frowning slightly.

"What's your assignment, Mr. Cutler?" she asked, leaning on the rail.

"McVinty wanted some spring photos for the May issue. He likes to boast how pretty Washington can be in the spring."

"Well, he's right. Springtime in Washington is wonderful. It helps you forgive it for being so stifling in July. My father always said spring is the season of optimism. He forbid gloom at our house. . . ." Her voice trailed off.

Will stood up, aiming his camera at her.

"Very nice."

She swung around. "Please don't take my picture. That isn't what your boss wants."

Will snapped the picture. "He said he wanted the pretty sights of the city," he said as he came up to her.

She frowned and turned away from him, back to the Potomac.

"You'll get too much glare from the water," she said irritably.

"You miss him, don't you?"

She nodded. Will leaned against the rail and let the silence do its work. After a time she turned to him.

"Let's go do the memorials. But no more pictures of me or I'll—"

He's smiling at me and standing too close, she thought.

"I'll take a cab home, you won't get my professional assistance, and your pictures will turn out lousy. Then McVinty will fire you, and hire me!"

He stepped back in alarm. "Such optimism!"

She laughed and put her arm through his. "It's springtime, Mr. Cutler!"

They spent three hours walking slowly, laughing, watching the tourists, taking pictures along the mall and at the memorials. It was a day Emilie Morgan would never forget. She framed certain moments in her mind, and saved them to think over later.

On the mall they stopped for hotdogs from a vendor.

"Have you taken any pictures without me in the background, sir?"

His mouth was full as he shook his head.

"McVinty is going to scold you, Will. He'll say you simply took pictures while you were out on a date! Not very professional."

"He appreciates a pretty girl as much as he does the Washington Memorial, Emilie. Don't fret."

She started laughing. "You've dribbled mustard down your shirt."

He groaned. "Aw . . ."

"Serves you right for taking pictures of an unwilling model. Very ungentlemanly. Let me have your handkerchief."

"I can do it."

"Let me." She was standing close as she blotted the mustard. He could smell her hair and see the dark, glossy highlights. She felt him looking at her. Their eyes met and, for a moment, Emilie thought he might lean forward and kiss her. But it was a fleeting look. She stepped back, handing him the cloth. Her smile returned.

"Here. I wouldn't blow my nose on it though . . . or maybe you should," she said saucily.

She turned and walked away, with him laughing behind her.

At the Lincoln Memorial they were separated by a group of school children and their guide. Emilie listened to the guide and smiled at their questions. She looked up to find Will. She could see he was listening closely. In that frame of time, she thought he looked younger, with the brown hair falling over his forehead and the mustard stain on his shirt. He was not darkly handsome, or strikingly handsome. He was . . . kind and . . . it was his personality that made him pleasant looking. *Like Gary Cooper*, she smiled to herself. *Her . . . own Gary Cooper*. It startled her that she should feel this interest and attraction for this man. This was only their second time together. Across the heads of the children, they looked at each other. She noted he didn't smile. One of the children leaned forward to touch the foot of the monument. She nodded at him with a frown to take a picture. It would be a great picture. He stepped back and aimed.

Then they were alone; the crowd was gone. Will started walking slowly around the inside of the building, reading the walls. His steps sounded hollowly on the floor. Emilie remained at the statue. Sunlight filtered between the columns: warm, quiet, golden. Emilie always felt she had stepped into a special place when she came here. She went out to sit on the sunny steps. It could not have been a more beautiful day! Finally Will came to sit beside her. He looked thoughtful. "Will, have you never been here before?"

He glanced away. "Sure, when I first came. But I didn't . . . really read the walls. I've never seen anything quite like it before." He looked down at the pool which reflected the Washington Monument. "All that scripture and reference to God—it's pretty amazing."

"They're going to put a memorial to Jefferson across the Tidal Basin. I've seen a drawing of it. It should be magnificent. But for me, I don't think anything could top the Lincoln. I've always loved it."

"What's the Tidal Basin?"

She looked at him a moment, then pointed. "The lake there. You see, when it's finished the Capitol, the White House, and three monuments will form a cross. That always impressed Dad."

"It impresses me."

"Can I ask you a very personal question, Mr. Cutler?" Emilie asked smiling.

Will frowned for only a moment, not meeting her gaze. "Sure."

"What is your religious faith?"

He exhaled loudly and she laughed. "I thought it was going to be something really tough. I . . . would say I believe there is a God. I'm just not sure what He has to do with me personally."

"Your family?"

He fidgeted a moment. "Protestant."

She was quiet.

"Well, come on. I told you about me, what about you?"

"Do you really want to know? Or are you just asking?"

"I'm asking because I would like to know."

"We always went to the Episcopal church. When I was a little girl I read the Bible and said my prayers. Then ... I got older and didn't go to church as much, didn't read as much. Then, when I was 18, I was here one evening, rather late and I ..."

She stood up suddenly. "The sun's going. Let's go get some photos by the river again, then go eat."

"Wait. You didn't finish."

She shrugged. "I'll tell you some other time."

He was watching her, seeing she was forcing her cheerfulness. She pulled at the camera case. "Come on."

Later they sat in his car before her house. The gas streetlights of Georgetown were on, giving a quaint flush to the old houses.

"Would you like to come in for coffee?"

If I went in for coffee, I would want to pull her into my arms. That would tempt my restraint, he thought as he shook his head.

"Thanks, but I better be going. I have an early-morning appointment."

She was looking into her lap, feeling slightly rebuffed.

"I'll bet your picture of the little boy in front of Lincoln will be the one McVinty likes best—and I'm not in it."

He smiled. "I'm sure you're right, but the one with you by the Potomac will be my favorite."

"I had a very enjoyable day, thank you."

"Me, too."

She could hear the crickets in the twilight. She looked up at the house. *So dark and empty. Yes, it was just as well Will refused me.* She felt the tears come to her eyes.

"You have come along at a time when I needed ... a new friend. Thank you for taking me out."

He was surprised by her candor for a moment. He didn't know what to say. Then she got out of the car and hurried up the steps.

• • •

"Well, I think we can conclude that he's interested in you."

Emilie lay in bed the next morning talking on the phone with Bess.

"You are used to guys who paw you on the first date. I don't think you can hold Mr. Cutler to the same standard, Bess."

"I guess not. He didn't even attempt a kiss in the car, and he didn't say 'see ya' this time. I don't know if he's regressing or progressing."

But Emilie couldn't share with her friend the looks she and Will had exchanged during the day. There had been something unspoken between them.

"I think he's lonely, Bess, as lonely as I am."

"I need to meet this guy, Emilie. You're too . . . tender right now to be a judge of anything. This guy could be a total cad taking you for the proverbial ride!"

"So he needs to be approved by the sharp eye of Bess Bennett, authority on all things masculine?"

"Exactly."

"Actually, Bess, he's very sensitive and kind. I don't think he could be a cad in disguise."

"Still, I want to meet him."

"I don't know if I'll ever hear from him again."

"You will. If he's lonely and you're lonely, he will want to be lonely together."

Emilie was laughing. "Bess, you are so ridiculous."

"Do you like him?"

She stared into the ceiling. "Well . . . I wouldn't have minded if he had tried to kiss me."

"She likes him. Gary Cooper and Senator Sam have been replaced. Then you're probably uninterested in the want ad I saw in the paper this morning."

Emilie yawned. "I haven't seen it."

"Well, it involves screaming kids, hard-to-please mothers, and a camera . . ."

• • •

"You've been scowling into your coffee cup all morning, Will," Stephen Greenberg said. The two sat alone in the "rescue" office.

Will shrugged. "Just thinking, I guess. I haven't seen my family in awhile."

Stephan nodded and returned to the German newspapers they were translating. But Will couldn't be distracted from his thoughts: *Emilie as they walked along the mall, fresh, happy.* He could see her face plainly in his mind as she had looked up at the Lincoln Memorial, eager and innocent. For a moment he'd been reminded of another girl. . . . *Last night, walking along the Potomac with the air full of the scent of cherry blossoms, when they had stopped. . . .* He shook his head. He couldn't allow this attraction to . . .

The phone rang and soon Stephan was talking excitedly to someone on the other end. He turned to Will.

"New York. Weitzman has been given an appointment with Roosevelt for next Friday. Now the president will hear some truth from Europe. They say we can submit a report to send along with him."

"That's great."

Stephan returned to the table. Will poured himself another cup of coffee. "Have you ever spent much time over at the Lincoln Memorial, Stephan? I mean, have you read everything that's on the walls?"

The older man nodded. "When I first came here. I haven't been over there in probably five years or more. Why?"

Will was scratching his head. "Well, I've never seen anything quite like it. Scripture all over the walls . . ." His voice grew a little excited. "Did you know that the memorials are all laid out in the shape of a cross? It's pretty incredible."

Stephan was watching him with amusement.

"Seeing it for the first time, huh?"

"Yeah, I guess you could say that."

Stephan pulled a file toward him and flipped it open.

"Does this sudden interest have anything to do with the diplomat's daughter?"

Will's hands were jammed in his pockets, the scowl creeping back to his face. "She told me about that stuff."

"So you made contact with her, obviously. How come you haven't given us a report yet?"

"I felt there was nothing significant to report to you. Thomas Morgan died eight weeks ago from a heart attack. So that contact is out."

"So she went for your story? Working for McVinty and all that?"

"Yeah. What's the saying?" Will searched the ceiling, then snapped his fingers. "Hook, line, and sinker."

"Hasn't tripped you up on anything?" Stephan leaned back with pleasure on his face.

Will shook his head.

"Well, Will, I think congratulations are in order. You've done very well. You're a fast learner. No doubt about it, you're an asset to our group. You've brought us information very relevant and current. I'll tell you, Rosenberg is very impressed."

Will relaxed and smiled. "Thanks. Think I might meet him soon?" Rosenberg was the leader of the group in Washington, a respected yet removed figure from the day-to-day operations of the bureau on Fourteenth Street. He formulated policy, contributed heavily, and met with other highly placed Zionist leaders.

"Mr. Morgan was a good lead. We understood he was definitely anti-Nazi. But the daughter may prove valuable to us, too, so keep up the pose." His eyes narrowed a bit. "In cases like this, it can be difficult not to let emotions or passions of the moment interfere with a higher purpose."

Will stood casually, leaning against the table, his face a mask. Stephan looked back to the file, pointing at a black-and-white photo of Emily Morgan and her father. "Quite a looker."

Will shrugged and reached for the Berlin paper. "Not bad."

16
A Journey of Two Hearts

It became the pattern of her days: a day or evening spent with Will, followed by several days of silence. Bess explained that this was the young man's way of keeping Emilie interested.

"A primitive tactic, but often highly effective," she said.

"You make it sound like a tribal mating ritual!" Emilie laughed.

"There are similarities. You should be very chilly to him the next time he calls. Two can play this game. You must show him you're no pushover. Tell him you have a date."

"But I don't!"

Bess's eyebrow arched and her smile was a little wicked.

"I shall arrange it . . ."

But Emilie remained uncertain of Will's feelings. Very interested and complimentary in his tone, he would often suddenly tell her she was pretty. *So he has noticed me beyond my photography skills.* But perhaps the fact that he made no move to touch her or communicate further intimacy meant he wanted a brother-sister relationship. Or perhaps to show himself too interested somehow showed a weakness. Not knowing did not alter the fact that Emilie

Morgan looked forward to his further entrance into her life, no matter how sporadic. Still, her vanity and the ancient courtship strategies did not lay entirely dormant within her.

"Hello, Emilie! Let's meet downtown for lunch."

"Oh, hello, Will. I have other plans for today, sorry."

A pause. "All right. Then how about dinner? We could go to the movies afterward. *Desire* is showing at the Metro, with Marlene Dietrich and—"

"I'm sorry, Will, but dinner won't work either. And I don't like Marlene Dietrich. She's German."

A longer pause. "I'm not sure I have the right number. Is this Emilie Morgan?"

"You know it is!"

"What's the problem then? You sound kind of . . . hostile."

"There is no problem."

"All right. *Desire* has Gary Cooper in it too. Didn't you tell me he was your favorite?"

"I may have."

She did not miss the exasperated sigh on the other end of the line. She smiled to herself.

"So, are you sure tonight won't work?"

"I'm positive. I have a date for tonight."

"Oh . . . How about tomorrow night? . . . Emilie?"

"You mean tomorrow night would be convenient for you, Mr. Cutler?"

"Well, yes."

Emilie counted to 20. "I'll expect you at seven. Goodnight, Mr. Cutler."

He arrived promptly at seven the next night, smiling innocently and friendly on her front step just as he had that first day. She looked from his face to the bouquet of flowers.

"I don't know what I did, Miss Morgan, but am I forgiven?"

She laughed and reached for the flowers. From that day on, through the balmy spring and summer, he called or came by to see her every day.

● ● ●

Will sat alone in the darkened rescue office. It was nearly 11:00, but through the open window poured light and noise from the street below.

He went to sit on the windowsill and watch the traffic and the few pedestrians. A breeze drifted up the corridor of Fourteenth Street, stirring up the nighttime heat. He felt tired and headachy. He knew, however, that there was no point in going to his apartment a few blocks to the east. He couldn't sleep. He looked over the city, picking out the obvious landmarks that he had gotten to know better over the last few weeks. The city was less strange and foreign to him now. He was grateful to her for that. He glanced to his left, toward Georgetown. Was she asleep? Was she lying in bed awake thinking of him? He turned to look at the phone on the table across the room. He could call her, have her voice in his ear in less than a minute. He knew she wouldn't resent it if he woke her. *She'd scold me a little*, he smiled to himself. Then he thought of the meeting that had broken up only an hour ago, and his smile faded.

"Will, I told you when you first made contact with her not to let personal interest get in the way of your work. Your work is with us."

"I know all of that, Stephan. I'm not saying I won't do this. I'm saying I don't like it."

The group waited tensely. Stephan moderated his tone.

"Look, we all understand. She's a pretty girl and you've fallen in love with her and now—"

Will laughed shortly. This group had taken him in when he was a stranger to the city. They hadn't laughed at his awkwardness or naivete. He didn't want to falter in his duty or lose their respect. "I'm not in love with her," he said slowly. "I never said that. She's a nice girl and I have enjoyed going around with her, period. But this plan, I . . ."

They were all watching him. He could feel sweat trickling down his back. "She . . . she trusts me. And it could be dangerous, very dangerous. If the Nazis find what's she's carrying we all know what could happen."

"This is the best opportunity we've had in months to get money and papers into Berlin, Will. We feel with all the visitors, athletes, and international media, the Nazis will be relaxed in their vigil. She should have no problem getting through."

"Will, think of the lives she'll be saving. Those passports can mean the difference between life and death for 40 Jews. And the money can be used for bribes to get others out of Germany," Isaac spoke up.

"We will be risking the life of . . . one young woman for many lives," Will said carefully.

Stephan nodded. "You have condensed it correctly, Will. It is a difficult sacrifice we may all be called to make in the future."

"But she won't even know she's taking the risk! Look, I've spent time with her. I think I can say she would do this willingly if we told her—"

Stephan's hand slammed the table, his voice harsh and impatient. "No! Mr. Cutler, she will not be told. We believe if she were to face the Nazis it would be better for her to face them with real ignorance and innocence than pretended feelings." His eyes narrowed at the young man. "If you cannot do this, we will set it up another way. She's a great plant, the daughter of a German diplomat, returning to her homeland. Someone will approach her to do this photography assignment in Berlin. Unemployed and an offer of a paid trip to Germany, she should be eager for it."

"I don't think she views Germany with much affection right now," Will said wearily.

"Exactly. This discussion may be completely academic," Isaac offered. "She may turn Will...or...whomever down."

"The higher-ups have approved this plan. This could be an excellent moral boost to the Zionist groups if we succeed."

They waited, watching him. He turned to the window. Yes, he had made the contact, but he had not planned for this to happen. He had not planned...He swallowed hard.

"All right....I'll set it up. But to make it real, I need at least a month."

Stephan nodded. "Fine. Just as long as she sails from New York by the end of July. We'll have our people take care of her bags in New York." He stood up and placed his arm around Will. "Don't worry, Will. She'll be fine. She'll never know about this, and you'll remain in her good opinion. When she returns, you can further a romance if you want."

Now, alone in the office, Will felt a wave of revulsion for what he had agreed to do. *They all thought it could go so smoothly: smuggle passports in the lining of a young American's suitcase. A holiday for her. But I know better. Emilie facing a roomful of Nazi interrogators?* He closed eyes against the vision.

• • •

It was another beautiful day. June had escorted the summer of 1936 in with mild breezes and sunshine. The city seemed to radiate a benevolent mood. Emilie was beginning to believe there could only be fair days when she was with Will Cutler. Every outing they had together had been marked by springtime loveliness. They had driven across the Potomac to the national cemetery at Arlington. Situated on a hill, the view was panoramic, and one of the capital city's finest.

They sat in the car for a moment.

"All right, you first," Will demanded.

"Well, my news is that I can't just go out like this anymore. I have an eight to five job now. I'm a working girl."

She expected a smile, but he was frowning.

"A job? When? Where?"

She smoothed her gray linen dress. "All right, it isn't the *Post* or the *Voice* or the Smith. . . ."

He leaned toward her slightly. "You don't have to sound apologetic, Emilie. A job's a job."

"I know that. It isn't exactly what I wanted, but . . . I'm taking portrait photos at Woolworth's. I have every other Saturday off. I'll be making less than I did at the Smith, but it isn't too bad." She shook her head and laughed. "Legs were no qualification!"

He glanced down at her legs, then outside. She watched him, sensing some mood change had suddenly come over him.

"No congratulations, Mr. Cutler?" She touched his arm. "Will?"

"Hmm? Of course I'm happy for you! And I'm sure they noticed your legs."

There he went, throwing in some comment like that, when she least expected it. After these weeks with him, it still made her blush.

"So why have you asked me to bring my camera for a date at Arlington National Cemetery?" she asked.

"You said it was one of your favorite places."

"You have a very good memory—it's almost frightening. Why here?" Finally he turned; his smile had returned.

"McVinty wants a few pictures of Arlington for the Memorial Day issue. He didn't want a file photo, he wants a fresh angle."

"So you want to borrow my camera?"

Will laughed. "No, he wants you to take them."

"Oh, Will, how gullible do you think I am? Why would Washington McVinty want me to take his photos?"

"Because I've told him about you and he's interested. He wants you to take some pictures as a trial."

Her eyes widened and she clutched his arm.

"I would smash a camera over your head if you're teasing me, Will Cutler!"

His smile didn't falter. "I'm not teasing you. I'm serious. Come on, let's get started."

• • •

They wandered among the rows of white crosses without speaking. In a way, Emilie forgot Will was even at her side. Suddenly her mother and father had come into her mind. It was a tranquil afternoon and she was missing them. She took a dozen pictures, while Will strolled, chewing on a blade of grass. He looked everywhere and avoided looking at her. *The sunlight on her hair as it tumbled on her shoulders* ... His mind wandered.

They met in the shade of the mansion.

"Get a shot of it yet?" he asked.

She nodded, looking up into his face.

Now it was his turn to blush. "What?"

"It was very sweet of you to talk to Mr. McVinty about me."

He shrugged and looked away. "I can't promise you he'll use them. Remember, I said he was picky."

"Still, it was very nice."

He glanced down at her. Clearly she was waiting to be kissed.He turned to the mansion. "Quite a place."

She turned to look. "I love Arlington like I do the Lincoln Memorial. I never look at the house, though, without thinking how ironic it was that they turned Lee's front lawn into a Union cemetery. I've never been able to discover if he was honored or outraged."

"Lee?"

She looked at him a little puzzled.

He shrugged again. "I admit I didn't do very well in American History in school. I was pulling girls' braids and drawing pictures."

"This was the home of Robert E. Lee."

"Which president?"

"Oh, Will! Quit playing the fool!"

Will looked a little uncomfortable. "He wasn't a president like Lincoln or Washington?"

Her hands were on her hips. "He was commander of the Confederacy—you know, the war between the states."

He gave her a little bow. "I give myself into your capable hands for the furthering of my education . . . in all respects."

Now it was her turn to blush and turn away.

● ● ●

The Heigh Ho Club was a favorite nightspot of Washington's young men and women. Prohibition had ended three years before, and now the cocktails and liquor flowed freely. Colored lights, quaint tables with little shaded lamps, a large dance floor, and a band that played the best of Goodman, Dorsey, and Miller made this the place to be. Some nights the locals were thrilled to get a fleeting glimpse of a celebrity or politician at one of the few reserved tables.

Will had been a little nervous about coming, though he didn't know why. He had danced very little and was certain it would show. He also knew he was under the microscopic scrutiny of Emilie's best friend, Bess Bennett. The foursome laughed and danced, but all along Will knew he was being sized up. It was confirmed when Bess's date, Jerry, asked Emilie to dance. As she left the table, Emilie smiled at him and rolled her eyes.

"Having a good time, Will?" Bess promptly asked.

"Ja. I mean, yes, of course." He toyed with his glass and looked to the dance floor.

"She's very pretty," Bess stated.

"Very."

Will had almost been startled by Emilie when he had picked her up for the evening. She looked glamorous in her ice-blue dress and pearls. He had never known a girl like this.

"She's very excited about taking pictures for this magazine you work for."

He nodded. "I hope it works out for her."

"Of course she may lose interest in photography altogether by working at Woolworth's. Lots of young men pass through there everyday."

Will smothered a smile.

"Emilie and I have been best friends since we were freshmen at Smith. We've been through a lot together."

"I'm sure you're a very good friend to her and concerned for her happiness," Will said straight-faced.

"Very concerned. With her father's death so recently I just can't bear the thought of her being hurt."

Will took a sip of his drink and gave her a smile.

Bess felt a little thwarted. She drew a deep breath and decided a more direct approach was needed.

"Emilie says your family is in New Mexico. Do you see them much?"

He shook his head.

"Parents can be so . . . funny about the girls their sons take out. Very particular."

"So I've heard."

"Are you a republican or a democrat, Will? Because Em is a strict democrat."

"I'm neither."

"You don't vote?" Bess asked, shocked.

"No. Maybe this year, though."

"Jerry's a big Yankee fan. Who do you favor?"

"The Redskins."

Bess calmly sipped her drink. "The Redskins are football."

He laughed as he stood. "I'm baseball illiterate." He leaned toward her, with a conspiratorial tone. "But I do know about girls." He came up to Jerry and Emilie on the dance floor. Jerry released her with a smile.

Will pulled her close, and her face registered a smile.

"What's that called that I just did?"

"Cutting in."

"I like that, cutting in."

Emilie was laughing.

"You are very dashing tonight, Mr. Cutler."

He spoke into her ear. "I've come to the Heigh Ho and found your mother waiting!"

● ● ●

Bess watched as Emilie cleaned.

"You could help, Bess."

"My concern makes me immobile."

They laughed together.

"Your concern makes you absurd. What are you so concerned about that you gave up precious beauty sleep to drive out to Georgetown for?"

"I did lose sleep last night thinking about your Mr. Cutler."

"Bess, you are perfectly hopeless," Emilie complained as she wagged the brush at her. "First you're worried that he isn't, to quote you, 'moving fast enough,' and now what is it?"

Bess crossed his arms. "He's so charming, he's suspicious!"

"That confirms what I've been saying. You are ridiculous."

"Emilie you are far too innocent and trusting. You really know very little about him. Did you know that he's never voted! Now I ask you why?"

"Well, I'm surprised you didn't ask him."

"Has he kissed you yet?"

"No."

"Em, you like him very much don't you?"

Emilie leaned back on her heels. "Only because I love you, dear Bess, can I tolerate this inquisition. Yes, I like him...very much."

"There's just something about this fellow that isn't quite right. And because I love you, Miss Morgan, I don't want this Will Cutler to hurt you."

Emilie smiled. "And I do not plan to be hurt, Miss Bennett."

New York City

Will Cutler and Stephan Greenberg stood in the farthest row of the arena. Away from the bright lights, they were almost in darkness. Instinctively they had chosen this distant corner to view the proceedings as if, like tentacles, the evil could reach out and grab them. It was not a capacity crowd that had come to Madison Square Garden this humid summer evening. Still hundreds of men were present to hear the speeches and raise their own impassioned voices. Will and Stephan stood unmoving and silent for two hours. Men in uniform had marched solemnly down the center aisle with the red-and-black standards proudly raised. The wild cheering had vibrated in the hall. Stephan glanced at Will and shook his head. The speeches began and were as predictable as they both expected. They left before the meeting ended.

Outside on the sidewalk, under the brightly lit marquee, Stephan drew a deep, cleansing breath.

"I never thought I'd see it. I need a drink."

Will could still hear the blasphemous, shrill oratory. It seemed to echo in his head. How had this happened here? The Nazis had come to America.

● ● ●

It was a drizzly evening as Emilie worked in her kitchen. She felt silly that she was nervous. This was the first time she had cooked for Will, and the first time they had been alone in this house for any real length of time. She fixed the table with the best china and linen. Slender ivory candles gave a graceful light to the table. She stood back and appraised it critically. Was this overdoing it? Too formal? Would it make him nervous? He was due at six—only five minutes away. She had time to change and move the dinner to the den. Cozier there. Would he like that better? Or would he be pleased with the effort she had gone to?

Bess isn't the only ridiculous one," she teased herself. She left the table as it was.

An hour passed and still he had not arrived.

"Have I been stood up, Jasper?"

Then he was at the door, looking terribly tired and . . . boyishly in need of attention.

"Hi."

"Are you all right?"

"Yeah. Sorry I'm late. The train was late."

"Where have you been?"

"New York. McVinty sent me up there to talk to some advertisers." He stood in the hallway, looking into the rooms. She watched him.

"This is nice," he said wearily.

"What?"

He gestured toward the room. "This . . . home."

He looked back at her, feasting on her with his eyes without embarrassment. She stepped back, her voice a little shaky.

"Supper's ready."

It was a quiet meal, without their usual banter. She could see he was troubled.

"Everything's great. You're a good cook, Emilie."

They took their dessert into the den. Emilie brought the candles in. He took a big mouthful of strudel.

"Verdict? I haven't made it for years. It was my mother's recipe, straight from Germany."

"It's very good. As good as my mother's."

Emilie laughed. "Well, then I've received the highest compliment a girl can get."

They sat at opposite ends of the sofa, and he began to relax.

"I'm surprised you made this. I have noticed an anti-German attitude in your conversation. Do you want to tell me what it's about?"

Now Emilie grew pensive. "I don't really have an anti-German thing. I . . . I'm just very disappointed with how someone over there treated my father. I don't know who's responsible, I just know it broke my father. He had given his country the best years of his life and they . . . stabbed him."

She told him all the lawyer had told her. He listened intently. "What did you say the company was called that he worked for at the end?"

"Farber. I think my Uncle Josef—"

"The one who's a doctor in Berlin?"

"Yes. Anyway, I think perhaps I should write to him. Maybe he knows what happened. . . . I'm not really angry at Germany. I'm angry at someone over there." She sighed and shrugged. "I don't know . . . I do have good memories of the years we lived there. "My father didn't want to go back after mother died."

He stretched. "How good is your German?"

She told him he looked tired and needed a haircut and why hadn't McVinty used her photos in the May issue—all in German.

"You sound like a Berliner," he laughed.

"Danke, Herr Cutler."

"Be patient with McVinty. I told you he's eccentric. Besides, he paid you for the photos even if he didn't use them. He said they were good."

"Being paid was fine, but using them would be fulfillment."

As they sat on the floor with a backgammon board between them, he returned to his usual, teasing self. Emilie was soon laughing as he described a few commuters on the train.

"You are trying to distract me, Mr. Cutler. I see your strategy, but it won't work." She studied the board intently. "There! You're on the bar."

When he didn't move, she looked up. He was not even looking at the board. His voice was barely above a whisper.

"I try not to notice how pretty you are, Fraulein Morgan. Tonight...I want to stop trying."

"You are so unexpected, Will." She looked to the board, almost afraid of his intensity. "Saying things that surprise me, showing up at my door . . ."

He reached across the board to capture her hand. She looked up.

"Why do you not want to notice that I'm pretty?" Her voice was husky.

But he could not answer her. He pulled her to him with sudden desperation.

I wonder if Bess will be thrilled or alarmed that the suspicious Mr. Cutler finally kissed me? Emilie wondered later.

● ● ●

Finding courage was not something Will had ever had much difficulty doing. But this was different. He could hardly concentrate on the movie. He felt angry that he couldn't properly enjoy the sensation of having Emilie Morgan leaning into the shelter of his arm. He was tempted to steal a kiss in the darkened theater, when other couples were obviously doing more than eating popcorn or watching the screen. He knew she would be embarrassed if he tried such a thing.

Emilie was animated as they left the theater, entwining her fingers in Will's hand.

"Gary can never do a better film than that. *Mr. Deeds Goes to Town* is now my favorite movie."

"You liked it for the background," Will offered.

"Partly, but Deeds was very charming. . . ."

He looked at her from the corner of his eye. "So you're in love with this guy, huh?"

"Hmm . . ."

"What does that mean?"

They had climbed into Emilie's car. She slid across the seat toward him. "You figure it out."

Even in the darkness, she could tell he was embarrassed.

"Where do you want to go now?"

She was fingering the hair above his ear.

"Doesn't matter . . ."

He cleared his throat nervously. "How 'bout the Lincoln Memorial?"

She laughed. "The hotdog vendors aren't out."

"I have something kind of . . . special to tell you . . . and I'd like a special background."

She straightened up instantly.

They strolled along the moonlit mall, other couples passed silently by them.

"All right, enough suspense. You've brought me to my favorite place in Washington. What do you have to say, Mr. Cutler?"

For a moment she saw a flash of sadness cross his face, but it was soon replaced with his wide smile.

"I will expect a very big kiss for this. I just want you to know that up front."

"Such conceit!"

He took her hands. "Do you know what's happening in Berlin in about four weeks?"

"Berlin, as in Germany?"

He nodded.

"Well . . . no . . . wait! Aren't they holding the Summer Olympic Games there this summer?"

"Well done, Fraulein Morgan."

She gripped his hands. "You're going! McVinty wants you to cover the American team!"

His throat tightened as he shook his head. "Better than that. He wants . . . Emilie Morgan to go to Berlin to cover the games for the *Mount Vernon Voice*."

"Will . . ."

"It's the chance of a lifetime for you, Emilie. A dream assignment."

"But . . . but Will he's never even met me."

"And he doesn't really care to. He liked your work; he saw your portfolio. He's impressed. He gave me the authority to offer you this assignment."

"But why wouldn't he want you to go?"

"He has other things for me here. I don't have a passport and you do. You have family there—your uncle—I don't. You speak fluent German, mine's rusty. He thinks a woman's perspective on the games would be unique. He's impressed that you're the daughter of a diplomat who had the impeccable taste to like the *Voice*. He sees you're a professional photographer and I'm just a hack. Like I've told you, there's no predicting the ways of Washington McVinty."

Emilie felt breathless. "Will, I . . . feel bad for you."

"Don't be silly. I don't care about going to Germany. I'm happy for you."

"I don't know what to say."

"Say you'll go, then move your lips my way."

● ● ●

They sat under the pear tree, tired and dirty, as late afternoon sunshine painted the back garden a soft emerald and gold and the house a mellow wine and cream. In the distance, a muted melody of someone mowing their lawn, a dog barking, and a car honking several streets over moved through the wind. Emilie leaned against the tree trunk with her eyes closed.

"I've always thought this was a beautiful house," Bess sighed. "Every bit as lovely as Dunstan or Blair House. This house is like your folks . . . dependable and dignified."

Emilie smiled.

"Remember when we drank whiskey here the night prohibition was repealed?" Bess laughed.

"I forgot that it was whiskey. I do recall that you were fine the next morning and I was sick for two days. I longed desperately for death."

"You were such a lovely green . . ."

"Such sympathy!"

"I remember when your father planted this tree. Your mother wanted it closer to the house. You told them their arguing was 'mortifying' in front of your friend, and they looked very shocked and stopped immediately."

"I think that was the only time I ever heard them argue. And mother won. They were of that proper German stock that said arguing was very undignified." Emilie laughed. "So, I might disappoint them, since Will and I spar all the time!"

Bess did not reply. Emilie glanced at her.

"Miss Bennett, do you still have an undecided opinion of Will?" Bess did not turn at first, and Emilie was surprised. She had expected a swift judgment.

"Bess?"

"Oh, Em . . ." Bess was crying as she leaned against Emilie's shoulder. "I know you like him, and he's fine. I really am happy for this chance of a lifetime . . . to go to Germany . . . all expenses paid and..and to take your pictures . . . but he is making you go away so far! It's like you're going to the other side of the earth!"

Emilie smiled and squeezed her hand. "I am going to the other side of the earth, Bess, but I'll be back. What a dear friend you are."

Bess blew her nose loudly. "I know, you'll go over there and meet some German lord or prince and become very rich and sophisticated and forget all about your friends back home."

"You've got your countries mixed up, dear, it's barons in Germany. I'm going to take excellent pictures for Mr. McVinty and make him proud he hired me, and nothing more. The men won't impress me because . . . none of them are senators or look like Gary Cooper. I'll tell them I don't find Nazism romantic. I'll be back by the time the leaves are turning in LaFayette Square."

Bess stood up stiffly. "Let's finish entombing the house so we can go eat."

Emilie rose and put her arm around her friend's shoulders.

"My practical Bess returns!"

Two hours later they finished, everything tidy and clean, packed and locked. Bess stood holding Jasper as Emilie slowly drew the shades in the front room. Bess was watching her.

"I guess I really shouldn't worry about you falling for some German baron since there's Will Cutler to come back to."

Emilie perched on the edge of a chair, her face growing thoughtful. "Everything's happened so fast. I'm sailing for Germany in two days . . . I . . . I will miss him. It's as though we were just beginning to have something. I don't know where it will lead, but . . . I wanted to find out. Now I suppose it's just on hold. We'll both wait."

"If it's meant to be then you'll know when you get back. I wish I could go to the station with you in the morning. O' Crewes just won't let me off."

Emilie gathered up her suitcases. "Don't worry about it; I can take a cab. It will be fine."

"Why isn't Mr. Cutler taking you since it is he who—"

"Uh oh . . . it's Mr. Cutler again. We said goodbye last night. He just didn't want to go to the station. I understand."

"Coward," Bess mumbled and Emilie laughed. "Did he give you an appropriate-to-the-situation goodbye kiss?"

"Bess, what will I do without your blunt prying for a month?" But Bess simply stood facing her, hands on her hips, unrelenting.

"He didn't kiss me. He was sort of . . . stiff—cool and brotherly." When she saw Bess roll her eyes, her voice was hurried. "Honestly Bess, I think he just didn't want to show me how much he was going to miss me. Come on, I'm ready to lock up."

They carried Jasper and the bags to Bess's waiting car. Bess stopped, her smile evaporating. "Em, should I also be worried that you're going over there with all those rabid-sounding Nazi types? The newsreel at the Lowell the other night showed these very angry-looking soldiers all over the place."

Emilie lifted her chin. "Worry not, Miss Bennett. Those hard-faced soldiers will be impressed with this German-American photographer who has come to see their splendid Olympic Games. We shall get along beautifully."

"Isn't bratwurst German for baloney?"

● ● ●

It was the first time she'd been to Union Station since the afternoon she had come to pick up her father. There, clutching her purse and camera in the crowd of early-morning commuters, Emilie Morgan felt the tears sting her eyes as a rush of loneliness and anxiety replaced her excitement. Everyone was hurrying past, a current of purpose and energy, saying goodbye or saying hello. She was half-inclined to jump on a bench and shout, "I'm going to Berlin! To the summer games!" She laughed to herself. They would just look at her and shake their heads, and continue on, unimpressed. *Don't spoil the beginning of your great adventure, Emilie Morgan.* She drew a deep breath and pushed her shoulders back.

The New York train was boarding and she headed that way.

"Miss Morgan!"

She turned. Will Cutler was hurrying up to her.

"Herr Cutler . . ."

He came to stand very close, looking down at her.

"Practicing already, huh?"

She nodded. "You said you couldn't come."

"I found a way. I . . ." He cleared his throat and looked away a moment.

"Did you sleep in those clothes? You look terrible."

He searched her eyes. "I came to say, that is, to remind you to, that you should be careful . . . over there. We've both read about the Nazi government. It can be pretty . . . rough."

"A famous German-American photographer is nothing to trifle with. One wrong move and I will plaster their photo on the cover of *Life Magazine!*" she laughed.

He was not smiling as he clutched her arm. "Emilie, I'm serious. We get reports on how ugly they can get. You have to watch what you do and say. You have to take them seriously!"

"All right, all right," she returned a little cooly. She glanced toward the train. "I have to board. Did you come all the way down just to caution me about Nazis?"

He jammed his hands in his pockets. "Well, I repeat what I said last night. I think you're going to do a great job . . . for the *Voice*. I'm proud of you."

She softened. "Thank you, Will."

His eyes lingered on her hair and face.

She reached up and placed her hand against his face. He pulled her into his arms and held her tightly. He seemed to radiate desperation. The porters began their final call. He pushed her back at arm's length, searching her face.

"Thank you for coming to see me off, Will."

He nodded. "I'll be here when you come back."

She waved from the steps of the train. Her smile and eagerness had returned. But to him, she looked very slender and small and young standing there in her trim blue dress. *Too fragile to be heading into Nazi Germany.*

"Goodbye, Will!"

"Auf Wiedersehen, Emilie."

•   •   •

The driver spoke over his shoulder. "Where to?"

Will sat staring into the traffic.

"Hey, the meter's runnin'. Where to?"

"Hmm?"

The driver drew a deep breath. "I said, where to?"

"Oh . . . take me to the Lincoln Memorial, please."

New York City

Emilie hoped this was not an ominous prelude to her voyage and adventure. The porter had been calm and certain.

"We'll find your bags, Miss Morgan, we sure will. The 'Anthem' ain't never lost nobody's bags before, and ain't gonna start now. Probably just been sent to the wrong cabin."

Emilie chewed her lip and looked down the companionway.

"Well, I have my purse which has my passport and my camera, so it could be much worse."

By evening the lost luggage had been found. Emilie smiled and thanked them for their efforts and found everything as neatly as she had packed it. Missing nothing, but added to by 40 precious passports and 1500 German dollars.

17
Homecoming

Chartwall, England, Summer, 1936

The painter at the canvas was applying the final touches to a flaming sunset with vibrant flourishes. He stood up stiffly and stepped back, hands thrust into the pockets of the smock, to admire his work. The long, smoldering cigar was snatched up and clamped between the beefy jaws, as the head wagged in approval. How he loved to surprise his critics. They grudgingly admitted he had talent and several paintings hung in the Royal Academy of Art—landscapes that were depicted in bold, brilliant colors. He loved painting and he loved writing, both were an outlet to his endless current of energy and creativity. He rocked back on his heels in satisfaction—Winston Churchill was very pleased with his efforts this late summer afternoon. When the sound of laughter finally penetrated his artistic nimbus, he laid his brush down. He had not entirely forgotten Clemmie's afternoon tea in the garden. He sighed with reluctance, like a child being pulled away from his world of toys.

He plodded down the garden path to the emerald lawn where a table had been placed under the shade of a huge oak. He paused to watch some young people near the tennis court, romping and laughing. He looked at Clemmie in her lovely gray silk dress, passing the teacups. He looked back to his feet, and smiled. *Not a luckier man in the commonwealth than he*. The women spotted him and he waved, then joined them. His wife came up to him, giving him a quick peck on his cheek.

"Thank you for joining us, Winnie."

She raised an eyebrow and tugged gently on the lapel of his smock to remind him. Sheepishly he pulled off the paint-spattered uniform. He adjusted the blue bow tie and smoothed his white shirt. He gave the guests a nod and smile. Winston was capable of teatime chitchat in an amiable fashion, but it was a light, unsubstantial confection for him. Politics and world events were his real meat and drink. So he listened to Lord and Lady VanDemire with a mild face, inserting his blunt opinions appropriately while his mind raced on other topics.

"...we leave next Friday. We'll stop in Paris for a few days. I won't appear in Berlin in dowdy rags!"

Lord VanDemire stretched and yawned. "Yes, Amanda, your closet is full of nothing but rags. I've spent a small fortune on rags!"

Clemmie Churchill and her guests laughed. Winston spoke abruptly with his mouth full of cream puffs. With the smear of jam on his chin and crumbs down his shirt front, he looked like an overgrown schoolboy bolting his sweets. "Did...you say...Berlin, Amanda?"

Clemmie's smile froze but her voice remained smooth.

"Darling, Amanda's been saying they're going over for the Olympic Games in Berlin. Her cousin Jack is on the equestrian team. Haven't you been listening?"

He licked two pudgy fingers. "Berlin...so, you're off to see the grandest show on the continent! The most illustrious show on earth!"

Lady Churchill and her visitors exchanged strained smiles.

Winston nodded. "Yes, I've read all about the splendid preparations the Nazis are putting into this—quite impressive."

"You aren't one of those who thought Great Britain should boycott the Games are you, Winston?" Lord VanDemire asked, his walrus mustache quivering with shock.

Churchill leaned back, his mood expansive, his eyes snapping. Lord VanDemire could not have put a more pleasing and palatable question to him.

"You know very well I am of the minority, James. It was my counsel that we should not participate in Berlin. And being in the minority, and not having the singularly myopic vision that many of my esteemed fellow countrymen have, my counsel was not adopted. Hence, the fine athletes of Great Britain will participate in the shadow of the swastika. Likely they will return home with glowing accolades for the stunning efforts of Herr Goebbels and Göring and the fuehrer."

Amanda VanDemire's laugh was a nervous twitter.

"Really, Winston, it's only the Olympic Games, not a political rally."

Clemmie Churchill's eyes closed for just a moment. Amanda had handed the pariahlike statesman a feast, a banquet. Churchill's feet plopped to the ground, and his posture became steel straight, his voice, a modulated growl.

"Herr Hitler and his gallery of rogues are using these Olympic Games to divert the attention of the world from the harsher aspects of German life! The ink on the Laws of Nuremberg is hardly dry—not even a year has passed. Do not think the glamor of Berlin is the real Berlin. You'd do better to stay in Paris."

"Winston . . ." his wife soothed. The VanDemire's were looking alarmed. The tales of the eccentric Winston Churchill were being proven true on this quiet English lawn.

Churchill's chin rested on his chest; he looked menacing underneath his brows. "You can dress a sow in a pink tutu and satin slippers and you still have a sow, Amanda. Remember that when you step off the train."

An embarrassed silence settled over the little group. Clemmie sighed. *This was typical. Winston would settle into a gentler tone in a short time.* But he was looking past them to where the young people played. His lips jerked forward in thought. Though his brow was still heavy and thunderous, his voice was slower and softer. Clemmie looked closer. *Winston sounded . . . sad!*

He shook his head. "Herr Hitler is making speeches about peace . . . while he's arming Germany for war."

On Board the Anthem

Emilie had little time for shipboard conversation. She spent most of her time reading the thick folder of notes she had compiled. Will had not told her any particular athletic event Washington McVinty wanted her to photograph, so she would try to cover all of them! She tried to learn the names of all the athletes on the American team, and the prominent ones from other countries. She could usually be found in a white wooden deck chair, her eyes closed, saying, "Jesse Owens, track and field; Lutz Long from Germany . . ." She cleaned her camera at least once a day and rechecked her film. In her notes she also reviewed her knowledge of the Nazi government and the names of all the cabinet: Goebbels, Heydrich, Göring, Hess, Himmler. . . . She walked the decks thinking over her memories of Germany, sorting what she had experienced as a young girl from everything her parents had told her.

They were passing through the channel with the white cliffs of Dover on the port side. They were clean, stark white, and sharply defined by the blue waters and soft-blue skyline. She closed her eyes and breathed deeply of the tangy air. The breeze ruffled back her shoulder-length hair as she reviewed the travel plans: *France, then Belgium, then western Germany from the seat of a train*! She was excited at the prospect of seeing so many different sights even before she arrived in the capital of Germany for her assignment. *This life of a traveling photographer just might become a narcotic*, she reflected. The little house in Georgetown might stay closed up longer than she originally planned. *Bess would protest loudly*, she smiled, *and say, "I told you . . ."*

She pulled out her camera and took a picture of the cliffs. Then she walked around the ship. *Going back to Germany . . . Mom and Dad would be very pleased*. They had loved their homeland, though they had not lived there for much of their adult lives. Emilie knew they had wanted her to love it, perhaps through an umbilical-like connection. She viewed her life in Germany as a distant, largely irrelevant part of her personal history. *Isn't my future in Washington? I know the styles, the slang, the American perspective. Germany won't be as foreign to me as it would be to Bess Bennett, but it's still an unknown equation*. She thought through all of this as she walked. She also thought of her Uncle Josef whom she had not seen in over three years. He had written her, of course, with sympathy for his brother's death months ago. Tacked on the end of his letter was a concern for her future and a vague invitation to come to Germany someday.

"I am coming, Uncle Josef," she smiled. "And you will be so surprised to find me on your doorstep!"

The last evening on board she retired to her cabin early. She stretched out on her bunk and let the motion of the ship lull her into relaxed reflection. Glancing at her leather camera bag, she thought of Will Cutler. She thought of him every day since they'd said goodbye at Union Station less than a week ago. She began a slow mind's journey of their relationship: every time they had spent together, their conversations, their kisses.... She thought of the day they had taken pictures along the mall, Will with mustard down his shirt and a sudden shared intimacy.... She had asked him about his faith, but she had stopped when he pressed her about hers. Though she trusted him, she couldn't share it with him. She couldn't tell him about that evening at the Lincoln Memorial when she was 14. She had never told anyone. Funny she should think of it now, again. An experience over 10 years ago but still vivid when she demanded it from her memory, and yet still a mystery in its meaning.

She rolled over and turned out her light, returning to thoughts of Will to quench her nervousness of landing in France the next day. She soon fell asleep. After several hours, she awoke abruptly. Switching on the light, she saw with disgust that it was only 2 a.m. She turned off the light and lay back down in the darkness, wondering what had wakened her. *A dream? A sound? No... just a very clear thought: I'll learn the answer to what I experienced that evening years ago... in Berlin.*

● ● ●

In less than six hours the Anthem would be steaming into the port of Calais, France. Emilie Morgan, standing at the rail of the promenade deck, reviewed her travel itinerary in her mind. Disembark at Calais, take the train to Brussels, Belgium. Change trains there. On to Essen, Germany. Change trains at Hanover, on to Berlin. She pulled out the little leather book, consulted it, pleased that she had memorized it perfectly. She smiled, *If only the rest of the trip would go so smoothly.* But she suspected it wouldn't. She had spent some time on the voyage brushing up on her French. Even though she would only be passing through the country by train, she wanted to be prepared. Then there was the matter of foreign currency and keeping up with her luggage.... She watched the parallel landscapes as they moved up the English channel, eagerly and nervously. Her life had changed so dramatically in the last few months....

Berlin

The meeting had begun at 9 a.m. and now, just after two in the morning, it was drawing to a close. Of the seven men gathered at the Chancellery, only Adolf Hitler looked alert and energetic. The others were tired and sagging, their voices subdued. Not one among them would suggest the meeting adjourn until the next day. The long meeting confirmed what they all had known for a long time: Adolf Hitler was a tireless, sacrificing leader imbued with supernatural resilience.

"I am very pleased with all of the preparations we have discussed today. These Olympic Games will be the most spectacular and lavish of this century! Germany will be long remembered for hosting this event with unparalled glory. We were dishonored when we were barred from the games of 1920 and '24. This will restore our honor!" His chest seemed to swell and his eyes were glassy. "Not one nation has boycotted like they threatened, not one!"

"Even the Jew-lover Roosevelt was not able to persuade his country to withdraw," Goebbels laughed. The others joined him in weary imitation.

Hitler gave them a rare smile. "Ja, he is an impotent, crippled old man. . . . Now, that brings us back to the discussion we had earlier. I have listened to all of you carefully and have reached this conclusion: Not only will we display Berlin in all its magnificence, we will remove the signs concerning the Jewish vermin from all of Berlin and the surrounding countryside." He leaned forward. "Every single Juden unerwuenscht. Find a warehouse and have them stored. They will be brought back out after the last journalist and visitor has left Berlin."

A sinister and arrogant sound of laughter greeted this proclamation.

"No beer hall or park or restaurant or shop. The train stations must be especially clean. All of the road signs. None of these anywhere." He held up a neat white sign with bold, black lettering: Jews not welcome.

They all nodded in unison.

"Return the Jew books to the shelves, take the papers off the street corners," Hitler sneered.

"Let the Jewish swine think they have a little holiday," Heydrich added with a cold, reptilian smile.

"Ja, ja," Hitler agreed eagerly. "You are all responsible to see these signs are removed. We want all our visitors to feel welcome, to be impressed.

They should understand we, of all European people, are the most reasonable!"

The room erupted in laughter.

The Farber Estate

He walked across the grounds silently, his hands behind his back, head up, posture very correct. A terrier trotted at his master's side, equally observant and proud. While the man did not wear an officer's uniform or an SS uniform, his bearing was proper and radiated authority. Heinz Mueller, who walked beside him, could not help but think of Irwin Farber and the first I.E. Farber. They always walked in this commanding way. The old gardener was surprised and disappointed; he had never expected such a change in the youngest Farber son. He had to admit though, this youngest son had not changed in his pleasant tone to him. He was relieved of that.

"Everything looks impeccable, Heinz. You've managed the new staff very well."

"Danke, Herr Max."

"We'll be expecting our guests to arrive in 10 short days. I'll be out from Berlin two days before, for final preparations."

"Yes, sir. It is good to have the house opened and enjoyed again."

"I agree with you completely, Heinz."

The young man turned and headed for the house. The old gardener lingered, watching the tall, straight form. *Ja, it was good to have the house open. . . .* But he had not expected it to be open to this. Even Marta was nervous. He shook his head and returned to his work.

Max gave the inside of the house the same circuit of inspection he had done outside. Percy remained in his own precise reviewing position. Rudi Schmidtt, new head of the Farber house staff, was at his employer's side. Max looked in every room. Schmidtt then lined up the staff of maids, butlers, and kitchen workers in the long, front hall.

"As I just told Heinz outside, everything looks perfect. I am very pleased. As you know, we will have a houseful of guests after the ceremonial opening of the Games. There will be no distinction in the Farber house—every guest is important and will be treated with the utmost courtesy." His chin went higher. "We all want this time to bring honor to the great Third Reich, and I expect you to do your part." Then he smiled. "You're doing a great job, keep up the good work."

One of the new maids, a young woman at the end of the line, gazed timidly at Herr Farber. So tall and blonde and handsome, and that smile . . . she suddenly felt lightheaded.

Max turned and entered the library. Rudi followed him, carefully closing the door. Max went to the deep leather chair and sat down. Percy jumped to a window seat, as if waiting for another assignment. Rudi stood casually, eyeing his friend.

"Max, I'm glad everything meets your approval. . . . You know how grateful I am to you for giving Magda and I this position."

Max smiled. "It was a purely selfish decision, Rudi. I'm guaranteed great meals from the best chef in Berlin."

But they both knew the real reason he was here. The Gestapo had "visited" their establishment only hours after Max had sent an unmarked van to collect them.

Rudi Schmidtt was a man as tall and broad as his employer, only dark and swarthy where Max was blond and fair.

"I hardly imagined that day you showed up to captain the rowing team you would someday become my rescuer," Rudi smiled. "The children are happy here. I can't thank you enough, Max."

"You and your family will be welcome here as long as you want. Heinz and Marta are getting older—they needed you and Magda to help out. When times change you will be free to return to the city to provide Berlin with fine food—if you wish."

Rudi looked away a moment, emotion making it hard for him to speak. "Max, everything is going smoothly with the preparations for the weekend, but I have to tell you . . . Magda is a little nervous."

"Why, Rudi?"

"You have half the Nazi cabinet on the guest list!"

"Only Heydrich and Goebbels have accepted." Max drew a figure on the desk. "I refrained from inviting the fuehrer. It won't be easy for me, either, Rudi, but Magda shouldn't worry. She's going to have to get used to Nazi guests in this house."

"I know, Max, I know. . . . It's just hard. These kind of men were hunting us, and now we'll be under their noses."

Max leaned forward. "Rudi, I have to give this party. I need the prestige it will garner me."

"I understand that, Max," he said tiredly. "Magda will just have to trust us."

"You haven't told her?" Max asked quickly.

"No, no. She thinks like the rest of the staff, that you are a good-hearted Nazi, a little on the absent-minded side."

"Good. How many are on staff now?"

"Including the grounds staff, 24."

"Does the staff know that Magda and the Muellers are Jewish?"

Rudi shook his head. "I don't think so. I've had a long talk with Heinz about it. He's angry and proud, but he understands."

Max nodded. "He's served the Farber family for over 40 years."

"Max, if something slipped, if someone said something...you know, and someone like Reinhard Heydrich demanded to know why you have Jews on your staff...like our old soccer coach used to tell us, we must be prepared for the plays we did not prepare for."

Max looked away. "I am prepared, Rudi. If that happens, I will be very surprised...and indifferent. You will be required to be the same."

Again, because of the long hours they had spent talking all of this over, they understood each other perfectly.

"You can trust me, Max," Rudi said, pausing at the door. "I offer you this advice though. Stop smiling at young Mary Ghent. Everytime you do, she almost faints."

Max motioned him away with a tired smile. Percy laid his head in Max's lap, looking up with sympathetic eyes.

"So, we put our hand to the plow, Sir Blackney." He looked out the window, "and we will not turn back."

Alexanderplatz Station, Berlin
July 29, 1936

Josef Morgan hated to be in a hurry. It went against some inner timeclock that had directed him all his life in a predictable, pragmatic speed. But this rainy summer morning he really didn't want to miss his train to Geneva.

"Almost there," Max said from the wheel.

"I can imagine they're upset over at the Propaganda Ministry with this rain," Josef chuckled. "Berlin could hardly present an impressive face if the Games are soggy!"

"And I know you'd be deeply grieved if that happens," Max laughed.

Josef shrugged and looked through his wallet. He avoided discussions with Max over Nazi matters. It had subtly changed their relationship over the past six months and had come between them, though Josef loved Max as a son as he always had. Max, in turn, could find no man to respect as much as he did the old doctor. And because of that deep affection and respect, Max dare not tell him the truth. Only Rudi could know—even in these early years of Nazi rule, when terror was gloved and veiled, Max instinctively understood the importance of a small, tight circle of confidence.

"Of course I'd be sorry for you if it rained on your gathering next weekend, after all you've put in to it," Josef added.

"Everything does look pretty nice. We have huge tents for the lawn, quartets, and all of that. Found out yesterday that the Lindberg's are going to come."

"As in Charles Lindberg?" Josef asked with obvious surprise.

Max nodded. "Charlie and his wife, Anne. They're touring Europe and are coming here for the Games. Göring is hosting them."

Josef glanced out the window, freshly grateful he was going to be out of the capital city for nearly a month.

"You'll be missing some sights Josef, like nothing your medical convention could possibly provide! Great entertainment!"

"Yes Max, I'll be missing a month long case of indigestion, too." Max leaned back and laughed heartily.

Alexanderplatz Station
August 1, 1936

Morgan would have been perversely pleased. The rain showers had dissipated, but bequeathed a lead-colored sky over Berlin. The humidity soared. Men and women looked moist and wilted even in their finest clothes. Undoubtedly the lords in the Chancellery were frustrated with this untimely revolt of nature. Yet the international crowds came, each Berlin train station disgorging hundreds of wide-eyed athletes and coaches, spectators, and a small legion of reporters and photographers. Hotels were full and restaurant lines snaked to the street. The capital city merchants were gloating—and exalting Adolf Hitler.

When the two o'clock train from Hanover pulled into Alexander-platz with rusty wheezing, the platforms were soon thronged. The bright posters of the Olympic rings and huge welcome signs greeted the weary travelers. One young woman, clutching a bulky leather case in one hand and purse in the other, started down the platform looking surprisingly refreshed and unwrinkled. She was making swift and careful observations of the terminal, the prominent signs, the surge of excited visitors around her. She paused just inside and drew a deep breath. Across an ocean and a slice of France and Belgium, into Germany, with her wits, her money, her camera, the *Mount Vernon Voice* photographer had arrived. Emilie Morgan had returned to her homeland.

Four young men stood in various points around the terminal building, and another roamed the platform, searching faces. They had been at this position for two days, in shifts, at the arrival of each train. It was an intensely boring—and important duty. One of them, smoking continually and leaning casually against a marble pillar, saw her first. Instantly alert and inwardly boasting, he knew he would win the money they had pooled together. He quickly consulted the photograph he had carried in his pocket for the past ten days. *Looked close* . . . He sauntered up to her. "Hello, fraulein, welcome to Berlin!"

She was surprised. She had not expected to be greeted in English. "Hello. Thank you . . ." Her tone was cautious.

Bess had told her to be wary of strangers!

"Bess, as soon as I leave Union Station, everyone will be a stranger!"

Her bright eyes squinted knowingly. "But some will be stranger than others. . . ."

Emilie gripped her purse and camera bag tighter.

"Your luggage will be there," he said, pointing down a corridor. "Of course, there will be some delay as the Nazis must go through it. Have a pleasant stay in Berlin, fraulein."

Unconsciously he had fallen back into his German tongue.

"Danke."

He tipped his hat and slipped into the crowd.

Emilie immediately dismissed the incident as she hurried to find her bags. The corridor led to a large, crowded, noisy room. An SS officer stopped her at the door. He looked at her with a tight, obligatory smile and spoke in clipped German.

"Your papers, fraulein."

She produced her passport and papers. He scanned them in a bored fashion. His eyebrows suddenly vaulted upward.

"Ah, you are a photographer! For the Games!"

He was beaming and confidential, now.

"Ja, I am a photographer."

"From America!"

"Ja."

Heads were turning in the line in front of her.

"We have reserved a special room for our foreign correspondent guests. We want them to pass through our inspection points as quickly as possible. Please follow me. Allow me to carry your bag, it looks heavy." His eyes swept over her with a smile.

Before she could protest, he had taken it and was leading her down another hallway. They entered a room not nearly as crowded as the first. A long table ran the length, behind which stood four men wearing the black SS uniforms. They were inspecting luggage. In front of them, a row of wooden chairs paralleled the table. No standing in a long line here. The chairs were filled by other reporters. Emilie stood straighter. She was in a room of her colleagues! Her nervousness returned. Only one chair remained; she took it, perched on the edge, and watched for her baggage.

"Can I get you a cup of tea or coffee, fraulein?" Her Nazi guide asked, pointing to a table in the corner.

She could feel the eyes of the other journalists turn in her direction. She could imagine their thoughts, *Preferential treatment.* She could hear whispers and caught the word "broad" and "young." She felt herself color. Her voice was cool. "Nein, danke."

Emilie could see her guide's boast had been an empty one. The Nazis were maddeningly slow in their inspection of luggage. An hour passed slowly in the stuffy room. She was horrified to see they examined each personal article thoroughly. She leaned forward slightly—there were no other women in the room. Her undergarments were going to be pawed over and viewed by a roomful of men.

She leaned toward the man beside her, hoping he spoke German or English. "What are they looking for?"

He did not bother to turn. His heavy French accent was filled with disgust. "They are Nazis, mademoiselle."

She expected more, but he had retreated to his own absorbed waiting.

"They are Nazis," suddenly Emilie felt like laughing. Forty minutes later, with other correspondents arriving behind her, she saw them bring out her two suitcases. At first she was not sure they were hers. Her cases had been neatly closed and locked when she had last seen them on the Hanover train. Now, one of them looked a bit battered—and a length of white strap was hanging out of the crack.

Emilie jumped from her chair and hurried to the table.

"What has happened to my luggage?" she blurted.

The men behind the table glanced at each other with ill concealed amusement. One of them consulted a clipboard.

"Fraulein Emilie Morgan, I presume?"

"Ja."

His hawkish face bent closer to the board.

"From Washington D.C., United States of America. Photographer to the . . ."

"*Mount Vernon Voice*."

"Ja, ja . . ."

"Look at my suitcase! What happened?" she demanded again.

The room was noticeably still and silent. One of the officers pushed open the lid; the lock was broken. Emilie gasped. Her clothes were a tumbled mess. The men at the table exchanged a look, the reporters in the chairs behind her leaned forward.

Her voice was tight. "I saw my suitcases when they were taken off the train and carted into this building. They were locked and undamaged. Now they come out looking like this!" She searched through her things, feeling their eyes and their smirking smiles as she came to her lingerie. "Why has this been done?" Her tone did not match any inner bravery.

"Fraulein Morgan, we have not gone through your luggage. This is the first inspection we have made. Now, if you will kindly let us do our work, you may catch a taxi to your hotel and begin enjoying Berlin."

"Your . . . people have been the only ones who have handled my luggage. Look, look at the lining! It's in shreds!"

"Unfortunate. Now." He motioned for his men to begin their search. Emilie was thoroughly disgusted. She watched them rifle through her garments. They opened her cosmetic bag.

"Do you suppose you could tell me what it is you are looking for with this ... ravaging?"

She heard a short laugh behind her, but the Nazis were not smiling. She felt a presence at her elbow, looked around and saw a tall, unsmiling man. He wore a midnight-black uniform, trimmed in silver braid with a red, black, and white arm band. Knee-high, mirror-shiny black boots and a black peaked cap completed his uniform. She quickly searched through her mental notes on the Nazi government. *Which police agency was this*? Her knowledge was sketchy. *Gestapo*? From the corner of her eye, she could see the four men behind the table stiffen.

"What is the meaning of this delay?" he asked coldly.

Before Emilie could speak, the man behind the table spoke up.

"Fraulein Morgan's luggage was damaged on the train. She is upset."

The Gestapo agent ran a cold eye over Emilie. Her hot words died in her mouth. "Are any of your personal belongings damaged or gone, fraulein?"

At that moment, one of the younger SS men held up a slip. The Gestapo officer snatched it from his hand.

"Fraulein?"

"I ... don't think so. Only the suitcase—the lining is ripped. Someone went through my things."

"Perhaps the locks broke when the bag was transferred from the train," the Nazi behind the table spoke up calmly. "The contents fell out. The baggage handlers did not take the time to properly fold your things."

"And perhaps their pocket knife just ripped the lining," Emilie stated with equal calm.

"May I see your papers, bitte?" the Gestapo man asked curtly.

She sighed as she presented them. Less than one day in Germany and she'd already shown these papers a dozen times.

He snapped them up and drew out his own notebook. He swiftly wrote something down on his pad, then turned to Emilie with a frosty smile.

"We apologize for this damage and that your belongings suffered in the reich. Please present this receipt at this address and you will receive reimbursement."

"Danke."

He handed her another paper. "All journalists and photographers are to appear at the Propaganda Ministry on the Wilhelmstrasse tomorrow at 9 a.m. sharp for a meeting with Herr Goebbels. He will help to make your stay during the Games even more pleasant."

Someone behind her snorted. She took the paper and nodded. He clicked his heels in proper Prussian fashion, and glanced to the waiting correspondents and the Nazis at the table.

"Proceed at a faster pace. We should not keep our guests waiting."

"Ja, sir."

The man left. By now the other Nazis had finished with one case. Emilie could see the Nazi leader was irritated. His tone was brusque as he motioned and called for another reporter to come to the table. Before closing her damaged case, he held up a thick book: *Gone With the Wind*.

"American decadence," he murmured and tossed it back in the case.

His pale-blue eyes met Emilie's. "Heil, Hitler, Fraulein Morgan. Enjoy your stay in Berlin."

● ● ●

Out of the terminal, Emilie took a long look at the city skyline. The sun was coming out in soft, warm, brilliance, the clouds dissolving. Closer at hand, sleek taxis waited at the curb in an efficient line. With her battered luggage piled around her, her hat a little askew, Emilie knew she looked less than impressive and professional.

She whispered to herself. "Well, we survived that little squabble Bess—now, Berlin!" Taking a deep breath, she was ready to move on—exhibiting the priceless blending of German persistence and American optimism that was her heritage. She eagerly hailed a cab and was soon settling into the seat with a contented sigh.

"Where to, fraulein?" the driver asked cheerfully.

She gave him the address while pulling off her hat and running her fingers through her hair. Her excitement returned. She was going to see her uncle!

The office of Dr. Josef Morgan on Friedrichstrasse was as his niece expected. A small, brick-front building tucked between a shoe shop and green grocer. She smiled. It was as unpretentious as her uncle. Green lettering edged in gold adorned the plate-glass window: Dr. Josef Morgan.

She leaned over the seat to the cabman. "I'll have to see if he's here first. I don't want to take my luggage out, and you can see it's been a bit damaged. Would you mind waiting?"

"I'll wait," he grumbled, pushing a greasy-looking cloth cap over his forehead.

The door swung open ringing a shopkeeper's bell. She quickly took in the small waiting room: plain, well-worn chairs, a desk, a lamp, two framed medical decrees, and an oil painting of a placid sea. It was quiet, empty, and smelled quite properly of antiseptic. She stood a moment looking at a smiling picture of her uncle and another man on skis. Then she heard a muffled laugh and the dark green curtain that hung before a doorway parted. A young woman in nurse's whites emerged, adjusting a wayward lock of blonde hair.

"Guten Tag."

"Guten Tag," Emilie returned.

"May I help you?"

"Ja. I'd like to see Dr. Morgan if he isn't with a patient."

The nurse opened her mouth to speak, but the curtain parted again. This time it was a man. He was adjusting a loosened tie and straightening his hair. The three exchanged quick glances. He was tall and strongly built, tanned, blue eyes set in a squarish face, thick blond hair. Emilie immediately thought of Bess. She always had a word at her command to describe a man like this: *knockout*. Emilie felt the full strength of the roguish look he gave her.

Max had been in a silly, flippant mood for several days. He had come to Josef's office to pick up the mail and found Helga in a playful mood herself. They had been kissing in the back room when he'd heard German words spoken in a soft woman's voice in the waiting room. He'd become instantly curious.

He was startled—she looked vaguely familiar as he did a quick inventory. *She's pretty: deep-auburn wavy hair, a heart-shaped face, blue eyes, very dark lashes. Yes, very dark and long. Full, coral lips. Average height. She's wearing a tan suit and cream-colored blouse*. A quick look, nonchalant of course, told Max she had legs she need never complain about. *Young and very pretty*. He smiled.

"Is Dr. Morgan in?" Emilie asked, ignoring his inspection, looking to the nurse.

"I'm Dr. Morgan," Max spoke up cheerfully, extending his hand.

Helga, the nurse, cleared her throat loudly.

"You are Dr. Morgan?" Emilie gave a puzzled look at her little notebook in her hand.

The phone suddenly rang shrilly in another room. The nurse gave Max a frown and disappeared through the curtain.

"Ja. Now . . ." He walked to the desk and flipped open the appointment calendar. "You have an appointment . . . is it frau or fraulein?"

Oh, he's smooth, thought Emilie with an inward smile. She would be as absurd as he.

"It is fraulein. I don't have an appointment. I was merely hoping you could see me. I've been told you are . . . very sympathetic."

He gave her a slight bow.

"Please sit down."

"Danke." She smoothed her skirt, still feeling his eyes. "You don't remember me, Dr. Morgan? We met some years ago."

The disarming smile did not falter.

"No, I'm sorry I don't remember—though that is very strange for me since I remember pretty women with . . . professional thoroughness."

"Professional thoroughness . . ." Emilie repeated softly.

"Now, please tell me how I can help you, fraulein."

"Just Emilie if you please."

"Of course."

Max was enjoying himself hugely. He drew a pad of paper before him. "Now . . ."

"Well, you see, I was diagnosed with . . . lumbago six months ago. In the last few weeks I've . . . felt . . . my condition deteriorate. My own doctor is away and I hoped . . . I did hope . . ."

Tears seemed to be forming in the blue eyes. Max grew instantly uneasy.

"I hoped you could give me something for this terrible pain," she continued softly, "morphine or something. . . . Please help me, Dr. Morgan, please!"

Emilie bent over, shaking with sobs. Max was horrified.

"Oh! . . . please . . . now, there, there . . . I . . . Fraulein Emilie, I . . ." He patted her hand awkwardly.

Suddenly Emilie went limp against the desk. Max stood up.

The nurse entered. "Max! What has happened? Oh, you idiot with your games! She's fainted!" The nurse bent over her.

Emilie sat up, laughing.

Max was wiping his forehead. "You!" he gasped. "You were acting!"

"Ja ... Dr. Morgan."

"Well, you see, I ... I ... ."

"Well, Max?" Helga was laughing now, too.

"I don't scare easily, fraulein, but you have shaken me." He slumped back to the chair. "I am not Dr. Morgan."

"I know that."

"You know?"

"I'm Emilie Morgan," she smiled, "Dr. Josef Morgan is my uncle."

18
Let the Games Begin...

The cafes and tea shops along the pretty, tree-lined Unter den Linden were crowded at the social hour of four o'clock. Government workers were done for the day, and added to the already swelling crowds of visitors. A holiday feeling was in the air contrasting with the typical somber, pragmatic Berlin. The skies were a beautiful vault of cloudless blue, the temperature was mild. The newspapers declared this was "true Adolf Hitler weather." The world had come into the courtyard of the emerging Third Reich. They would see athletic prowess and competition, and they would leave admitting Nazism had replaced the dour-faced Germany of the 1920s.

Knowing the cafes would be crowded and feeling no impulse to impress the pretty young American, Max Farber took Emilie Morgan to one of his favorite shops on a lesser-known Berlin street. They were seated at a small black, marble table. The waitress, knowing the blond man on sight, brought fragile cups of steamy chocolate and a plate of sugar-dusted pastry.

Max gave a depreciating shrug and smile. "Your uncle hasn't been able to convince me that sweets are such a terror to one's digestion."

Max had smoothly adjusted after the shock Josef Morgan's niece had given him.

Emilie, however, had not recovered from the disappointment of finding her uncle out of Germany. Suddenly she felt very tired. *I need a bath and a long sleep*, she thought as she stared into her cup of chocolate.

"I'm very sorry you missed Josef by one day. I'm sure you're disappointed," Max offered.

The gentleness of his voice pulled her eyes up to see him. *Uncle Josef's best friend, Max Farber. The man in the ski picture . . . one of the richest men in Germany. What else has he told or written to me about him over the years?* She didn't have much to draw from.

"Thank you." She drew a weary breath. "I am a little disappointed. I wanted to surprise him."

"Well, I can assure you, you would have done that. We could send him a telegram—I know where he's staying in Geneva."

Emilie frowned into her cup. "Well . . ."

"Come on, try your chocolate. It will lift your spirits."

She smiled. "I have to think . . . I mean, whether to contact him or not. I hate to take him away from his convention; it's probably like a vacation to him."

Max chuckled. "More than you know."

Emilie looked at him a little puzzled.

Max leaned back. "Let's just say Josef is not caught up in the fever of these Olympic Games which has gripped our city. He has no interest in them."

"Really? That surprises me."

"The Games themselves are all right—we went to a few days of the Winter Games last year in fact. But he doesn't care for the . . . way they are being promoted."

"And how are they being promoted, Herr Farber? I've only been here a few hours, remember. I'd very much like to know what my uncle thinks."

"Our leaders have used this opportunity to display the glories of the Third reich as much as an arena for sports competition."

"And Uncle Josef objected to that?"

Max smiled. "His words were 'vulgar and insincere.'"

Emilie stirred her chocolate. She had noticed the gold enameled swastika against the collar of his cream-colored shirt.

"And you? What do you think? I'd be interested in another Berliner's opinion."

"You are only a photographer?" he asked.

Emilie laughed. "Nothing you say will be put in print."

"Well, I think there is nothing wrong with the perspective the government has taken. It has helped the economy of Berlin. It has given the citizens a dose of excitement. To borrow a journalist's phrase, I think Germany has gotten some 'bad press' in the international community lately. I think the government wants to change that. I see no harm in that."

Emilie had begun to relax. "By 'bad press,' you mean the Nuremberg Laws and the occupation of Rhineland?"

Very pretty, and not brainless. Max gave a slight nod and sipped his chocolate.

"Now, may I put a question to you, Fraulein Morgan?"

She nodded in return.

"I would be interested in a German-American's opinion of the Third Reich."

"I admit I don't have much of an opinion. My father followed events in Germany, and he didn't care for Hitler's rise to power. But, after a time, we hardly talked about it."

"You have my condolences on your father's death. Josef told me many times what a great man his younger brother was."

Emilie's eyes suddenly filled. She looked away and was relieved he understood and was quiet.

Finally she turned back to him. "Despite my first run-in with Nazi officials at the train station, I have no opinion," she restated. "I've come to form my opinions."

"I see . . ." He selected a large pastry. "Your run-in at the train station?"

"Oh, they went through my suitcases a little roughly. The locks were broken and the lining was cut. Nothing was damaged or stolen. They were rather humorless," she shrugged.

"Humorless . . ." he repeated.

"Are you a Nazi member, Herr Farber?"

"Ja."

"And my uncle?"

"Nein."

Emilie finished her drink. "Well, I suppose I should go to my uncle's place. Tomorrow will be a big day! Could you take me there?"

"That would be convenient—your uncle lives with me."

"You? I thought he lived near his clinic?"

"He did until a few years ago. We thought it was better for him to live with me on Tiergartenstrasse. Two old bachelors and Percy."

"Percy?"

"My canine companion."

Emilie took her time to speak. "Well, I would be grateful if you could take me to a hotel, since my uncle is out of town."

Max had leaned back. "Hotel rooms have been booked for six months. Is there some reason you won't consider staying at your uncle's house?"

Emilie blushed. He knew very well what the problem was—he just wanted her to verbalize it. Bess rose up in her mind. *Would Bess be shocked or...* One swift glance at the handsome German, and Emilie knew exactly what Bess Bennett would advise. Emilie smiled.

"There is no reason why I shouldn't stay there. I'm sure my uncle would want me to. Danke."

● ● ●

Early evening had not thinned the crowded streets. Max drove the Mercedes slowly to his house across from Tiergarten.

"How much do you remember about Berlin?" he asked her.

"Brandenburg Gate and the park. I remember Vienna better."

So Max became a tour guide and pointed out the government buildings, great churches, and theaters. They drove past the ruins of the Reichstag, the Aldon Hotel, the Chancellery, Propaganda Ministry, the American embassy, and Gestapo headquarters.

"Shall I pop in there and ask why they frisked your bag?"

Emilie laughed. "No thank you."

Along the Kurfurstendamm the car came nearly to a halt. The crowded sidewalks had overflowed into the streets. Emilie swiveled in her seat to get a better look.

"I haven't seen crowds like this since inauguration day back home! When you slow at the intersection, do you mind if I take a few pictures?"

"I am merely your driver, Fraulein Morgan! Snap away as you please."

Finally Max pulled in front of his home.

"Here we are."

Emilie was not surprised. It was a two-story brick, snuggled tightly against the next house. This was obviously one of the city's wealthier residential sections.

"The park at the end of the street?"

"Tiergarten, Berlin's pride," Max answered as he opened the car door for her. "Please forgive me for taking so long to get here, I know you must be very tired from your journey."

"Oh, no, I enjoyed the tour. It will be helpful."

He drew the two cases from the car and started up the steps. At the door they both heard the whining.

Max grinned. "Percy. It's a hard thing being adored like I am, it makes separations so hard on the old boy."

Emilie laughed, discovering the flippant side of Max Farber in a very short time.

In the hall, Max commanded Percy to sit. The dog obeyed instantly, but could not contain his pleading whine.

"Sir Percy, this is Josef's niece, Fraulein Emilie Morgan. Can you say, welcome to Germany?"

Percy gave one short bark.

Emilie dropped to her knees, laughing.

"Percy, offer your paw."

Emilie took the offered paw. The dog was wiggling and licking and ecstatic. Emilie laughed with delight.

"I apologize for his ... affection," Max said seriously. "He does that when he sees a pretty woman."

When Emilie finally stood, Max was smiling at her. Suddenly she realized she was truly alone with this bachelor. Propriety flashed into her mind. It hadn't been difficult figuring out what was going on behind the green curtain in Josef's office. She glanced down the dim hallway. "You don't have a housekeeper?"

His smile began in his eyes. "She comes in once a week. Josef and I eat out or I cook." He picked up her bags and started up the stairs. Emilie nervously followed. He entered the study and turned on a light, then led her further down the hall. "That's my room, Josef's is there."

He opened another door. "And this is your room."

Emilie had half-expected a room of heavy masculine furniture, but it was a beautiful room with a cream carpet and cerulean accents. He went to the window and pushed back the lace curtains.

"You have the best view in the house," he said cheerfully.

She came to stand before him. It was a beautiful view of Tiergarten: trees and lakes and gardens.

She turned. He was watching her with a smile, then he went to the bathroom and brought out a big folded towel.

"We have a nice deep tub to soak away traveling fatigue!"

"Thank you . . . so much. I feel a little overwhelmed. It's all so lovely, I didn't expect . . ." She glanced at the four-poster bed.

"Did all of this belong to someone?"

"Some of it is from my country home. My mother picked these pieces out. I'm glad you like it."

He turned and walked to the door. "Well . . . is there anything else I can get you? Something to eat or drink?"

"Oh, no, thank you, I'm fine."

"Since I was going to the Games anyway, may I escort you? I have some excellent seats at the stadium—or wherever your press passes take you. I could be your assistant."

Emilie smiled. "Well, I wouldn't want to monopolize your time. I have to be at the propaganda ministry at 9:00."

He made a face. "Hardly seems the way to begin an enjoyable time in the city," he shrugged. "Well, we'll talk it over at breakfast." His hand rested on the doorknob; his eyes went over her in the same way they had at the clinic. Emilie clutched her hands behind her. "You know," he said thoughtfully, "I just had an idea. When the Games are over next week, I could drive you to Geneva to your uncle. You could have your surprise!"

"You would do that? Don't you have to work?" Instantly she colored, furious with herself.

He smiled and gave a little bow. "Work? I have an allergy to the word. You could see your homeland this way. . . ." He looked up at the ceiling a moment. "It could be a kind of homecoming—besides the one Berlin has given you."

Emilie relaxed. "You are very kind."

Now he looked embarrassed. "Well, goodnight. Come along, Percy."

But the dog remained on his haunches, whining and appealing to Max with his deep, liquid-brown eyes.

Max glanced at Emilie who was smiling, and frowned.

"What's this? A mutiny?" he asked gruffly. "You're throwing me over like that?"

"I really don't mind," Emilie said.

"This is scandalous, Percy. You hardly know her!"

Emilie burst out laughing and called the dog. Percy came to her, lay down, and put his head across her feet.

"The rascal will want to sleep on the end of your bed."

"I can tell him all my first impressions of Germany."

Their eyes met a moment. Max backed up, closing the door, saying, "Now I know I'm going to have trouble sleeping!"

● ● ●

Sunrise came over the rooftops of Berlin pearllike and it pushed through the lace curtains of the second-floor bedroom of the Farber house with a gentle and pleasant insistence. Emilie stretched, assured herself it was still early, and curled up on her side to awaken slowly and think over the past 24 hours. The warm little burrow Percy had made at the end of the bed was vacant. She vaguely remembered getting up and letting him out when he whined at the door during the middle of the night.

Her eyes rested on her suitcase across the room. She hopped up and brought it back to her bed. Both the lining of the lid and the back were torn. She felt them with her fingers. It was not a jagged cut—smooth and even, as if done with a knife. Why would someone cut her case? She picked up a small leather folder then. It contained photographs. She lay back, looking at the photo of Will Cutler standing in front of the Lincoln Memorial . . . smiling. She frowned. *Is he anything more than a good friend? Were our moments of passion purely physical need . . . But he held me so tightly at Union Station. Almost—desperately.* She smiled to herself and looked at the window with the day growing, *to have someone love and want you desperately....*

• • •

She could hear Max Farber singing something as she came down the stairs. She smiled as she heard Percy inserting an occasional howl. She glanced into the lower rooms, richly carpeted, elegant, quiet. *One of the richest men in Germany, inherited money—an allergy to work....*

"Marriage is the thing," Bess had said. "All the better if the man has money."

"So which is more important, Miss Bennett, marrying for love or money?"

"Or love of money ... just don't snag an old man, Em, one that dribbles down his yellow beard."

She could imagine Bess surveying the Farber house, and the Farber man, and coming to her decision with typical swift bluntness.

"Money first, Em, then love.... With a man that looked like that it wouldn't take long!"

"I've come only to take pictures and see my uncle," Emilie whispered to herself as she pushed open the kitchen door.

Max stood at the stove, an apron around his waist. His fork stopped in midair as he took in her full length. She wore a yellow dress with a broad white collar, her hair was caught at the base of her neck with a yellow ribbon. She looked as fresh and clean as a summer morning. Max shook his head—he hadn't meant to stare. Emilie turned and looked behind her. He turned back to his stove. "Please don't get in the line of vision of Germany's track team. We have enough competition with Jesse Owens."

"You know, Herr Farber, I think the Nazi officials at the train station could take some lessons of charm from you."

"Ah! You will have to understand: Most Nazis take the wrong things seriously and make the serious things of little importance. It is a curious defect that happens when they pull on their polished boots."

She vaguely wondered what things, if any, Max Farber took seriously.

"Your breakfast, fraulein!"

She sat down. "Thank you. This is very nice of you."

"Cooking is one of the few labors I enjoy."

Percy came up to her, sitting and looking at her longingly. Emilie and Max smiled at each other across the table as he poured her coffee. "He jilted me in the middle of the night," Emilie said. "So you see, his loyalty is still intact."

A reply came to Max's lips, but he squelched it.

"So tell me, fraulein photographer, how I can assist you in capturing our splendid Games?"

She drew out her leather notebook with the official Olympic schedule she'd been given at the station. She sketched for him what she wanted to do. He asked her questions and soon they settled into a comfortable discussion. She was telling him about working for the Smith and getting laid off, her job at Woolworth's, her assignment for Washington McVinty's magazine. She made only passing mention of a friend named Will, who had secured her the job.

"Have you ever been to the United States, Herr Farber?"

Max shook his head. "The one continent I've never visited—a neglect I hope to remedy someday. So, if I understand, your desire is to photograph every event."

Emilie laughed. "A little too ambitious?"

"Only if you can be everywhere at once."

"And I'd like some photos of the American team as they explore Berlin, as they react to Berlin."

"Perhaps I can help there, also. I have those things called connections. And then there's my party two days from now."

"Your party?"

"At my country home outside of Berlin. Goebbels and Heydrich will be there. The Lindbergs and a few of the athletes from the American swim team. Now, if it's Adolf Hitler you want, my box is near his at the stadium."

Emilie had to control her mouth to keep it from falling open. This was what was called "a plum," and it had dropped in her lap. An influential man that could steer her into an impressive photo essay. She had not had any expectations near to these opportunities.

"Did you say the Lindbergs?"

He nodded. "I called my housekeeper this morning and had her prepare you a room. I thought we could drive out after the opening ceremony tomorrow night."

"You ... continue to overwhelm me, Herr Farber, I don't know what to say."

He rose, gathering up their things. "You'd better get ready—you don't want to be late for your indoctrination by Herr Goebbels. But you know, if I am going to be your assistant I really think we should drop this Herr Farber and Fraulein Morgan business don't you?"

• • •

The Ministry of Propaganda occupied a huge building of Roman classical design on the Wilhelmstrasse. Before the advent of Adolf Hitler there had been no recognized propaganda bureau. The architects of the Third Reich had seen the importance of such an institution, and so a building had been converted and remodeled with the passion of its first—and only—minister, Dr. Paul Joseph Goebbels. Like so many of the men that surrounded the fuehrer, Goebbels was a man of a singularly obscure and unpromising background. But Adolf Hitler had seen potential and genius in the slight, dark-haired man during the infant days of the Nazi party. Goebbels was a man with a passion similar to his own— a man who could see the vision of a new Germany. Germany as ruler of the European continent; Germans as the master race.

So Goebbels gloried in his power and position and fed the good people of Germany a daily diet of half-truths and lies. He was considered Hitler's closest confidant. He had only to walk across the street to the three story, L-shaped Chancellery to have the German leader's ear. He had been given control of all German newspapers and radio, all culture and the arts. It was his charge to keep both German and foreign journalists in observance of Nazi policy—both defined and subtle. These summer Olympic Games would be his greatest triumph to date.

• • •

Max dropped Emilie off in front of the Propaganda building. She told him she would take a cab back when she was finished. Pausing on the steps a moment, she snapped a picture of the entrance. She turned and caught the Chancellery with garish golden eagles clutching swastikas above each entrance. The balcony where the fuehrer often stood for reviews was empty, save for a single Olympic flag that fluttered lazily. *What if the man himself suddenly appeared, posing perfectly for me*? Someone brushed past her, reminding her what she had come here for. She hurried inside.

She showed her press pass to the guard at the door and was shown to a large, ornate room where other journalists stood waiting. She glanced around the room—a sea of unfamiliar faces. Most of the men were middle-aged. They gave her a cursory look and returned to their own personal meditations. Emilie looked down at her perfect white shoes. Herr Farber thought her pretty, but now she was wishing she looked a little older and more professional.

A thin, dark-haired man with a slight limp came from a side door to the raised platform. His eyes swept the room and he smiled. He wore a dark suit. *I wonder if he isn't terribly hot*, Emilie said to herself. She could not see his face clearly because she was standing so near to the back. He welcomed them briefly, then began a 30-minute tribute to Adolf Hitler and the glories of the Third Reich. His voice was shrill, and Emilie thought his gestures a bit feminine. His speech moderated then, telling them they must observe all Nazi policies concerning press releases to their respective countries.

"We call it censorship back home," someone near Emilie muttered.

Photographers near the stadium box of the fuehrer were permitted to take his picture only when the SS officer in attendance gave them permission. If an SS officer anywhere in Berlin asked them not to take a certain picture, they were to obey him on penalty of having their film confiscated. But, of course, that would most likely not happen—they were, after all, honored guests of the reich. He smiled and gave a short bow to terminate his speech. Emilie didn't feel inclined to take his photograph when he moved away from the podium to pose in front of the huge, blood-red banner. She had seen her first Nazi leader and found herself unimpressed.

● ● ●

"Excuse me," a man said, as he came up beside her when she turned to leave Goebbels' throneroom. He stuck out his hand.

"Jake Harrold, Rueters News Service."

He was a short, heavy-set young man with a thick crop of wavy, red hair. His New York accent was heavy, and Emilie couldn't help but smile.

"I'm Emilie Morgan, photographer for the *Mount Vernon Voice*." Giving this credential still caused her a little self-conscious blush.

He nodded. "I was behind you in line yesterday at the train station during baggage check."

She instantly remembered the display of the lace-trimmed slip. "Oh."

"I thought you handled yourself very well during their little search routine."

She laughed, "Thank you. You're from New York?"

They were slowly walking down the long tiled hallway, the crowd of correspondents all around them.

He nodded. "Brooklyn. When I first came to Germany, I practically hugged any American I came across. Your German is very good."

"My parents were German and I was born here—but I've lived in the States most of my life."

"I've been here 18 months. I took a break last month to go home. You have to get out of Germany every so often to keep your sanity and perspective, know what I mean? Your first visit to Naziland?"

"Yes."

"I guess it can be pretty startling for a visitor. Nazis like to do things in a big, splashy way."

"I've never seen so many banners and flags," Emilie agreed.

He nodded. "I don't think people back in the States have a clue what Naziland is really like. We try to tell 'em, but I'm beginning to think they really don't want to know."

They turned down a corridor leading to the massive front entrance.

"You notice any Gestapo-types hanging around your hotel?"

"Actually, I'm staying at my uncle's home."

His eyebrows shot up. "Now that's a classy angle. I'm at the Adlon: great food, but it's a little crowded now. All the bigwigs come strutting by. 'Course if there were Gestapo hanging around, with you being new, you probably wouldn't notice them. They like to blend in, know what I mean? Look for a guy unsmiling, wearing black, and reading a day-old newspaper and you have a goon on your tail."

"Why would the Gestapo have me watched?" Emilie asked with a little laugh.

He gave her an oblique look without turning his head.

"You look like a smart da-, girl, one that doesn't scare easy."

"Well, I hope so."

They had come to the steps and the sunshine. Jake Harrold glanced at his watch. "I have an interview with the American ambassador in 40 minutes, so I have to hustle."

"You can't leave without telling me why you said what you did. That would be very ungallant of you, Mr. Harrold."

"Call me Jake. Well, first of all, having the Gestapo interested in you isn't the end of the world. They keep close tabs on all foreign correspondents. I've had 'em shadowing me from assignment to assignment plenty of times. You have to know how to deal with them. They're all pretty paranoid—like their tearing through your bags yesterday."

Emilie had come to realize this friendly reporter from the States had a mind that sped from topic to topic with few breaths in between. She also felt she must suddenly play the country's defender.

"Well, I don't know if they did or didn't." Her voice took on a slightly righteous tone, "but I'm unwilling to cast an immediate judgment on them. They can't all be unsmiling—"

"Thugs."

"I can't believe that—not all of them. Germany is a highly civilized country. This is the country that has given the world Bach and Beethoven."

"And Hitler and Goebbels and the Nuremberg Laws."

Emilie crossed her arms. "You were starting to tell me why I am suspect in the Gestapo's eyes."

"Simple. I saw what you didn't yesterday. The Gestapo guy was interested in your damaged bag. He didn't think his people did it—they aren't that sloppy and obvious."

"Then who did?" Emilie hadn't planned to divulge this to a stranger, but she wanted a perspective to this also, and Jake Harrold seemed to have a lot of answers. "I looked at it last night. It looks like it was cut with a knife."

"That's what he would like to know. Why would someone go through the bag of an American photographer? Maybe she was bringing something into the country and—"

"Like the rest of the room, I think you saw everything I was bringing into the country—even my dangerous copy of *Gone with the Wind*!"

He held up his hands laughing. "I'm not saying I think you brought anything into the country. I'm saying *they* could be interested if they think someone else was interested. Main thing with them, Miss Morgan, is don't take anything off of them. But be careful."

Will Cutler's warning was echoing suddenly in her mind.

"I gotta go. We journalists hang out at the Adlon or The Tavern on Lutzowstrasse. I'm sure you'll get a few wolf whistles and propositions, but we're largely a harmless lot. There are a few other dames in the crowd, like Susan Meigs. She's British and older than you."

"Thank you, Jake. I feel... accepted even though I'm so painfully new at this."

He touched her shoulder. "Yeah, you're pretty green lookin'. But us Yanks have to take care of each other, you know what I mean? You can come with me when the Games open up if you want. I've got some good passes and seats."

"Thank you, that's very kind. But I... I met, I mean a friend of my uncle's has offered to show me around...."

Harrold's eyes narrowed as he waved for a cab.

"A German?"

"Well, yes."

"A Nazi." He smirked a little. It was not a question.

Emilie thought of the gold enamel swastika on Max's jacket.

"Actually, he is, but he isn't at all like you described. He *does* smile and he doesn't wear black."

"I said that was Gestapo. But SS, Gestapo, or just plain Nazi-Party boy, they're all cut from the same cloth."

Emilie smiled. "I don't think so."

Harrold opened the door of the cab. "I didn't get your address. Look me up at the Adlon!... Sure he's interested in showing you Berlin. He'll only show you the topside though, know what I mean?" The cab sped away, with Emilie lingering on the sidewalk.

What did he mean?

●　●　●

Though the Olympic Games of 1936 had been presented to Germany in 1930, three full years before the Nazi government had taken power, Adolf Hitler was determined to receive all the accolades for their overwhelming success. To such an end, he was willing to dip into the national treasury as he saw fit. So now Berlin had a beautiful new stadium outside the city. As early twilight fell over the capital in diluted purple and ivory, the crowds that had swollen the streets all day surged toward the stadium. The opening of the tenth Olympiad was only an hour away.

Emilie had been infected with the expectant excitement of the vast crowd around her. Every seat in the huge stadium seemed to be filled. Athletes from 55 nations had assembled on the field in neat rows behind their respective flags. Emilie managed a few pictures of the American team on the field before Max led her to his box. The dirigible "Hindenburg" hovered over the stadium, a swastika clearly emblazoned on its side. There was no mistaking who owned these Games.

She glanced around. Everyone looked so happy. She knew she was surrounded by European wealth and aristocracy in this section of private boxes. Women in silk and wide hats, men in crisp whites and natty ties. Max looked impeccable in his line suit and navy tie. "So are you impressed yet, fraulein?" he asked, leaning down.

She looked up, smiling and nodding. She knew she looked like a wide-eyed girl. At the moment though, she didn't care.

Two rows below them in a box next to the stadium rail, the fuehrer had taken his place. She was surprised to see him wearing a heavy black-leather coat. *Do Nazis have a thing for black leather?* she wondered. His face was pasty looking. *So this was the great man of Germany.* She recognized the diminutive Goebbels at his right side, but didn't know the heavy-set, smiling, uniformed man at his left side. She leaned toward Max.

"Who's he?"

"Hermann Göring, Reichmarshal and commander of the air force." Max lowered his voice, "He has this penchant for uniforms."

Then a man on the platform in the center of the stadium field addressed the crowd, opening the ceremonies. The German anthem was played. Max nudged her, whispering. "He'll be coming down here in a minute or so. Got your camera ready?"

An expectant stillness fell over the crowd. Emilie felt like everyone was holding their breath. She glanced up at Max, and he winked at her. The crowds turned their heads to the steps that paralleled where Emilie and Max were waiting.

A blond, tanned, and well-muscled young German appeared at the top of the steps. He wore white shorts and a white sleeveless shirt—and he carried the Olympic torch. Emilie raised her camera as he prepared to descend. She would have an excellent shot: the young man with the smoking flame held aloft, the eager faces of the crowd. Then like a wave, without a word exchanged or signal given, the crowd raised their arms in a stiff salute. He passed her, within two feet, a young man solemn and proud. Emilie thought he could be no more than a teenager. He jogged to the far end of the field and up the small flight of steps to the beacon.

Emilie's eyes swept the crowd near her. The arms remained raised, some faces smiling, some etched in concentrated firmness. She was a little shocked at this display of Nazi fervor. She stirred a little uneasily at her thoughts and cast a sidelong look at Max. He was staring forward, his face in a hard cast she recognized from the crowd—but oddly not his own. His arm was pointing toward the flame. Emilie sat down.

The ceremonies continued with the review of the athletes before the fuehrer's box. The crowd had sat down and the excited chattering and laughing resumed. She could hear them calling out the names of athletes, the destined stars of these games.

"Are you all right?" Max asked.

"Just a little warm." She didn't look at him.

"Did you get a good shot of the runner?"

Only then did Emilie realize she had not taken a picture of the runner. She had missed her excellent shot.

● ● ●

The road from Berlin was nearly deserted. Emilie sat back in the rich leather of Max's Mercedes and chided herself for her sudden gloom. It was not the way to begin a stay in Berlin. She was determined to be a nonpartisan, unbiased observer to the scene: nothing more, nothing less. She wouldn't carry any taint from American newspapers or American journalists...or even her own father whom she had always respected.

"Are you feeling all right, Emilie?" Max asked. "We'll be there soon."

"Yes fine...just a little tired."

She hoped she could rally herself once they reached Max's country estate for it was her desire to settle in her bed and begin a letter to Will Cutler. It would be a long one, for she had so much to tell him.

"You are so quiet," Max continued.

"Well, I suppose I'm a little disappointed about missing the shot of the runner coming down the steps. It was silly of me to get so . . . so distracted by the crowd. It wasn't very professional."

"I'm sure there will be other opportunities for good pictures." Max glanced at the young profile in the shadows of the car. He knew what had kept her from taking her picture, but he said nothing.

Percy crept up from the backseat and laid his head on Emilie's arm. Emilie ruffled his ears.

"I've never seen him take to anyone so quickly. I think he's smitten with you, fraulein."

Emilie laughed. "Well, I'm smitten with him. He's quite a gentlemen."

"As my companion, he's required to be. Only one of us can be a rogue!" Max laughed.

His joke made her think of the man she had met in the stadium before the ceremony had begun. He had come up to them as they entered Max's box.

"Maximillian!" It was a deep, gravelly voice. Emilie had turned to find herself regarded by a heavy set man, with close-cropped, gray hair, wearing a dark suit. A tall woman stood slightly behind him. Though she was smiling, it was a tired smile, and Emilie decided there was sadness lingering in her eyes.

In a swift glance, Emilie saw a shadow pass over Max Farber's face. There was a sudden, forced cheerfulness in his voice.

"Guten Tag, Katrina."

"We saw you had a guest with you," the older man said, his eyes piercing into Emilie's.

Max turned. "A most pleasant surprise, Irwin. This is Fraulein Emilie Morgan from the United States. She is Josef's niece. Emilie, this is my oldest brother, Irwin, and his wife, Katrina."

"Welcome to Germany," Katrina Farber offered.

"Danke."

"You have come to visit your uncle?" she inquired.

"Ja, even though he's out of town. I'm on assignment to photograph the Games for an American magazine."

"How fascinating!"

Emilie smiled, and wondered why Irwin Farber was staring. Max touched her arm, indicating the seats.

"I'm so sorry we can't make your little weekend party, Max," Katrina continued.

Max shrugged. "I understand perfectly."

"We've heard you've improved the place greatly."

Max bowed. "The staff has done the work."

"So where are you staying, Emilie?" Irwin's wife asked. "The Aldon or Kaiserhof?"

Emilie glanced at Max, and he spoke up for her.

"The Farberhof. Her uncle's home."

The eyebrows on Frau Farber's face lifted and lowered in agitation. "Well, really, Max, I think it would be better if she stayed with us. Don't you agree, Irwin?'

"You are welcome to stay with us until your uncle returns, fraulein," Irwin said briskly.

"Thank you, but I—"

Max leaned toward the couple, his voice conspiratorial.

"Percy has taken guard on the end of her bed . . ."

Frau Farber looked wholly shocked and stepped away to fan herself.

Now, in the car, Emilie suddenly burst out laughing. Percy whined.

"What is it?" Max asked.

"Herr Farber, I do think you enjoy shocking people."

"Whatever do you mean, fraulein?"

"Percy guarding my bed!"

Max laughed deeply.

"I don't think they approved of me, exactly," Emilie smiled.

"It is your association with me, fraulein," Max continued laughing.

"He's not very . . . well, you two aren't much alike, are you?"

"A small understatement!"

Emilie tried to remember what her uncle had told her of the Farber family history.

"You have another brother?"

Max nodded. "Eric."

"Will he be at your party tomorrow?"

"No. He's in the military and he's off on the fuehrer's business somewhere."

"The Rhineland, perhaps?"

Max looked away from the road. Emilie noted he was not smiling.

"I don't know," he said.

Emilie turned to watch the countryside in darkened purple shadows with only an occasional spark of light from a house in the distance. *So the Farber family isn't one big happy clan? Irwin certainly had not looked happy—nor his wife.* Emilie had felt like she had been thoroughly scrutinized by Irwin and then found distinctly wanting. She didn't have to know much about their past to know that these brothers were uncomfortable around each other.

The car slowed and came to a stop before two stone pillars and a set of black iron gates.

"And so we have at last arrived." Max's voice had returned to its good humor.

• • •

Karl Beck, Max's personal secretary, returned to his apartment from a preGame party with a cheap bottle of wine and a personable young woman. His only concern was that his landlady might hear the young woman's giggling as they climbed the stairs to the third floor. The old shrew would just love to stop them and deliver a lecture—and she'd smell the liquor. It could mean a higher rent or possible eviction.

Beck quickly closed and locked the door. The woman hopped on the couch, still laughing. Beck was pulling off his tie when the phone rang. Having such a limited social life, he knew instantly what this call could mean. He waved an angry hand at the girl, signaling her to be quiet.

"Ja?"

He expected the rough, without-greeting voice.

"Beck, Maximillian was with a girl tonight. Did you see him?"

"Nein."

"Well, it was Emilie Morgan. She's staying with him."

"How convenient for Max," Beck returned laconically.

"Find out about her, her plans. Find out from Max whatever you can."

"All right . . ."

"She's Thomas Morgan's daughter."

Beck was now alert. "I see . . ."

"I want to know the real reason she's come over."

"She might tell you if you asked her," Beck ventured easily.

The phone went dead on the other end.

Beck smiled. "Guten Nacht, Herr Farber."

He joined the woman on the sofa, physically with her but mentally back on the phone call. An imperious knocking at his door, and the woman groaned while Beck cursed.

"We could have gone to my place. It isn't like this—Stadtbahn!" Beck frowned at her as he opened the door. A man stood in the darkened hallway. Beck turned and spoke sharply over his shoulder.

"Go wait in the bathroom!"

She opened her mouth to protest until she saw his face. Beck could look very menacing. After she retreated, he permitted the man to enter. They, too, did not exchange greetings.

"I want you to find out more about this woman," the visitor said, passing a slip of paper to Beck. He unfolded it: Emilie Morgan.

"Who is she?"

"A woman from the States. Says she came over to take pictures of the Games."

"But you think . . . ?"

"What I think doesn't matter to you right now," the man snapped irritably. "She is staying with your boss. Someone tore up her bag before we had a chance to look through it. Find out why."

He turned and left without a backward look or word. Beck smiled as he crumpled the paper. *So this Emilie Morgan was something of an interest . . . to Irwin Farber, Max Farber, and the Gestapo of Berlin. A most intriguing American. . . .*

19
Games

From her second-story bedroom window, Emilie could see the rose garden that formed a perfectly clipped oval in front of the grand Farber house. She could see the white gravel circular drive. She could see the side lawn that was bordered by a stand of poplar trees and the opposite lawn that stretched to another band of trees two miles distant. She felt that besides the sheer luxury of the room this was the most advantageous room Max could have selected for her. She could watch the sleek, black Mercedes, touring cars, and convertibles come up the drive. She could see the guests disembark in a swirl of chiffon, broad hats, and white summer suits. Emilie Morgan was suffering an unexpected attack of nerves. She had barely adjusted to Max Farber's friendly generosity. His Berlin house had whispered his wealth, this house that he had brought her to last night, with its staff of formally dressed servants, fairly shouted his prosperity. And now, the "cream" of German society, Nazi high officials, and a sprinkling of celebrities were coming to his very doorstep. She was a young, naive American girl with a good strong German accent but no real knowledge of contemporary Germany. She was an amateur with a camera—and she felt every inch of it.

Max gave her a tour of the house and grounds after their breakfast together. They didn't feel or notice the raised brows and smiles that were given to their backs as they passed by the staff. *A young girl and Max nearing 30. . . . Was he too old for her*? some of them speculated. *Of course, she would hardly care about his age once she realized this was one of the richest men in Germany*, they chuckled behind their hands. *Well, it was high time Herr Max settled down. . . .*

Max led Emilie down to the edge of the river.

"My staff is a little nervous this morning. Did you see Berta jiggle the cream for you at breakfast?"

Emilie nodded. "Why are they nervous? I'd think they would be used to this kind of grand party."

Max sat down on the low stone wall that edged the river, and looked out over the water. "Actually, this is the first party that's been given here in years. I can't even remember when the last one was. . . . Long ago . . . Father never gave one after mother died. And the house was closed up for years before I took it over."

"What did your mother die from?"

"Tuberculosis."

"How old were you?"

"Eight. And your mother?"

"She died of cancer when I was eighteen."

He tossed a stick in the water, not looking at her.

"Then that gives us another point in common. We are orphans."

There was something in his voice, something she had not heard before. A tiredness? A sadness? Then he spoke again, and she realized he had forgotten she was standing behind him.

"I wonder sometimes . . . if they had both lived . . . what they would think of their youngest son. . . ."

Emilie was tempted to turn and walk quietly back to the house and leave this man who was a stranger to his own private thoughts. But she stood there, thinking how likable Max Farber really was. A full minute passed. Then he stood up, hands in pockets, head slightly tilted. He turned and saw her and smiled.

"Well, I'd better go back up to the house to get ready for those people descending upon Farber house ready to eat my food and drink my champagne."

Emilie matched his tone. "The price you pay for popularity, I suppose."

• • •

Just before noon, the cars came down the long drive. In the distance, from her open window, Emilie could hear the strains of violins playing from the lawn, the tinkle of glassware, and women laughing. She saw the Lindbergs when they arrived. Of course Emilie knew them by sight—they were celebrities in America, front-page stuff with Charles' solo flight in '27 and the tragic kidnapping and murder of their infant son only four years earlier. Anne Lindberg was slender, looking up at the big house with a mixture of curiosity and pleasure. Her tall husband stood beside her before he led her up the stairs. Emilie leaned forward, the famous aviator still had that boyish look with thick, brown hair falling over his forehead. Emilie turned to her writing table and scribbled down a description of Anne's dress. Bess would be astounded. Emilie stood, alternately watching from her window and messing with her camera. There was a knock at her door. "Come in," she called.

Max's head came around the door. "That's what I thought. Why are you hiding out up here?"

Emilie blushed. "I'm not hiding out, Herr Farber. I'm just finishing up a few letters."

"Grab your camera and come on."

"Max, I'm not going to bring my camera along. That would be very rude, not to mention unprofessional. Your guests have had their pictures taken since they arrived in Berlin, and I'm sure they are tired of it."

"Hardly. How do you think the famous get famous?"

"Well, to be perfectly honest, it didn't really dawn on me until I saw them arriving, I didn't bring a dress for a party like this."

"What's wrong with what you have on?"

She shook her head laughing. "You don't understand. They are in jewels and satin. I'm dressed fine for running around Berlin, but—"

He shook his head. "Tsk, tsk . . . Just a minute."

He was gone, returning a few minutes later. He closed the bedroom door and now Emilie's eyebrows nearly elevated. He came up to her.

He held a string of pearls in his hand. "Put these on and you'll have your jewels."

"Max, I can't wear these. Don't be ridiculous. Whose are these?"

"Some heavy-set woman's who's drinking my champagne—maybe Magda Goebbels." He shrugged and headed for the door. "Hurry up, fraulein."

She stood in the middle of the room. *Such an eccentric and kind man. Bess would wonder why he wasn't married. I wonder why he isn't married*...She placed the necklace on the table and left her room.

With so many people, Emilie realized she could drift through this party largely unnoticed—or at least she felt like she was. She forgot her plain dress while taking in this extravagant scene. She had never imagined she would be at such a gathering. Goebbels was there, as Max had promised, sitting in a white, iron-claw chair, laughing with a group circled around him. *He still looks feminine*, she mused. She sat and listened to the music awhile. She strolled and sipped champagne and was happy that the weather was so perfect for Max's outing. She stood on the fringe of groups, listening, thinking. Across the lawn she looked up and found Max smiling at her. He nodded to her and she raised her glass. He frowned when he saw she hadn't worn his pearls. She shrugged and turned away to get herself a dish of sherbet. The afternoon lengthened and died with mellow sunshine and the melody of Mozart on the breeze. It had been a delightful afternoon. The party would surge inside as darkness came and there would be dancing in the great ballroom. Most of the guests would leave for the night, but some would stay in the rooms that had been prepared for them. The party would continue when the sun rose the next day, with lawn croquet, boating, horseback riding, and rowing on the river.

The sun was slipping like a yellow disk behind the line of trees. Emilie had stolen into the library for a little quiet. She closed the door and found she was not alone. Mrs. Lindberg was sitting in a window seat. Her smile came slowly, and Emilie was struck at how very young and fragile she looked.

"I suspect we had the same intent," she said.

Emilie nodded. "A little quiet. Do you mind if I join you?"

"No, come in. You're American!"

Emilie thought of Jake Harrold's words and smiled.

"Yes. I'm Emilie Morgan," she said as she sat down.

They talked for almost an hour.

"Anne, what do you think of Germany?" Emilie felt bold enough to venture. "I mean, the . . ."

"Naziism?"

Emilie nodded.

"I trust you wouldn't print or repeat what I say," Mrs. Lindberg said slowly.

"No, of course I wouldn't. I ask you as one American to another. I don't have any real interest here, beyond this assignment and my uncle. I want to form my own opinion, but I want to weigh what others think, too. I'll figure out what I think at the end."

"Well, I think the Nazi government has improved the economy and morale of Germany. That is no small thing. Have you seen the autobahn? I was here in the '20s and it was a very dismal, depressed country. They are growing powerful.... Every country has a right to that ... if they respect other countries' powers. I admit I see the improvements and I ... wonder what may be beneath it—or beyond it."

The topside of Berlin as Jake Harrold had called it, Emily remembered.

"At the ceremonies last night, when the runner came ... they all raised their arms like they were machines or puppets. It had a very odd effect on me," Emilie told her.

Anne smiled. "I felt the same thing. Then, later, at our hotel, when I mentioned it to Charlie, he reminded me, Is it so different from our own pledge of allegiance? When we go see the Yankees and the anthem is played, we stand and cover our hearts and look to the flag. Was last night so different?"

Emilie shook her head. She hadn't thought of that.

"Well, I'd better go," Anne said rising. "Charlie will be wondering where I've gotten to. I've enjoyed our conversation immensely. It's nice to think of another American in the house tonight," she laughed.

"I'll have to introduce you to my husband, but I confess he'll be a little edgy when he finds out you're a photographer."

Emilie didn't have to ask why. Most Americans knew the flyer had a profound distrust of newspaper people after the death of his son.

Emilie remained in the library awhile longer. She could hear through the doors that the guests had come in now, and dinner would soon be served. She tucked her feet under her as she sat in the window seat, leaning into the rich folds of drapery with her chin on her knees, thinking.

The panel doors slid open, and Emilie decided Max had come looking for her again. But the tall, blond-headed man was not Max. He walked into the room, not bothering to look right or left. He slowly pulled off his gloves and hat and tossed them to a chair. He wore a dark uniform that Emilie didn't recognize as the SS. He was looking at the gold framed oil painting of the last generation of Herr and Frau Farber that hung over the fireplace. He stood with his legs slightly apart, hands behind his back. *Very confident*, Emily noted. *And he's been in this room before.*

Later, when she had gone to bed, Emilie wondered why, like a naughty child, she had pressed herself deeper into the window seat instead of speaking up and introducing herself. But this man . . . for some reason she felt a little afraid. She didn't want him to turn and see her—surely it wasn't the uniform. But he did turn, as if her fear had reached across the room and alerted him that he was not alone. He turned and his eyes rested on her.

They were cold, pale-blue eyes. A hawklike nose that, to Emilie, marred his otherwise classic features. She didn't know that Adolf Hitler regarded this man as the epitome of physical German perfection. This was the Aryan model—much like Max Farber was. She could see he was comfortable with his evaluation of her. Emilie, like any girl, liked to be admired, but this man was . . . undressing her with his eyes. She slipped off the seat, smoothing her dress. He smiled then: It improved his face only a little. He stepped forward.

"I thought I knew everyone Max had invited. I do not believe I know you, fraulein."

"I'm Emilie Morgan."

He had come up to her now, towering over her. He reached down and took her hand, bending over it with a kiss. Emilie refrained from jerking it away.

"I am Reinhard Heydrich, Fraulein Morgan. An old friend of Max's." Emilie drew her hand away and stepped back.

"Are you new to Berlin? Like Max, I . . . pride myself on knowing all the pretty girls of our city."

"I'm from the United States."

"Ah! How charming! You've come for the Games?"

"Ja."

His eyes swept over her hair, her face, her neck . . .

"I'm sure you will find our Games most impressive."

"I'm sure."

"You know, it just occurred to me—I have an extra pass to some of the track and field events and the swimming. If you need them, I could...I would be happy to escort you."

"Thank you, but I already—"

"I thought it was you, Reinhard. I couldn't quite tell from the voice, but the words were a dead giveaway." Max stood smiling and lounging against the doorframe. "Glad you could make it. Dinner's about to be spread."

The officer stepped back from Emilie, his chin tilting, the amusement evaporating from his eyes. He regarded Max for a long, cold minute.

"Good evening, Maximillian."

"Is Lena with you?"

Reinhard cleared his throat. "No, she sends her regrets. She's a little fatigued from the day."

"Pretty close to her time, isn't she?"

"Ja."

"What are you hoping for this time, a boy or girl?"

"Since we have one of each, it doesn't really matter." He gestured toward Emilie. "I was getting acquainted with your American guest. Very lovely. How did you meet Max?"

Emilie was annoyed, so her voice was distinctly frosty. "Through my uncle."

"Ah...well, as I was saying, if Max, here, can't show you enough sights, as an ambassador for the reich I would be happy to."

Max dug into his pockets, nearly snorting out loud.

"Where are you staying?" Heydrich continued.

Emilie drew a breath, forgetting Max. She looked at this man directly. She also forgot to be afraid of him. Her smile was tight. "You know, Herr Heydrich, I'm not quite used to such forwardness. American men aren't like this."

He laughed loudly. "And you've been with Max?" He gave Max a wink.

If Max was ruffled, he didn't show it. His voice was little more than a drawl. "She's turned you down, old man. Let's go eat, shall we?"

• • •

Max knew it would be well after midnight before he would be able to go to bed, and probably longer before he actually fell asleep. That is, if sheer physical exhaustion could overcome his mind's deliberations. It had been a very long day, not so much from the need to supervise, for Rudi Schmidtt had taken care of that without a flaw. Max had only to saunter and gossip among his guests. Years ago, such an activity, wouldn't have fatigued him nearly so much. But now he was constantly on an inner alert, listening, committing fragments of information to memory, and carefully framing his replies and flippancy in a more calculated way.

This evening, he sat at the head of the long table, smiling and laughing—and watching his guests with carefully concealed observance. To his guests, he was unchanged: silly, casual, happy-go-lucky Max Farber.

Emilie was seated a few chairs to his left, between Magda Goebbels and a young military officer. Heydrich was at the middle of the table. Emilie avoided the frequent looks he sent her way. Lindberg and his wife sat across from Heydrich. Max had introduced Emilie as they had come to the table, partly to make her more comfortable and partly to diffuse any more Heydrichlike encounters like he had witnessed in the library. Emilie felt the full strength of every eye in the room upon her. Though inwardly trembling, she held her head up and smiled.

"This is Fraulein Emilie Morgan from the United States. She is here to cover the Games for an American magazine. Some of you may know her uncle, Dr. Josef Morgan. Her father was Thomas Morgan, a distinguished servant in Germany's diplomatic corp. Fraulein Morgan was born in Germany."

She glanced up to see Charles Lindberg giving her a frown. Frau Goebbels captured her attention, managing to eat from the Farber bounty while asking Emilie her complete and unabridged history. Frau Goebbels was delighted to be seated by this unexpected novelty. Emilie ate sparingly and tried to keep up with the animated woman, half-listening to the table gossip that swirled around her.

"So, Max, where is Leni? Shouldn't she be seated at the end of your table?"

Already Emilie recognized the smooth voice of Heydrich. Those around Max were attentive to his reply. He glanced up and smiled.

"The fuehrer has Leni working, as you well know, Reinhard. And, as you know, Leni, if she were here, would sit wherever she liked." Laughter greeted this. Emilie watched as Max took a long drink of his dinner wine. The melody of laughter and the clank of silver returned. Frau Goebbels was telling Emilie about the party Göring had hosted the night before. When she finally paused with a mouthful of trout, Emilie leaned over in feminine curiosity.

"Who is Leni?"

Frau Goebbels was flattered. She brought her head close to the younger woman's. "Well, she is Leni Riefenstahl, Max's latest conquest. Though I have to admit, I've always felt Max prefers flashy blondes."

Emilie's brows rose at this. "What is she doing for the fuehrer?"

"Only directing a film about our Olympic Games, capturing every magnificent moment on film. Joseph says it is a triumph. Leni is very . . . liberal and independent."

"Have you known Max long?"

"Only forever." Which was a Nazi edition of the truth.

Emilie was poising another question when she overheard a question directed to Mr. Lindberg.

"So, Mr. Lindberg, what do you think of the American track-and-field team?"

Lindberg took his time to wipe his mouth and glanced around the table. "I think they're every bit as good as the other teams represented."

"Including Germany?"

He nodded. "Including Germany."

Polite laughter followed this.

The propaganda chief, Emilie noticed, had spoken very little throughout the meal, an obvious contrast to his voluble wife.

"You are saying then, Herr Lindberg, that you expect the American Jesse Owens can beat Lutz Long?" Goebbels was watching him, swirling his wine glass and smiling. Lindberg leaned on the table with his fingers laced. "Well, I think they're a pretty even match. It should be a good contest."

Goebbels nodded benignly.

"How can a black man and a white man be an even match?" Heydrich asked with a slight laugh.

Lindberg looked at his plate a moment. Emilie looked at Anne. Her smile had frozen. Emilie looked up at Max. He had leaned back in his chair and appeared very relaxed. She felt a twinge of irritation.

"I think in athletics, in this contest, Owens and Long are very near each other in abilities." Lindberg lifted his shoulders. "I fly airplanes, that's more my speed."

Another titter of affected laughter. When it had died down, Emilie, neatly arranging her forks, spoke up.

"As I am new to Germany, Herr Heydrich, perhaps you would be so kind as to explain to me what the difference between a white runner and a black runner is. Why are they not evenly matched?"

If Emilie had stood up and shouted death to Adolf Hitler it could not have had a more chilling effect on the table. Emilie calmly forked some fish and bit into it, looking to the SS officer.

"Because you are new to the reich and I am always eager to help a visitor, especially a pretty one, I will tell you. And if it is unsatisfactory, I'm confident Herr Goebbels can further enlighten you." Reinhard smiled a smile of perfect white teeth. "First of all, the American runner, Owens, is here because our fuehrer permitted it. He has done very well in other contests, but he has not faced our Lutz Long. I know your parents were German, therefore you are of pure German blood. You have returned to Germany, your true homeland—you are part of the master race."

A dozen things leaped to Emilie's tongue, as a blush creeped up to her hairline. He had not answered her question. There were powerful men and women in this room, and she should not risk offending any of them—even the obnoxious Heydrich. She had only come to take pictures...hadn't she? Their arrogant beliefs were...

She wished she could speak just to Heydrich and, later, she might find him alone, but that held even less appeal than having nearly half the table looking at her. She spoke calmly and slowly.

"As you pointed out, Herr Heydrich, my parents were German, and I was born in Munich. They taught me a great many things that I'm proud of, and one of them was to avoid being narrow-minded. Men were judged on their heart and their character, not on their physical strength or the color of their skin. God created all men...in His image. If my parents were in the stands to watch the Games, and I wish they were, we would simply see runners on the field, and one of them would win. This would only mean that one had reached the finish line first."

She reached for her wine and saw that Anne Lindberg was smiling at her.

● ● ●

In the late afternoon of the following day the guests of Max Farber began their lavish gratitudes and goodbyes. The long row of cars turned to go back down the drive, leaving a wake of white dust and sudden quiet. Separately the household staff and the master of the house drew a collective sigh of relief. Max immediately yanked off the narrow tie and sauntered through the empty rooms. Filled ashtrays and stains on the carpets . . . He hoped his party had been a success. He found Rudi supervising the kitchen staff in the mammoth washing chores.

"I don't need anything for dinner tonight. Have everyone assemble this evening, so I can thank them."

"Yes, sir. And the young lady? Won't she want dinner?"

"The who? . . . Oh! Fraulein Morgan." He had seen only glimpses of her during the day, and for a moment had forgotten her. He hadn't spoken to her more than a good morning since he'd found her in the library with Heydrich the evening before.

He yawned deeply. "Do you know where she is?"

Rudi's wife, Magda, spoke up. "I saw her and Percy on the back lawn, heading toward the river."

"Put us something together to munch on, will you, Magda? I think a little picnic on the Spree would be in order."

He did not see the look husband and wife exchanged.

● ● ●

The river was clear and sparkling with a haziness over the opposite bank. Emilie was sitting under the shade of a huge tree near the water. She had been tossing a stick for Percy, when the quiet, soft stir of the water had finally lulled her into closing her eyes. She was thinking about Will Cutler. She didn't immediately hear Percy whine or feel the shadow fall over her.

Max supposed it was considered rude to watch someone sleeping, but at the moment he didn't care. He was watching her as he would the sunset or any other lovely woman—in detached appreciation. *She is pretty*, Maximillian thought. But he had erected a barrier around his heart the day Elaina had said they couldn't make each other happy. It hadn't lessened his enjoyment of female company, however. He just would not pursue marriage. And now, especially with this mission he had given himself, it was impossible. *Besides, isn't she too young for me?*

Percy's barking finally woke her. Max was at the edge of the water getting a boat ready to launch.

"The party's finally over, fraulein. Come rowing with me!"

"Can we take Percy?"

Max straightened. "So you've taken a fancy to my dog, have you?"

Emilie laughed. "My friend Bess would say it's love at first sight."

"Here you are, Herr Max." Heinz and Marta Mueller had come down to them with a small basket. Marta was watching the pretty young American with ill-concealed beaming.

"Danke." Max helped Emilie into the boat then got in also. Heinz pushed the boat off gently, and the older couple waved.

Marta was discreet enough to wait until the boat was out of hearing distance.

"I remember the last time Herr Max went rowing with a lady. He came back looking very sad."

Heinz rubbed his chin. "Ja, ja, that is true."

"They make a lovely couple. I wish they would fall in love. Herr Max needs to settle down and give this old house the voice of children."

Heinz put his arm around her plump shoulders and kissed her cheek. "You are a romantic, my dear."

Marta sighed. "Ja . . . I wish our Wilhelm would find such a lovely girl."

The boat slid around the bend of the river, lost to their view. Heinz drew a tired breath, he would be content just to know where their youngest son was.

●　●　●

A boat gliding silently along a river of polished glass, with a countryside on either side that was still and tranquil, and verdant green—how could there possibly be a more romantic setting? A poet of any generation or an artist with a palette would be stirred to capture the setting, Emily realized, and settled back against the cushions with a contented sigh. The party, for the most part, had been thrilling, but she was glad it was over. Tomorrow would begin hours of work, pressing through the crowds for a decent shot, so this little voyage was a welcome thing. Max handed her a glass of chilled fruit juice and a plate of bread and cheese. Again, Emilie felt that sweep of gratitude.

"Max, this is so nice. I... well, you've made my first few days in Germany very special."

"I'm glad it has been pleasant for you."

Emilie watched the shore, and the silence stretched for many minutes. Max rested on his oars and watched his property sliding by.

"Your party was a great success. I heard many people admiring it as I walked around," Emilie said finally.

"Good. They should not be too surprised that Max Farber can give a decent party."

Emilie didn't know how to interpret this remark since it wasn't said in the usual teasing tone. "You mean because of your wealth?"

He looked a little surprised at her frankness. "No, because they expect Max Farber can do little else besides give a party."

Now she looked surprised.

"Don't misunderstand, I'm not crying in my cup. Let them think what they will."

Emilie reached out to pet Percy for several minutes.

"Do you work with your brother Irwin in the company?"

Max laughed shortly. "He lets me think I do. But I started a farm implement plant in Bremen and one in Hannover. He thinks of it as my hobby."

"Why farm tools?"

"It interested me. Besides, it is what the original Farber Company produced. My great grandfather, I.E. Farber began it."

"And what does Farber make now?"

"Irwin could give you a tidy answer on that. Most of the business is in chemicals. He's branched out into synthetic oil and rubber in the last few years."

Emilie carefully filed this information in her mind. Now was not the time to ask about her father.

The evening deepened and a breeze ruffled the waters.

"It's very beautiful here," Emilie said.

Max dipped the oars and slowly turned the craft back toward the estate. "I've loved this river . . . forever, I guess. I've spent a lot of hours by myself on it. When I was a boy I fancied I could sail all the way to the Mediterranean. I dreamed about adventures . . ."

Emilie was putting the picnic basket back together and giving leftover bits to Percy.

"But I can say that I've never sailed with a lovelier companion." Emilie was growing used to this Farber charm. She could parry it as swiftly as he could deliver it.

"Not even in your imaginary adventures?"

"Not even then," he smiled. "You know, there will be talk from the female side of my guest list on you being my houseguest. You may run into a few of these speculations."

"And I will tell them the truth. I came to see my uncle and take pictures, nothing more—no offense intended."

"And no offense taken. I . . . am merely your host."

Emilie smiled. "And after all, there is someone named Leni Riefenstahl."

Max cleared his throat, "Well, yes. Surely there is a young man back in Washington, D.C."

Emilie hesitated only a moment and nodded.

"There you see!" Max leaned forward conspiratorially. "The tongues can flap, and we will know the truth."

So their understanding was sealed. There would be no interest beyond mere friendship. They landed the boat and finished picking up.

As they were walking up to the house, the lights reached out to them in the darkness. Emilie felt tired, content, and eager for the morning. Max's tone startled her.

"I feel it my responsibility to tell you that Herr Heydrich is a powerful and ambitious man." He stopped and looked at her fully in the face. "He is a man I wouldn't trust. If you come across him at the Games or in the city, I encourage you to be very prudent in your words to him."

Her hands went to her hips. "You mean be afraid of him?"

"No, Emilie. I said be prudent in your speech."

"I had to say something after that taunt he gave Lindberg. And there was Lindberg looking afraid and embarrassed!" She shook her head.

"No one else was going to speak up and say how absurd his notion of race is!"

Max stood looking at the ground, his hands in his pockets. Emilie could not see his face clearly in the shadows. She did not want to put a voice to the obvious question. She liked this friendly German, her uncle's best friend. He had been so hospitable, so charming. She wasn't sure if she wanted to know if he agreed with the pompous Heydrich. She waited a moment more.

Her voice sounded like a small girl to him. It wrenched through him. "Do you believe it, Max?"

"No. But I still believe in my government. Do you agree with everything your President Roosevelt does?"

"Probably."

"But if you didn't, if there were say, an opinion he had against Japan that you didn't agree with, would you no longer support him?"

"No, but I think this is larger than foreign policy! This is a way of viewing men and women."

"It is not large to me. If it is wrong, it is in small comparison to the whole, which is good."

"I'll have to think about that. Goodnight, Max. Thank you for the ride."

Max stood frowning deeply, as he listened to her steps echo through the tiled hall. Marta Mueller, who was shaking out her tea towels, had overheard the last of the exchange. So the sailing had not gone so smooth for Herr Max. Perhaps he should not take a woman on the river until he had her safely married . . .

• • •

Emilie chose the starting line of the 100-meter dash, rather than the finishing line, for her shot. This was the first appearance of the American, Jesse Owens. He was the only black man in the row of ten athletes, one of whom was German. Emilie watched as Owens stretched, then nervously lowered himself into the block. The stadium crowd came to their feet, many of them shouting the name of the German runner. Emilie was close enough to see the beads of sweat forming on Owens' forehead. She could see he was nervous, but he was smiling also, as if he were enjoying himself. The American track coach called out a final word of encouragement. Emilie looked toward the stands. It was not difficult to pick out the fuehrer's box. All the men wore hats and black coats. Autograph seekers crowded under the box. The starting shot went off. In a matter of seconds, Jesse Owens had his first gold medal; the German runner came in fourth.

• • •

Emilie finished her shots of the swimming finals, and was feeling the desire to return to Max's house for a quick shower before the afternoon events, when someone called to her from across the parking lot. It was the newspaper man, Jake Harrold. He was smiling as he came up to her.

"Hello."

He jerked his head toward the pool. "You finished?"

"Yes."

"Our ladies' team would have done a sight better if they hadn't kicked Eleanor Jarrett off," he frowned.

Knowing he probably had the answer, she asked. "Why did they?"

He tipped his head back as if he were thinking. "Kept boasting her training diet was caviar and champagne. The coaches weren't amused. But I thought, heck, if it helps her swim like a fish and defeat these German competitors, I say let her do whatever she wants!"

"But they didn't consult you," Emilie laughed.

"Naw . . . Say, I'm finished for awhile. How 'bout lunch?"

Emilie glanced toward the stadium. Max was there somewhere with the photographer Fraulein Riefenstahl.

"Well, I have a friend . . . he might wonder what happened."

"Aw, come on, you're a big girl. I'd like to compare notes."

And suddenly Emilie did want to be with the newspaper man and away from Max's tether.

"All right."

"Good, 'cause I could sure use a beer."

• • •

The Tavern, Berlin's watering hole for foreign journalists, was everything Harrold had boasted: crowded, with everyone talking at once under a fog of cigarette smoke. Harrold graciously introduced Emilie to over a dozen reporters and photographers. As they were all bolting their meals and talking, they gave her bland, cursory attention. A few however, spoke their minds, with their mouths full. "Kinda young, aren't ya? I'm surprised ol' Washington McVinty would send a kid over."

"I'm hardly a kid. I'm 24," she replied defensively to one reporter's comments.

The reporter grunted and sank his teeth back into his drippy beef sandwich.

A woman reporter had smiled and offered her hand, then loudly asked, "How many propositions have you gotten from the SS or Gestapo?"

They were watching her. She reddened. "None."

She was thankful when Harrold steered her to a small outside table. "You don't look like you'd enjoy your meal with all that smoke."

"Thank you."

He pulled off his thick glasses to polish them with the end of his tie. "You really haven't had any SS tryin' for ya?"

Emilie could laugh now, and shook her head.

"And they say my eyesight is bad!"

They ate and talked over their meal. Emilie found herself telling this near-stranger all her impressions. Harrold listened carefully and inserted his own observations.

"So that explains it. No wonder you haven't had anybody tryin' to pick you up. This Farber guy's been with you all the time."

"Well, not the whole time. Not now." Hesitantly she told him about her encounter with Reinhard Heydrich.

He gave a low whistle. "Man, you move fast!"

Emilie laughed delightedly. "I didn't do anything."

"You get close to Lindberg and Goebbels! And Heydrich makes a play for you? He's a smooth one all right. I think your friend is right. Be polite and steer clear of him."

"Why? Other than being a married man with a . . . roving eye, is he really that bad?"

Harrold was now comfortably picking his teeth.

"Göring is fat and silly. Goebbels is paranoid and dillusional. Himmler's an ambitious exchicken farmer. From what I've picked up, Heydrich's being groomed by the fuehrer himself to take over the SS. He's very cool and tough. I hear a few . . . whispers that he's more than lecherous—he has this sadistic, cruel streak. Don't draw attention to yourself."

Emilie remembered his cold, marblelike profile as he had stood inspecting the Farber library. Harrold's words were not hard to believe.

Emilie toyed with her salad. "My friend, Herr Farber, he—"

"The youngest one?"

She nodded.

"Sure, I've heard of Max. He always makes the social pages."

Emilie wasn't sure she wanted to know anymore from Harrold's extensive knowledge of Berlin personalities.

"So, you've heard of him."

"Bachelor Farber always with a different dame on his arm. Driving
around town in a convertible with a dog in the seat behind him. A few
years ago he was tight with Elaina Heydrich."

"Reinhard's wife?" Emilie asked, shocked.

"His sister. Max is a Nazi Party boy but not near as ambitious as big
brother Irwin. He's a likable guy, kind of on the inane side."

"He's very kind and generous," Emilie defended. "He doesn't strike
me as this hard-hearted type you cast all Nazis as, though."

"Not yet. They aren't all like that . . . yet. A lot of them go along for
the ride. Believe me I know, I've been talking to 'em for nearly two
years. Hitler's given them a show and promises and full bellies. Though,
in Farber's case, that hardly matters. He's in it because it's the thing to
do."

Emilie studied her plate. "After Heydrich made his speech about
Jesse Owens and race, Herr Farber said it wasn't a big issue with him.
Maybe because we live outside of Germany, we don't see it as they do."

Harrold snorted. "I'm tellin' ya, if he said that, he's taken it hook,
line, and sinker. What Goebbels and Hitler spoon out, they swallow. If
they said the earth is really flat, your Farber friend would be afraid to
sail to the edge of the horizon. If they said Americans really evolved
from apes, he'd serve you bananas at breakfast tomorrow."

Emilie was laughing. "I've got that pure German blood, though."
She sobered then. "At the opening ceremonies . . ."

He shook his head with disgust. He already knew her thoughts. His
voice was laced with irritation. "The torch lighting has always been a
symbol of goodwill, now they've turned it into a show of blatant Nazi
pride."

"We say the pledge of allegiance at a Yankee game," Emilie said
slyly, remembering the Lindbergs.

"Don't be dopey, it isn't the same thing."

"We feel pride in our country; they feel pride in theirs."

He shook his head vehemently. "You haven't been here long enough to understand. Your smooth Farber heir has just shown you the pretty Berlin sights. He—"

"Well, what else is there?"

He glanced around, lowering his voice. "You don't understand. You don't understand what the Nazis are really like."

"And I don't think they are all alike. Max is as different from Heydrich as . . . Look, if things aren't as they seem—you called it the topside of Berlin—then show me what you're talking about. Being a German, I should know the truth."

"You're a spunky kid . . ." He saw her face. "All right, all right, maybe if you stick around after the Games—if you still want to—but not now. Anyway, I have to go."

"Why do you stay in Berlin if you dislike the Nazis so much?"

His grin was wide. "They make things real interestin'."

• • •

Emilie had politely told Max the next morning she would not need his assistance or escort at the Games any longer.

"I think I can get by on my press pass all right. I'll just catch a cab home in the evening."

She had scooped up her film and camera bag, missing the crestfallen and disappointed look he had given her. He sat stirring his coffee, feeling rebuffed. And he suspected it was over his acquiescence to Nazi racial policy. He sighed. So be it.

"Today's the big day!" she called cheerfully, as she left. "Auf wiedersehen, Max!"

And so it was a big day for many Germans. The eyes of the world were focused on this contest. Owens had captured three gold medals. Today he would try for the fourth when he went against the favored German, Long.

As she expected, the fuehrer and his companions were on their feet. She could pick out Max's white suit in the stands. A woman in white was beside him. She turned and stepped as close to the jump as she was permitted. Long had taken his jump and the stadium roared. Owens came to the plate, poised, and ran. The judges hurried forward with their tape. The cards came up. The American had landed farther again. To Emilie's surprise, the crowd again erupted in cheering. She raised her camera and shot as the German jumper came and put his arm around the black man. They were smiling and laughing. Then Long led Owens around the track to the cheers. Emilie lowered her camera, a little stunned. She hoped Harrold was somewhere in the vast crowd taking note. She hoped Reinhard Heydrich was in the crowd as well....

The track coach had joyously thrust a small American flag in Emilie's hand. She was laughing and waving it—and forgetting entirely she was supposed to be an impartial observer. From the stands, Max was watching her and smiling.

20
Collisions

1937

A cold rain and a raw wind slanted and slammed against the windows of Max Farber's Berlin house. The red and yellow city lights looked like melted pools of color against the dark December night. The streets themselves were rivers of oily black. While not sufficient yet for skating, the River Spree was crusty with ice. It was such a night to stay close to home fires, and more so, because it was Christmas Eve.

Max had tempered the library fire to a moderate roar, and at one point, Emilie was actually fanning herself and threatening to open the windows. Max and Josef exchanged a look that contained only a single communication—women! Josef was lounging in his favorite leather chair, a Berlin paper lying idle across his lap, his thoughts far from this room and only coming back from his meditations when one of the other occupants summoned him. It could not be said at the moment that his thoughts were exactly filled with festive and yuletide cheer. He had read the fuehrer's latest speech delivered to the Reichstag that morning. It was angry, impudent, and full of threats toward the independent government of Austria. The fuehrer had spent considerable time explaining to his docile audience that Germany needed more "lebensraum," living space. She needed to expand her frontiers. It seemed to the doctor that the German Chancellor's disinterest in foreign matters for most of the year was now drawing to a close. He also appeared occupied with economic matters inside the borders of Germany.

But the lack of interest in foreign affairs had been a well-designed, deceiving one. Josef, like so many, of course, didn't know that.

Max was strolling around the room with a smug expression, his hands thrust into the pockets of his silk jacket. Emilie was bent over a chess board, ignoring Max's posturing.

"Perhaps you should fetch fraulein Emilie a white handkerchief to wave, Percy. She's looking desperate."

Josef chuckled and Emilie looked up to roll her eyes.

"Josef, don't you have anything in your bag for a case of terminal arrogance?" Emilie asked her uncle. She moved her knight. "I am far from desperate, Herr Farber, and it's your move."

"My move! How . . ."

Emilie stood and stretched.

"You've met your match, Max, might as well admit it," Josef provided.

"Hmmm . . ."

"I'm going to bring up the refreshments now," Emilie said. "Max looks like he needs reviving."

Max continued to study the board as the doctor studied him. Percy followed Emilie downstairs.

"Your dog has lost his heart to my niece," Josef observed mildly

"Hmmm . . ."

Josef leaned back, thinking of that summer day when he'd come into the hotel lobby in Geneva to find Max smiling broadly, like a big kid, with a slim young girl standing beside him. She seemed to hesitate only a moment before she propelled herself into his arms. How surprised, then, how glad he had been to see her. Now a year-and-a-half had passed and she was part of their household, putting their bachelor days on the shelf for a time. Her voice, her laughter, her laundry on the line, the smell of her shampoo and perfume, her own little cooking feats, her camera case, her photos, her pumps on the floor, her excitement, her silences when she was thinking filled their lives. Their walks together in Tiergarten, her pampering him with a hot lunch at the clinic. . . . The daughter he had never had. . . . And he was the father she missed. Berlin could be dreary to Josef Morgan even though it was his city—and now a city with an imposter's face—but it was infinitely dearer to him now that she had come and stayed.

Percy sat on a stool to watch the mistress of the house as she prepared a tray with tempting treats. He made no effort to control his tongue that lolled in expectation. If Max came down and saw such obvious imploring, he'd scold. With the young woman humming over the stove, he knew he'd get a few bites if he were only patient. The American had a distinctly pampering way that had sealed his devotion for all his canine days.

Emilie was stirring the schokolade and humming "Silent Night." She had prepared the tray knowing all the proportions and preferences of the two men waiting upstairs. She knew this kitchen now...as she had known the one in Georgetown. Georgetown ... under the little tree up in the library was a brown-wrapped package from Bess. Bess who was no longer Bennett, but Adams. Emilie smiled. The letter that had come with the package had been drenched in bliss and domestic tranquility—Bess had once said all problems could be solved with marriage. So the newlywed myopia continued...

Emilie couldn't deny that despite her acclimation in Germany, she missed her voluble friend. Emilie had persuaded her to come over the previous summer. Bess's observations of Germany, Max Farber, and Adolf Hitler had been, for Emilie, a much needed dose of hilarity. But now that seemed so long ago. And the letters came infrequently now. Bess had built a new life for herself, just as Emilie was. The tether to the United States had grown thinner as time stretched on.

Emilie stopped humming. She arranged the tray things a little absently now. Percy looked on with growing alarm. Emilie could not think of Bess...without thinking of Will Cutler. He came into her mind at odd, unexpected times. It used to be every night when she crawled into bed. Sometimes when Max said something teasing, it reminded her of Will. At first, it had been almost everytime she had picked up her camera. Now...now, like his letters, her thoughts traveled across the Atlantic less often. His letters were kept in an upstairs bedroom drawer, the last one postmarked August. The letters were kept beside a neat file of the Olympic Games photos. Her copies...but what did it matter. Those she had sent had never made the magazine. He had written that the irascible McVinty had changed his mind, but a check had been sent, giving cold and hollow satisfaction to the American photographer who had looked eagerly for her first magazine photo essay. Will's letters had been formal and newsy, and little else. After a time, and a season of tears, she had stopped looking for more than friendly topics. There was no passion, no promise. She took a long walk on the Farber country estate one weekend and saw her future was Bess and Gary Cooper on Friday nights and her days at Woolworth's. She decided to extend her stay in Germany. And after a few weeks, with the obvious affection of her uncle and the friendship of Max, the stay lengthened. A job taking photos for the American embassy, and Emilie Morgan had taken root in the homeland of her parents. Josef had been pleased, proud, and declared it was fitting. Though missing Bess and hurting from a romance that perhaps had never really been a romance, Emilie was happy this Christmas Eve. Percy was now whining with such energy he was about to topple the stool. He brought Emilie back to the kitchen. She laughed and gave him a pinch of sausage roll.

When Emilie returned to the library, she found Max weighing her package to him in his hands. Josef was puzzling over the chess board.

"Max, put that down! You can't do that before Christmas!"

"I've eliminated the possibility of a tie."

She took the package from him and returned it to the tree. She stood admiring the little evergreen that she and Max had hunted for and brought home together. With the tiny lit candles and tinsel it was beautiful. Her face grew shadowed, and Max, standing beside her, wondered what she was thinking of. That American she had spoken infrequently and casually of and now never mentioned? Even Max knew the letters to Berlin from Washington had not come in months. But he didn't feel, even in their close friendship, he could ask her about it. She glanced up, momentarily startled that he stood so close and looked so . . . It was Max. She cleared her throat.

"It's always so important to have family at Christmas," she said softly.

He nodded slowly.

They talked and laughed over their food. Josef read the Christmas story from the Bible. Outside the storm raged, but they were warm and comfortable. At midnight, they toasted each other.

"Do you like Christmas any better now, Max?" Emilie asked. He had told her the year before that Christmas holidays had not always been pleasant at the Farber home.

His blond head was bent slightly. Even Josef expected a flippant answer. Max fingered his glass. Emilie looked at her uncle and he shrugged. The fire crackled into rich red embers. Finally Max spoke, looking up and smiling, "Ja, I like it better. I think you have made it better." His eyes held her a moment. "Wouldn't you agree, Josef?"

Josef took Emilie's hand and kissed it. "I would say she's made everything better."

"Certainly the sausage rolls," Max added.

"Enough you two. Such flattery—"

"Will certainly get me permission to open a gift," Max said as he returned to the gift he'd held earlier.

Emilie shook her head. "You're terrible."

"It is officially Christmas."

Josef and Emilie watched amused as Max tore off the paper. He glanced toward the wall near his desk.

"I don't know how it could be better than last years'."

The year before, Emilie had placed three small black-and-white photographs in an elegant frame and given it to Max as his Christmas gift. One photo showed the German athlete Lutz Long as he prepared to jump. The second photo showed Jesse Owens as he began his run down the narrow track toward the winning leap. The third photo showed the two competitors smiling, with their arms around each other. Max had said it was her best photos of the Games, but he would not invite any of his Nazi friends into his library. "We've decided none of them have the impeccable taste I do," Max had said.

Emilie had made a sour face. "Well, we've decided they don't have something. . . ."

He brushed away the paper. It was another framed picture.

"I apologize for a lack of imagination, Max," Emilie laughed. "You're hard to buy for—the man who has everything!"

Josef observed with his critical eye a fleeting shadow that crossed Max's handsome face.

"Do you like it?" Emilie ventured a little timidly.

Josef stretched to see. Emilie knew Max's love of astronomy, his passion for the moon. With her camera, she had caught a full moon as it hung luminous over the river that lapped the edge of Max's boyhood home. The moon and his country home in one photograph.

Finally, he looked up. "Ja, it is . . . very nice." He nodded. "Very nice."

He reached for a gift for Josef and Emilie.

Josef was pleased with a richly bound book of verse. Emilie opened her gift slowly and with a little trepidation. There was no predicting what the rich young man would lavish on her. Last year, it had been a camera. But this package was thin and slender. She opened a black velvet case. It was a beautiful string of pearls.

"Max . . ."

"You rejected them once, I think on the excuse that I was nearly a stranger. Well, we're old friends now, so you must take them."

Emilie felt awkward. "Max, this is too much."

"And why, pray tell?"

"Because these were your mothers' pearls. They are to go to a Farber bride."

Josef tugged at his chin and looked at the floor. *Ah, these young people. . . . I'm getting too old to understand*, he decided. He had given up hoping these two would do the sensible thing and fall in love. It seemed so obvious—except to them. When he looked up, Percy was looking from face to face, as if he watched a ball being tossed back and forth. They both looked distinctly embarrassed. Josef stood stiffly.

"I'm going to bed. Frau Leiberman wants a Christmas baby and she usually gets her way. And I want to be in fine mettle for your feast tomorrow, so goodnight. Merry Christmas one and all."

Emilie kissed him. "Goodnight, Uncle Josef."

Max still sat, watching Emilie. "Let's try them on."

"Max . . ."

"Jewels are cold and ugly and useless in a velvet box, fraulein. They are meant to be held against something warm and living and . . . lovely."

He stood behind her and she shivered as she felt his breath against her neck. This was the almost legendary Farber charm she had heard of and experienced since she had come to know him. *I can't let it go to my head*. She felt a little dizzy with daring.

"But as I said, it was meant for . . ."

"And as I have said, I'm a confirmed bachelor, so they are meant for you."

She couldn't know that he had closed his eyes for a moment.
She turned around. "Well . . . all right then, if you insist."
He gave her a slight bow. "I do insist."
She stretched up on her toes to kiss him on the cheek.
"Danke, Max. Merry Christmas."
He watched her leave. *The man who had everything?*

• • •

Two nights later, Emilie padded down to the kitchen to let Percy in
from the enclosed back garden. It was nearly midnight and she knew
Max was at one of his holiday parties. She privately held in contempt
these gatherings of Nazi high officials. Josef had gone to bed. She
stopped, surprised, before the closed kitchen door. A thread of light
could be seen under it. She could hear low murmured voices. Who? She
tensed. *Surely burglars wouldn't announce themselves so blatantly. And
Max was notorious for very late nights.*

Suddenly the door swung open. Max was framed in the light.
"Emilie?"

Emilie reddened with embarrassment. How did he know she had
been standing there? Max must think she had been eavesdropping. If he
did, he didn't betray it in his typical, smooth manner.

"Did you need something?" he asked.

"I . . . remembered that I hadn't let Percy back in," she stammered.
Percy stood at Max's leg. Emilie knew then how he had been alerted.
Max moved back to reveal he was not alone. A thin young man now
stood beside the kitchen table.

"I heard voices and I . . ."

Max led her in. "Emilie, I don't believe you've met my brother. Emilie, this is Eric Farber. Eric, this is fraulein Emilie Morgan."

Emilie was startled. He looked as unlike Max as the older, grizzled
Irwin did. He was slightly taller than Max and much thinner. He wore a
Luftwaffe uniform and highly polished boots. His hair was lanky and
brown. Only his blue eyes bore any resemblance to his brother. But
when he gave her a tired smile as he bent over her hand, she decided she
liked his face. It was kind.

"Delighted to meet you at last, fraulein. Max has told me so much
about you."

Emilie laughed a little nervously. "Oh, no. I hope it's all been good."

She knew the society circles of Berlin still raised an eyebrow over this unconventional arrangement: an unmarried young woman living with the rich bachelor—even if her uncle lived there, too. She knew what many of them must think.

"He merely understated your beauty," Eric said.

"Well, the Farber charm strikes again," she returned.

The three laughed.

"It was nice to meet you. Goodnight." Emilie backed from the kitchen.

The men exchanged a look, then smiled. Max refilled Eric's coffee cup.

●   ●   ●

"Now I see why the tongues have wagged."

Max sat back down with a heavy sigh. "As I said before, we are friends, Eric. You can make a play for her if you like."

"I have a girl."

Max raised an eyebrow. Eric, so quiet and reserved, had never had a girlfriend before as far as Max knew. But since they had never really been close, he supposed there were likely many things about this man that he didn't know.

"I met her in Wilmershaven. She's a fine girl. We ... we've talked about marriage. Perhaps this summer."

Max slapped him on the back. "Congratulations." He drew a long drink of hot coffee, eyeing his brother in the uniform.

"This must help take the sting out of leaving the Luftwaffe."

Eric gave him a thin smile. "I was pretty disappointed not to get to fly. It was the strangest thing, though. Every time we reached 5,000 feet, I'd black out."

"Not something Herr Göring would allow in his fine German pilots, I would think," Max inserted.

Eric chuckled. "Exactly. But it's turned out for the best, though I didn't think so at first. Now I'm going into a medical corp. Just the direction I've always wanted to take."

"Dr. Farber ... Josef will be pleased," Max mused, and looked to the ceiling. "A Farber son finds his calling at last."

"And you, Max? How goes it with Irwin?"

"It goes as it always has. Irwin lets me toy with the business. When I came back from Brazil, I started up a few farming implement plants. We just opened one near Cracow. I think it amuses Irwin. It's like pocket change to him. It also keeps me out of his hair. So I put in a few hours at the office, look to my farming plants, sign the papers that Beck puts in front of me. A tidy arrangement for everyone." He waved a limp hand in the air.

"And that is what you want for the rest of your life?" Eric asked with unexpected earnestness.

"I don't look past tomorrow," Max returned easily.

"For the first time in my life, because of Anna, I want there to be a tomorrow . . . for us."

Max studied him a moment. "And why shouldn't there be a tomorrow?"

Eric shook his head, and Max instinctively knew his brother was troubled and burdened. He had seen this look before.

Finally Eric lifted his eyes. "Max, you hear things. You're in the party now, you must know . . ." He lowered his voice. "Germany is gearing for war."

Max's heart was racing. Here was the confirmation he had been seeking for months, and it was going to be laid neatly before him.

"I hear rumors," he admitted casually.

Eric swallowed hard. "They aren't rumors, Max. The fuehrer says Germany needs more room."

"I've read *Mein Kampf*, Eric. Certainly it's boring reading, but it's his . . . vision. Getting from vision to reality can be a great leap. Great leaders always tell their countrymen they must go on conquests. It makes them popular. He—"

Eric silenced him with a look. He glanced around the kitchen as if he were suddenly troubled with the prospect of hidden ears—or microphones.

"Max, this isn't ranting and posturing. There was a meeting two months ago in the Chancellery with Hitler, Göring, and the generals' Brauchitsch and Raeder. Hitler pretty much laid it out. He's going for Austria early in the spring. That's why he's having the Austrian Nazis stir things up. It's a bold move like Rhineland was. He's even put a red circle on the map of Czechoslovakia."

"How do you know this, Eric?" Max asked calmly.

"I just know, Max, trust me," Eric replied tiredly.

"Why are you telling me? You have doubts about our leaders' high goals?"

Eric looked him in the eye. "I have to tell someone. And, yes, I am having doubts. And you don't go around advertising that. I hear the generals are nervous about this, too. They don't think Germany is ready for any kind of military confrontation. I don't know, Max . . . I will go along with it. Of course, in loyalty, I must."

Max's face was impassive. "Of course. Well, stop worrying, Eric. Concentrate on your girl."

Eric leaned back. "Life is that for you, eh Max? Pure enjoyment? I envy you. No worries, no risks, no troubles—"

"Beyond deciding what color tie to wear in the morning, ja."

Eric stood, draining off the last of his coffee. *Have I said more than I should have? Even if this is phlegmatic Max,* he wondered.

"I would have thought none of this would really be news to you, Max."

"At parties I avoid boring politics and such. Social events are for pleasant and more satisfying pursuits." He winked.

"I meant from Farber's involvement you should be more than aware." Eric pulled on his gloves and gray woolen coat. "Unless Irwin really does keep things hidden from you." He sighed. "The last war swelled the Farber treasury, I suppose it will do it again. No one could accuse Irwin of being ignorant of opportunities. Where do you think he gets this passion for making money, Max?"

Max shrugged. "Who knows? I'm just enormously grateful," he said as he saw Eric to the door and said goodnight.

The youngest Farber son sat for a long time alone in the warm kitchen. His head sunk to his hands. He fervently hoped neither Josef nor Emilie would put in a sudden appearance. He felt tired, lonely—and angry.

● ● ●

The night watchman of the new Farber office building on Unter den Linden had already gone through the first tour of the five story building for the night. Now, at 9:30, he settled in at the reception front desk for his coffee break. He carefully measured brandy into his cup. He would have preferred to have added a little more, but there was always the possibility of Irwin Farber suddenly breezing through his private entrance and up to his office for late-night business. This happened at least once a week. It still surprised the watchman though he had been here over six months, to find himself face-to-face with the solid, frowning Farber in the corridor. He had supposed men who were as rich as Irwin Farber didn't have to keep such long hours. You paid others to do your work when you had that much money. Farber had bluntly told him there was to be no liquor consumption during his shift on penalty of immediate dismissal. But tonight was New Year's Eve. Of course, the business magnate would not come in. And why shouldn't he have some comforting spirits as every other fortunate Berliner was doing. So he spiked his coffee and went to the outer vestibule where he could look up and down the wide boulevard. Cars were bumper to bumper, lights shone from nearly every building. A grand party tonight, and he had to work. He sighed with envy.

Of course it was not quite as bad as the old workman who pushed the heavy bucket and mop down the long tile floors. The watchman glanced at the wall clock. He had greeted the old man 30 minutes ago. He should be on the third floor by now. He yawned and went back to the desk. He felt a wave of benevolence. He'd go up in another 40 minutes and share his coffee.

The cleaning man was not on the third floor as his fellow worker had estimated. He had hurried, two steps at a time up to the fourth floor. His arthritic stoop had instantly vanished when the elevator door closed on the watchman. Hurriedly he unlocked the door to the suite of third-floor offices. He did not trust the lights and only used the pocket lamp he had concealed in his dirty overalls. He went to the office of Karl Beck. After a succession of keys, he unlocked the door.

He stopped a moment in surprise. He had not been here in nearly two years. He did not remember this expensive decor. A bar had been added in one corner. He drew the heavy drapes closed and seated himself at the desk. He drew a sigh of relief—it was unlocked. He felt through the top of the drawer, his fingers finally brushing across a key. He smiled.

The filing cabinets slid open after he unlocked them. He glanced at his watch. He knew that in 20 minutes the watchman would begin his rounds. He glanced at the locked office door and refused to imagine what would happen if Karl Beck entered. But he was counting on this night of revelry to distract the ambitious secretary.

He had only a vague idea of what he was looking for. He would find some notation that would lead him along a trail to the answer he suspected—and dreaded. He was not surprised at the thoroughness of the notes. After searching through months of files for the year 1935, he came to what he was looking for. He glanced at his watch. He needed more time. He slammed the file closed and hurried back down to the third floor. The watchmen was just getting off the elevator when the janitor stepped through the door of the stairwell.

The watchman bristled with authority.

"What are you doing, old man? Where have you been?"

The janitor croaked for a laugh. "Ja, ja, you caught me." He bent over his bucket.

The watchman came to stand before him, hands on hips, frowning and imperious. "Tell me!"

"I went up to the fifth floor. I confess. I took my break a little early. I wanted to see the city lights from the hall window. Have you seen the city from there? It is all lit up tonight like, like a Christmas tree! So many cars...ja, the good fuehrer has made our city prosperous."

"You wait till your done with your work before you go sightseeing! Do your job!"

"Ja, ja, of course you are right. But you should go up there, so many lights . . ." He pushed the mop forward.

The watchman stood watching him a moment more, something nagging at his mind. Something about this old man...same greasy overalls, same bent back and gray hair....He turned and went back down the elevator. The janitor waited five minutes before he repeated his performance of the earlier hour. He dashed back up the stairs—he knew that from the front desk any elevator use would be detected.

He returned to the file cabinet. He wished he could smuggle these papers out, but he could not afford to do that yet. After another 20 minutes, the trail he had sought lead him to a single sheet of paper. It was dated May, 1933. Four years ago.

Four years ago...He looked at the sprawling signature at the bottom. His own. Max Farber closed his eyes.

• • •

In her almost two years as a resident of the Third Reich, this was the biggest party Emilie Morgan had been to. And the first time she had been escorted by someone other than Max Farber. Ambassador Wilson, head of the American embassy, had approached her with the polite proposition that she be a date for his son visiting from the states.

"He's engaged to a lovely girl, so you need not worry."

Emilie frowned to herself. *Why would I worry*?

Still she dressed with typical feminine care, knowing from Berlin society pages that this New Year's Eve party at the Kaiserhof Hotel was considered the select Berlin party of the year with guests from German high society and also Nazi officials—even an appearance by the fuehrer himself was possible.

She twirled in a display of white satin before her uncle, Percy, and Max who happened in.

"Very, very beautiful," Josef nodded approvingly.

Max, lounging against the doorframe, had an unexpected sullen appearance. They looked to him for an equally enthusiastic compliment. But he stood, observing Emilie with a strangely critical eye.

"You will shine in the Nazi galaxy tonight, I'm sure," he said in a laconic tone.

"Thank you . . . I think," Emilie laughed.

"What do you know of this Wilson fellow?" Max asked.

"Well, I know he's on parole for triple murder in the States. He's an avowed communist and he's a drug addict. I think we'll have fun, though."

Max kept a poker face.

"You're doing a very good big brother imitation, Max," Josef said slyly.

"My thoughts exactly," Emilie agreed. "Will you be at the Kaiserhof with . . . fraulein Riefenstahl?"

"The Kaiserhof will be too crowded with uniforms and monocles and heavy women trying to claim a dance after too much champagne. No thank you. I prefer something more intimate." He bowed.

"Oooo," was all Emilie could comment.

"Have a gay time, fraulein," Max said as he prepared to exit.

"And a Happy New Year to you, too, Max."

As soon as they were alone, Emilie twirled once more for her uncle. It had been a long time since she had splurged on such a gown. It had been a long time since she had dressed up and felt elegant and...Suddenly she thought of a long ago night in the Heigh Ho Club with Will holding her close...

"He was certainly in a sour mood," Emilie sniffed.

Josef nodded with reluctance. He had noticed the same thing. *Something was bothering his young friend, something he has not shared with the doctor.*

"Well, I suppose we could speculate that he was jealous he wasn't escorting you."

Emilie frowned. "Are you serious? Don't be silly, Uncle Josef. I'm wearing his pearls," she finished lamely.

Josef shrugged.

Emilie pulled the brush through her hair once more in front of the hall mirror. "Why has Max never married, Uncle Josef? I mean he's young, rich, charming, and handsome. My friend Bess would say he's a top catch." Emilie sat down on the deeply carpeted stairs beside the older man.

"You're his closest, oldest friend, you must know," she pressed.

Josef studied the fabric of his pants.

"We are close, Emilie. You know I've loved him all these years as if he were my own flesh. I've watched him grow...I've seen many of his little triumphs. Did you know, for example, that he's an excellent pianist?"

She shook her head. "The piano is always draped at the country house. I guessed it was his mother's."

"No. It was part of the house from another generation, but Max taught himself to play. His father didn't approve, but Max kept on despite that, despite his brother's teasing. He kept on until his mother asked him to quit...to please his father. He was very good. He told me once he wanted to be a concert pianist when he grew up. So I've seen his triumphs, I've seen his tragedies as well. His childhood was far from happy. I'm telling you this to explain my answer to your question. I think Max avoids the commitment of marriage because he's afraid to love and be hurt."

Ralph Wilson was then at the door, and Percy barked furiously. Emilie was saved from comment—but she did not forget the conversation.

• • •

Max stood resplendent in a black tuxedo at the entrance to the Kaiserhof ballroom. His hair was brushed to shining, his face a little pink from scrubbing. He greeted a dozen friends in typical fashion, accepted a glass of champagne that he downed quickly. He had some vague hope it would cool his rising temper. He scanned the room. All the Nazi notables: Göring, Himmler, Hess, Goebbels. He did not see the fuehrer. He spotted Elaina Heydrich. He greeted her affably and invited her to dance. Soon he had her laughing like old times. Once again she felt the firmness of his arms. But she was married now to a rich Italian count. While they danced and chatted, Max continued his search of the room. There were hundreds of partiers present. Emilie was resting between dances in the congenial company of Mrs. Wilson. Ralph had gone off to get them drinks.

"Look there, Emilie, isn't that Max Farber?"

Emilie looked. "Yes . . ."

"Who? . . . Why that's Elaina Heydrich he's dancing with!"

Emilie appraised the elegantly dressed woman in Max's arms. She wasn't heavy set. She wasn't wearing a monocle. Had she had too much champagne?

"I can't remember her married name," Mrs. Wilson continued. "It's so hard to pronounce anyway. I wonder if her husband is here to see her dancing with such a handsome young man. But they say the marriage isn't a happy one. Maximillian can be such a rake, he—"

She stopped abruptly, coloring to the neck of her dress. For a moment, she had forgotten who this young woman was living with . . .

Max left the dance floor. He was still looking across the crowded room. If he did not find him soon, he was going to leave.

"Stoking the old . . . flame, Max?" a voice came at his elbow.

Max turned reluctantly. This was not a night that he wanted to see, much less speak to, Reinhard Heydrich.

"Reinhard . . ." They watched Elaina depart. "Just saying hello, actually."

"Leni with you?"

"No."

"Ah, your little . . . houseguest. There she is, dancing with the American ambassador's son."

Max finally spotted Emilie in the crowd. She looked like she was having a good time. Fresh and young in her white satin. He had never noticed the glossy highlights of her hair before. He forgot the tall officer beside him. Reinhard seemed to read his thoughts.

"Ja, she is beautiful. Tempting in a virginal sort of way."

Max grabbed another champagne from a passing tray. He had taken a great risk this cold December night in his janitor charade. He had learned a terrible truth that had shaken and sickened him. He felt a guilt that wounded him. He must control his temper in the face of this arrogant, rapacious man. Reinhard represented all the hurts of the past, too. But there would be challenges—many of them he suspected—in the future when he must keep his cool and expected mild manner. This was Max Farber.

He sipped his drink.

Reinhard leaned a little closer. "I envy you, Max. She's been stirring me ever since I saw her in your library. I'm a man of varied . . . tastes. I've never had an American woman before."

Max thought of a thousand replies. "Hmm . . ."

"You're turning red, Max. I'm not going to steal her . . . unless she comes running to me," he chuckled. "How could I possibly refuse? A German-American alliance could be very enjoyable."

"Yes, those days of stealing are long over, Reinhard. The pony was the last time. . . . I see Irwin, I've been looking for him all night. Say hello to Lena for me. Happy New Year, Reinhard," Max called as he walked toward Irwin.

Max led his oldest brother to a private dining room in the hotel. They faced each other across a long table.

"Make it fast, Max. I don't want to keep Katrina waiting."

Max gripped the back of a chair until his knuckles whitened.

"No, this won't take long at all. How long has Farber Company been under contract with the government to make armaments?"

Irwin did not betray his surprise, nor did he attempt to lie.

"You can see a detailed report tomorrow."

"I want answers now, Irwin. Neither of us will be leaving this room until I have them."

"Threats do not become you, Max." But Irwin's tone was a little shaky. "The contract was begun in 1935, officially. Farber plants have been manufacturing for three years."

"What exactly?"

The elder Farber licked his lips. "Tank turrets and guns."

Max looked to the floor. His voice was a controlled rage.

"Where?"

"Hamburg and Kiel."

"Plants you made sure I never visited. Armament production is a clear and flagrant violation of the Treaty of Versailles. You know that. If any representative of the Allies found this out, your precious money-making monster would go bust and you'd be sitting in jail. The Company would go down and everything our family has put into it—not to mention the people it employs."

"A frail argument, little brother. The government of Germany does not recognize the despicable Treaty of Versailles. I could tell the prime minister of England or the president of France myself what Farber is doing and what could they do against the great Third Reich? What did they do about our occupation of Rhineland except snivel and whine? They can't touch Adolf Hitler!"

"Napoleon's generals thought the same thing, Irwin."

He laughed hollowly. "I am Farber Company, Maximillian. Me. I control it. You know that. Eric knows that. The synthetic oil, the rubber, the tank parts, the guns, they make the company rich, they will make Germany great." Irwin's eyes narrowed. "Surely this immature outburst doesn't suggest disloyalty to the Third Reich. That would be disturbing, Max. I'm not sure how the Gestapo would feel about this, if they got wind of it."

Max straightened. He studied Irwin with an expressionless face, his thoughts bitter. *Everything he said was true. Irwin was the victor again.*

Irwin pulled out a long cigar, smiling with a final taunt.

"What does all this matter now? You signed the agreement. Production is well under way. Your bank account swells each month."

Max's voice was tight. "I did sign the paper . . . but I..I didn't know what it was."

Like an echo rising up in his mind, he recalled Josef's concerns so many years ago. "You must take more interest, Max. You can't leave it all to Irwin."

"You mean you signed a paper you didn't read first?" Irwin mocked.

Max felt as if he were choking. "Yes, and you and Karl knew that. You did this together."

"It's time for me to get back to the party. I think it would be best for both of us if we forgot this entire conversation ever took place."

Max's voice dropped to a near whisper. "It isn't supposed to be like this, Irwin."

But Irwin brushed past him without a word. He didn't care if Max meant the activities of the company or the relationship between brothers. Either way, it really didn't matter.

● ● ●

Max wanted to slip out of the hotel unnoticed. He certainly didn't feel like going back into the loud, bright, ballroom. But suddenly he thought of Heydrich's predatory look at Emilie across the room and he wanted to make sure she was all right and still in the company of the neutral Ralph Wilson. It didn't take him long to find her.

Emilie had been standing in a small group with Ambassador Wilson, his wife and Ralph, and a few others, when Heydrich, Ribbentrop, and Adolf Hitler had approached them. Pleasantries, introductions, and New Year good wishes were exchanged. Emilie found herself face-to-face with the German leader. She had seen him from a distance, now she stood looking into his dark eyes. He smiled and extended his hand.

"Mine fuehrer, this is fraulein Emilie Morgan," Heydrich said pleasantly.

Emilie was tongue tied. How was she to greet this man?

"It's nice to meet you," she said at last.

He bowed slightly. "You remained in Germany," he said.

So he knew about her. This was like, like Roosevelt knowing her by name! Why should such an important, busy man like the fuehrer know that she had remained in Germany after the Summer Olympic Games?

"Ja."

"She is part of my very capable staff," the ambassador smiled.

And a most lovely addition," Hitler said softly. He was staring into her eyes—which left her feeling distinctly uncomfortable. She had heard the leader had this almost hypnotic quality over women. She glanced up at Heydrich. He was smiling, too, possessively and intimately. This man made her sick.

"America's loss, our gain," Hitler chuckled. He finally released her hand. "Now, in Germany, you can gain insight into the true character of this nation. Often when one lives abroad a distorted perception can occur. It is perfectly understandable. America, I'm sure, is a fascinating place." He gave a swift, amused glance to the ambassador. "But it is vastly different from Germany."

Instinctively Emilie knew he was referring to her father's refusal to support the Nazi regime. So he knew everything, of course. Emilie forgot she was speaking to the most powerful man in Germany. At the moment, he looked like a flabby-faced waiter in a black suit.

Her voice was steady and even. "My parents were always loyal to Germany. They loved this country to their dying breath. My father...gave the best years of his life to serve Germany."

The ambassador's eyes shot up in alarm. Mrs. Wilson suddenly felt lightheaded. Emilie didn't feel the slight pressure Ralph applied to her arm.

"Of course, of course," Hitler soothed.

Then the leader turned slightly and spoke casually to the ambassador. Emilie could feel the eyes of Heydrich upon her. In her anger, she looked boldly up and stared at him until he glanced away. She gave her attention to Hitler's words. Apparently the two men were involved in some discussion of the American president. They seemed to have forgotten—or ignored—the inappropriate environment of their casual conversation. Emilie quickly realized the fuehrer was intent on this discussion, and that Wilson looked distinctly uncomfortable.

"Let me explain this for you, Herr Wilson."

Emilie stepped forward slightly, captured by Hitler's condescending tone.

"Herr Roosevelt is the leader of a vast nation of immense wealth. He feels responsible for the history of the whole world and the history of all nations!" His voice was well-laced with sarcasm.

Heydrich and Ribbentrop chuckled.

"I, sir, am placed in a much smaller and modest sphere. I took over a state that was in complete ruin. I have conquered the chaos in Germany. The conditions of the Untied States are such that Herr Roosevelt has time and leisure to look at problems beyond his borders."

From the corner of her eye, Emilie could see the ambassador's mouth was pulled down into a hard, compressed line. She sensed he was very irritated—and holding his tongue. Emilie wished the fuehrer had not chosen to vent his sarcasm on her president.

Hitler thrust his hands into his jacket pockets, his legs wide apart. His head was wagging vigorously.

"With men such as yourself to prudently advise him, I trust Herr Roosevelt will use wise judgment in this soon to be new year. He need not concern himself with the affairs between England and France and Germany. Let him serve his second term with the interests of America...only."

"I lived in Washington, as you know," Emilie cut in, before the ambassador could speak. She was smiling, her voice sweet and calm. "I don't think President Roosevelt has a great deal of leisure time. He faced a great economic chaos during his first term. He's worked very hard. I think he's a generous man that would like to see all nations prosperous and at peace. I think that would be his reason for, as you said, sir, looking beyond his borders.

"I would not presume to suggest to him how he should govern his country. Meddling is not something I think becomes a great statesman," Hitler countered easily.

The Chancellor refocused on the young woman in front of him. His eyes traveled down her—and Emilie felt sudden coldness.

"I think, Fraulein Morgan—" Wilson began.

"And of course Great Britain and the United States have always enjoyed a close relationship—allies in the last war," Emilie ventured rashly.

Hitler flushed a bright pink.

"Well, of course, they had their little spat in the beginning," Wilson inserted nervously.

Heydrich leaned forward to the fuehrer's ear, but he spoke quite clearly. "You see, mine fuehrer, American women are bolder. They speak their minds...something I personally find very attractive."

"You have not been in Germany long enough to understand, fraulein," Hitler said tightly. His eyes had almost closed to reptilian slits. "I will allow for that. Like your parents, you were in America too long. Now as a good German woman, loyal to the reich, you must understand. Your fine German blood will reassert itself, I am confident." His eyes drifted to her neck. "You are a picture of Aryan beauty. I am proud of that."

He bowed and moved away.

Heydrich stepped forward, grasping her hand. He leaned close to her ear. She could smell the liquor on his breath.

"I can help you learn."

"I'm here to claim my dance, fraulein," a jaunty voice sounded behind her. "Tsk, tsk, Reinhard, neglecting Lena again?"

Max swept Emilie to the dance floor.

"I think you're making an enemy," Emilie said with a glance over her shoulder at the fuming face of the tall SS officer.

But Max did not reply. She looked up. His face was as hard as Reinhard's. Before the dance was over, he guided her through an archway to a corridor, down the hall, and then to his car.

"Max, Max! What are you doing? Where are...? Max, I'm with the Wilsons! You can't! This is very rude!"

He pulled her in the car and slammed the door. He drove in stone faced silence. Emilie sat with crossed arms.

"I don't know what this, this little tantrum is about, Max, but I don't take kindly to being abducted!"

He drove to the house. She hurried up the steps, intent on complaining loudly to her uncle.

"If this is about jealousy, then, then . . ."

He unlocked the door, his voice harsh. "Don't be ridiculous."

One small light glowed in the hallway. Max tossed his homburg and silk scarf to the bench, his hands on his hips. Emilie faced him, waiting. "Well?" she demanded.

He took her by the shoulders. His grip made her wince. She was shocked by the intensity and anger in his eyes.

"You little idiot!" he said in an acid voice, "a foolish American idiot!"

She felt like she'd been slapped.

"What in the world possessed you to speak so impudently to the fuehrer? Didn't I warn you once about talking like that to powerful men? Have you lost your mind?"

She shook herself free of his grasp, her anger flaming to life as his had. "I am not afraid of your little German Chancellor with his goofy-looking excuse for a mustache! I am not under his spell as so many are!"

"You should be afraid, you child!"

"You are afraid! Well, I won't be! He can strut and shout and work himself into a frenzy till...I won't be a mindless Nazi machine! He's leading Germany to war, he's after the Jews, he—"

Max's voice was calm. "You are spoiled and stubborn. Josef should never have allowed—"

"Allowed!"

"Yes, allowed you to stay after the Games were over. He should have sent you back to the states. He is under your spell!"

"Listen to me, you, you arrogant Nazi! No one packs me off! I am an adult and my uncle is a gentleman, something that is very, very rare in Germany these days!" She took a step back. "I simply spoke the truth to Adolf Hitler tonight, that's all. I didn't swoon and drool over him. He's foolish if he thinks he can march and bully and Roosevelt will stay silent. If he gets greedier and England gets involved, he'll draw in the United States. Doesn't he know his history? Isn't your brilliant fuehrer smart enough to realize that? I said the truth to his face, instead of what he wants to hear, and you carp at me."

"You call him my fuehrer, my chancellor. While you remain in Germany he is yours also. You are under his government's authority, not Franklin Roosevelt's. I repeat, you are spoiled and willful. If you can't learn to control your mouth—"

"What is this? A Nazi threat?"

"You don't understand how foolish it is to speak the way you did tonight. That is all I am trying to tell you. People can be sent to prison for saying less than what you did tonight."

"And that is a government you are proud of? What honor!" she taunted. "Then you heard what he said about...my...father."

He came to stand close to her, his eyes boring into her.

"Has it occurred to you to wonder why and how he knows so much about you? About your father? If you don't control your tongue you could be sent away. I've heard enough sedition from you. Don't think your American citizenship or your youth or your gender or your beauty will protect you from the Gestapo. Quite the opposite. Think of your uncle. Where will your daredevil attitude get you? In a prison cell or worse. Think about that tonight, fraulein, before you sleep. If you cannot stop your spouting off, I will personally see that you are sent back to the United States."

She paled. She had never seen this side of the flippant, happy-go-lucky Max Farber. "You can't do that," she replied barely above a whisper.

He had gripped her shoulders again. "I can and I will."

He turned on his heel and left her.

When she undressed for bed later, she found the red marks his fingers had left imprinted on her skin.

21
The Night of Breaking Glass

1938

Without the sound of a rifle shot or a drop of spilled blood, the country of Austria ceased to exist. In German vernacular it became Ostmark. It was no longer an independent European nation. In the springtime of 1938, it was absorbed into the growing geography of the German reich. For Adolf Hitler it was a high political triumph. He had added needed "lebensraum" and seven million citizens. More importantly, he had gained a strategic foothold for his future designs. His followers were ecstatic! Great Britain and France had done nothing—Hitler was a genius.

Proclaiming peace while making ready for war, building his countries' military offenses, and ruthlessly pursuing the enemies of the reich were no longer disguised or denied. It was 1938, and the shadows of night were growing.

● ● ●

Emilie Morgan had had over a year to become accustomed to the anti-Jewish signs that littered the landscape of Berlin. The signs were part of the city now—like the bold Nazi posters and swastika banners. And the men in uniform were everywhere.

Goebbels' propaganda broadcasts were heard each day on the radio and in the paper. German life was Nazified in every area. Accustomed to them, but hardly indifferent, it was where she parted sentiment with so many fellow Germans. She could remember the first sign she had seen. In the little camera shop off the Kurfurstendamm. She had gone there to have her film developed after the trip to Geneva, two weeks after the closing of the Summer Games. "Jews Not Welcome." She had come to a standstill just inside the doorway, shocked.

The woman proprietor, whom she'd struck up an acquaintance with had greeted her in the typical friendly fashion.

"Heil, Hitler, Fraulein Morgan! Is something wrong?"

"Your sign,' Emilie pointed, "it wasn't there before."

The woman's warmth evaporated instantly. She drew herself up with suspicion. "Nein, it was not. But it is now. Is there a problem?"

Emilie bit back her impulsive words. She didn't want to draw attention to herself. The woman was appraising her very coldly.

"I have this film to develop," Emilie said slowly.

The woman took it, her eyes continued raking over the young American. "Are you a Jew?" She demanded crisply.

Emilie met her eyes and she shook her head.

She left the shop and walked. *The signs are everywhere. How could I have missed them*? She stopped in the middle of the sidewalk. *The Games were over. The foreign press had gone home....*

Then there had been the afternoon she and Josef had driven out to Max's for the weekend. Josef had drifted off to sleep in the seat beside her. She had taken a wrong road and was about to awaken her uncle when she slowed for a rural intersection, a sign posted on a wire fence caught her eye, painted in vivid red.

Caution! Drive carefully!
Sharp curves ahead!
Jews 75 kilometers!

That had been the beginning. Without a great deal of thought, Emilie had begun her own little secret photography. She did not know what her uncle would have said; she knew Max would protest. So she did not tell either of them. Only Percy had driven out with her the following day to photograph the sign when no other traffic or people were in sight. She wanted to photograph the signs in the city as well. That was far more difficult. There were military and Nazi officers everywhere, not to mention plain-clothed Gestapo. It became a little game for her. Pretend innocence and a casual way as she caught this anti-Jewish virus her homeland was infected with. What she would do with these photos she had no idea. Of course, over time, it became more than just offensive signs.

The Jews began to have faces.

She saw women in threadbare coats hurrying to buy food from the few stores that still served Jews. A face hurried past her on the street, white with fear. *Was this a Jew*? She heard snippets of gossip in the embassy. Suicides, Jews wanting to leave Germany, deportations...

On her way home from the embassy one day, she had sat idly staring out the window of the streetcar. At a corner she had seen three men in SS uniform surround a woman, her two young children, and a teenage boy. The streetcar was halted for a moment with the tableau in vivid reality a few feet away. A hundred or more witnesses, silent. The SS men had slapped the woman and shoved the teenage boy to the concrete. One soldier kept his polished black boot on the youth's head. The children were crying. Emilie looked around. The driver had riveted his eyes to the street. Some people had buried their faces in the newspaper. Some averted their eyes to the opposite side of the street. But some looked. Emilie began to stand in horror. A hand pulled her back down to the seat.

"Why are they doing that?" Emilie gasped in the deathly still streetcar.

A sharp voice answered from a seat in front of her.

"They are Jewish swine."

"But the children," she stammered.

"Jews," the voice countered.

Emilie looked around wildly, her heartbeat thudding in her ears. How could this... the hand squeezed her arm. She glanced sideways. An older man was beside her, with tears in his eyes.

When she reached Max's house, she had hurried up the steps and rushed to the bathroom to be sick.

She had lain in her bed later, weak and staring up at the ceiling. What if she'd had her camera with her? Would she have dared? And if she could, who would want such pictures?

Her eyes circled the room as she tried to steady her emotions. Her room for these two years. Max...they did not play chess in the evenings much anymore. He was rarely home. He had not apologized for that night months ago when he had bullied and threatened her. Josef had been at a loss to explain it. She could see this sudden change had grieved her uncle.

"He has only told me he had to fire his secretary, this Karl Beck fellow. I personally have never cared for him. I think it has wounded Max to do this."

"But why?"

Josef shook his head sadly. "All these years he trusted Karl . . ."

So someone else had let Max Farber down. Emilie meditated on this and found it softened her anger. So he was hurting, betrayed again. She could understand that. Perhaps his anger that New Year's night had been nothing more than excessive concern for her safety. She should be flattered. So she tried the old teasing and chumminess with Max, and he responded. But it was different now, the old way had gone. All three in the house on Tiergartenstrasse had felt it. *What would Max say about this brutality I've witnessed? About these insulting anti-Semitic posters?* Now he was a stranger. She didn't know how he felt.

Her thoughts changed course again. She thought of the American newspaperman Jake Harrold. What had he said? "I wonder if they care what we write . . . if they care what Naziland is really like." She had not seen him since the summer of the Games. She sat up suddenly. If he were still in Berlin, surely he would know what to do with her photographs.

● ● ●

The easy conquest of Austria had only temporarily satisfied the territorial appetite of Adolf Hitler. He now turned his voracious eyes south. He had surrounded Czechoslovakia on three sides. Within this nation resided three million Germans. From his pinnacle in Berlin, the fuehrer demanded these Germans be placed under his control. But the Czechs had no intention of submitting to this bullying as their Austrian neighbors had done. They would fight. France vowed to support the Czechs. Britain pledged support to France. So in the autumn of 1938, the German chancellor had pushed Europe to the precipice of war. Peace had lasted on the continent only twenty years.

Emilie had never seen her uncle looking so depressed. Staring into the fireplace since the end of their quiet supper, he had been uncommunicative all night. Had he lost a patient? Then Emilie remembered her own father, this man's brother, his look of frailty and fear and . . . She left her chair and knelt on the floor beside him.

"Please tell me what's bothering you, Uncle Josef."

He stirred from his reverie as if seeing her for the first time. He smiled and stroked her glossy hair.

"Emilie, perhaps it is time you went back home," he said gently.

She was startled. "Home? You mean the United States? This is my home, here with you!"

He sighed. "And you've brought such sunshine into my life. . . . I would hate to see you leave, but I can't be selfish."

"You're talking nonsense. Why should I leave?"

"Emilie, this madman is dragging Germany into war," he said with sudden passion. "We all know that. Herr Hitler is like, like a compulsive gambler. With each country he grabs, he tosses the dice again. That's what all this rearmament business means. The only ones who can stop him are the generals and they may be nervous about what he's doing— even disagree with him—but they're a bunch of spaniels! They aren't stopping him!"

They were silent together several moments.

"So you see, Germany may not be safe for you. My homeland is changing before my old, tired eyes. I can't do anything . . . but I can keep it from hurting you."

"I lost my father and mother. I don't want to lose you Uncle Josef. We can face these changes together."

Washington, D.C.

The cabinet meeting had lasted nearly four hours. The president had been up since five. Now he sat alone, except for his dog, Fala, who kept leaping at the south lawn window. He was admittedly tired, but alert with a restless, impatient energy. He was watching the slow descending shadow of evening creep over the south lawn, it was a tranquil scene. He felt anything but tranquil. When he heard the door behind him open and close, he didn't bother to turn his chair. He knew who it was. Fala went yapping to greet the newcomer.

His secretary handed him the single sheet of paper wordlessly. He perched on the desk, nudging the dog with his shoe. Roosevelt read swiftly. He was not surprised with the contents of the paper, but he was angry. Impatiently he snatched up his cigarette holder, peering critically through the smoke at his young secretary.

"Well?"

"Sickening," Harry grunted.

Roosevelt chuckled and nodded with satisfaction.

"The British should be thoroughly disgusted and embarrassed with Prime Minister Neville Chamberlain," Harry amplified. "Peace for our time. He waves this paper with Hitler's scrawl on it and supposes it's something binding? He can't be serious. Munich agreement my—"

"He is serious," Roosevelt broke in calmly. "He thinks he's saved Europe from global war. It would almost be funny if it weren't so deadly serious."

"So Hitler says he just wants the Germans in the Sudetenland and no more...Ha! He'll wait a few months and then take over the rest of the country. Chamberlain's handed Czechoslovakia to Hitler on a platter."

The president nodded and referred to the paper. The meeting between the leaders of Britain and France and Hitler was over. They had given in to the fuehrer's demands. Czechoslovakia would be gone in record time.

"I read that quote of Hitler's and thought I was going to throw up," Harry continued.

"Yes, it is rather remarkable."

"Pure horse hockey...if you ask me."

"Right again, Harry. It is pure and unadulterated. That's what I told my cabinet all afternoon." He peered at the paper, quoting the German leader. "'This is the last territorial demand I have in Europe.'"

Roosevelt laid the paper down slowly, looking back to the lawn, and shaking his head.

"Grab a pen, Harry, it's time to write another letter to Winston."

Paris

The young man who was wandering the streets of the French capital looked exactly like what he was—a homeless, nearly penniless vagrant.

He was thin and hollow-cheeked, his clothes were cheap and worn. He had had a series of menial jobs, but his own inner restlessness had driven him from them. He worked long enough to provide himself with money to eat, and little else. He slept in alleyways, and park benches and under bridges—all within sight of the Eiffel Tower. He attended meetings with communists and various government protesters in smoky cellars. All of them were passionate about their convictions, all of them wanted to overthrow their government. He had been that way once. Now—now, he didn't know. Everything had changed since he'd fled Berlin almost three years earlier. So much...he no longer felt young and ambitious. He felt old and tired and used up. He was nagged by some vague depression. This was not what he had intended for his adult life—certainly not what his mother and father would have wanted. They would have been horrified.

Horrified...now he was horrified. He slumped down at the base of a chestnut tree in one of Paris's finer parks. He was unaware of the looks of disgust he received from passing Parisians. He smelled as bad as he looked. Reluctantly he pulled out the much folded letter from his shirt pocket. Again the tears came, though he thought he had exhausted his portion of tears. Soon he was sobbing. The looks changed to pity: a ragged, weeping young man—it was enough to tear at the hardest heart.

Through his crying he reread the letter, though by now he knew the words by memory. It was from his aunt who was in hiding. She had written to tell him his parents had been deported to Poland—along with 10,000 other Jewish Germans. His old father and mother shipped off in a filthy cattle car...he felt like he could retch his empty stomach onto the grass.

After an hour, his tears ceased and his mind seemed to clear for the first time in many, many months. He looked at the brilliant blue skyline. He didn't feel the crisp November air through his thin jacket. He carefully pulled out his money and counted it. Enough.

In another hour, he managed to bath and shave. He had his clothes cleaned. He had a heavy meal and drank nearly half a liter of cold wine. With the last of his money he bought a gun and ammunition. It felt heavy and comforting in his pocket. His energy reasserted itself. He felt that old vibrancy. He began walking toward the German embassy.

Just after noon he entered and politely asked the receptionist if he could see Ambassador Welczeck. No, he did not have an appointment.

He waited while she disappeared with a frown through the door to an inner office. He hummed to himself. Revenge against the persecution of Jews in Germany. At long, long last. He thought fleetingly of his friends from those days in Nuremberg—Wilhelm and Peter would be pleased and proud. His boasts were no longer empty ones.

The secretary returned without the ambassador. This was an aide to the embassy however, Ernst von Rath.

The German gave the young man a superfluous glance.

"May I help you?"

"Ja."

He pulled out his gun and fired at nearly point-blank range. The man slumped to the floor in a fountain of blood. The receptionist screamed. And Herschel Grynszpan smiled. He had finally killed his first Nazi.

Bern, Switzerland

If the staff of the Hotel Bellerive au Lac, Bern's finest hostelry noticed the increase in foreign visitors, particularly from the neighboring German reich, they did not betray it. This capital city with the picturesque Alps in the background drew tourists, international financiers, and diplomats alike. Switzerland was a choice meeting center for the European community with its friendly citizens, it natural beauty, its fine food and wine—and most importantly, for its neutrality. Surrounded by temperamental and often aggressive neighbors, Switzerland provided an island of peace, a place of discussion, a refuge.

A man arrived in the plush hotel lobby just after dinner was being served in the elegant dining room. He could hear the music of silver and china, he could smell some tempting scent. He had not bothered with the lukewarm food on the train from Germany, and now, though very hungry, he was too keyed up to eat. He looked out of place in his cheap, worn-looking gray suit. He could feel the looks he drew. The porters and guests looked at him haughtily, and he smiled to himself. As he selected a corner sofa, the head concierge came up to him. "May I help you, sir?"

"Just waiting for a friend, thank you."

The concierge ran a cold and unforgiving eye over this tall, dark-haired man.

"Clothes truly do make a difference, wouldn't you agree?" the man laughed.

The concierge turned sharply. Max continued to laugh to himself, he'd been here a dozen times before, and had never been treated this way. He picked up a Swiss paper and pretended to read. The British prime minister's enthusiasm for the agreement with Adolf Hitler did not make interesting reading for him. It was already old news. He was too absorbed in his own thoughts anyway. He'd had the long train ride from Munich to decided how much he should say to this man he was meeting with. Yet he'd decided on little more than a superficial identity change. The main thing was that he be taken seriously and that what he had to say would reach the ears it needed to reach and something could be done.

But it had been more than that that had occupied his thoughts on the train ride from Berlin. Max had sat brooding and watching the countryside slipping by without really seeing it. He was about to embark on another new direction in his life. It was the right thing—but it was also the hardest thing. He knew too well what could be said about him by his fellow countrymen. He was turning traitor. For a man like Maximillian Farber, with his family's history deeply imprinted in his soul, this was the toughest thing he had ever done. But he was not alone—and that gave him a slight degree of comfort. He glanced at his watch. He had entered the lobby at exactly 1 P.M. He had waited 30 minutes, unobtrusively reading the paper. He looked up. The porters and concierge had forgotten him. He got up and hurried to the nearest elevator.

Edourde Schulte greeted Max warmly as he pulled him into his hotel room. "You made it," he smiled. They had not seen each other since that night at Göring's five years before.

Schulte looked at him critically. "It looks like the Berlin train added a lot of soot to your hair. And can this be Max Farber in the cheap suit and scuffed shoes!"

Max laughed. "I'm supposed to look like a factory worker in his only Sunday suit."

"Which means you stood out in the lobby."

"But not as Max Farber—who is known here." Max pulled off the thick eyeglasses and slumped into a velvet chair. "Is it still on for 2:30?"

Schulte nodded and sat down. He had always liked this young man. "Any problems coming?"

Max shook his head. "No, other than the streets of Berlin were packed as I tried to get to the station. All the SS and Werchmat battalions were parading in the streets with this latest coup of our fuehrer's. They were in high spirits. Hitler made the little Englishman back down."

Schulte sighed. "Ja, I saw it also before I left. So he gets a slice of the Czech pie. He'll lick his fingers then reach for the rest."

Max stood suddenly and went to a sideboard. "I need something to drink."

Schulte watched him with a frown. "Max, are you having second thoughts about coming here?"

Max swished the ice in his glass. "No ... I ... I've just been thinking on the train. Perhaps too much thinking, Edourde. But we both know we'll be regarded as traitors if it is learned we've come to Switzerland to talk to an Englishman. I know it's right ... I ... ." He shrugged and drained off his drink.

"I understand exactly how you feel, Max. We may be regarded as traitors now, but later, perhaps quite the opposite. Who knows how all this shall end?" He leaned forward. "But we both know Germany will be destroyed from within or without if Hitler keeps on this course. The military leaders don't have the backbone to oppose him right now. The people are giddy over Rhineland and Austria and now Czechoslovakia. The only way to oppose this evil regime is through warning and assisting potential victims of it. And to warn those in other countries that Hitler makes no idle threats."

Schulte stood. "He must be stopped now while there's time."

"Of course you're right."

Schulte put his arm around Max. "You and I, my friend, regrettably, are caught in this age-old conflict between moral principle and patriotism. We both love our country. You are a man of honor, such as your father was—on that alone I know you will do the right thing."

Max was peering at the floor. *Honor* ...

"Let's go to our appointment Max. We don't want to keep our Englishman waiting." They left the hotel.

Schulte stopped him just before the outdoor cafe.

"Remember, you are Herr Franken and I am Herr Schiller."

"How close is this man to someone in authority over there?"

"He has the ear of the Duke of Hamilton whom I met during the Olympic Games. The Duke can hopefully get to someone higher up, perhaps even Anthony Eden who is wise to Hitler."

"Someone like Herr Churchill might be better."

"Churchill's a political leper right now, out of power. If more of his countrymen saw things like he does, you and I probably wouldn't have had to make this long trip to Bern."

"Ja, Herr Schiller."

The Englishman was waiting for them at a small corner table. He was already enjoying his Swiss meal. The introductions were made and Schulte began the discussion. Max said nothing.

Finally the Englishman leaned back, giving the younger German a thorough scrutiny.

"Now, Herr Franken. What can you add to this information?"

Max had not appreciated this man's unfriendly brusqueness. The Englishman had listened to Schulte without apparent enthusiasm—and even a shade of suspicion.

"I can add only that Adolf Hitler will not be satisfied with the Sudtenland. Britain should understand it will only be a matter of time, very little time, before the Wehrmacht marches into Prague. Your prime minister's Munich agreement will be as worthless as this paper napkin."

"Seditious words from a German," the Englishman countered testily.

"I'm here, sir, because I love my country. As much, perhaps more, than you love yours. At some point, if Hitler's ambitions aren't thwarted, your homeland and mine may be facing each other over a battle line."

"You agree with this, Herr Schiller?"

"I agree completely."

"How do you know Herr Hitler's ambitions exceed the Sudtenland? He has told Chamberlain this is his last territorial desire in Europe. Are you calling him a liar?"

Schulte spoke up before Max. "Herr Franken is far more a gentleman than I. Ja, we are saying he has lied to your country, to Europe, to his own people who are blindly following him. Lying."

"Proof," the Englishmen said bluntly.

"What?" Max gasped.

"Proof of what you say. I can't go back with just your opinions."

"I hardly think the risks Herr Schiller and I have taken to get here are supported by mere opinions!" Max snapped back hotly. Schulte laid a restraining hand on his young friend's arm.

"I have a family member in the Luftwaffe," Max said crisply. He has personal knowledge of Hitler's ambitions. The code name for a surprise attack on Czechoslovakia is 'Code Green.' General Blomberg drew it up last summer—"

The Englishman was gaping, and even Schulte looked surprised.

"But . . . last summer? Are you certain?"

Max ignored him. "Kietel is in on this, too. All the big generals. They will move swiftly. Hitler has said it must be carried out this year. This little posturing with Chamberlain is only a delay. The forces are in place ready for the go ahead."

"But, but, that would mean . . ." the Englishman sputtered.

Max nodded. "Ja, you understand now. If everyone honors their obligations, that would mean a war in Europe. That would mean war for Great Britain. Take that opinion to the Duke."

● ● ●

They were walking back to the hotel. Max had forgotten his hunger and now he felt only fatigue. Schulte eyed him appreciatively.

"You did very well, Max."

"Think he's convinced?"

"I think so. I've met with him before; he likes to appear very hard and demanding.

"Edourde, can I ask you a personal question? Don't answer if you'd rather not."

"Certainly. Go ahead, Max."

"Do your wife and daughters know about this? About the true nature of your feelings?"

"Heidi does. We are too close to keep anything from each other. She is afraid of the risks I'm taking, of the things I know, but she knows it is right. We cannot sit on our hands or say nothing. The girls? No. They only know I go to my Nazi meetings with a half hearted devotion. I tell them it is very boring. We don't want them to know until they have to." He looked at Max as they drew closer to the train station. "And you?"

"I had a discussion last night with Josef. He's very upset about what Hitler's doing—leading us to war. I acted disinterested at first, and then sort of defended it."

"I can see how that has bothered you, my friend."

"Ja, he . . . he is disappointed in me. But you see, Edourde, he's my closest friend—like a father to me. I don't want to put him at any risk. If anything happened, if they questioned him, he could honestly say I was a loyal party member, that I support the aims of Hitler."

"But you must endure his disappointment."

Max nodded. "I have told you about Josef's niece that lives with us. I can see it in her eyes, she thinks the same thing about me. Growing disgust."

"It is a difficult path, ja."

Max stopped. "Edourde, all these things I've said today, that sound like worries...I know I'm doing the right thing."

"I understand, Max."

They had come to the train station.

"You sure you can't stay over? We could take in a little fishing on—"

"I'd like to, Edourde, but I need to get back."

"Max, do you have any Jewish friends?"

"Ja, a few, why?"

Schulte looked at the train a moment. Now his face was shadowed. He looked back to Max and smiled wearily.

"In the banking business, like you in Farber Company, I've built up contacts in many areas. I've heard through a friend in the SS that something is building up over this assassination in Paris."

"Building up? Concerning the Jews?"

"Some type of retaliation," he smiled wryly. "Nazi style. Tell your Jewish friends to be careful for the next few days. I don't know anymore than that."

"Nazi style . . ." Max murmured. "Reinhard Heydrich has just been appointed to the number two position in the SS, just under Himmler. So, it will be his style. . . . Even more reason for me to get back. Auf Wiedersehen, Edourde."

Berlin, November 9, 1938

Reinhard Heydrich despised Joseph Goebbels. But, since the propaganda minister was the "pet" of the fuehrer, he kept his true sentiments for the man well concealed. But their discussion this cloudy, crisp November night had been untypically brief and void of contentions. This time they were in complete agreement.

"Spontaneous demonstrations throughout the reich are to be organized and executed by the good German people against the Jews in response to this heinous crime in Paris," Goebbels demanded.

"When?" Heydrich asked without emotion.

"Tomorrow night," Goebbels smiled. "Our fuehrer demands it. So you have a lot of work to do, Herr Heydrich. Gute Nact!"

Heydrich was not resentful of this enormous and sudden project given him. *It will be a showpiece of my devotion and efficiency. It could even unseat Himmler*!

Soon the teletypes across the reich, to all SS headquarters and police stations, were humming. Slightly edited messages were sent to local fire stations.

> *Fires started in Jewish homes, businesses and synagogues are to be allowed to burn as long as there is no threat to German life or property.*
>
> *Apartments and businesses of Jews may be destroyed, but not looted . . .*
>
> *Police are not to interfere with demonstrations . . .*
>
> *Jews—especially rich ones—are to be arrested and sent to local prisons or shipped to the camps. . . .*

It was nearly sunrise before Reinhard had finished his plans. He had worked all night, but such enthusiasm for his work had disguised his fatigue. He leaned back in the deep leather chair, smiling, and well satisfied. He, like Max Farber in Bern, had done his best for Germany.

• • •

Josef had gone out just after dinner to meet a patient at his clinic. He had pulled on his coat and told Emilie not to wait up for him. Max had left before she had gotten up that morning, so besides Percy who sat faithfully beside her, she was alone in the house. She'd eaten a lonely meal in the kitchen, then gone up to her bedroom and listened awhile to the BBC radio broadcast. Goebbels would not approve. The British Broadcasting programs were highly frowned upon in the Third Reich. *They'll probably be outlawed soon*, Emilie thought prophetically. Emilie preferred this station over German radio. She enjoyed the music which ranged from classical to jazz. Even the commentators sounded more interesting and cheerful. German radio gave you little more than heavy Wagnerian opera, Hitler's latest speech, or Goebbels most recent praise of Nazism.

Darkness had fallen when she tired of the radio and drifted to Max's study. She flipped on the desk lamp. She had been in this room a hundred times, still she strolled along, looking at the pictures and bookshelves. Occasionally she picked up a volume. Max Farber seemed to like adventure stories. She smiled as she analyzed this. The young German must have this secret inner longing to be the bold, courageous hero, rescuing damsels in distress, finding hidden treasures, fighting off pirates...while he appeared to be a pleasure loving, indifferent soul. "Who are you really, Max Farber?" she said aloud. Startled at her own voice, she swung around to the doorway, embarrassed that Max might be leaning there. But she was still alone—and only Percy, sitting in the window seat, was watching her.

She seated herself behind Max's rich oak desk. Theater ticket stubs, a brochure of fishing trips in the Mediterranean, a carefully folded paper airplane, a half eaten apple, a train schedule to Switzerland. One of the departure times was circled. She looked closer. *Had Max gone to Switzerland without telling them? Skiing already?* She began to absently tidy the desk. As she deposited the apple core, she saw a container: a small bottle of black hair coloring. *Empty, used.* She had not seen Max's hair any way but blond. *Had he used this? Why? Had he gone to Switzerland like this? Max in disguise.* In her boredom, she was a little intrigued. She leaned back in the deep leather chair.

She didn't notice that Percy was no longer watching her. He had turned his attention outside the window. After a few minutes, Emilie was aware of some distant noise. *A party in one of the nearby houses? An accident out on the street? No...this sound was not close, not on Tiergartenstrasse. Perhaps on the Unter den Linden. An impromptu Nazi parade?* Emilie frowned. The Nazis were great lovers of parades. Especially ones at night that could be dramatized with torches and searchlights. *No, this wasn't exactly a sound like that, not the usual cheering. This was* . . . Emilie froze. This sound, so muted, carried on the wind, was like moaning and weeping. Her eyes suddenly riveted on the opposite wall. A huge splash of orange had suddenly appeared there. Emilie went swiftly to the window.

Percy was trembling and whining. She pulled him into her lap.

"What is it, boy? What's going on?"

Across the skyline of Berlin, she could see smoke and fires—huge fires. Her first thought was of Hitler's most recent gamble, as her uncle had put it. Had Czechoslovakia retaliated? She pulled Percy closer. "It's all right, Percy. . . ."

But Emilie knew instinctively that it was not right. Something terrible was happening out there. She watched a moment longer before she hurried to her bedroom. It gave a view toward the Tiergarten and the business center of the city. The huge park was in darkness, but the city itself was alive with light—too much light. Only then did she realize she had not heard a single fire siren. She went to her uncle's bedroom for a different view. She could see some of Max's neighbors gathered in small groups, gesturing toward the brushed-orange heavens. With Percy following her, Emilie rushed down the stairs. In the foyer she snapped the leash on the dog and went outside.

It was a chilly November night. Now she could hear the sound better, but it was still indistinct. It was an eerie sound that made her scoop Percy into her arms. She went up to the group of neighbors, but no one knew what was happening. Like her own face, theirs were pale with worry.

Back in the house, Emilie locked the door and leaned against it a moment. The radio. She ran back up the stairs to her room. But the station was still playing the same dull opera. *If this was an attack of some sort, or . . . or an overthrow, wouldn't there be some radio bulletin?* Back in the library, she quickly dialed Josef's number. *No answer. Is he on his way home? Has something happened?* She went back to her bedroom window. There was no way she could tell what was going on. And she needed to know that Josef was safe. She pulled on her coat as Percy's whining increased. She knelt beside him.

"Now, you'll be fine. I'm just going to go out and see what's up." But his whining only increased as he laid a paw in her lap. She had never seen the animal so agitated. "It's all right, Percy. I'll be back soon, and Josef or Max will be here, too."

Her eyes fell upon the camera. She glanced back to the window. A night like this—something important was happening. She tumbled her camera bag contents onto the bed, grabbing her smallest camera and flash. It all fit tightly into her big coat pocket. She gave Percy one last hug before she closed the door.

She had made this walk many times toward the Wilhelmstrasse and the American embassy. Her heart was pounding in a mixture of fear and excitement as she turned the corner.

Five minutes later the Mercedes pulled up in front of the house. Max hurried up the steps, stopping suddenly at the front door as if struck. From inside he could hear ... Percy was howling!

"Percy!"

The dog bolted through the door when Max opened it. He dashed down the steps. For a moment, in the darkened hallway, Max was stunned.

"Percy!"

Percy was already at the end of the street when Max's voice reached him. He hesitated, and looked back. He could see Max coming down the steps, jogging toward him. The dog looked back to the city, quivering and whimpering. But he sat until Max came up to him.

"Percy, what the devil has gotten into you?" Max picked him up, only then realizing the dog was shaking as if terribly cold.

"What happened to him, Max?" an elderly neighbor had come up to him.

Max had turned and was walking back to the house.

"I don't know. He just shot out of the house like a cannon when I opened the door. He's never acted like this before."

"Must be the commotion in the city. Somehow it's bothering him. Never been a night like this before," the older man said.

They looked each other in the eye a moment. Max nodded.

Back in the darkened house, Max locked the door and stroked the dog until the whining had quieted.

"Josef? ... Emilie?" He hurried up the stairs with Percy behind him.

Every room was empty and dark. He stood in the library and saw the orange reflection on the wall. He went to the window. Unlike Emilie, he had a good idea what was burning: Berlin's largest synagogue.

He went to Emilie's room, his heart beginning to race.

"Emilie?"

But the room was empty. He switched on the light. The made bed, the camera case—empty. He leaned against the doorframe, closing his eyes. "No, Emilie . . ." he whispered.

Two streets away from Max's house, Emilie found the eerie quiet and near desertion evaporate. The streets were crowded and noisy. She stopped. A riot! Shouting, yelling, anger . . . Some people stood watching like her. She joined a group of men and women who stared as two dozen men surged down the wide avenue, their shouting was raised on the clear night air.

"Death to Jews! Death to Jews! String up the swine!"

Emilie kept walking toward the smoke and glow of the fire. As she drew closer, the crowds thickened. She turned a corner and stopped as if she'd walked into a wall. A huge building was on fire, flames lapping greedily, shooting high into the sky. She pushed herself through the crowd to get closer. She was at the front of the edge of the crowd. It was a synagogue. She watched as two fire trucks on either side were showering water on the two buildings beside it. Not a drop was used on the Jewish place of worship. It took a moment for her to understand. They were allowing it to burn, allowing it to be consumed in flames.

Trembling, she prepared her camera. She lifted it. A burning synagogue with no effort to save it. She snapped the picture. Someone was murmuring behind her, but she ignored it. She turned her camera to the group of laughing SS men near the fire. The flash caught their attention. They looked across the street and one of them pointed. Emilie pocketed her camera and backed up. Turning she ran down the street. Someone shouted behind her.

● ● ●

Max had an idea where Emilie Morgan would be heading. He could only hope she'd be too shocked or frightened to lift her camera. On foot he felt like he could catch up with her. She would want to find Josef— and Josef's clinic was surrounded by Jewish shops. While the crowds were thick, Max hurried his pace.

● ● ●

Emilie pressed herself into a crowd of spectators. She turned to the woman beside her, her voice lowered.

"I don't understand what's going on. What's happened?"

The woman's forehead wrinkled. "Did you not hear of the Jew who killed a German diplomat in Paris?"

Emilie nodded. She had read the lurid account in the paper.

The woman swung her arm toward the street.

"We are showing our outrage. Jews cannot do this despicable kind of thing and get away with it!"

Emilie was caught like an object in a current, as the crowd surged through the streets. It became dangerous now, and Emilie pushed herself against a brick building, her hand covering her mouth in horror. She could feel the weight of the camera in her pocket. This was madness—it couldn't be real. Then she knew the sound she had heard, that Percy had heard before her: the high, thin sound of shattering glass mixed with screaming.

Men were throwing furniture into the streets and breaking storefront windows, pulling the merchandise into the streets, setting small fires. Lights were on in upper apartment windows, a chorus of men cursing, children crying, mothers screaming filled the air. Emilie felt her knees weaken. SS gangs were laughing and roaming the streets. They were spattered in blood....

At the sight of the blood, she thought of her uncle. His clinic... with an effort she pushed away from the wall and stumbled farther into the city.

• • •

As Max jogged through the crowds to find Emilie and Josef, he could not help but note the success of Reinhard's evening. Policemen stood at nearly every intersection, with folded arms and smiling faces. He saw looting and arson and men pulling other men into the streets to beat them. This was Germany. His homeland.

He was only three blocks from Josef's clinic when he spotted her. Even though she was at the end of the street, he knew it was her. He yelled, but his voice was lost in the confusion. There were SS men everywhere, shouting, brutal, and drunk with bloodlust. *A woman alone, even an Aryan one...*

She pushed herself into a darkened doorway to rest. Her lungs were burning and she felt lightheaded and nauseated. If only she could reach Josef, to have his arms around her, to tell her this wasn't real. Across the street a shop was being ravaged. To the chorus of yells and curses, the SS had pulled a man and woman into the street. They were kicked, the woman's dress torn. She was on her knees pleading and they laughed. The man began to beg and they spit on him. A flash of light stopped them. They looked around wildly, but in the crowd they did not see her at first.

Emilie had never been so terrified in her life. If they saw her. She stepped out of the doorway and began walking—just around another corner must be her uncle's clinic. But in the darkness she'd misjudged. And she had been seen.

She began to run, the camera banging painfully against her thigh. She glanced back. Two SS men were coming after her, weaving through the crowd, pushing people roughly aside to reach her. She could feel the tears rising in her eyes.

When she turned the corner, she realized she had not reached her uncle's street. And the men behind her would surely catch her. She didn't have strength to run anymore. Then an arm reached out and yanked her into a darkened doorway. She opened her mouth to scream but a hand covered her mouth.

Max had seen the camera flash. Grimly he knew exactly where it came from. He saw the faces of the men—their surprise, their anger. He glanced at the doorway and turned, running back to the head of the street. He found the alleyway, bolted some fences, and ran harder.

Emilie willed herself not to faint. The arm whirled her around roughly. The hand still covered her mouth, but she was looking up into the face of Max Farber. Her eyes widened. Before she could form a clear thought, she heard the running steps behind them. They would find her. Max pushed her into the corner of the doorway. He grabbed at the collar of her shirt and opened it. Then he leaned against her, his eyes coming closer. Was this really . . . Max? Unsmiling and angry and . . . He was kissing her! Kissing her with the same roughness he had grabbed her with.

"You! You there, a . . ." The demand broke off into laughing as Max slowly turned. Emilie lowered her head.

"What are you yelling at?" Max asked languidly. His voice almost sounded sleepy to Emilie. "Shove off and leave a fellow to his business."

"We are," they panted, "looking for a woman, she ran this way, did you see her?"

"I heard and saw no one, I'm sure you can understand why. Now, go back to your looking," he winked, "and I'll go back to mine."

"No, no, not like that. She had a camera."

"A woman running on the streets on a night like this with a camera? How singularly unusual! Now, if you'll excuse me."

He turned and resumed his kissing. He heard their retreating steps. Emilie heard them, too.

Finally, he pulled away and looked down at her. The lazy smile was gone again. His face was stern. She felt like a teenage girl who had broken curfew with the face of her father to greet her. She was surprised again when he reached up and carefully buttoned her collar. Then he reached into her coat pocket and pulled out the camera and transferred it to his own. She opened her mouth to protest, but fell silent. She pushed away from him and stepped onto the sidewalk. She could smell smoke. Glass crunched under her feet. She had never seen so much broken glass. She looked back to the doorway, he was watching her. "We'll have to walk home. There's no point in trying to find a cab."

She looked back down the street. "I have to find Josef and make sure he's all right."

"I called him before I left the house. He's at the Jewish hospital, helping out. The clinic was too dangerous. Now, let's go. You left Percy in quite a state."

She didn't care for the curt tenor of his voice. But, since he had just rescued her, she didn't feel she could protest too loudly. He took her arm, and firmly steered her home.

• • •

Emilie was too weary to speak. They walked home in silence, ignoring the madness around them: the small fires, the shouts and screams, the trucks that lumbered past with grinning SS men and their cargo of Jewish misery. Emilie was too numb to think about where they were being taken. The house was still dark when they entered, but the phone began to ring, shrill and impatient. Max dashed upstairs. Emilie followed slowly, her feet leaden. Exhausted, she knew it would be a long time before she would able to sleep this night. This night . . . When she entered the library, Max was hanging up the phone.

"That was Josef. He wanted to make sure I had found you. He's staying at the hospital tonight. He'll be home in the morning."

Emilie stood in the middle of the room, pulling off her coat with effort. She stood staring at the floor, unseeing, uncaring that Max was watching her. She dropped to the floor like a broken doll and Percy came and curled in her lap.

"Can I get you something to drink?" Max asked.

She shook her head without looking up. Max cleared his throat.

"Your uncle was very worried about you tonight. You shouldn't have gone out."

He waited for her protest, but she said nothing as she stroked the dog.

"Emilie, I . . . you should consider returning to America I think." At that, she looked up, and the hurt in her eyes stabbed him.

"Germany is the land of my parents. I was born here. Uncle Josef is here. I've made this place my . . . home," she said softly.

"I understand," he fumbled.

"You understand, Max?"

"Ja, I do. But this Germany is not the Germany of your parents . . . for better or worse. And not the Germany for you."

She drew a deep breath. "You are a member of the Nazi Party, you support this government. You've told me this. Do you support what is happening out there tonight? I thought you were different from them, Max, but I have to ask bluntly now. Are you in agreement with what they are doing out there . . . to the Jews?"

He measured his words carefully. "No, I don't like it. I am not in agreement. But Emilie, I must be loyal to my government."

She stood up shaking. "I'm sorry, Max, but after seeing what we both did tonight, I find such loyalty disgusting and cowardly."

He ignored her, his voice crisp. "As I pointed out to you once before, if you cannot support Germany, you should leave Germany."

They eyed each other for a long moment. She nodded to his coat that he had tossed over a chair. "I'd like my camera. please."

He reached into his coat slowly and drew out the camera. He weighed it in his hand a moment, then opened the back and pulled out the film, exposing it to the light—destroying it.

Emilie turned whiter.

"You . . . you had no right to do that."

"I'm sorry. But it was not . . . prudent of you to take these photographs tonight. They can put you in danger, whether you like that fact or not."

"I can't believe this arrogance! Actually, now that you've declared what a diehard party boy you are, I can believe it!"

He shook his head. "I'm doing this—"

"You have no right to tell me what pictures I can take and what I can't take. I don't tell you how to run your life. Is this how you treat a friend?"

His voice was patient. "I would like to think that we are friends. And that you will trust my judgment as a friend."

"I've already documented your fine party standards."

"Then you have made a mistake," he said tightly. "I do not mean to bully you, this is for your own good."

"Danke, Herr Farber, but I will trust myself or my uncle to watch out for my good."

"Do you think Josef would have agreed with you going out tonight? Have you forgotten you were being chased?"

The horror of the night, the fear, swept over her. She did not feel like she could spar with this man any longer. He was a mystery; she didn't understand him. At this moment, she didn't care about trying. He had rescued her—she could not ignore that even if he angered her. She brushed back her hair and tiredly gathered her coat. He handed the camera to her.

"Thank you for coming after me and," she stopped a moment as she remembered the kiss. *Angry and demanding . . .*

He walked up to her. "Please don't be mad at me." He reached out an unsteady finger to touch her cheek. "I used the methods those men would understand. Yet . . . I . . ."

He leaned forward and kissed her. Not demanding and hard this time.

Her hand flew out and slapped him. She stepped back, surprised with herself.

He was rubbing his cheek, a slight smile playing about his mouth. He covered the tension of the night, the fears, the anger, the disappointment, with the flippant tone she knew so well.

"From the school of Scarlett O'Hara, Fraulein Morgan?"

Her eyes narrowed. "I have just added rudeness to your arrogance," she said cooly.

He bowed as she turned and left the room.

22
Honor Has Two Voices

New York

The snow, piled in soft mounds, always made him think of the pastries his mother coated in thick sugar. He was flying over the hills on a sled he had built with his brother. He was gripping the steering rope of the sled as it sped toward the bottom of the hill toward his brother who was waiting there, cheering him. Then, halfway down the hill, a girl stepped out from behind a tree. She plodded through the snow to stand by his brother. She was not smiling, not cheering. He glanced away to avoid her look, to continue to enjoy this ride through the piercing winter air. When he dared to look at her again, another girl had joined her. She was unsmiling, too. He sawed on the rope to swerve the sled away from the group of three—to speed past them. Why should they ruin his ride? He and his brother had been having such fun before they came. Nothing somber or serious, just fun—as things should be.

But as hard as he pulled on the rope, it would not turn. It seemed to be driven by a will of its own. And the will was directing it toward the three people waiting at the bottom of the hill. He was frantically trying to turn, yet strangely fascinated with the two young woman who were watching him. Their faces were coming closer, and he felt a vague gladness at seeing them both. It had been so long. The dark-headed one, the youngest of the two, was crying.

Will Cutler sat upright in his bed breathing hard, and trying to focus on the room. The snow and hill, his brother, the two young women... they had vanished. He groaned and swung himself out of the bed. He went to the gas radiator and turned up the heat. Then he went to the window and pushed back the blinds. Snow was falling on Manhattan. He caught a glimpse of the Hudson and imagining how cold it was sent a shiver down his back. He hopped back into bed until the small room warmed.

He lay staring at the ceiling, thinking over the odd, unexpected dream. Of course, it was because he had not seen his family in so long. Here it was a little over four weeks until Christmas and he was missing them. He would not be able to spend this Christmas with them either. Again, he would be in a city of strangers. He glanced back at the window. The first real snow New York City had seen this winter. In the early hours as it came down pristine and fresh and beautiful. But he knew what it would look like in a few hours—gray and slushy, black crusts along the sidewalk. Not like back home where it lay in unmarred folds of pure white.

Emilie Morgan had been the first girl in his dream, looking just as she had the last time he had seen her at Union Station. The only difference now was that she was frowning at him. He sighed, it was no mystery to figure out why.

Will had enjoyed the dream because it had brought him his brother. It had taken him out of sterile, cold New York to a place familiar, a place he trusted. It took him out of the grim reality that had stalked him since he had bought the New York World newspaper from the boy on the corner of thirty-second street. The news had thrown him into shock, followed by a stupor. Everyone in the group was reeling from it. With cynicism they had chided each other—why should anything surprise them that happened in Nazi-held Germany? Nothing should shock them—not even this.

Will Cutler had stood on the sidewalk of thirty-second street as people rushed past him. He was gripped by the front-page story. A Jewish German named Herschel Grynszpan had killed a high Nazi official in Paris. He'd immediately been seized and returned to Berlin to await trial. Will had an idea of what the trial would be like—and what the verdict would be. This young Grynszpan didn't have a chance. He'd disappear without a trace.

Three days later, one of the group had rushed into the diner where a few of them were gathered. He brought the latest newspaper edition, almost wet with fresh ink. Front page again: Riots in Germany against the Jews.

"Throughout Germany at least 900 shops destroyed . . . 171 houses destroyed . . . 119 synagogues set on fire, another 76 completely destroyed . . . 20,000 Jews arrested. The death count still incomplete. . . . Reports of looting and rape . . ."

The group could speak of little else. Everyone was collectively horrified. What had their small efforts really amounted to? What did they need to do now? How could they reach out to those suffering in the Third Reich? How?

Will felt empty. The shock and horror had drained him. Suddenly he felt useless, impotent of even revengeful fury. He rolled over on his side and thought of Emilie Morgan again.

He had not loved her—not really—if he were honest. He'd been attracted to her. Of course, you'd have to be a stone not to. She was enjoyable to be around. He had used her and when it was over he'd felt too much guilt and frustration to try to hold on to her. His future was too uncertain for a relationship with a woman.

But the dream had suddenly clarified everything for him. He sat up again, ignoring the still cold room. *I do have a future. I can't run away any longer. I'll go to Germany now.*

Berlin

Karl Beck could not forgive Max Farber for firing him. He had given him so many years of hard work and dedication, catered to his whims and fancies, picked up all the things the young bachelor dropped when he scampered off to another European playground. *Max and that idiotic dog.* He had done so much. He had kept Irwin at bay when Max had forgotten something. Yes, he had been an effective liaison between the volatile brothers. And this was his thanks? Max had entered his office grim-faced and blunt. He was fired. And no, he did not have to offer him any reason. Here was a month's salary until he found other work. Within a week, Beck had found other work.

The only drawback was it didn't have the luxuries and the fine office that working for Farber Company had. The pay was not near as good. But Beck was confident that in a matter of months that would change. He would better himself without the aid of scheming Irwin Farber or silly Max Farber. He would not have to tolerate the curt rudeness of Irwin any longer. He was on his own now, and so much the better. And now, crossing to his desk, he sensed he had found not only a way to improve his own position, but a potential way to strike back at the foolish Max Farber.

Beck had been a Nazi Party member for years, and a Gestapo informer nearly as long. His position in a successful company, his contacts, even his social circles had made him prime Gestapo material; his total lack of scruples had been an asset. It was a minor position, but that would soon change. *No more hunting Jews and doing menial office tasks. I'll be with the big boys. I'll show them their investment was well made!* he swore to himself.

He leaned back and scanned the notes one of his subordinates had innocently placed on his desk.

"Emilie Morgan, daughter of former diplomat Thomas and Anya Morgan, both deceased, niece of Dr. Josef Morgan, 'houseguest' for over two years of Maximillian Farber. Photographer at the Olympic Games in '36, now working as a minor staff member at the American embassy."

Beck pulled the paper closer. A small notation made two years ago. *Her luggage had been gone through before SS or Gestapo had had a chance to examine it. Obvious amateur work. Possible contraband? For who? Who had removed it? Possible Jewish support based on comment at dinner party also during the Summer Games. Still not a registered member of any German women's Nazi organization. Pro-American sentiment made to fuehrer at a New Year's Eve party.* Beck pondered the facts.

Was this important, useful information? the subordinate wanted to know? Should he file it away?

One final entry, the most recent, caused Beck to sit up straighter—and to decide this would not be filed away to gather dust. He smiled with great inner satisfaction. A young woman had been seen on the streets of Berlin the night the retaliations against the Jews had begun. A woman taking pictures. Then the woman had vanished—but her brief description sounded very much like the pretty German American.

Beck leaned back in his chair, thoughtful. *There is one man who would be very interested in this file. Very interested.* And such a man would help Karl Beck climb in the ranks of the Gestapo.

• • •

By early 1939, Max Farber had distilled his efforts against Hitler's Germany into two main directions. He regarded his homeland as Hitler's Germany—the true Germany had been deceived both innocently and willingly. And it was for him and men like Schulte to revive the true Germany. That meant destroying the reich. From the inside as Schulte had pointed out. By the new year he knew without doubt that Adolf Hitler meant to lead Germany to war and to dominate Europe. He also knew Hitler meant to destroy the Jews under his control. The year would bring dramatic events to his country. Hitler would not be content to swallow up surrounding countries so effortlessly. It was time to flex the new muscles of the German army for the world to see and understand its power. From his sources and conversations with Eric, Max knew Poland was Hitler's next target of conquest.

So Max worked to expose this intent to the world outside the reich. Now his reputation as a European traveler served him well. His business contacts provided diplomatic contacts. Under assumed names, and often disguised, he carried information to them. If only they would listen and stop this posturing little Austrian they could prevent a European war. *If they would only try . . .*

Over a late night conversation, Schulte had been uncharacteristically pessimistic.

"If it comes to war, Max, it will make the Great War look like a schoolyard tussle."

Max nodded. "Surely the French and British will move. They can't sit and watch Poland taken. They'll have to come in!"

"And if we were prophets we could probably see that that will draw in the United States. Roosevelt won't remain neutral forever."

Max thought back to Emilie's words to the fuehrer and allowed himself a smile.

Schulte and Max had become close in their work against the reich. But Max did not tell his friend about his other work with the new enemies of Germany. There was enough danger between them already. But he suspected Schulte knew and was likewise helping the persecuted people. On a cloudy, cold January day a large green truck pulled up to the curb with screeching brakes. It was in a poorer district of the capital city. Those on the street looked up furtively, those in their apartments looked between scarcely parted curtains. The squeal of brakes meant an arrest. It had become a common sound and sight in the city and throughout Germany. A neighbor, a friend, the man and woman who ran the store on the corner, suddenly gone.

A man in an SS uniform stepped from the truck. He stood a moment, as if he were staking out his territory. He pulled off his leather gloves and snapped them against his arm. He did not appear in any hurry. He was full of authority and confidence. When he emerged five minutes later from the apartment he was rushing two families in front of him, directing them to the back of the truck. His voice was sharp. "Schnell!" The driver closed the gate and threw down the canvas. The SS had obviously ferreted out another group of Jews who had been hiding since that night in November.

The officer gave a defiant glance up and down the street before he climbed into his truck. He had performed his task smoothly and efficiently. The truck roared to life and sped down the narrow street.

Inside Max was pulling off the SS hat and wiping his forehead. Cold or not, there were beads of perspiration on his brow. Suddenly he laughed. Rudi Schmidtt gave him a sideways glance.

"How can you be laughing?"

"I'm not as cool at this as I'd like to be. I'm sweating like a hog in this wool uniform. Blackney never sweated. A beautiful actor."

"Who?"

"Haven't you ever read *The Scarlet Pimpernel*?"

Rudi shook his head.

Max loosened the top button of his tunic. He jerked his thumb toward the back of the truck. "They all did very well—acted perfectly terrified."

"For some of them, I doubt it was acting."

They had driven through several side streets of the city. Rudi slowed. Max's car was parked at a corner. By now, Max had peeled out of the uniform and stuffed it into a fine leather suitcase.

"When you get them to the house, get them settled in. I'll be out tomorrow, hopefully with enough papers."

At the corner, Max hopped out. "Tell them not to worry."

Rudi nodded. "Good night's work, Blackney!"

• • •

The SS headquarters just off Wilhelmstrasse was always a building of activity, night or day, with many men passing through the doors. This afternoon it was no different and Karl Beck, in a simple gray suit and hatless, made no distinction in the crowd. It had taken him nearly a week to secure an appointment with the high and mighty SS chief and he was distinctly irritated with the slight. *Perhaps I should have kept the information for myself, and used it to act alone. I could hold great power over the Farbers!* It was a heady thought. *Still, it didn't hurt to try to work with a man like Reinhard Heydrich.*

After an hour wait, he was admitted into the inner office. His irritation was freshly fueled. He had already decided the posture to take with this man who was only slightly older than himself: an attitude of cold authority. *Men like Heydrich did not respect sniveling pushovers. And men like Heydrich did not trust anyone. So tread carefully*, he reminded himself.

Heydrich looked up from a cluttered desk to scrutinize the former Farber secretary. It was a perusal that brought a rush of red color to Beck's face and he hated himself for the weakness. Heydrich waved him to a chair.

"You are a difficult man to see, Herr Heydrich," Beck said as he drew out a cigarette.

"I am a busy man."

Beck nodded slightly. "As I am myself."

"Then I'm sure you will condense your information and get directly to the point." He glanced over a paper. "You were secretary to Max Farber?"

Beck nodded. "For fifteen years."

"And he fired you. Why?"

"You would have to ask Herr Farber that."

Heydrich squinted. "I am asking you, Herr Beck."

"I do not know. He didn't bother to tell me. But I didn't come here to discuss my work with Herr Farber."

Heydrich's lips thinned and he said nothing. Only then did Beck notice the icy blueness of the two eyes that were trained on him. Beck felt a twinge of nervousness. He had heard rumors of this man's hardness. He was a dangerous man.

Beck cleared his throat. He pulled out a paper from his pocket. He held it. "This has come across my desk and I thought it might interest you."

He did not extend it, nor did Heydrich reach for it.

"And why would your little piece of paper interest me, Herr Beck?"

Beck smoothed the paper on his knee. "Because it concerns Herr Max Farber."

"Herr Farber is under the scrutiny of the Gestapo?" he laughed. "For what? Not having that dog on a leash in the Tiergarten?"

"The Gestapo is willing to cooperate with the SS in matters that may compromise the reich."

"And your superiors approve of this cooperation? Or is this a personal mission?"

Beck leaned his head against his hand studying the powerful man before him. "My information concerns Herr Farber's houseguest—the American woman, Emilie Morgan."

Though no muscle twitched or expression was altered, Beck knew instinctively he had struck a nerve. Perhaps it was because looking at this man was like looking in a mirror.

Heydrich stood up and reached for the paper. He read it swiftly. Again, his face was impassive. Finally he looked up at Beck. It was a cold smile. "Ja, you did well. I am very interested. We will keep this confidential between us." He stood up again to terminate the interview. "I will remember this cooperation, Herr Beck, between the Gestapo and the SS. Good day."

● ● ●

Five days had passed since the night of breaking glass. For three days after, Berlin had been caught up in the violence. The newspapers and radio urged the good citizens not to worry—this time of purging was for the best and would soon be over. The papers also described this violence as a rightful revenge against the Jews that was sweeping across the Third Reich. Goebbels had raged that the Jews would be wise to understand what was happening, what it really meant for them. While the violence had graphically revealed the Nazi contempt for Jewry, it also made a second equally chilling announcement. For Jews, all exits and escape routes out of the Third Reich were sealed.

Together Josef and Emilie read that some German businessmen had been bold enough to complain at the destruction and the financial loss. Who would pay for this? In the Chancellery, the solution was arrived at with predictable swiftness and brutality. Let the Jews pay.

Emilie stood looking out the window of her second floor office at the American embassy. It had been a slow, quiet morning. She felt a sense of restlessness as she went to the window a dozen times during the day. Up and down Wilhelmstrasse everything seemed normal—traffic and pedestrians moving constantly. Life as if nothing had happened—as if the synagogues were still not smoldering a few streets over. As if there were no weeping. And many storefronts looked like gap-toothed victims of a bully's fist.

Through the embassy network, Emilie heard the fuehrer was outraged and angered at the international reaction to the retaliation against the Jews. "What business was it of their's," he screamed. His stormtroopers had only had a much-needed fling. *Only a fling* . . .

Emilie felt suffocated in the office. Everyone was so subdued and withdrawn. None of them had ever witnessed anything like this. During the lunch hour, the ambassador had the embassy doors locked and gathered the trusted staff into an inner office. They listened to the news of Germany's riots over the BBC.

"At least they know it happened. At least they know on the outside," one of the staffers said glumly.

"Yes, they know," Ambassador Wilson nodded.

Emilie thought of her photographs that could have given further testimony. Could have . . . Should she have given the other film to this American official instead of Jake Harrold?

She stood watching the late afternoon traffic when the ambassador came to stand beside her.

"About ready to head home, Emilie?"

She nodded. "Yes, sir." She turned to him. "Roosevelt knows about this, doesn't he?" She searched his face.

Wilson smiled tiredly. The past few days had been so long—nothing like anything he had seen in his years of diplomatic service. Mrs. Wilson was nervous and wanted to go home.

"The president has no idea what a loyal supporter he has here in the heart of the Third Reich. Perhaps the next time I see him, I will tell him. He knew a few hours after it all began. Rest assured, Emilie, he is watching the situation very carefully." He looked past her to the window. "And Mr. Churchill. Not everyone is sleeping. . . ."

Josef encouraged her to take a cab home from work now, the streets were still unsafe and he was nervous. But out in the bright sunshine, with the lure of a crisp fresh wind, Emilie could not resist walking. It would do her good. It was still light. She knew Josef would be at the clinic, his clientele had swelled, so she would not worry him. And of course, Max Farber didn't matter.

She was halfway home when she approached one of Berlin's largest Protestant churches. Many people were hurrying up the stone steps. She could catch snatches of music when the doors opened. She found herself almost pulled in. She stopped a woman near her.

"Is there a special service tonight?"

The woman gave her a friendly smile. "Ja, Pastor Bonhoeffer is the guest speaker tonight."

"Oh . . ."

"Will you come? He is a wonderful man. It is late, though."

Emilie hesitated. She had not thought of spending her evening in a stuffy, crowded church. But now . . . The woman was watching her, nodding in encouragement.

"Well, all right. I suppose for a little while."

They could only find seats near the back, and once she sat down, Emilie forgot about everything else. They sang the old familiar hymns, and it seemed to her they filled the great hall with one united voice—not raised in anger or pride now. Tears gathered in her eyes and she closed them. A peace, unexplainable, swept over her. She needed to be here. She wished Josef was at her side. He needed to be here, too.

Then a man came to the platform. He was younger than she expected. He was tall and broad, balding yet blond. He seemed at ease as his eyes swept the silent expectant congregation. He began to speak.

"Germany is a proud country with a rich heritage, a country of many fine and noble traditions. But if a country is built on nothing more than blood and race it is nothing more than a pagan land. There is nothing noble or dignified about this new emerging Germany."

The congregation stirred. Emilie was spellbound.

"These new changes are unhealthy, they are wrong for Germany. It pollutes her honor, her history. Things are terribly wrong. A few nights proved that graphically.

"Look to your heart. Ignore the clamor around you, the threats, the lies, the shouting, and listen to your heart!" he said emphatically.

He was clutching the edge of the podium, leaning forward, pleading. "If a government is built upon suspicions, on neighbors turning against neighbors, if books are burned because their authors are on some unapproved lists, if a country shames itself by trampling its weakest member . . . such a country is not fit to rise, but must be brought low. Dignity and honor must not be replaced with brutality and arrogance. . . . I will conclude this evening with the words of my friend Pastor Martin Neimoeller. As some of you may know, he has been seized by this government for speaking out. Like many of you, he trusted in this government for a season. Then he stopped listening to the lies and he listened to his heart. And, my friends, he heard the truth. He said, 'God is giving Satan a free hand so that it may be seen what manner of men we in Germany are.' What is our answer to that question?"

Emilie had to wait for some time after the service for the crowd to thin around the young pastor. Finally she approached him suddenly a little nervous, as she twisted her purse handle. But his pleasant face and smile soon put her at ease.

"Gute Nacht, Herr Bonhoeffer."

"Gute Nacht, fraulein," he bowed with a smile.

"I wanted to come up and tell you how much I enjoyed—no, that isn't quite the right word, how much I needed to hear your message this evening. It's the most reasonable thing I've heard since I arrived in Berlin."

"Ah, you are a visitor to Berlin?"

She smiled. "A visitor who has been here since the Olympic Games. I came over as a photographer. My father heard you years ago when you were in New York City. I remember you impressed him very much. He told my mother and me you were perhaps one of the few voices of truth left in his homeland."

Bonhoeffer slowly pulled off his glasses to polish them.

"Your father's words are very kind. You are American then? I thought I detected a slight accent."

Emilie laughed. "And here I've been thinking my accent was thoroughly Berliner. I've been very proud that no one knew I'd spent most of my life in New York City and Washington, D.C."

He smiled. "If I hadn't spent some time in America, I wouldn't have known. You can trust me with your secret, fraulein."

"Emilie Morgan."

They shook hands. "Welcome to Germany, Fraulein Morgan."

"Danke."

Two men then came up beside the pastor, their voices lowered.

"You about ready, Dietrich? I think we should use the back door." Bonhoeffer frowned a moment, then his voice became amused.

"I'm sure they are at the back door as well. Besides, I am not going to slip around like a criminal. I have nothing to be ashamed of."

"I know that, Dietrich, but you were pretty blunt tonight. I'm a little surprised they didn't storm in here."

Bonhoeffer turned back to Emilie. "The Gestapo have nothing better to do than follow me around." He shrugged. "What a boring occupation."

"The Gestapo follow you around because of what you said tonight?"

"Ja. They carry my words back to the ears in the Chancellery and the leaders squirm there. Ja, a little protestant pastor makes the high and mighty squirm." He laughed as he drew on his heavy coat and hat.

"Pastor Bonhoeffer, could I ask you a question?"

"Certainly."

"How can this church be filled tonight, and no one got up and left, yet these same people, they were . . . they saw what happened . . ."

"You are a very observant young woman. A few of us are going out for coffee, would you like to come along and we can talk? I can't guarantee I can answer all your questions."

Emilie exhaled loudly. "Danke, you are very kind. I would love to come. After this past week, I need to talk with someone . . . who . . . really cares about what is going on."

"You are not afraid to be seen with me by those men who wait in the shadows in their black leather coats?"

She shook her head. "I am not afraid."

• • •

Max appraised her a moment in the shadowy foyer. Emilie looked happy. He had not seen this look for many days. Since...And as she greeted him, he could not hear any veiled hostility in her voice. Emilie could see her uncle was very troubled and saddened by the night of broken glass, so she kept her anger toward Max Farber hidden, pretending that it had never happened. Max, though he suspected her motives for the charade, was still grateful. It had hurt him more than he fully understood to see the contempt for him in the young woman's eyes. She was foolish and independent and impulsive. It was bound to get her in trouble—if it hadn't already. For Josef's sake, he had tried to protect and help her. Anger and a stinging slap had been her reply. He allowed that the kiss was an impulse he should have ignored. Even Percy would probably have advised him against it. Perhaps he should just let her alone to her own headstrong ways. If she fell...

"Emilie," he said in greeting.

"Hello, Max!" she smiled brightly, lapsing into English. Just like those first days.

"You had a good day at work?" He asked as he slowly descended the stairs.

She looked thoughtful a moment. She pulled off her hat, running fingers through her hair. "Actually, no. It was a very boring day."

"Oh."

"But it was a wonderful evening. And you? Did you have a nice evening?"

He nodded. "Ja, it was all right." He could not conceal his curiosity. "The streets are still—" he stopped. She resented caution. "Where did you go to have this wonderful evening?"

"Max, I think I ended up at one of the safest places in all Berlin!"

"Ja?"

"A church! I was walking home when I saw people hurrying in. I had every intention of going past. I honestly didn't feel like being around people. But as I passed, I heard a soloist...I felt like I was supposed to go in. So, I did! Pastor Bonhoeffer was speaking. You have heard of him?"

Max smiled indulgently. "Ja, everyone has heard of him."

"Do you think Adolf Hitler has?" she asked teasingly.

"Most certainly," he chuckled.

"Then I wish he'd come to one of the services and listen."

"Did the service go this late?" Max pressed.

"No," she admitted slowly. "Afterwards, I wanted to go speak with the pastor, I felt like I should. So I did. He is very friendly and nice. We talked a bit and he invited me out for coffee." Max's eyebrows went up.

"Alone?" he blurted.

She crossed her arms, her head tilted appraisingly.

"There were others."

Max shrugged. "Of course, I only meant . . ." He kicked at the carpet with his toe.

Emilie spoke slowly, watching his face. "If he speaks tomorrow night you should go. We could go together, Josef, too."

Max continued to study the carpet, and as the silence lengthened Emilie could not help but feel a little rebuffed. Finally he met her eyes.

"You are very impressed with this man," he said simply.

"Yes, I am. My father called him a voice of truth in Germany. I found him . . ."

"Ja?"

She stood up from the bench, gathering her things. She was no longer smiling. "I was only with him a few hours . . . Dietrich Bonhoeffer is a man of courage. Gute Nacht, Max."

● ● ●

Two nights later both Emilie and Max were heading out the front door together. Both appeared in a hurry, and Emilie thought Max seemed unusually agitated and preoccupied. She didn't really want to ask him for a ride, but the weather was stormy and she couldn't see any cabs nearby. She was tying a scarf around her neck and giving Percy an affectionate goodbye.

Although he was dressed in plain, dark clothes, Emilie ventured a guess. "A party, Max?"

"Not tonight." He locked the door behind them and hurried down the steps to the car. Emilie felt a little piqued. He wasn't even going to offer her a ride. Thunder and lightning split the night sky.

"Do you suppose I could trouble you for a ride?"

He stopped with his hand on the car door. She usually didn't want his help or advice. He bit off a sharp reply. He pulled up his coat sleeve and glanced at his watch.

"Where?"

Emilie was definitely nettled. "The clinic."

"Sure."

They rode in frigid silence for several minutes.

"Uncle Josef and I are going to dinner with Pastor Bonhoeffer. Would you like to join us?"

Max kept his face rigidly forward. "Danke, but I have other plans tonight."

"Do you have some . . . reason for not at least hearing what this man has to say?" Emilie asked with a little asperity.

Max turned to her, giving her a smile that was rare these days. Only then did she notice he looked tired. *I wonder why*, she mused quietly.

"Why should I go hear him when you can tell me what he says? It's a far greater pleasure to look and listen to you than some balding pastor."

She smiled in spite of her irritation. The charmer had reasserted himself. "Max, he . . . I think you would like him. What he says, he says better than I ever could."

"You underestimate the power of beauty, Fraulein Morgan."

She laughed. "Stop! Won't you come? Bitte? It would please Josef."

Max frowned and didn't answer. Dressed as a factory worker, standing at the back of the church, he had heard the pastor. His heart had swelled with pride to hear a German speaking with such authority and integrity.

Emilie turned to look out the window.

His voice was low and hesitant. "You know, Emilie, I hear things at parties and at my club. Your pastor is considered a . . . threat to the government. He cannot continue his speeches and expect the Gestapo or SS to ignore him. And those around him—even in an audience or small dinner party may be subjected to interrogation."

He could see her posture stiffen. His own voice hardened.

"Of course you are now angry with me. I tell you the truth, and you grow angry. Can't you understand I am trying to keep you out of harm's way? And now you're dragging Josef into danger."

"I am not dragging anyone! He wanted to come!"

"Bonhoeffer will be arrested very soon. I would hate to see you swept up in the—"

"Arrested for telling the truth! A new crime in Germany? Please stop. I can walk the rest of the way."

"Don't be ridiculous. We're almost there. You are the most stubborn woman I have ever known."

"And you are the most, the most—Max!"

They had turned the corner and could clearly see Josef Morgan's little clinic. The front window was smashed, the sidewalk showered in glass that sparkled like scattered jewels in the streetlights.

Max's voice was stern as he brought the car to a halt a few yards from the clinic. "Stay in the car until I find out if it's safe."

She was suddenly trembling and had no thought to disobey him. She watched him hurry, then carefully pick his way over the glass. She could see the shadows of people inside. What had happened to her uncle? It seemed like hours, but it was only minutes before an older woman left the clinic and motioned to Emilie to come.

Emilie stopped in horror at the doorway. The clinic was in shambles. Every piece of furniture smashed, the pictures ripped from the wall. Emilie looked around in a daze. It appeared as though someone had stepped through the frames. She looked up. Max was watching her from the doorway to the inner office. His face was pale and hard.

Wordlessly he pulled her through to the examining room. She cried out and sagged against Max. Her uncle was huddled in a chair, looking like a frightened child. His face was distorted with bruises and cuts. His lips were swollen and one eye was closed. A ragged gash was bleeding freely across his forehead. Max gently pushed her away.

"Do you want to treat him here or at my house?" Max asked.

Only then did Emilie understand there were other people in the room. She looked around wildly. Helga the nurse, the older woman, and a man. She recognized them. They lived above the clinic. The woman was crying.

Helga was gathering things into a bag. "Let's take him to your place, Herr Max. You never know . . . they might return."

"Of course." Max walked to the doctor and stooped down. Emilie could barely hear his voice and tears gathered in her eyes. She had never heard Max so gentle.

"You look a little weak, doc, mind if I carry you?"

The doctor looked as if he were going to faint.

"Ah, Max . . ." he returned in a wheezened voice.

"You've carried me half a dozen times," Max smiled.

The doctor shook his head slowly. "Where is Emilie? Is she all right?" Then he slumped into a faint.

Max scooped him up without effort and carried him to the car. Helga followed. Emilie searched the room, all the cabinets were destroyed, the fine instruments smashed, the medicines dumped into coagulated pools. She forgot the older couple and spoke aloud.

"Why? Who would do this?" she whispered.

The couple came close to her, taking her arm.

"They beat him up. We heard their cursing and shouts. They beat him because he had treated Jews. That is why they did it to good Dr. Morgan."

● ● ●

Emilie had been for a brisk walk with Percy in the Tiergarten. Even leafless and frozen, she thought it a beautiful park. And, of course, Percy found no limit to his energy or things to bark at and chase. She had been in the house for a week. Helga had attended her uncle, and he had urged her to get out for a walk. He had stroked her cheek.

"You are pale and there are shadows under your eyes. You see I am much better. Go out and drink in some fine February air for me, ja?"

Though she was reluctant to leave him, he had been right. She did need the walk. The house seemed to surround her with her own anger and emotions. Max had been quiet. Of course he was upset—that was obvious. Their conversations were brief and general—there was no discussion of the beating Josef had suffered, just commonplace things like the weather and food and Percy's latest trick. It was then her thoughts wound their way back to Will Cutler. It surprised her. She realized that he entered her thoughts because she needed someone to talk to, someone to let her describe all she had seen in Germany, all that it stirred up within her. There was no one to talk to—no Bess, no Will. She felt as if she were smothering in loneliness and frustration and fears. Why had Will Cutler dumped her?

Later that evening she went to her room to write a letter to Bess. She froze when she opened the drawer. The neat stack of photos she had taken over the past few months was gone. Hurriedly she searched through the other drawers. Had she moved them to the closet or under the bed and forgotten? She searched there. They were gone. She sat down on the edge of the bed stunned. Someone had been through her things. She could feel her cheeks burn with anger. Calmly she opened the door and tiptoed to her uncle's room. He was dozing. Helga had left. She drew a deep breath and entered the library.

Max was seated on the floor making adjustments on his telescope. Lenses and parts were scattered around him. His face was etched in a concentrated frown, and hair was tumbling over his forehead. He needed a haircut she noted. And sitting there, with Percy licking his ear, he looked like a boy of 12. She hardened her heart—he was not an innocent boy of 12, far from it. She cleared her throat dramatically. He looked up. She pulled the paneled doors closed and he raised an eyebrow. Even Percy sat up in expectant rigidness. Did he smell the smoke of battle in the air?

They stared at each other a long moment, and Emilie knew from his look he knew why she had closed the door.

"It seems I am forever saying 'how dare you,'" she said without preface.

He looked back to his tools. She watched his hands a moment and vaguely wondered why someone who never worked had such chapped, cut-looking hands.

"I'm going to try to be civil to you, Herr Farber, for my uncle's sake, and because this is your house and I'm a guest and have been for so long. Tonight, I realize, it's been too long."

He looked to the window.

"I could go in there right now and awaken my uncle and I think he would be as outraged by this as I am."

Still he was silent.

"He . . . loves you like a son, but I know he would be disappointed in this."

He began polishing a lens. "I understand your passion right now, Emilie, but I think you should leave Josef out of this. This is between you and me."

Her voice was trembling with anger. "Then you don't deny it! Well, at least that is honorable."

He stood up, facing her, hands in his pockets.

"I took your photographs and destroyed them. They were in my house and they brought danger here. If I found poison or some type of explosive I would do the same thing for the safety of myself and everyone under my roof."

"You destroyed my film that night, and now these pictures. I find it repulsive that your loyalty to Adolf Hitler has driven you to such despicable depths."

"We have covered this territory before, and you spoke eloquently. I see no reason to go through this again."

She hated that he could see tears rising in her eyes and hear it in her voice. She wanted to be strong in this dramatic moment.

"You are right, Herr Farber, there is no point in discussing this. I only want to say that I will be leaving in the morning. This latest arrogance has only proven that I should leave immediately. I talked earilier with Helga, and as soon as Josef's ready he wants to go to Italy. It will be a good place for him to recover from Berlin."

She looked down at Percy a long moment, then back to Max.

"Thank you for your hospitality these past years."

She turned and slid the doors open.

"You destroyed my photographs Herr Farber, but you did not destroy the negatives. An American newspaper man has them in his protection. So your pillaging my room really doesn't matter."

She was crying openly now.

He shook his head. "That was a mistake, Emilie," he said softly.

"That's your opinion. Guten Nacht, Max."

23
"It Happened One Night..."

The spring of 1939 had been unusually cold and damp across Germany and much of Europe. So, when the first, mild, fragrant breezes of summer blew, they were greatly welcomed. But even balmy weather could not draw the tourist crowds to the ocean resorts, to London, to Paris, to Brussels, to the Alpine lodges, for a tense expectancy settled over the continent that summer of '39. From palaces, to the corner bus stop, from Downing street and the Champs Elysées to the smoky beer halls in Munich, to Rome, to the salons in Moscow, it was felt. The farmer, the fisherman, the housewife, the pastor, the young men and women in the universities, the officer, the man that delivered the milk in the wagon, they all listened and watched and waited to see what would happen from that new throne in the ancient German capital. Would there really be war? The poppies were blood-red in Flanders, reminding them that if the German chancellor moved on Poland, all of Europe would be consumed in the greedy flames of war. Young and old held their breath that last summer of peace.

Lena Heydrich had the good sense to know that when her husband was preoccupied with his affairs at work she should expect little attention from him. What little Reinhard had achieved in his Hitler Youth Group or the mark Inga had made in school or the status of Werner's cold or the triumph of Gerta's first step she kept to herself with maternal possession. Lena Heydrich was keeping a lot to herself these days. Reinhard was rarely home. In the dimness of their Mercedes, she chided herself. She should not complain—not as a good wife and loyalist to her country. Times such as these made demands on all Germans. Everyone must make sacrifices. The fuehrer had explained it all many times. She glanced at her husband. *His features were so perfect.* She sighed with contentment. These were the best times of their marriage.

Heydrich gripped the steering wheel and stared ahead, cooly efficient but driving mechanically. He was not thinking of his wife or children or mistress. He was agitated and grateful Lena was not prattling. He was distinctly irritated that he had to go to the Chancellery when he preferred to go home and sleep. It had been a long, tiring day at his office. That very afternoon the fuehrer had stood waving his arms, spittle flying from his mouth, his face an alarming red.

"I shall find a reason for starting this war! Whether the world believes it or not amounts to nothing!"

One more day in a string of long days. But of course, he had the clear understanding that he was in an inner circle plotting war. And plotting war was a consuming, demanding, and exhausting task. But to have to sit through a third showing of this American film that Hitler had taken a fancy to was absurd. He could practically say Gable's lines. He knew when to expect Hitler's high-pitched, delighted laugh as Colbert and Gable are separated at night by only a thin, wool blanket. Hitler loved that part. Heydrich then realized he could drift off to sleep in the little private theater of the Chancellery and no one—except Lena perhaps—would know.

He pulled out a slim, silver flask and took a long drink. He didn't offer any to his wife since she carried their fifth child. He glanced at her. She was smiling in her furs. Even if she were providing children for the Fatherland like Hitler was constantly urging, he found his wife's bloated appearance offensive. But a few drinks relaxed him and eased the ache in the back of his neck. It was not the complex problems of this invasion of Poland that was troubling Reinhard Heydrich now. He was a small architect in that. Hitler, Göring, and the generals were making that map. He had a fresh problem within the SS that challenged him. Such a challenge that Heydrich was fervently hoping Himmler or the Gestapo had not gotten wind of it yet. He must solve this one swiftly, efficiently, and quietly on his own. It could prove very embarrassing to him. This was the kind of knotty situation that could topple a man in a regime like this one. It was not difficult to imagine Himmler's biting invective or Hitler's seething rage. His mind went back over the few details known.

He was leaning over his desk as he reread the report. His junior officer stood at rigid attention before him.

"Then what you are telling me is that there have been three separate incidents in the last six weeks, here in Berlin, of two SS officers arresting Jews, then never reporting their removal to headquarters or to the camps."

The officer nodded. "We have no reports of sending them out. They appeared at each site only hours before the intended raid."

"And two incidents in Munich, one in Frankfurt."

"Yes, Herr Heydrich."

"And these were left at the sites." Heydrich fingered a small scroll of paper wrapped in a scarlet thread. Carefully he unrolled it. It was a scrap no bigger than one inch square. A German flag—the one flown prior to the advent of Adolf Hitler—had been drawn in the center.

Heydrich tossed it down and leaned back, pressing his fingertips together and looking at the man before him with the contempt that was earning him a reputation.

"It would appear we have a little charade going."

"That is what I thought, sir. That is why I hurried this to you."

"And what else did you think to solve this?"

"I, well, I, wasn't sure. I'm not sure how to approach this."

Heydrich laughed coldly. "That is why I am where I am, and you are where you are."

"Yes sir."

"What we have is at least two people posing as SS officers. Most likely they are part of some sort of resistance group. This little signature they leave proves they are traitors—probably communists more interested in embarrassing the reich than saving Jewish lice. Clever amateurs." He laughed again. "How can they possibly think they can get by with this? How many Jews are we talking about?"

"Between 20 and 30, sir, as well as we can estimate."

Heydrich stood and walked to his office window.

"Very foolish to put yourself in my gunsights: stealing SS uniforms, posing as officers of the reich, aiding Jews." He shook his head as he addressed the unknown imposters. "Very foolish."

He swung around. "I want all intended raids in Berlin, Frankfurt, and Munich placed on my desk within the hour. Not one raid will be approved until I see it first. We'll be waiting for our duo of fools."

He tossed him one of the scrolls. "Take this and have it analyzed."

"Yes, sir."

"I also want a list of every officer and every secretary who has access to the raid lists. I want background checks. Obviously there's a leak somewhere. Of course, you understand this is all confidential. You report to me only. If anyone asks questions, bring me their name and I'll take care of it."

"Yes, sir."

Heydrich continued in his detached, cool tone.

"Perhaps the fuehrer will want them publicly executed when they are apprehended. Perhaps a guillotine at the Brandenburg!"

The young officer shuddered. "Ja, Herr Heydrich."

● ● ●

He walked from the Potsdamer station to the Brandenburg Gate without stopping. He had sent his one suitcase on to a modest hotel near the center of Berlin. A man carrying a suitcase along the city streets would undoubtedly stir notice that he did not want. With SS on nearly every corner, he would be stopped, papers would be requested, questions asked. For now, he wanted to blend into the capital city, to look and listen, and to quickly understand contemporary Germany. Reading about it in selected, diluted, and edited doses in America was a different education. This was the real school of learning. And he'd better learn it fast.

The first success had come in passing easily through the ports of entry into Germany, then Berlin. His papers identified him as Dieter Voss of Berlin, a 26-year-old German medical student who had studied in America at a New York City University, but was now returning as events in his homeland intensified. His papers were impeccable. In fact, he'd been treated with mild respect by the examining SS officer—here was a young man ready to serve in the medical corp of the fuehrer's army. To interrupt his medical career was the kind of patriotism and devotion the fuehrer applauded. With a cheery "Heil, Hitler" the young man was absorbed into the crowd and caught a train east for Berlin.

He had seen the black-and-white pictures in the American newspapers and the flickering newsreels before the main attraction in movie houses. He knew what to expect in the Nazi fortress, but reality is always more potent than a picture. He was prepared for Germany's steady march to the starting line of war, but still he was surprised with the crowds of military men on every street, in passing trucks, in the shops, and in the taverns. Everywhere were men in green, while the civilian population stood as somewhat sober, stunned spectators: "Well, of course, Hitler and Göring and Goebbels were right with all they said, weren't they? The country of Poland itself was an offense. Chamberlain and Reynaud were dummkopfs without the genius of their Adolf Hitler. Of course he was right. We should not worry."

He turned left from the gate and crossed Unter den Linden. Only now did his confidence and composure suffer a tremor. He had seen her face in that dream. Now, he could see her with his waking eyes. If she were still here. He had never been on this street before, yet he found it with little problem. She had described it in her first letters to him. He walked down the sidewalk, his head slightly down, giving the house of Max Farber a quick glance. Also as she described: a rich neighborhood. But he saw no sign of life from the windows. A quiet house like the rest along the row. He turned at the corner and retraced his steps a final time. What if she happened to be there and looked out her window at that moment?

Would Emilie Morgan recognize Will Cutler with his newly acquired mustache and gold-rimmed glasses? He turned and walked toward his hotel. At an intersection, he stopped with a group of other pedestrians as a line of traffic passed.

• • •

Emilie Morgan had never seen so much traffic in the city before, except when the Nazis were holding one of their many parades. But this was just an ordinary middle-of-the-week morning—and her first day back in Germany after eight weeks on the Italian coast. She glanced at Josef who was watching the streets with studied interest. She bit her lip with a touch of anxiety. Had this return been too soon? Was he ready for the heavy Nazi touch again? He still seemed so thin to her. While the rest and fresh air, the absence of fear and anger had healed him, the months of clear, sunny air had defined the new lines of age on his face. She had to face the fact that Josef was growing older.

"Are you sure you want to go back, Uncle Josef? I mean . . . after all that has happened? You don't have to go back."

He squeezed her hand. "I'm 65 years old, so I can confess I always envied my brother when he found Anya. So long ago, but I can remember when I first saw her. Well, my envy grew when I saw you that first time looking up at me from your basket. Now I have you worrying over me, and I find, in the end, I did not need to envy after all."

"We can't go back there and have the chance—"

"Emilie, I'm no hero. I won't put myself in front of the SS, but I won't refuse to help someone who comes to me—Jewish or precious Aryan. I won't. I took an oath to try to save life."

"If you treat Jews you are putting yourself in front of the SS. As soon as you go back, they'll be watching you."

"Then I'll be more careful."

"Uncle Josef . . ."

"Emilie, look at me. I must go back. It is my place. I only agreed to go to Italy so we both could recover. But I must go back." His voice took on a new strength that mocked his frailty. "This is the time for Adolf Hitler and Herman Göring and all the rest. It is the time for the three men who beat me." He looked into her eyes. "It is the time for the Jews to be under attack. Even if I go back to Germany to suffer with them, that is because it is the time of Josef Morgan." Tears filled his eyes.

"Their businesses have been boycotted, their children cannot go to school, but they still get sick, they still have babies. These poor people—I must help them."

"We must help them."

Emilie would never forget their talk, and how he had held her against his chest as she wept. She felt closer to him then—closer than she had ever been with her own father.

She looked to him again and he smiled. "Busy streets today," he commented mildly.

She nodded and looked past him. For a moment someone at the corner . . . The car behind her honked, and she moved on.

"It will be good to be home. I'd imagine Max has cooked up some fine feast for us. Percy will be a mess of slobber," Josef laughed.

When she didn't respond, he turned. "You haven't changed your mind?"

She shook her head. "Getting my own place is the right thing to do. That way Percy won't be torn between who to sleep with," she added lightly.

"Max will be disappointed."

Emilie didn't answer. She had never told her uncle in those quiet months together what had happened between her and his best friend. As Max had sagely pointed out, it was really between the two of them and not Josef. Josef had suffered so many disappointments with his country, his fellow citizens, fellow doctors. She would not wound him with the truth about his friend.

He could live with Max as they had done, bachelors together. But she could not live with the Nazi.

● ● ●

For a man with a pleasure-loving, lazy, carefree reputation, Max Farber had never been busier. His eyes were shadowed and he had lost weight. Long nights of planning with Rudi, transporting Jews to safety, providing food, clothing, shelter, false identity papers, and traveling passes, hiding Jews at his country estate until they could begin the long, treacherous journey out of the reich were taking its toll.

Max and Rudi stood at the bottom of the stairs to the Farber wine cellar. Seven Jews were hidden there, made comfortable by cots and food, and the presence of two tall men who looked at them with kindness and compassion. Receiving protection and help from strangers. It was a new, frightening, challenging experience for the Jews of the reich. An old man came tottering up to them, his rheumy eyes rimmed in red. He reached out to grasp Max's hand.

"How can I thank you? I have nothing."

Rudi stepped back and watched his friend's face.

"You . . . you have helped me, sir," Max replied gently. "Now try to get some sleep. You and your wife will leave tomorrow for Belgium. You will be safe."

"Could you not tell me your name, sir? My wife and I want to pray for you. We will pray for you the rest of our days."

Max swallowed hard. "My name is . . . Herr Blackney."

"Jehovah go with you."

Rudi walked Max to his car. "You sure you can get them to the station without any problem? I wish I could stay and help you," Max said.

"We'll be fine. Max, you look awfully tired. Can't you—"

"I have a 9:30 train to catch. I'll sleep on the way."

"Where to now?"

"Geneva."

"Then I shall echo the words of our old guest downstairs. Jehovah go with you."

• • •

There was little rest for Max as the train sped through the darkness of Germany. His mind was too active for sleep. So many details to go over, asking himself if he had forgotten anything, making mental notes of what he must do when he returned. His extensive social contacts had gained him quiet, unobtrusive access to other Germans who were finally, slowly, growing discontent, then alarmed and revolted, finally coming to complete opposition to the Nazi regime. Max had spoken with two generals and a Gestapo officer. It had been the greatest lift of encouragement he had had in many lonely months. He was not alone: there was Schulte, there were others. Enough others and they might make a difference. And all the while they lived under the ax of possible discovery. Discovery then certain imprisonment then probable death. *An adventure*, Max mused, *as deadly as the fictional Englishman had played in The Scarlet Pimpernel.*

As busy as he was, Max had never really been as personally satisfied as he was now. *Strange*, he mused, *how all my efforts are connected to something grim and dangerous, but I feel useful . . . needed.* He stared out the window, thinking suddenly of Emilie's disdain. *Cowardly.* It had stung him worse than anything she could have possibly said. He shrugged, sitting alone in the train compartment, *They need me, I need them . . .*

In Geneva, he made the contact after looking in on Farber Company concerns. He met the man as they strolled along the lake shore. They had met twice before, and Max trusted this man. Likewise, the Englishman had been impressed with the young German's manner and quality of information. Max made such a strong impression that the man had taken Max's words to the first lord of admiralty, Winston Churchill. The prime minister and foreign secretary—while finally recovering from their blindness to the German chancellor—were still vacillating on a response to the threats from Germany.

"We are frustrated with England's apathy. We don't understand why they are giving into Hitler's aggression," Max said with a touch of desperation.

"The prime minister wants to keep England out of a continental war—that is his first concern."

"But he will get the very thing he wishes to avoid if he doesn't stop Hitler now. Was Hitler satisfied with Austria or Czechoslovakia? Does London think he will really be satisfied with Poland? He has a voracious appetite. He'll be standing on the edge of France looking over the channel ready to plant a little swastika on the cliffs of Dover! Doesn't the prime minister understand that?"

The man rubbed his eyes wearily. "What do you want our friend to know?"

"Tell him Hitler is not invincible. If England and France will only flex their muscles, his confidence will be shaken. He can be toppled. Tell him . . ." Max glanced around. "Tell him Case White will go into effect the end of August, September the first at the latest."

"Then—"

"He will invade Poland. And he won't stop. Tell Churchill that."

Max was so preoccupied with these heavy thoughts that he didn't notice a man move from the shadows at the train station to follow him.

●   ●   ●

Emilie surveyed her apartment with satisfaction. Her own place, her own mistress, with no one going through her things or commenting on the hours or company she kept. And if she kept busy, loneliness could be held at bay. The only drawback was being away from her uncle, but she was confident they would still be together almost every day. Their relationship had a new element now—they were working together.

He had compiled a list of all the Jewish patients he could remember that he had treated over the years.

"What has happened to these poor people? Little Sara Shraeder was doing so well with the iron tablets I was giving her. What about Frau Weller's pregnancy? There were some complications. . . ."

Emilie patted his hand. "That's what I will find out."

"But they probably have gone into hiding. Ah, Emilie, it will be so dangerous for you to make inquiries. People will look at you with suspicion or fear. I am committed to helping, doing all I can, but I confess I see such difficulties. Even Max is bound to wonder, to ask questions."

"That is why our arrangement is so perfect. He has set up a little clinic in the house so you won't die from boredom and provided you with a few perfect Aryan patients. A doctor for a few overweight Nazi maidens in the home of a proper Nazi." Her voice was unmistakably scornful.

"Now, Emilie, you must admit it was thoughtful of him. He knew I wasn't quite ready to be put out to pasture—to sit in a rocker and read medical journals," he smiled.

"All right, he's thoughtful. But he doesn't know his thoughtfulness has helped us by providing you with a reason to keep ordering medical supplies. You'll work on his clients and I'll be the go-between for your old ones. The Gestapo won't be interested in either of us."

He nodded slowly, still thinking of this deception toward Max.

Emilie watched his face a moment, her voice a little hesitant.

"Last night I was reading my Bible. Josef, the Jews are God's chosen people, the apple of His eye." Her voice grew excited. "It says those who bless them, He shall bless, and those that curse them, He shall curse."

Josef nodded. "No matter the danger or peril . . . and God will give us strength. He will help us."

"Yes, I think He will."

• • •

These days it was not easy to find Dietrich Bonhoeffer—even if you had the ferretlike skills of the Gestapo. His friends could see he was in constant danger, so he was moved from city to city across the reich, encouraging in private, speaking in public, urging Germans to open their eyes, to stop this madness. So for Emilie it was not a simple matter of going across the city to speak with him. But finally, after several weeks of searching, she was able to get Bonhoeffer word that she had hopes of speaking to him. One dark, stormy night—the proper theater for such a meeting—he came to her apartment. Though exhausted looking, he exuded his boundless energy and confidence.

"Fraulein Emilie, you are well?"

"Ja, thank you. Please sit down. May I get you coffee?"

"Nein, well, yes. But I cannot stay long. I have a train to catch."

"Thank you for coming to see me. I know you're very busy."

He nodded. "Ja, very busy these days. But indeed, not too busy for a pretty—" He stopped abruptly, blushing across his full face as a boy of fifteen would. He looked at her a moment in silence. He was a shy man in such affairs of the heart, but a man who must speak the truth.

"If there were more time, Emilie, if things were not so difficult now . . . I would wish we could get to know each other better. You might even see beyond a bald pastor too old for you. . . ." He laughed at himself.

"I don't know about that, age isn't a requirement for me . . . but ja, Herr Hitler has made romance a luxury in the reich these days."

"There is no young man?"

She shook her head slowly.

"Sometimes I listen to gossip, you know it can be an amusing and a pleasant diversion. I heard your name connected with the Farber heir once."

"My uncle lives with him. I lived with both of them when I first came to Berlin. That's how such gossip started. But there was never anything between us. He's a nice man, but not my type. A little immature and irresponsible. Besides, he's a Nazi."

"Ah . . ." He glanced at his watch. "As much as I'm enjoying your company . . ."

"Well, you see while I was in Italy, I had a lot of time to think about what's happening here. I had to find my responsibility in all of this. I confess I thought of persuading my uncle to go back to the States."

"That is nothing to be ashamed of. I myself was in New York for over a year and finally knew my place was back here."

"He truly is going to try to destroy the Jews isn't he?"

Bonhoeffer's face fell. He stared at the carpet for a long minute. "I will tell you the truth as I understand it. This man is like an anti-Christ. It is my Christian duty to try to stop him—whatever the cost."

"And I . . . feel the same way. It is my duty. I suppose that's why I wanted to speak to you, to tell someone I knew would really understand."

He reached out and took her soft hand. "And you are afraid."

"Yes, I'm terribly afraid."

He smiled then, giving youth back to his lined face.

"You will keep my secret, Emilie. I am afraid, too."

"You are?"

"Ja. But where I go, God goes with me. Where He leads, I follow. I never go alone. What task He puts in my hand, He equips me. I take great comfort in that. You should, too."

"I've never told anyone this. It happened many years ago when I was a girl. I was at the Lincoln Memorial in Washington, D.C., and I was so impressed with it. I was alone and suddenly I felt as if someone or something was speaking to me. Not with a voice I could hear with my ears. I know this sounds very strange."

"Not at all."

"I closed my eyes because I was a little afraid. I saw myself like in a waking dream. I was older. I was on the steps of the memorial and there were people reaching out to me, people I didn't know. They were sad and afraid and I was terribly frustrated because I didn't know how to help them. Then they were gone, and . . ." Tears filled her eyes. "That voice seemed to say, 'I love you, Emilie Morgan.' I looked back to the memorial and thought suddenly of Lincoln helping the slaves to freedom. I knew that someday, somehow, I was to help someone—or more than one—who needed me. Pastor Bonhoeffer, I think now . . . that dream, those were Jews. I want to do something to help them."

He stood, tears in his own eyes. "You have shared your heart, Fraulein Emilie Morgan, and I will never forget that. You have encouraged me. He will show you how to help, ja, I believe he will." He leaned down and kissed her cheek. "With such as you, how can Hitler possibly succeed? In the long, dark hours before us don't forget that. In the final hour, he cannot win."

● ● ●

Two impressions struck Emilie with unexpected force when she saw Max Farber across the room. He was wearing dark pants and a white dinner jacket, he had a glass of champagne in his hand. She had seen him in this pose many times, exuding wealth and elegance, confidence and good humor. But she did not expect to be so struck with his handsomeness. *He was* . . . She glanced away a moment, trying to separate her feelings about him and his physical presence. Look at him dispassionately as her old friend Bess would. *One of the nicest-looking men I've ever seen. Built just perfect. Perfect.* She shook her head and turned her back on the Adonis across the room, inwardly laughing at herself.

Emilie was surprised at the total lack of military discussions at this gathering. She hadn't heard the word Poland a single time. Yet half the men in attendance were in spotless uniform, as if on parade, as if to give the civilian population confidence. She drifted among the chattering groups laughing and smiling and sounding like a devoted Nazi maiden. A little champagne helped her pull it off.

She had spoken to Heydrich when she had arrived. He had bent over her hand and kissed it. He smiled broadly and told her he was so glad she could come. It had been so long.... She smiled and moved away with the Beckwiths. An hour passed and Emilie was grateful Heydrich seemed to have forgotten her. His eyes had roved over her neck and shoulders, lingering, almost possessive. She had had an impulse to slap him.

But Heydrich had not forgotten her, anymore than you could forget the pleasure of some sweet delicacy you had just sampled. He played cooly and with patience. He cursed under his breath when Max Farber appeared with his sister, Elaina. He watched Emilie with a calculating eye: her every move, when she laughed. He filled his glass with something stronger than champagne and realized this German-American woman had intoxicated him. It was a weakness he was not proud of, but one he could not deny. When she was standing alone for only a fraction of a moment, he was at her side, gripping her elbow. "Shall we dance, fraulein?"

"Herr Heydrich . . ."

He guided her to the floor, smiling.

"And how is Frau Heydrich this evening? I didn't see her here." Emilie looked past him, searching.

"She is at home resting. She must stay off her feet these days. Little Heydrich is quite a burden."

Nothing like big Heydrich, she mused, and smiled.

"And how many little Heydrich's is it now?"

She could see the smile falter just a fraction.

"Number five."

"Ah . . ."

"This party is growing tiresome—same faces, same inane jokes, same waltzes." He gripped her arm a little tighter. "We both came alone—"

"I came with the Beckwiths," she corrected easily.

"Let me take you to Habel's. It overlooks the river and we can have a private table and enjoy some quiet conversation."

"That is very thoughtful of you, but I must decline. I was enjoying the party and I can't stay out late."

"I see."

They danced in silence for several minutes before she realized he was steering her toward the open balcony doors. So smooth...

"Shall we take a bit of fresh air?"

Emilie had the distinct uneasiness she should not refuse this man again. She glanced around to find Max and, not seeing him, let Heydrich lead her to the empty balcony. He walked past her to the rail and lit a cigarette. She stood a few feet away, looking at the sea of lights from the city. Finally he swung around and she was startled by how very white his skin looked in the moonlight. It looked like...someone drained of blood. She shivered. He smiled and stepped closer. "You are staring at me."

She shook her head like a frightened child.

"You are afraid of me, just a little, perhaps?"

She found her voice, steadying it with effort. She had no real reason to be afraid or intimidated by this man. Besides there was a lighted room and people just a few yards away.

"Why would I be afraid of a married man and father of five?"

He laughed richly. "You keep casting up my marital status to me. It reminds me of Max." He cocked his head to examine her with amusement. "Do you think reminding me affects me, Fraulein Emilie?"

"No, I don't suppose it does."

"Some men look and want and only dream of having. I'm made of different stuff. I look, I want, I have." He shrugged.

She turned away to let him look at her profile. Suddenly she hated that she had worn this evening gown. A silly, foolish impulse.

"How is your hobby going these days?"

"My hobby?"

"Your photography."

"Oh. I haven't taken any pictures since Josef and I left Italy. Berlin hasn't much to offer after Italy."

"A pity...you have such talent I near."

Emilie studied the moonlight patterns on the ground, her heart racing.

"What does occupy you these days besides your work at the embassy?"

"You are not very clever at disguising that you know a great deal about me, Herr Heydrich."

He chuckled. "Not as much as I would like to know, fraulein."

"I think it's time to go back in."

"I think not." He pushed her against the rail and Emilie had the sudden realization that there was no one in the room who, seeing it was the SS chieftain Heydrich, would care to interfere.

"I can feel your heart racing."

"I admire a man who acts like a gentleman, Herr Heydrich—"

"You will call me Reinhard...A man who acts like Max Farber? A man who courts a married woman? You like his childish, spineless—"

"Bitte—"

Her back was against the stone rail, his body pressed against her, his breath on her face. "I am a man who likes the sport of a chase, you are doing very well."

"Stop!"

He was kissing her neck, and she thought she was going to faint. Finally, he whispered into her ear.

"Keep up this chase, I do enjoy it. But understand who I am and the power I have. It is better to have me by your side...than across from you...my sweet little photographer. Your beauty makes men notice... and follow you." He then lapsed into a string of vulgarity.

She found the strength to push him away, and deliver a punishing slap. Her ring caught him high on the cheek and opened a small cut that trickled blood. He stepped back, pulling out a cloth, watching her with measured eyes. "Another night? I do understand the strange currents in women." He bowed stiffly. "Gute Nact, fraulein." He paused at the balcony doors. "And I trust a smart woman such as you will not forget everything I said."

She watched him enter the room, pass through the crowd, then exit. She closed her eyes to try to stop the dizziness. She gulped the night air, fervently hoping no one would come out here. But someone sat in the shadows watching her.

Max cleared his throat loudly, his voice a sleepy drawl.

"Observe the moon, fraulein, it always has a calming effect on me." Her eyes flew open, searching the dimness for him. He was seated on the rail in the shadows across the balcony. He had been there, seen everything. She felt a heady mixture of anger and relief. She turned her back on him.

"The moon is in its last quarter . . . hard to believe it has no light of its own yet it shines with more beauty than any jewel. Yet a deceptive beauty, ja? No wind, no water, no air. Scorching in the day, freezing at night . . ."

He came to stand very close behind her, speaking softly into her ear. "As a good Nazi I really shouldn't quote an Englishman, but what is it Shelley wrote? . . . 'that orbed maiden, with white fire laden, whom mortals call the moon . . .'"

Like with Heydrich, she could feel his breath on her neck, but she wasn't afraid this time. His arm came around her, pointing.

"How is your astronomy tonight, Emilie? Can you identify that planet there, just to the left of our maiden?"

She shook her head.

"Venus."

It was not the moon that had calmed her, it was his smooth, familiar teasing voice. Max had stepped out of the shadows—again. She turned around and he stepped back.

"Welcome back to Berlin," she said.

"Danke."

His smile faltered. He stepped forward. "Are you all right?"

She nodded, suddenly feeling as if she might cry. She couldn't let herself get shaken so easily—not by some creep like Heydrich. She had things to do, important things that demanded steady composure and nerves and confidence.

"Will you take me home, please?"

They stopped outside her apartment, but Emilie didn't immediately leave the car.

"Thank you for the ride."

"It was my pleasure. You haven't been by to see Percy."

"I've been busy, Max. I'm sorry I slapped you that time."

He shrugged. "I see I got off lightly."

Still she didn't get out. Max turned in the seat and looked at her. He could smell her perfume. Her hair was piled up on her head. *Very glamorous.* Suddenly she didn't look like the innocent-eyed girl that had played along with his charade in Josef's clinic nearly four years ago.

"You look very lovely tonight."

She was still looking at her lap. "And you look very dashing."

"That dress . . ."

"What about it?"

"Well, it's too...small."

"Too small?"

"Revealing, too..."

She turned scarlet.

"You'll just get angry at me for saying it, but you really shouldn't wear something like that in a roomful of ... Well, like tonight, you just shouldn't."

"Women of the reich should always look their best and be a credit to their true and superior Aryan bloodline. Heydrich just had too much to drink."

"You are a ... a woman of the reich?"

"You told me that to stay in Germany I had to play in this league. While I was in Italy, sunning and relaxing I had time to think about that. You were right. I don't want to leave Germany, so I'll embrace all that Germany is. I want her to be a success. She should be the leader in Europe. I have a desire to be a part of history."

"And the treatment of the Jews?"

She shrugged. "I'm not a Jew. I won't personally persecute them, but, to quote a German scholar, I must be loyal to my government. Hitler has some greater plan that I can't fathom in my little feminine brain, but I'll trust he knows what's best."

Max was almost gasping. "I ... you have got to be teasing me."

"No Max, I am not teasing you."

"You truly feel this way now?"

"Truly. Aren't you pleased? We're on the same side now, we don't have to fight over politics."

"Why did you slap Heydrich? Why didn't you—"

"My personal life is my own, Max." Her voice was stiff. "I said I was sorry I slapped you, and I am. I was an emotional mess that night."

"Emilie, I don't understand much right now, but I think I do understand that you still underestimate Heydrich."

"Max, please don't start."

He leaned to her. "You are the most confusing woman I have ever met in my life, and I've met quite a few. Heydrich knew about your pictures, don't you see—"

"There are no pictures, Max. I don't care what Heydrich thinks."

"You should."

"Again, thank you for the ride. Now, would you bring Percy over tomorrow afternoon?"

● ● ●

Will had been in the city five days, alternately making mental notes of the Third Reich and thinking about Emilie Morgan. He had learned she no longer lived with her uncle and Max Farber. Since she was still working for the American embassy, he placed himself across the street with a newspaper and waited for her. Just before nine in the morning she appeared around the corner, wearing a blue skirt and white blouse and looking like she had on the steps of the Lincoln memorial. He stepped forward, his heart slamming in his ears. She hurried up the steps without seeing him. He wandered around the city for the rest of the day, got caught in a parade of the German army late that afternoon, and missed her departure from the embassy.

The following morning she didn't come to work, and he resolved to no longer be a coward. He really did want to see her closer than from across the street.

● ● ●

Emilie had been out most of the morning when her apartment buzzer rang. It must be Max bringing Percy. Perhaps she would invite him along and they could take the dog to the Tiergarten.

He stood nervously smiling and gripping the bouquet of summer flowers until he threatened to break the stems. He shouldn't have come. He should have called or sent her a note. This was too sudden, too cruel. The door opened.

"Hello, Emilie," he said after an uncomfortable length of silence. He spoke in English.

Of course she recognized him. It was Will with glasses.

"I'm sorry, I've shocked you. I should have sent a note first. Are you all right?"

She nodded numbly.

He was still standing in the hallway. "May I come in?"

She stepped back and opened the door wider.

He handed her the flowers.

"Danke. Thank you," she stumbled in confusion.

She laid them on the table, not bothering to look for a vase. They stared at each other across the room.

"You look great," Will said nervously.

"Why have you come to Germany?" Her voice was clipped and blunt.

He had rehearsed a dozen replies. Now he was uncertain which to choose. Seeing her pale, shocked face, he knew he must tell her the truth as hard as it was.

He drew a deep breath. "I work for a Jewish agency in the States and they smuggled me in to find out what's really going on. I'm scouting around, taking notes, acting like a reporter."

"That could be very dangerous."

"Ah, well...Emilie..." He searched her face. Suddenly it seemed like she was his little sister, wanting something from him.

"Why did you stop writing? Why didn't you answer my letters?" Her voice had become hoarse.

He looked at the floor a long moment.

"I did. I wrote you even after you stopped. I just...never sent them."

"Why?"

"I couldn't, Emilie. I...I felt so bad. There were things—"

"McVinty never saw my photographs."

He shook his head slowly.

"You never worked for him did you?"

"No."

She sat down. "You made all of that up. Why?"

"I—"

The apartment buzzer made them both jump. Emilie closed her eyes. Max. She crossed the floor with lead feet. Percy was whining on the other side.

"Guten Tag, Max. Percy!"

Percy had bolted against her, yapping and licking, and Emilie couldn't help from laughing.

"You rogue you! You have missed me, haven't you?"

"A weeping dog is enough to make the strongest man cry. It's been a trauma for us both."

Emilie was laughing. Then she remembered Will, just as Max saw him for the first time. She stood up.

"I'm sorry, I didn't know you weren't alone," Max said.

"Max, this is—"

He held up his hand. "Wait." He stepped forward into the apartment. "You are familiar to me...but it has been a long time."

Will was looking curiously uncomfortable.

"You can't know him, Max. He's from the States. He—"

"Mueller!" Max exclaimed with triumph. "Heinz's youngest son! It's been years!"

Emilie was slightly exasperated. The shock had worn her nerves thin at the moment. "Max, this is Will Cutler from Washington, D.C."

She turned, waiting for Will to contradict Max. But he was looking pale and strange. "Will?"

Will smiled tiredly then. "Guten Tag, Herr Farber. Ja, it has been a few years."

"I can't remember your first name," Max continued jovially.

"Wilhelm." Then he looked at Emilie, looked deeply into her eyes. She sat down again.

"My name is Wilhelm Mueller, Emilie," he repeated softly, as if he were sorry to have to admit it.

● ● ●

It was a gray, sultry morning with low-hanging clouds in Germany's capital city. The streets were quiet—almost somber—despite the news which greeted Berliners in the morning editions and over the radio. September 1, 1939, was a day most Germans would never forget. Twenty years before wild, patriotic enthusiasm with parades in the streets, cheers, bouquets of flowers, and waving flags had assured the German leaders the people were eager for war with their neighbors. Now the citizens seemed stunned, incredulous that many of them who had survived the crucible as young men would face it again—either in their own bodies or through their sons'. Was Poland really worth such a price?

While German citizens on the city streets appeared almost sluggish, their army was smashing across the Polish frontier with stunning speed and ruthlessness. From the skies, the air force was striking with impressive power, dumping bombs on bridges, railroads, troops, and cities. It was called the blitzkrieg and it was inaugurating a modern reign of terror for millions. The secret building of army, navy, and air force had been a success—a colossus destruction force was unleashed.

Two days later, Great Britain and France declared war on Germany. The Second World War had finally begun.

● ● ●

Rudi urged him to reconsider this rescue. It was far too dangerous.

"Danger is what this is all about, my friend," Max said, giving him a slap on the back. "Besides, I can't pass up this opportunity. Reinhard knows about the SS disguises and he's laying traps for me. But I can't sit idle. When I find out about a chance, I evaluate it. I've done that. I think I can pull it off."

He stopped on the threshold. "If you don't hear from me by midnight, move everybody out. Move the Muellers. Take Magda and go to my place in Frankfurt. You remember the name it's under and where the key is?"

Rudi nodded.

Max laughed easily. "Don't look so tragic, Rudi. I'll be back."

Rudi Schmidt wasn't so certain.

● ● ●

He typically moved under the cover of darkness, when vision could deceive, when shadows could conceal. But there wasn't time to wait until nightfall—only time to darken his hair and dress in very cheap, dark clothes. In the end, there was no time to affect a better plan to save these five Jews held in the empty office of a suburban train station. There was only time to offer the four guards money in exchange for five minutes of their backs turned. The lure of such money was enough to make them forget the looming menace of punishment. He talked smooth and fast and convinced them they could pretend the Jews had concealed weapons—but one of them temporarily forgot.

Max hurried the Jews into a waiting car with papers and clothes. He gave them money and directions. They thanked him profusely. Just as the car turned out of sight, the SS descended on the man who bribed them. He was on foot alone. The SS were now joined by five others. Rudi's worst fear for his friend had happened.

● ● ●

It was Percy who alerted them. They sat in the upstairs library eating strudel.

"This is the best strudel you've ever made, Uncle Josef."

"Danke. I just wish Max were here to enjoy it."

"So where is he tonight? The opera? The sportsplast to hear the fuehrer shout himself into a lather for a few hours?"

"He didn't say. He hasn't been home much lately. Not much more than to sleep. I worry about him. He seems so worn out when I do see him. I don't understand ... we used to talk."

"I'm sorry." Emilie leaned back, suddenly intrigued by what could possibly be occupying Max's energy and time.

Percy went to the library doorway, suddenly alert.

"He hears something," Josef said, sitting up. Emilie sat up also and listened.

"Probably the wind," she said, but her thoughts went immediately to the Gestapo.

A low whine came up from Percy's chest. Josef and Emilie looked at each other.

"He usually doesn't whine at the wind," Josef said.

"Well, maybe it's Max."

"He usually doesn't whine like this when it's Max." Josef went to the door and peered down the stairs to the darkened first floor.

Emilie stood beside him.

"Someone's in the clinic," Josef's voice was unruffled.

"Let's call the police," Emilie urged.

He shook his head. "There isn't time. I'm not going to let them smash up my things again!"

"Uncle Josef, wait!"

Percy backed up against their legs when Josef forcefully pushed the door open. Josef and Emilie stood rooted in shock. Max was leaning over the sink. Blood was splattered all over the floor. Josef regained his composure almost instantly. His tone was brisk, almost irritated. Emilie was a little surprised.

"Max, how could you imagine you could patch yourself up? Remember your fight with Irwin?"

"No ... no, I don't remember. I ... didn't want to bother you."

"Emilie, you're going to have to help me."

They eased him onto the examining table. Emilie felt a little weak—she had never seen so much blood.

Josef leaned over Max, smoothing the hair on his forehead, his voice tender. "Well, we are quite a pair, ja? Getting into scrapes like a pair of old tom cats."

Max gave him a weak smile.

Josef pushed the coat aside, then the shirt. Emilie turned away for a moment.

"Max, this is a gunshot wound!" Josef exclaimed.

"It ... is?"

Josef took his pulse and his blood pressure. He looked up at his niece. "Can you be my nurse, Em? I don't have time to call Helga."

"I think I can."

"Hold this while I get ready."

Max closed his eyes, but she knew he was awake. She gently pressed the cloth against his shoulder.

"I'm sorry ... you must assist in the ... aid of a Nazi, fraulein Morgan. Ah, but I forgot ... you have ... changed your ... spots."

"Be quiet, Max."

"Josef, can a leopard change his spots? Do you think?"

"You're talking nonsense, Max." Josef said brusquely.

"He's always talking nonsense," Emilie interjected.

"Is Percy here ... to defend ... me?"

At his name, the dog came to the table, standing on his back legs to lick Max's hand.

"There boy, good fellow. You're a loyal fellow, ja?"

"Max, how did this happen?"

His eyes fluttered open. "This? My memory grows so faulty ... after such tremendous blood loss."

"It hasn't affected his tongue, though," Emilie remarked.

"Max, this is very serious," Josef said, attempting a stern tone.

"Well, all right. I was shot by a jealous...husband. Elaina Heydrich's husband found us together. You know what tempers Italians have."

Emilie and Josef exchanged a look across the table. Max had closed his eyes again. Emilie felt a little wave of disgust.

"I lived among the Italians for nearly three months, Maximillian. I found them very courteous people. But any man—despite his nationality might get upset under those...circumstances," Josef replied tartly.

Max managed a feeble laugh. "All right, all right. I'll tell you the truth, then please fix...this. My shoulder is—"

"Killing you?" Emilie inserted wickedly.

Max's voice was growing weaker. "Josef, don't let her get near anything...vital. I had a little confrontation with the SS or the Gestapo."

"The SS or Gestapo? Why?" Josef asked. Worry instantly replaced shock.

"They...didn't like what I said, I suppose."

"They shot at you?"

"You know how some men like their toys."

"I'm afraid to ask, but what did you say?"

"I may have said something about how they almost make me believe in Darwin's theory of evolution."

"Maximillian, your very active sense of humor is going to get you into worse trouble than this if you're not more careful."

"Ja, more careful . . ."

Then he fell blissfully asleep, the first real rest he had in months. And as he slept, he left the doctor and the doctor's niece to speculate on why he had gotten on the wrong side of the German authorities. Emilie Morgan was determined to find out the true story of Max's escapade.

24
Moonlight Serenade

Though it was a bright sunny October day, the wind was strong, sounding to Emilie like pounding surf just outside her apartment window. But then, every sound seemed loud and magnified in the tense stillness of the room. She and Will were sitting across from each other, like two combatants in the ring, wary and uncertain. She had sent him away that first day, too upset and shocked to deal with any further revelations. But now he was back, and she wanted to understand with the hope this young man would no longer be such a stranger. Had they really walked along the streets of Washington, laughing like good friends? She had trusted him.

He licked his lips, glancing around the room.

"Thanks for seeing me again, Emilie. I know this isn't easy. I really wish I could make it easier."

"Just tell me from the beginning," she said in an emotionless voice.

He looked at his hands a moment. "The beginning ... where is the beginning? ... I ..."

She felt no sympathy for his discomfort. Seeing him so suddenly on her threshold stirred up the memories, stirred up the pain. Let him suffer a little as she had.

"Herr Farber recognized me because my father works for him. My father has been the Farber groundsman for over 40 years. When I was growing up, I played with Max once or twice though he was older. By the time I was 16 I left home."

"There is no family in New Mexico, no mother recovering from TB?" Emilie interrupted.

He shook his head, hoping she would not make these cold interruptions very often.

"I left Germany in 1935 because I had gotten into trouble with the SS in Nuremberg. I was a student there for awhile, then I dropped out. I—"

"What were you studying?" she asked in a slightly warmer tone.

"Journalism. But I didn't have the discipline to stay with it. I got a job with a Jewish paper—doing reporting, taking pictures, running errands, and such jobs. I also worked as a waiter. I liked my life, I didn't have any responsibilities. My friends and I had a good time." He cleared his throat nervously. "Things really started getting rough for the Jews in '35. I joined a resistance group, not because . . ." He stopped and looked at her for a moment. "Emilie, I'm a Jew."

She nodded.

"I'm not a religious Jew. I joined the resistance group because I didn't like what was happening; I didn't think it was fair. Jews are as German as anyone. So I got involved. I met a rabbi. . . . When things finally got too hot for me, I went to him, to say goodbye and told him that I had to leave Nuremberg. He made me take all the money he had in his pocket. It was pocket change for him, but it was over 300 dollars. Suddenly, I wasn't so limited in what I could do and where I could go. I went all the way to the coast and then I wandered down to the docks. I saw an American liner about to set sail. *America.* I had never thought of it before. Emilie, my life seemed so controlled in Germany because I was a Jew. I wanted to go where I could control things, where it didn't matter that I was a Jew. So I wrote my parents, bought a ticket, and sailed."

He stood up and went to her window and looked out.

"You sounded so American, so . . ." Emilie said softly.

"My brother taught languages at the university in Nuremberg, so my English was pretty good already. On the trip over I met a fellow about my age who had been to Switzerland to see a doctor there. He was dying of tuberculosis. I told him everything. We talked constantly and he gave me this sort of quick education on American culture. He was very kind to me. His name was ... Will Cutler."

"We got to New York and some men met me as I came off the boat. They wanted to know everything about Germany. I spent hours with them because they paid me for everything I could tell them. They bought all my German-made clothes and everything in my pockets. All I can tell you is they were with the United States government—intelligence people who were very interested in what was going on in Europe. I hung around New York for awhile working for them, picking up slang and American ways. They put me in touch with a Jewish agency. At first I didn't want anything to do with them. I was finished with the whole Jewish thing. It ... it was nothing but trouble."

His shoulders sagged under some sudden, invisible weight. He was silent several minutes.

"What happened then, Will—" Her laughter was strained. "I guess I should be calling you Wilhelm."

He didn't seem to hear her. "I finally looked them up. I was thinking of my father who I had disappointed so much. He would want me to meet these people. As it turned out, they, too, were very kind and helpful. Many of them were refugees from Hitler's reich. They thought I could help their group in Washington, D.C., so I was sent there. They paid me enough to get by on. It was all I could think of for awhile. I honestly didn't know what I wanted my future to be."

Again a long silence. They both knew the hardest part was coming.

"You didn't work for the *Mount Vernon Voice*."

"No. I made that up to impress you."

"You didn't know Helen?"

"Yes, I did. I met her at a party. She told me about you being German, about your father, and ... and it seemed like a good ... contact. The organization wanted me to pursue it."

He waited for her to say something, but she only watched him.

"We didn't know your father had died until that day we met. I was supposed to see if you still had any contacts in Germany that we might use."

"Use?"

"Emilie, we were trying to get things into Germany and get reports on the conditions of the Jews out. This was a rescue and refugee organization. We were only a small unit in the organization. All of us were trying to find ways to help the Jews in the reich and let the rest of the world know what was really happening in there."

"I see. So you were acting, playing a part. I remember Bess sounding some kind of alarm. Good ol' Bess," she finished bitterly.

"Yes, it was acting at first."

"Then an award for you, Wilhelm Mueller. You did very well. You convinced me."

It was as racking as he had known it would be. There was no detour around this kind of deception. He had to make a clean break with all the lies—then he'd be free to leave.

"Emilie, you have no idea how much I wish I didn't have to be telling you any of this, that it never really happened this way. But I have to tell you everything, then I'll leave."

"Did you arrange for me to lose my job at the Smith?"

"No, I had nothing to do with that. It just fit . . . in the plans."

"My father's death?" She stood, the gulf growing wider between them.

He paled, horrified that she could think . . .

"Emilie, no never, I couldn't."

"Finish it up, Herr Mueller."

"The assignment to cover the Games—we needed to get someone into Berlin."

"Why?"

"To smuggle in visas and money to the Jews—to help them get out. You had the perfect cover. No one would suspect you."

She had sat down. "Smuggled money and . . . My suitcase!"

He nodded.

Her voice came in a gasp. "It wasn't the Nazis—it was your people. They ripped up my bag. If the Nazis had found the visas, then I would be in a concentration camp right now—if not dead."

He gripped the back of a chair until his knuckles went white.

"I wanted to call it off, but—"

"But you couldn't."

He shook his head. "It was beyond my control. We took the risk."

She didn't want to cry in front of him.

"Please...leave. I know enough now. Just leave," she whispered. He dared to come and kneel in front of her.

"It was all wrong for me to do. I knew it then. I don't expect you to believe me now, but it became more than an assignment for me. I...I looked forward to those times we had together—all of them. You were very good for me. I was in agony until I heard from you in your first letter that everything had gone off as planned. You gave life to forty Jews if that's any comfort."

He stood up. "Emilie, I was wrong and I'm sorry."

He left then, quietly closing the door. Less than a minute later Max was there, standing in the doorway when she had not answered the knock. He had passed the distraught-looking Mueller on the steps. Had something happened to Emilie?

"You wanted to go with Josef and me to the country, do you remember?"

She nodded, not looking up. "I'll be ready in a few minutes."

He waited, hesitant. He knew she wanted him to leave.

"How has he hurt you?" he asked finally.

She looked up then, shrugging slightly. "What is left to hurt?"

1940

Max privately speculated that his contact within the Nazi hierarchy of Berlin was possibly one of the best and would be highly prized by those who fought against Nazism. It was a life vein into the reich nerve center that had come to him unexpectedly. He hadn't attempted to cultivate it, but was thoroughly gratified when it bore fruit. His contact had come to the painful realization that the attack on Jewish Germans was the single greatest threat to the country's dignity. Centuries of culture and advancement were being blotted out by a regime of barbarism. The Nazi informer and Max could not measure the danger of discovery against the hope for their country that their actions restored in them.

From this Nazi contact, Max was able to learn of impending arrests and raids against the Jews in Berlin and surrounding cities. Max knew he could not effect all of them, or even a fraction of them—he could choose only those that he and Rudi could manage together, within the short notice they received. He tried not to think about those he could not rescue—those Jews that waited in the cold, damp warehouses or the cattle cars praying for a miracle. And he found that each successful rescue fanned the flame of daring inside him. He grew bolder.

An absentminded doctor who removed five Jews from jail under the threat of a typhus panic, a priest who wanted to attempt a conversion of three young Jewish women, four Jewish children removed from an orphanage by a French diplomat . . . all provided opportunities for rescue. He struck in Munich, Frankfurt, Berlin. It could not last forever, but Max Farber had never been happier.

• • •

The men in the room had had enough experience with SS Chief Heydrich to prefer his tirades and his cursing to this stony, ominous silence. The chief sat at his desk scanning the papers in front of him. He had not said a word for over five minutes while they stood rigidly before him. He tapped a long gold pen over the lines of writing. Then he leaned back and stared at them. Finally he picked up the phone and gave a command. He stood up. "I gave you orders to find this . . . this actor." His voice was steady. "You are a disgrace to the SS. There are officers just outside this door who will escort you to the internment quarters until tomorrow. I will spend the rest of the day deciding whether you shall be shot at sunrise or merely imprisoned for one year. At the moment, I prefer to fill our prisons up with Jews and not careless, halfwits who cannot capture this man who is shaming the reich. You will share his punishment."

When they retreated, stumbling through the door in shock, he was alone. He went to his liquor cabinet and poured himself a liberal drink. This pretender had excellent inside information, access to passes, uniforms, schedules. Someone within his own territory was setting him up to be a fool. Heydrich was no longer concerned with the Jews that were escaping. This impostor was blatantly taunting him. Just an hour ago a scrap of paper with the flag had been delivered to his own hand. Someone was out to ruin his career . . . But the young officer had long since determined he would have a significant place in the third reich . . . like Adolf Hitler.

Reinhard Heydrich calmly sat down and pulled an empty pad of paper to his lap. He would think of all his enemies: those he knew had reason to taunt him this way. He would find the traitor.

• • •

The sun was a disk of opal wreathed in the morning mist, slowly thinning. It was a beautiful morning on the Farber estate, quiet and calm as it had been for generations. Who was in power in Berlin or how far south a war of men and steel clashed didn't seem to affect it. The designs and seasons changed, but the land remained. Sometimes, on a morning like this, old Heinz Mueller felt he had been here as long as the stoutest oak and beech trees. Mueller was as much a part of the Farber estate as any of the lords of the house—maybe more. He certainly knew it better and, perhaps, loved it more.

He had risen to putter about in the kitchen garden. There was no real need since there were now younger hands to weed the cabbages and thin the carrots, but Heinz had long since decided he'd be working with the soil until they laid him in it. He had been praying since the first light of dawn—another routine as sure as the sun rising. Each morning the same prayer concerns: Marta, Walther, Maria, Wilhelm, the Farber boys, Adolf Hitler, his country—and anything else that came to his mind. Lately, there were the frightened faces he had discovered in the cellar. He learned their names before they were slipped away in the night. When he thought of them, he invariably returned to pray again for the youngest Farber. How had he misjudged him those few years ago? Heinz was as proud of Max as if he were his own son. He knew the danger to Max—to all of them if their work was discovered.

Germany at war. He shook his head sadly. *So many young men sacrificed to the fuehrer's ambitions. Wilhelm would have been a prime candidate for the German army. Until they learned he was a Jew.* He squatted down to pull a worm off the cabbage. So it was better, perhaps, this way. Wherever he was, he was probably safe.

"Will I die before I see him again, Lord?" he whispered. "Just like Jacob, I long to see my son once again before I die."

He straightened up as the sun split the mist in dazzling radiance. He turned. Someone was coming around the house.

He dropped the hoe and stretched out his arms. He began to cry. "Bless the Lord, O my soul, and all that is within me, bless His holy name . . ." his soul cried out to God.

Wilhelm had come home.

In the Mueller home, the reunion was joyful. They hugged him and kissed him and cried over him all morning. Walther, settled in a small village north of Berlin, happened to be visiting, and his sister Maria was living at home. It was a happy reunion under the shadow of being a hunted people. They absorbed his stories of America with wide eyes and near disbelief. Wilhelm had been across the ocean, had seen the place where the United States president lived, and saw the woman with the torch in the harbor! They listened like people dying of thirst.

In the afternoon, Wilhelm and his sister took a walk down along the river.

"I wish you had stayed there, Wilhelm. It is so dangerous here. You were safe there," Maria sighed.

He put his arm around her. "Would you have your little brother a coward, Maria?" he smiled. He told Maria of his time in Washington, D.C., and the decision he had finally made. When he had seen Herschel's name in the paper those months ago, then read the revenge the Germans had taken, he had realized that he was running away from who he was and what his responsibility was. America was not who he was or where he belonged. He couldn't run away from being a Jew any longer. He didn't want to. It was an evolution he couldn't explain or put into words, but one he knew had occurred inside him. First he had to make apologies to Emilie Morgan. Next, he had to be restored to his family. Then he had to take his place beside his people—whatever that meant.

Maria was silent for a moment.

"Many have left, emigrated, but Father says we should stay. This is our home. I get scared sometimes, but I want to stay, too. Mostly, I just want it to be over."

"Someone I know said that once."

"What will you do now, Wilhelm? Are you home for awhile?"

He shook his head. "I still have someone to see—someone I knew an eternity ago . . ."

• • •

Emilie wanted to get the task over quickly, like taking a dose of un-pleasant medicine—before her determination failed her. The long drive to the Farber estate was what she needed first. The countryside, though absent of color and bloom, was also absent of Nazi flags. It was like driving through the winter countryside of Maryland as she'd done as a girl with her parents. Taking Saturday drives in their big blue Essex automobile. She thought of her mother and father then.

"What would you think about what I'm preparing to do?" she said aloud in the empty car, as she turned onto the Farber drive.

Rudi opened the door to the grand house, looking instantly nervous. "Fraulein Morgan, how...what a pleasant surprise."

"Guten Morgen, Rudi. I need to see Herr Farber."

"Ja, ja, or course. I will get him for you. Please wait in the library."

She pulled off her coat and gloves and stood before the library fire. Max was such a man of creature comforts. She studied the paintings to distract her nervousness. It was not working. She strolled to the couch. She could tell he'd been lying here: a rich wool blanket tossed aside, an empty cup and a plate of crumbs on the floor. Well, the servants were a little lax this morning. She spied the edge of a book under the blanket. What had Master Farber been relaxing with?

The Scarlet Pimpernel. She opened the cover and saw that her uncle had given Max this book on his twelfth birthday. She flipped through it, trying to recall if she had ever read it before.

"A classic I highly recommend," came the lazy voice from the doorway.

He stood in the doorway wearing a silk dressing jacket, his hair hurriedly combed.

"Guten Morgen, Max."

He came into the room with Magda following him. She gave Emilie a quick, nervous nod, set the tray down, and backed out.

"Your staff seems a little nervous at my unannounced visit."

Max smiled. "They didn't want to wake me—thought I'd be a bear. Please be seated and tell me what brings you from Berlin so early."

But she didn't sit. Max dropped into his desk chair, giving her an amused perusal.

"Max, I need to ask you ... something."

Only an eyebrow raised in response.

She took a long breath as if getting ready to plunge under water.

"My visa expires in 10 days. It isn't going to be renewed for some reason that I haven't been able to uncover. I've gone through all the channels, filled out all the papers, gone nearly to the fuehrer himself. My German birth helps, but restrictions have been clamped down because of the war. So ... so the only way I can find to stay in Germany is if I... The only way I can stay is if I'm married to a German citizen," she finished in a rush.

Max was leaning back in the chair, his arms crossed, smiling slightly. "A pity Reinhard is married."

She ignored him. Of course he would be flippant and rude.

"I'm asking, I need... I'm asking you to marry me."

He leaned forward, his blue eyes widened. "This is a marriage proposal?"

"Ja."

His voice took on the tone of a delighted child.

"This is my first! I'm very flattered, very, very flattered."

She looked away, rubbing her forehead.

"You don't have to make this more difficult for me than it is. A yes or no would be sufficient."

"You want me to marry you so you can become Frau Farber and stay in Germany."

"Ja."

He walked across the room and picked at the vase of fresh cut flowers, deliberately taking his time.

"What about Herr Mueller?" he asked casually.

"I repeat, you don't have to make this harder for me. I'm not asking Herr Mueller, I'm asking you."

He faced her, his voice smooth. "I think I should be entitled to one question."

"You have already asked one question," she returned sweetly.

"Touché, Emilie, touché! But you see I feel I must ask this, that I have a right to an answer. I've been a committed bachelor for now these many years. I'm attached to it with a particular fondness. Yes, I could not give it up easily," he sighed. He lifted his eyes to her. "I would need more information about my prospective bride."

Emilie rolled her eyes. "What, Max?"

"You want to marry, by your own definition, a cowardly lout—a Nazi—just to obtain German citizenship. That seems like a bitter pill to swallow. Why do you want to stay here so passionately?"

"I'm as German as you are, Herr Farber. I have chosen this as my home. I've explained that before."

He bowed again. "Indeed, you have. But I... suspect there is more."

"Your suspicions are wrong. I just want to stay in Germany."

"I'm a man who likes to play games."

"I've observed that."

"Ja," he laughed, "but I play best and enjoy it the most when I am fully apprised of the rules. It's very disconcerting to make a goal, capture a piece, reach the finish line, steal a kiss, and have someone cry foul! Very unpleasant."

Emilie was tapping the chair back with impatience. She should have expected this drawing out of torture. He would have it no other way. "What would the rules of this arrangement be, fraulein? The usual marital amenities?"

She felt herself blush. "Rules? Well, we marry in a simple civil ceremony. We continue to live our lives as we have." She raised her chin loftily. "Each to his and her own pursuits. A very practical and respectful relationship."

"Ah . . . very . . . charming words, practical and respectful—sounds cold and unfriendly to me."

"Yes or no, Max. I'm tired of your teasing."

"A business arrangement is what you want."

"If you want it in those terms, then fine. Yes, a business arrangement."

He regarded her a long time as she shifted uncomfortably.

"Are you quite certain about this proposal, fraulein? What a scandal if you found yourself liking me!"

"We don't need to worry about that, Herr Farber."

He leaned back and laughed deeply.

"I'm a little disappointed you didn't ask me on bended knee, but I accept your proposal, Fraulein Morgan. It should prove amusing."

● ● ●

Josef looked far more nervous than the groom. *It had happened so suddenly, so very suddenly. Max and Emilie getting married? He thought his niece had only a tepid affection for Max Farber, well-laced with disapproval and scorn. How had Max won her over? And how had Max been moved from his seemingly impenetrable fortress of bachelorhood? It is all very confusing. Apparently I'm too old to understand romantic adventures—but I'm not too old to see that Emilie looks properly*

*radiant in her cream-colored suit, and Max looks sharp in his tan suit.
They look just like figurines on top of a wedding cake!*

It was a simple civil ceremony in the pretty square of Dresden. Max
had succumbed to an unexpected bout of sentiment—his parents had
married here 50 years ago, and Emilie had agreed with little comment.

"Are you all right, my dear?" Josef asked. "You look a little pale."

She gave him a dazzling smile and kissed his cheek. "The bride is
nervous."

Josef leaned closer to her ear. "He really is a wonderful man, Emilie. Honorable and kind and decent. He'll make a good husband and a
wonderful father."

It was not difficult for Emilie to effect a blush. *A little Farber? Poor
Josef was still hoping after all these years and here I am going to disappoint him.* She sighed and looked quickly at Max across the room.
She thought of Bess, "Well, you got a looker, Em, no doubt about it.
Money, too, You're sittin' fine." The imagined conversation caused Emilie to smile. She strolled down the hall a little way as they awaited the
clerk.

Josef went over to Max who stood at the long tall windows that
looked down on the fountain and flowers. He patted Max's back.

"A little nervous?"

"Nervous? No. Just thinking about Percy. He wanted to be the best
man."

Josef chuckled. "I have the comfort of knowing, my friend, nothing—from Adolf Hitler to matrimony—can destroy your sense of humor."

Max let his eyes take in Emilie for just a moment as she wandered
down the hall. Josef watched her also.

"You're getting a lovely girl, even if I am a little biased."

Max nodded slowly.

"Love her with all your heart," Josef said with sudden intensity.

Max looked back to him. *Does he suspect this is an arrangement?*
He was saved a reply by the entrance of the clerk.

Max lost his look of casual indifference. Sham or not, he was about
to take a bride. Emilie looked straight ahead, repeating the vows in a
firm voice. She didn't appear to notice that his hands trembled slightly
as he slipped on the ring. She felt the coldness of the metal and looked
down. She had no idea what ring he had selected.

It was beautiful—far too...for an arrangement marriage. A diamond encircled by black sapphires, she thought and looked up surprised. He had entrusted her with a Farber jewel.

He was looking at her hand, his voice very low, and she thought, tinged with sadness. "This was my mother's. It was always meant for my...bride."

Emilie swallowed with difficulty. A swift kiss on her cheek, and Emilie Morgan, now Fran Farber, had received her desired citizenship.

• • •

While it was not well received in the Chancellery, still, it gave some Germans a private, slender thread of hope: Chamberlain's government had fallen, Winston Churchill was the new British prime minister. Emilie grasped the news with encouragement. The pudgy-faced Englishman seemed to understand the true and villainous nature of Adolf Hitler, his real menace to world peace. Now Churchill was at the helm of opposition. With the aid of her beloved president, Franklin Roosevelt, and Churchill in battle gear, Hitler could be stopped. She understood, like many, that the cost to stop him would be very high now.

Emilie watched and listened, as most other German civilians did with a sense of awe as the Nazi war machine rolled over and crushed Poland in 18 days. As spring bloomed in innocent riot from the channel to the Mediterranean, the German army and Luftwaffe took Denmark and Norway. The cherry and apricot trees blossomed, Holland, Belgium, and Luxembourg fell under the Nazi heel. Never in modern history had a conquering army moved so swiftly and powerfully. With Russia as his northern ally, the fuehrer directed his legions south—to the prize he craved the most. In only a short matter of time, the swastika would flutter along the Champs Elysées in Paris.

Even though it seemed the German army was unstoppable, Emilie Farber was not thinking of these grim events as she drove around Berlin. She had driven for over 30 minutes, turning, stopping, doubling back, watching in her rearview mirror to see if she was possibly followed. She shook her head. *The Nazis had effectively instilled paranoia in its subjects. People were always looking over their shoulders, lowering their voices—even if they had* Mein Kampf *imprinted on their souls.* She slowed near the entrance of the Berlin zoo; a man quickly jumped into the front seat beside her.

Jake Harrold gave her an appraising glance.

"So it's Frau Farber now, right?"

She nodded.

"No comment, no questions, no editorials," he chirped after a short silence.

"Danke. Now, what do you have for me?"

"Being part bloodhound—and larger part genius for getting past Nazi goons—I can tell you I found you two prizes, the Zimmerman family and Rabbi Weismann. The goons are really looking for him."

"Thank you very much, Jake. I can't tell you how much it has meant to me to have you as an ally."

"We Yanks have to stick together. Though now that you're this Farber dame, I guess I should be a little intimidated."

She laughed. "Hardly."

"You could have given me a scoop on why the young photographer from Washington married the Nazi playboy."

"There is no scoop and, as you told me once, you don't do society stuff."

She had turned down Kurfurstendamm and they both sat silent a moment at the influx of soldiers enjoying last minute refreshment in the many sidewalk cafes before departing for the front.

Harrold gave a low whistle. "Hitler's mighty men. Looks like they'll be sippin' bubbly in Paris any day now."

"Well, Churchill's in, so things may be looking up," Emilie said hopefully.

"Never thought this little corporal would get this far. Never thought I'd see a Napoleon in my lifetime," he said grimly.

"Come on, Jake, where's your eternal optimism?"

"When they pushed over the Maginot Line, it suffered a little. I like Paris almost as much as I like New York. I hate to see the goons tramping around there. And frankly, Emilie, I'm about fed up with this Jew baiting. The things I've seen . . ."

"Tell me the addresses and I'll drop you back at the zoo."

He told her and posed a question to her.

"How is it you're helping Jews with your hubby a Nazi? Does he turn a loving, but blind eye?"

"We do not discuss politics or things like that. I don't interfere with him, he doesn't with me."

"Cozy, cozy," the newspaperman murmured. "All right. Now I have a question for you—a favor to ask—sort of."

"What?"

"A few of my contacts have been picking up drifts of this problem for the SS, for Heydrich particularly. I figured that with you in the Nazi party crowd—and your husband's connections—you may have heard something."

"Picked up what?"

"Somebody's slipping Jews out of Berlin. Small packages at a time. He's dressed in disguise, mostly like an SS officer. Someone's acting like a regular pimpernel."

A pimpernel? Where have I heard that before? she wondered briefly.

"I haven't heard anything," she replied.

"Seems like he leaves these little scraps of paper with the old German flag drawn on them, rolled up with a scarlet thread around them. He's taunting the SS for sure. Gutsy guy, but headed for the ax if he isn't careful."

"Why do you want to know more about him?"

"It would make great copy back home. A German with some nerve, some spunk, and courage. It would be front-page stuff—and I wouldn't mind the byline."

She laughed. "Well, it would be great news for me, too. I don't know anyone like that, and I haven't heard of it yet."

She pulled up to the curb at the zoo. "But I will keep my ears open as you say."

"Your photos made it to New York. I'll let you know when I hear anything."

"Thank you, Jake. I'm grateful to you for taking the risk to get them out. As much as I'd like it, be sure my name doesn't get on them."

"Speaking of risks, Emilie, you know this helping Jews is—"

She smiled. "We both know, don't we, Jake."

Later that evening she and Josef found the Zimmerman family huddled in a damp, rat-infested basement on the perimeter of Berlin. They embraced the doctor and his niece with weeping. Seeing their surroundings, Emilie struggled with her own composure. She held the youngest child in her lap while Josef administered their medical needs. They had also brought the refugees food and warmer clothes.

"'We're working on identity papers for you, to try to get you to Switzerland, but it will take time."

Herr Zimmerman wrung Josef's hand. "You are not a Jew, yet you are risking . . . Ah, doctor."

Josef looked over at Emilie. She had never seen him looking happier.

• • •

Karl Beck was a very busy man. His official work with the Gestapo and his unofficial, personal ambitions kept him occupied most of the day and evening. He made social contacts for diversions and to hear gossip that might prove profitable. He had chosen a cold, calculating, sterile life for himself. Drawn into the Nazi system, nourished by it, like many Germans, the diet hardened him and seared his conscience. So when the cattle cars passed with Jews moaning and crying, Beck could look without protest or flinching.

Karl had determined he would become a valued employee of Farber Company. He had done that until he was fired. Now, he was determined to rise in the ranks of the Gestapo. He was on his way. And, he decided he would find a way to strike at Max Farber. After nearly a year, he added this ambition to his successes. The Gestapo was aware that information was filtering out of the reich to the British and French via neutral countries such as Belgium and Switzerland. German traitors were passing reich secrets. The age of espionage and counterespionage entered a new era. Gestapo agents were carefully planted in international watering holes and business centers like Bern, Zurich, and Geneva, to watch for German men and women on holiday or business who were actually selling pieces of Germany to Germany's enemies. In cities supposedly of neutrality and peace, the rate of dead tourists grew alarmingly in the reich years. One such agent recognized Max Farber, followed him, noted his apparent casual contact with a known English diplomat—and reported it directly to Karl Beck.

They arrested Max as he crossed the German border.

Munich

Emilie had purposely arrived at the prison only minutes before Max's expected release time. She wanted to avoid any conversation between herself and the Nazis. Now she stood in her raincoat staring through the small, black, rain-streaked window—her back to the desk where a lieutenant sat smoking and drinking schnapps and appraising the lovely young Frau Farber. For a few moments, Emilie forgot his presence in the small room.

Everything had happened so fast. Josef had taken the call from a Gestapo official. Max had been taken by the Gestapo as he reentered Germany. He was being held for questioning at the nearest prison, which was in Munich.

Josef was stricken as he repeated the brief message to Emilie.

"I don't understand... What has Max done?" he said slowly.

"I've just called the station. I can catch a train to Munich in one hour," Emilie said, while throwing clothes into a suitcase.

"How long will they detain him?" Josef wondered aloud.

"I'll stay there for however long they have him," Emilie returned with conviction. That made her uncle smile. *She must love her husband!* he thought.

A voice nearly caused her to jump. "Frau?"

Emilie turned reluctantly. The desk lieutenant looked to her exactly what he was: a small town nobody now swollen with power and pride. "You prefer a view of a stone wall to a little conversation while we wait together for your husband?" he asked with a toothy smile.

Emilie chose her words slowly and carefully.

"I confess I am not in much of a mood for conversation, sir."

His eyes narrowed and looked her over, lingering on her body in a way that made her blush with anger. *Nazis*, she decided, *had perfected a "wolf look" to an art.*

"I am a man familiar with women's moods," he continued smoothly.

Emilie wanted to turn her back to the window, but then she would feel his eyes on her back. Perhaps it would be better to face him.

He laced his fingers together, a smile lingering on his lips.

"I am also aware that a woman often asserts a certain influence over a man—wife over husband, mistress over lover. I say this to encourage you, Frau Farber, to use your influence over your husband. I understand he is known for his clever jokes in social circles—a clown—but we are no longer laughing. His jokes are far too disrespectful—"

"Nazis should not be so humorless, then. It isn't good for our international reputation," Emilie said with a slight smile. She instantly knew her mistake. Eric had warned her to be careful and say only what was necessary.

The man sucked in his cheeks in judgment. "Perhaps the advice should go to you as well, Frau Farber. You both would be wise to understand this. Lack of discretion—not controlling your tongues—could lead to painful lessons." His smile returned. "Your husband has tasted this. You're too beautiful a woman to have to be taught painful lessons."

Emilie felt weak inside. What had they done to Max?

She struggled to keep her voice level and calm.

"It is nearly 4:30, lieutenant. I was told Max—my husband—would be released at 4:00."

He glanced over his papers with a raised eyebrow. "Four thirty? I have the order here, it says 5:30. Another hour, then he'll sign this document and be free to go with you."

She knew he was lying.

"So please, Frau, sit down. You'll grow weary of standing, I'm afraid."

Emilie sat, suddenly aware of the very small office, the two locked doors, and the smell of liquor. He did not speak for several minutes as he studied the slender legs in front of him. Emilie studied the floor.

"You are eager to see your husband."

She nodded.

"But, of course," he leaned back in his chair, exhaling loudly. "I had almost forgotten, you and Herr Farber have not been married long. How long exactly, Frau Farber?"

"Eight months."

"Newlyweds, ja, I understand," he winked. "Being apart, even for five short days has been difficult for both of you. You have been neglected."

Emilie felt the hated blush rising up her neck. She was too angry to speak. He came around his desk to lean against it, his arms crossed. When Emilie lifted her eyes, she was staring into the paunch that hung over his brown belt.

"Join me for a drink, Frau, while we wait?"

"No thank you, lieutenant. I'll be driving back into the city and I'll need a clear head."

"A clear head, of course," he nodded. "Still, you should join me for one small drink. It would help you relax. I can see you are tense. You want a clear head for your husband, but really, I don't think you should count on him being much . . . company for you tonight, Frau. Being the guest of the Gestapo can leave a man tired, do you understand?"

He thrust the metal cup he'd been drinking from in front of her.

"Really, I don't care for any. You see, I have that American dislike of schnapps," she smiled slightly, shrugging, and hoping she didn't sound tense.

"Ah . . . and I am a poor host that cannot offer you anything else."

Emilie was beginning to feel trapped in the small room. It was stifling with body odor, stale cigars, and schnapps. She glanced at her watch. Forty more minutes.

He chuckled. "So eager . . . ja, an eager bride for her groom!"

Emilie was sickened.

"If your husband finds he has not learned his lesson and comes back to see us, well, you would be very lonely, Emilie Farber. Ja, very lonely at night. You would need a man to take his place."

Emilie stood up, nearly running into him.

"I will wait for my husband in the car." She walked quickly to the exit. "Please unlock the door."

His voice was amused. "Why, Frau Farber! What is the matter? We were having such a nice friendly chat!"

"Bitte." She was grateful her coat concealed her trembling.

"I will unlock the door, but first you will kiss me. Two kisses, Frau. One for releasing your groom, one for unlocking the door. Only two."

She swung around, her eyes blazing. "I find your behavior disgusting! You have forgotten the fine traditions of Naziism you are sworn to uphold. You are acting like some brutish Russian cossack! You forget that I am the sister-in-law of lieutenant Eric Farber and Irwin Farber."

He turned red, his eyes bulged. He looked like he was going to cross the room and strike her. The inner door suddenly swung open, squeaking on its hinges like a special effect from a Boris Karloff movie. A guard entered with Max close behind him. The desk officer was fuming at the interruption.

After five days in a Gestapo prison, Emilie had not known what to expect. Max was always energetic, athletic, unblemished, and she wasn't prepared to see him any other way. She stepped back into the shadows of the room as he walked slowly to the officer's desk. His face was darkened with the beginnings of a brown beard, dark circles were under his eyes, beside his mouth was an angry-looking red welt. *His mouth . . .* She winced as her eyes met those of the desk lieutenant's. He was watching her, smirking.

"Behold your groom, Frau Farber!"

Max spun around with more energy than he had shown when he entered the room. Emilie stepped forward nervously. His eyes went over her quickly, but Emilie didn't mind his appraisal. She was shocked at the raspiness of his voice. "Emilie! Are you all right?"

She didn't miss the eagerness in his voice or the gladness in his eyes. *And he had asked about her*!

"Ja, I'm fine," she said softly.

"Herr Farber." The lieutenant's voice was sharp. Max turned reluctantly. The officer pushed the paper across the desk.

"You must sign this paper. I will summarize it for you. It says you were treated well in confinement and that you will submit to any Nazi orders given you. It says you will cease from any anti-state activities immediately upon release. It says you will cooperate fully with the Gestapo in any future investigations. And finally, you are not to leave Germany without permission of the Gestapo."

Emilie tensed. She knew Max well enough to know that these conditions were insufferable to him. *Surely he would argue or protest*, she thought worriedly.

He stood staring at the paper as if he had not heard.

"You understand, Herr Farber?" the lieutenant sneered.

"Perfectly," Max replied softly. He picked up the pen and quickly scratched his name.

The Nazi was drumming the pen against the desk, watching his prisoner with hawklike eyes.

"May I leave now?" Max asked again in a quiet voice.

He motioned to the guard to unlock the door. Max took Emilie's arm to lead her from the room. The lieutenant's voice stopped them.

"Herr Farber, if you are brought to the attention of the Gestapo again it will not go so gently with you—I can promise you that. It will not matter what your last name is or who your brothers are. Do you understand that, Herr Farber?"

Max nodded. "Perfectly."

● ● ●

The gentle melody of rain filled the car as they drove in silence. Max had slipped into the passenger side wordlessly. He leaned back and closed his eyes. Emilie felt more nervous now than she had in the Nazi lair. *Max must have been hurt deeply to be so, so unlike Max*, she thought. She was afraid. When they arrived at the hotel, Emilie finally spoke.

"Max, are you asleep?"

He smiled faintly. "No, not yet." He sat up. "Where are we?"

"I booked a hotel room . . . rather than having to start the long drive back to Berlin tonight."

He nodded.

Though she was ahead of him, she knew he climbed the stairs as if it were drawing off the last of his strength. In the hotel suite, she took off her coat and nervously faced him. She had never been nervous with Max before. He stood, slightly hunched, hands in his coat pockets, his eyes fixed on the fire.

"Max, are you all right? Are you hurt anywhere?"

He shook his head and stepped up to the fire. He stood that way for a full minute before he turned to her. She was surprised at the sadness in his eyes.

"This room is very nice." He managed a thin smile.

"Ja, see—it even has a small kitchen. I wasn't sure how long . . . before they released you."

"You look worried, Emilie. Do I look so horrible?"

"No, I . . ."

"How did you come to the prison?"

"Someone called Josef."

He sighed and turned back to the fire. Still he had not taken off his coat. "Thank you for coming for me, but you should not have taken the risk."

"It was no risk, Max. I—"

"With the Gestapo there is always a risk. You should not have put yourself in such danger. Knowing you were safe gave me a measure of peace in there. If I had known that you were coming . . ."

Another time she might have flared at the rebuke, but not tonight. She sat on the edge of the sofa watching him. How could he say he was all right and unhurt with such a look on his face and that tone in his voice?

"Are you hungry, Max? I have some soup warming."

He shook his head. "No...not tonight." He swung around to look at her. Their eyes met. Was he looking at her with tenderness?

"More than anything right now I'd like a long, hot bath," he said finally.

"I'll go draw it for you. And I'll fix you some hot schokolade to enjoy while you soak," she said cheerfully.

He nodded and continued to look at her, almost as if he had not really seen her before. She hurried into the bedroom and he followed her. She began the bath and Max stood looking out the window by the bed. Then he turned and took off his coat. Emilie stepped back into the bedroom as he was taking off his shirt. It was gray and blood-stained on the shoulder. He looked up at her as he pulled off his shoes and socks.

"I have some clean clothes laid out for you in the bathroom," she said.

"I'll leave all of these clothes in a pile. Take them and throw them away. Don't leave them here."

She nodded.

"You have blood on your shirt," she said, moving toward him.

"It's just a cut."

"Let me see," she said coming up to him. "Josef would be horrified if it got infected or something." He had a gunshot wound on one shoulder, and now this fresh wound.

Slowly, with effort, he peeled off the shirt. The cut ran across his neck and over his shoulder. He sat down on the chair tiredly. In the bedroom light she could see the welt that went along his jawline from his mouth. "I'll put something on your shoulder when you get out of the bath, all right?" she asked in a trembling voice.

He nodded and headed for the bathroom. Emilie hurried to the kitchen for the Schokolade. He should be in the bath by now. *How...should I take it in to him? Nonchalantly, as if taking in Schokolade to my husband in the bath was routine. I did tell him I'd bring it to him.*

The bathroom door was open slightly.

"Max? I have your Schokolade. Max?"

"Hmm?" His voice was very sleepy.

She stuck her head through the door. He was nearly submerged in the high white tub. His head was against the side and his eyes were closed. The clothes were in a pile.

"Here's the Schokolade." She drew up a stool to the side and sat the cup down, her eyes studiously avoiding the tub—and the man in it.

"Danke." he murmured.

She scooped up the clothes. "I'll check on you in awhile. You're just sleepy enough to drown."

● ● ●

He sat on the edge of the bed while she stood beside him bandaging his shoulder. He was weaving back and forth slightly with exhaustion. His hair was damp, his skin pink from scrubbing. Emilie felt his nearness in a way she never had before. The robe he wore was pushed down to the waist. His hair was blond and curly on his chest. *A strong-looking, tanned chest*, she noted and tried not to let her eyes wander.

She cleared her throat. "Max, I'm done with your shoulder." She placed a finger lightly on the welt on his face. "Does this still hurt?"

But Max had fallen asleep leaning against her. She could hear the deep evenness of his breath. Suddenly the strain of the evening was telling on her. Gently she laid him down in the bed and covered him. She stood looking at him. There against the pillow, asleep, he looked like the Max she knew—a man at peace.

But Emilie didn't have the ease of falling asleep as the man in the bedroom had. She lay on the sofa staring into the crumbling red embers and listening to the rain. She hoped the sound of the rain could somehow reach Max in his sleep and wash away the terrible things he had been through. She replayed the events of the night slowly in her mind.

His surprise at seeing her, a moment of gladness in his tired eyes, then the look of utter exhaustion and sadness as he stood by the fire. His words that he found peace in knowing she was safe, the look he had given her as if he were drinking her in with his eyes. His childlike dependence in her. Suddenly Emilie forgot Max Farber was a despised Nazi. There in the darkened living room, alone with the sound of fire and rain, it didn't matter.

It was a long time before Emilie Farber finally fell asleep, but not before she discovered she had fallen in love with her husband.

• • •

He stood in the doorway in his robe, his hair tousled. It was late afternoon the following day. He'd been asleep nearly fourteen hours. Emilie had stood beside the bed half a dozen times through the day to make sure he was all right. The same look of peace and calmness was on his face—like a boy sleeping with untroubled dreams. This must have been how he looked to Uncle Josef when he'd met the Farber heir as a child. She longed to touch him, but was afraid of waking him. *How would I explain my hand on his forehead or resting lightly on his chest?* she smiled to herself.

She looked up, startled, from the table where she was writing.

"Do you feel better, Max?" He didn't look much better to her though. The wound by his mouth was growing purple, his face looked gaunt under the beard.

He nodded and smiled slightly. "I'm half-starved."

"I'll have it ready in 15 minutes. Just sit."

He sat on the sofa, his bare legs stretched to the fire. She brought him the food on a tray. He sat up surprised.

"This looks great!"

"You think all I can do is snap pictures, Herr Farber?"

"No," he lowered his voice. "I know you can do a lot of things."

She sat beside him while he ate. Neither spoke. *I don't want him to talk if he isn't ready.* She frowned. *Maybe he doesn't feel he can talk openly with me.*

"That was very good, Emilie. Danke."

"There's more."

"No, I'm full."

He was staring into the fire.

"How does your shoulder feel?"

"Sore. I don't remember you bandaging it."

"You fell asleep while I played nurse. I suppose I could have done anything to you and you wouldn't have—" She turned red with embarrassment. "I could have performed an appendectomy and you wouldn't have felt it," she continued hurriedly.

He smiled and leaned back, closing his eyes. *Yes, the teasing Max was gone. This man . . .* She felt shaky around him. She studied his profile without shame. *Strong chin, high cheeks, long brown lashes.* While she preferred him clean-shaven, he was still handsome unkempt.

She spoke, imagining he could hear the beating of her heart. *Could he tell, if he looked, that I want to lean close and kiss him*? "Max, how did you get that cut on your jaw?"

He reached up to finger it, then rolled his head to face her.

"I think the British call it being cheeky. The SS goon that interrogated me had this riding crop he was fond of. When he didn't like what I said, he used it."

"Oh, Max, I'm sorry."

He was surprised at her tone. "It's all right. It doesn't hurt much now."

"It may scar."

He shrugged. "Another one."

"Like the one above your left eye," she said gently. She was telling him she had looked very closely at him. *Did he notice*?

But he had looked back to the fire. "Irwin and I had a few run ins when we were growing up."

Uncle Josef had told her there had been more than a few.

"Do you want to talk about what happened? If you don't, I understand."

Another deep sigh. "I can tell you what happened to me in that place Emilie. I can't tell you what I saw, and what I heard . . ." She thought he would say no more.

"The first two days I was kept in a cell with a guard. They didn't give me anything to eat or drink. They wouldn't let me sleep. When I'd start to doze off, the guard would kick me awake. The third day they took me to a room to ask me questions. That lasted most of the day. They gave me water for each question I would answer. The last two days they put me in another cell that had no light, no window. I did have some rodent companions. They made it a little difficult to sleep. Then today—or yesterday rather—they came and said I was to be released. It was not nearly as bad as it could have been."

After he had asked her a few questions about Josef, they lapsed into silence. Then he was yawning.

"Thank you for the Schokolade last night. I do remember that part. You were pampering me."

"You're welcome, Max."

She said his name so softly that he turned to look at her. The room was dim and shadowy. The smoothness of her cheeks and neck... Something warned him he should not say this, but he ignored it.

"When I saw you in the lieutenant's office," he hesitated.

This Max was so different... or was this the real Max? She felt pulled by his words. She leaned a little closer.

"Ja?"

His eyes swept her face. "I was surprised that you were there. But I thought you were the most beautiful woman I had ever seen."

Time seem suspended. *One kiss?*

She saw a frown pass over his face. *What has he suddenly remembered? Something I said about our marriage arrangement?* He ran his hand across his face. "I think I'll go shave and go to bed."

They both stood. She gathered up the dishes.

"I can take the couch tonight," he said.

"No, really, I'm fine there. You need another good night's rest."

"Are you sure?"

She was hurrying to the kitchen. "Uh huh . . ."

"Well . . . Gute Nacht, Emilie."

"Gute Nacht."

● ● ●

The storm clouds had finally dissolved over Southern Germany. The allied bombers could find their targets now: the lights of Berlin. Just before midnight, they came over, two dozen flying in perfect formation, the ground defenses caught unprepared. Emilie awoke as the first bombs fell. She was disoriented at first. Where was she? What was happening? Distant rumbles . . . Planes? She sat up and went to the window. Nothing. The sounds of thunder seemed to be coming closer. She hurried into the darkened bedroom. Max was already standing at the window that faced the center of the city. His arms were crossed. She went to stand beside him.

"Max?"

He didn't turn. "The Allies. The fuehrer said this would never happen." His voice was almost angry-sounding to Emilie.

They could see searchlights cutting arcs in the blackness. "Should we go to a shelter?"

"No, they seem to be hanging over the industrial section. I don't think we need to worry. Are you afraid?"

Standing there with him tall and strong beside me, how could I be afraid? she thought as she shook her head. "No, it just frightened me when I woke up to it."

They watched for several minutes.

"I think that's about it," Max sighed. "Goebbels will have some explaining to do in the morning."

He turned. They were facing each other. She had forgotten to grab her robe. The white smoothness of her skin seemed to shine. He could smell some pleasant scent. *His ... wife.* He stepped back.

She walked to the door, paused, then turned to face him.

"Max," Emilie's voice was shaky. "Max, I don't want to be alone tonight. I'm afraid—not of the planes ... but of being alone."

He spread his hands out, silent.

"Tonight I'm your wife," she said as she took one step toward him. She reached out for his arm.

His voice was shaky too. "You will ... make me forget things I shouldn't forget."

She ran her fingers lightly across the line of his jaw. Tentatively he reached out and touched her shoulder. She drew closer and laid her cheek against his chest. It was warm. She smiled to herself, she could feel his heart racing. His hands were in her hair as she lifted her face to him. The kiss lasted until Emilie was breathless.

"My husband," she murmured, "we will forget together."

25
Before Night Falls

Nuremberg, Summer 1940

Nothing had changed about the old city that Wilhelm could see as he stepped off the train. Was he glad or disappointed? He couldn't tell, the flood of memories was too strong. Five years had changed him though. Since the SS had such an active interest in him, he had bought a cheap hair coloring and darkened his hair. He'd put the wire-frame glasses back on. It wasn't much of a disguise, so he walked through his old haunts a little nervously. He didn't want to be recognized. Like the streets of Berlin, a young man not in German uniform could cause unwanted speculation, so he was very careful. He walked past the university, his old apartment building, ja, the narrow streets were the same. He approached Handel's cautiously, peering into a shop window across the street as he watched in the glass. The same tables, the dark, green-striped awning. He held his breath as the rotund Handel appeared from the back, carrying a tray and chatting with a table of patrons. Wilhelm watched him. He had been a trusted friend ... still, he should just turn and walk away. But the feeling of total separation, of wanting to make some contact with his past, pulled him across the street. He slipped into a chair, burying his face in a paper.

Handel greeted him, took his order, and didn't recognize him. Wilhelm, like a young boy, was pleased. He sipped his beer and ate the bratwurst and thought how odd it was to not have a recognized past. *I could start over. Start over doing what*? He had mulled this over from Berlin to Nuremberg. He had thought of many things and decided on none. He lingered over his meal, ordering a second beer while the lunch crowd waned. Finally, he was alone with Handel.

"This bratwurst is pretty good, but my mother always made better. You don't put in enough spices."

Wilhelm looked innocently at his plate. He had always teased the owner with this complaint in the years he had worked for him. Handel's eyes widened. He started to speak, and Wilhelm shook his head. The big man looked like a sausage about to burst.

"How's business?" Wilhelm asked casually.

"Good, good." Handel was gaping as if Wilhelm had walked back from the grave. He lowered his voice and kept sweeping. "We thought they had gotten you."

Wilhelm asked about several of his friends and, with reluctance, of Widerstand.

"The SS broke it all up. There has been no resistance in the city since . . . Then Simon was taken to a . . . camp, I heard."

Wilhelm winced.

"You know about . . . Herschel?"

Wilhelm nodded.

Handel took the empty plate. "You look well, Wilhelm. But you could be recognized again. They would not care that five years has passed. They wanted the author of those leaflets very badly."

"They didn't rough you up anymore?"

He laughed. "They like Handel's beer and bratwurst too much!" He peered at the young man, his smile fading. "What are your plans?"

"I don't know yet," Wilhelm admitted reluctantly.

"You should not stay in Nuremberg. Can't you go home?"

Wilhelm stood up, tossing his money on the table.

"I have to find out about someone. Auf Wiedersehen Handel."

● ● ●

By nightfall he found what he had come for. Sitting on a darkened bench in the square, he felt sickened. He had expected the worse; he had found it. He stood across the street from the rabbi's house. It looked exactly the same—until a German officer and his pretty blonde wife emerged through the doors. With a sudden heaviness he made discreet inquiries. The old rabbi had been taken by the SS when they purged Nuremberg. He was last seen in the back of an open truck full of Jews. They most likely were taken to the camps. That had been over three years ago. He was probably dead.

The woman who owned the bookstore looked at Wilhelm with touching concern.

"You saw them take him?" Wilhelm asked.

"Ja, I remember. Rabbi Bergmann had such nice white hair."

"What about the young girl, his granddaughter? Was she taken at the same time?" He didn't realize he was holding his breath.

The woman was puzzled. "No, I didn't see the young girl. Perhaps they came for her earlier or later. One tries not to watch . . ."

"Maybe they didn't take her," Wilhelm mused aloud. "What about the housekeeper? Did you see her?"

A man passed on the street outside. The woman frowned.

"Do not ask me any more questions. Please be on your way, young man.

• • •

It had been a very warm afternoon, without a breath of wind, so Emilie was grateful when sunset came and a slight breeze drifted up from the river like a whisper. Max had arrived at the estate just at dinner, joining Emilie and Josef at the table with a cheerful greeting. Emilie watched him at the head of the table, across the expanse of white linen and crystal, as he teased and told amusing stories until Josef was doing more laughing than eating. She smiled to herself. Her husband had a talent for relaxing a person or situation with his charm and wit. *Her husband . . . She mused to herself. What would Bess think of their arrangement that moved along with a current of courtesy and detached companionship . . . and nothing more?*

"Emilie found the river very cold when she went swimming this afternoon," Josef was saying. "Percy didn't mind the temperature, though."

"Hmm . . ." Max commented. He observed his wife with seemingly indifferent glances—except he was aware that her hair was piled up like it had been the night of the party when Heydrich had assaulted her. That night when she had worn the blue dress that was so. . . .

"I noticed the lights were on at the Heydrich estate when I drove by. They're probably here for the weekend." He took a drink of his wine. "If Reinhard happens to go rowing and you happen to go swimming I'd imagine he'll say something about finding a mermaid in the River Spree," Max smiled.

But Emilie was in a world of her own thoughts.

"Emilie?" Josef asked.

"Oh. Excuse me, what?"

Max repeated his comment.

Emilie felt a little annoyed. Why did Max persist in this continual reference to her and Heydrich?

"It would be nice if it rained tomorrow, wouldn't it? Everything is so dry," she replied.

Max smiled and returned to his meal.

"Reinhard was over this afternoon," Josef inserted blandly.

Max looked up, his fork in midair.

"He came over to present his congratulations to Frau Farber." Josef looked up at the ceiling. "He's turned out to be such a big tall man after being such a skinny little runt of a baby," Josef laughed. "He always looks so smug, as if he's about to devour something."

"Which explains why he's risen so high in the SS," Emilie added. She and Josef laughed together, but Max was not laughing and not smiling.

He was trying to appear disinterested. He was really irritated with himself that he had brought up Heydrich's name. But he was far more irritated that he had not been home when the Nazi officer came calling on Emilie. Of course Heydrich came without his wife—of course he came when Max was absent. Max downed his wine.

"If you'll excuse me, I have a headache," he bowed to them and left the room.

Josef watched him leave, frowning.

"Your husband appears to be a little piqued."

Emilie squirmed at the word husband.

"Herr Heydrich seems to always put him in a sour mood. Living side-by-side . . . has it always been this way, Uncle Josef?"

Josef nodded. "There was trouble when they were boys. Reinhard was aggressive even then."

Emilie's tone was haughty. "Max should control his emotions. He's a grown man after all. Heydrich can't snatch his toys away."

Josef gave her a long look. "No, not his toys. But I suspect my friend doesn't like the devouring look his wife receives from this old nemesis."

Emilie gave a nervous laugh. "You mean like jealousy? No, I don't think so. Max would be indifferent to something like that."

"You really think so?" Josef commented quietly.

• • •

It was just before midnight. Emilie awoke from a dreamless sleep. She lay there a moment, perfectly still, wondering what had disturbed her sleep. The room was quiet, a river of moonlight pouring in through the open balcony doors. She pushed herself up in the huge bed. *This had happened so many nights . . . since that night.* She would fall asleep only to waken in the middle of the night, restless, wide awake, unable to drift easily back to sleep. *I am sleeping alone in this big bed in this big room in this big house, while Max sleeps alone in his big bed in his big room down the hall.* She propped up her knees and leaned her chin on them, thinking. *Have I mistaken my own feelings? Were they artificial in a sweep of passion? Did I mistake the tenderness in his eyes and touch?* She had asked herself these questions a hundred times since that night in the hotel in Munich.

He had been gone the next morning with only the briefest note saying he had important business. A very impersonal note . . . when she had wanted so much more. He had not even whispered that he loved her. It had been over a week before he appeared again, cheerful and friendly— as if that night had never happened between them. They went back to their platonic relationship, their arrangement. That was all he wanted. She felt a hurt she had not felt since Will Cutler—but this was worse.

Then she heard it and realized this was what had tugged her from sleep. *Music. Music was coming from somewhere downstairs.* She paused. She had listened to her newest Glenn Miller record on the player in the grand ballroom earlier in the evening. *Did I leave it on by accident?* She went to the balcony. She could hear the music clearer. It was not the record player. She grabbed a robe and, barefoot, slipped down the stairs of the great Farber house.

• • •

She pushed open the huge gilded door of the ballroom, stopping in the shadows. Max sat at the piano with a single tall candle. His back was to her. He finished playing the music she had listened to earlier—the new Miller tune, "Moonlight Serenade." She was shocked. He had apparently been listening from the library and, hearing it once, had picked it up perfectly. He followed with another piece, classical—and also very well done. He played for nearly 30 minutes without stopping. Emilie stood pressed against the gilded wall. Then he stopped abruptly, hunching over the keys as if in pain or sadness. Emilie instantly forgot her earlier irritation. *Something was wrong... with her husband.*

"Max?" she said softly.

He swung around as if touched with electricity and stood up.

She was surprised with his appearance. He was always so carefully groomed, but tonight his white shirt was untucked, his hair was tousled.

"I heard the music and thought perhaps I'd left the phonograph on. What were you playing? It was very beautiful."

"'Schubert's Serenade.' I'm sorry I woke you."

"I'm not sorry. It's the first time I've ever heard you play. It was beautiful. Josef told me how good you are."

He turned as if uncertain, running his hand along the smooth black wood of the grand piano.

"Why don't you play more often?"

It took him so long to answer she thought he hadn't heard her. His face in profile was inscrutable, except to express that he was upset. "Playing brings so many memories. It has been a long time... since anyone told me I... could."

"Well, you could make new memories if you played for me."

He turned and looked at her. He looked past her where the moonlight poured in through the French doors. *The moonlight wrapped itself around her in a shimmering veil. She looks like she looked the other night—when I should not have looked.*

"You were picking out Miller's 'Moonlight Serenade.' I could put it on... and we could dance."

He looked away, shaking his head.

Emilie had vowed to herself she would not make a move toward him as she had before. He must come to her, assure her that it was mutual. "Max, I'm sorry if you were upset about Herr Heydrich coming over this afternoon."

He looked down at the tile floor.

Her voice was light. "He is an arrogant man, nothing more. Power has gone to his head. He—"

"You have forgotten that night, Emilie? He will not stop till he has you. His marriage vows mean nothing to him nor do yours."

His voice was cold and hard.

"Well, what can he do, sling me over his shoulder in some abduction?" she returned lightly. She studied his face. "Would you care if he did, Max?"

He gripped her by the shoulders. "Do not talk that way."

"Max, why . . ."

He knew instantly what her words meant. He drew a steadying breath. "That . . . night . . . I am flesh and blood—"

"So am I. I'm not too proud to admit it stings a little to wake up and find yourself abandoned."

He pulled her against his chest. "I did not abandon you," he said hoarsely. "I simply had urgent affairs I had to deal with. Being in prison for several days left some things undone. I—"

"What kind of urgent affairs?"

"Party business. But, Emilie, we made an agreement and, I think, for the time, while . . . while things are so uncertain in our country we must . . ."

She stepped back. "I think I understand what you're saying, Herr Farber. Forgive me for interrupting you. Gute Nacht, Max."

I've lost Josef's respect. Now I'm losing her love just to keep her safe. Does this mission have to have such a high personal cost? he agonized.

"Emilie, wait—"

At that moment, Rudi stepped into the hall. Magda was behind him weeping, and outside the sound of a car on the gravel drive brought with it swinging lights into the house as the headlights shown in the window.

Rudi gave a swift look at Emilie, then to Max.

"It's Heydrich. He's come for the Muellers."

• • •

Heydrich's posture was one of a conquering general—cool, composed, confident—as he stood in the bright hallway of the Farber manor. At just after one in the morning, he wore his impeccable black uniform and knee boots. He took off his hat, his hair gleaming under the chandelier. They all seemed struck mute.

"Darling, did you forget to tell me you invited Reinhard over for light refreshment?" Max said with amusement as he leaned against the balustrade.

Emilie couldn't find any words, stunned by Heydrich's appearance on their doorstep and Max's word of endearment.

Max shrugged and yawned. "I think she meant one in the afternoon. Lena could have come with you then," he stated to Reinhard.

Heydrich did not smile. "This is not a social call, Max."

Max's tone took on a chilly tenor. "No? Well, I hope then there's a good reason for waking us up."

The officer pointed at Max. "You sleep like that, Max?"

"You woke my household, Reinhard."

Heydrich had known Emilie was in the hallway, but since this was business he had given her only the briefest look. He allowed himself a longer look. Max gritted his teeth. Emilie felt exposed in her gown and robe, but couldn't leave with this tempest brewing.

"My apologies, Frau Farber."

"What's this about, Reinhard?" Max asked curtly.

"This is about harboring Jews in your household."

"There are no Jews in my household," Max replied evenly.

"Heinz Mueller, his wife Marta, his son Walther, his daughter Maria. They are all on your property and are your servants. They are Jews. I have come for them."

"Your information is wrong this time, Reinhard. The Mueller's have been here for years—you know that. They are Christians."

Reinhard shook his head. "They are Jews. I have known this for some time, and I have overlooked it for the sake ... for my friendship with Irwin. Walther Mueller was apprehended tonight. He admitted his family is Jewish."

Max turned to Emilie. "I think you'd better go back upstairs, bitte."

She clutched his arm, ignoring Heydrich's leering, appealing to Max with eloquent eyes.

Two SS officers emerged from the back of the house, pushing the three Mueller's before him. Heinz met eyes with Max and smiled.

"Are you a Jew, old man?" Reinhard asked sharply.

Under the harsh lighting, he looked old and frail to Max. He would not survive long at a camp. Young Maria had terror clearly etched across her face. Marta struggled against tears. Max looked away.

"Ja, I am a Jew. I am a completed Jew. Do you know what that is, young man?" he asked the tall officer.

"I do not care what a completed Jew is. Jewish lice is Jewish lice."

Heinz appeared to not have heard. His voice was clear and ringing. "My family and I are proud of our Jewish heritage. But we have seen the light that is God's only Son, Jesus Christ. We believe in God the Father. We believe in His Son who died for the sins of the world. We belong to Him. We are in His hand, and nothing can snatch us out."

Reinhard smiled. "Danke, Herr Mueller, for this little education. It appears you have educated your employer after these many years."

"As I said, I didn't know they were Jewish," Max said tiredly.

"What do you plan to do with them, Herr Heydrich?" Emilie asked.

"They will be sent to Berlin until they can be moved to a camp."

"But you see, you ... know they have been a part of my husband's family for many, many years. They are like family," Emilie continued.

"Family, Frau Farber?" He shook his head, chuckling. "A Farber would not have a Jew in his family. You understand this since you are now a woman of the reich and a Farber, ja?"

"Ja, I understand."

He nodded.

Heydrich nodded at the officers.

"Max, please do something," Emilie appealed again.

Everyone in the hall looked to the young man still lounging at the rail. Rudi, the Muellers, Emilie, Reinhard, the SS officers. Josef stood at the head of the stairs.

Max yawned deeply. "I understand your sentiment, darling, I really do, but Reinhard is right."

The officers pushed the Muellers through the open front door into the night. Max started up the stairs.

"Next time, could you conduct your business at a more suitable hour, Reinhard?" He reached out and took Emilie's hand. "Gute Nacht."

The door closed and Rudi locked it. The cars could be heard down the drive. Then the summer night became quiet and ordinary again.

Emilie wrenched her hand free from Max.

"You can't be serious!"

"Emilie, please—"

"Not 'darling' now?"

Max turned, looking down at Rudi who waited.

"Rudi," he said simply, and the young man moved down the hall.

"Max, this is abominable. As Emilie says, you must do something," Josef said coming down the stairs.

Emilie looked triumphant.

"I'm sorry this woke you, Josef."

"Never mind that, Max. You can't let them take the Muellers away!"

"Josef, there is nothing I can do. He is within the law—"

"Law! Ha!"

Max sagged against the rail. "Look, I know it is . . . hard. But they admitted they are Jews. I can't change that."

"What has happened to us, Max?" Josef whispered hoarsely.

"Josef, please . . ."

Emilie was crying. "You could . . . have paid him. You have enough money. You could have tried that. How can you let this happen to someone who has served you like that?"

He looked at her a long time, not caring that Josef stood nearby. She was very beautiful to him. He looked without shame. Somehow he knew, this was the last long look of her he would have. Like a blind man about to lose his sight, he looked.

"I do understand . . . but Reinhard would not have taken my money. There was no point in offering it. That is not what he wants." He reached out and ran a finger along her cheek, surprised she didn't pull away.

"Remember that I am sorry, Emilie."

He slowly climbed the stairs to his room.

Nuremberg

Wilhelm found that his old skills of survival had only been dormant in those years in the States. Back in Nuremberg, he fell into the old routines of streetlife—living day-to-day, uncertain where his next meal would come from, looking over his shoulder, sustained by nervous energy. And sustained by the hope that somehow Natalie Bergmann had survived the Nuremberg liquidation and was still alive. In his mind, she represented the best of Germany and she must live! He had to find her or find out what had happened to her. Then he could figure out what his future in the Third Reich was supposed to be. He had gone to the woman at the bookstore because it was near the rabbi's house and because the rabbi had once said this neighborhood was very kind and unimpressed with Adolf Hitler. But the woman was clearly afraid, caught in the struggle between heart and mind. So Wilhelm racked his own brain to try to remember the housekeeper's last name. If he could find her, surely she would know where the young girl was. Sitting on a bench in the square he remembered how it had been that last summer, their one day alone together, her happiness at being out of the confining house. Five years. Suddenly he sat upright. Five years! He wasn't looking for a girl of 16. She was 21 now. He called himself a dummkoft and hopped off the bench. If she had escaped and concealed her Jewishness....No, she would have left the city. But he could not really see her as a young woman of 21 making decisions, living this hidden life that he led—she had been so sheltered. How could one like that survive? At that moment, Wilhelm felt such despair he was tempted to give up. Then he remembered Hilda's boasting of the best store in Nuremberg to buy food fit for the rabbi's table. He moved quickly down the street.

● ● ●

With the last of his money he bought his information. He would beg, borrow, or steal to get to his next destination. The clerk was very happy to answer his questions for a few marks. "Of course I remember the rabbi's housekeeper," he said wagging his head. "She was punctual and at the store as it opened each Friday. She was a little imperious at times, discriminating, but always generous with her approval." The little man shrugged and grinned, looking up at Wilhelm with a confidential wink, he noted that he had overlooked that she was employed by a Jew. Business was business no matter what Goebbels said.

"Do you recall her last name?"

He stroked a grizzled chin. "Let's see . . ."

"The old rabbi was taken away of course," Wilhelm said in a bland tone.

"Ja, ja, so I heard."

"Where did Frau Hilda go, have you seen her in Nuremberg?" he asked eagerly.

"Oh, no. I remember that very well. She came in to say goodbye and to thank me for such fine produce and said it had been a pleasure—"

"Where was she going?" Wilhelm demanded.

"Hmm... she was upset, very agitated. She said that she was going to her sister's in... in... was it Munich? Or Berlin? Hmm... no, no it was Munich."

"And her name? Her name!" Wilhelm was leaning over the counter. The old man's eyes sparkled. "You are very eager for Frau Hilda," he laughed.

"Ja, I am. Now, please, think of her last name."

More chin stroking. Wilhelm slammed the money on the counter.

"There is no more."

"Wiesner. Ja, that was it, Weisner."

Wilhelm hurried to the door.

But the man kept on talking as if Wilhelm had not moved.

"I hated to see Frau Weisner leave, ja, ja. She was one of my best customers. But she said it was best for her granddaughter. She was ill—"

Wilhelm's hand froze on the doorknob. He swung around.

"Her granddaughter? You said she was alone!"

The old man looked offended at Wilhelm's tone.

"I never said that. You didn't ask me if she was alone. Her granddaughter stood right where you are, looking pale and ill. Yes, Frau Weisner wanted to take her to a doctor in Munich. She was a pretty thing, just stood there twisting a violin case in her hands. Very sad, ja."

• • •

Emilie felt listless and drained when she awoke the next morning, dully staring up at the ceiling, trying to comprehend what had happened only hours earlier. *If only it had been a dream, a nightmare. Reinhard looking so triumphant, Maria Mueller so afraid, and Max so indifferent.* Her mind swung back to the ballroom: *Max playing the piano, then looking like he might take me in his arms...* She dressed quickly and hurried downstairs. The ballroom door was closed.

She opened it, stepped in, closed it, and stood where she had the night before. The vast room was empty save for the piano and the candle, looking empty and lifeless as if the music had never been played, as if this room had been closed for years—that she had not stood here and tried to tell her husband what was in her heart. And she had failed...

She went to the French doors that looked out on the garden and opened them, letting in the morning freshness. *Heinz's garden, his prize. How had he spent the early hours of the morning while his master slept so comfortably in his grand house?* Emilie felt the shock reassert herself. In all the things she thought about Max, she had never thought he could stoop so low. *Apparently Nazism has infected him as deeply as it has Heydrich....*

The house was so quiet, so tomblike. Suddenly, unexplainably she felt like she was in the big house alone. She jogged back up the stairs to see if Josef was ready to take breakfast with her on the patio. They could console each other, think together of how they could help the Muellers—and how they could remain in the house with such a despicable man. She found his room empty. She looked across the hall at Max's room. Could Josef be in there trying to persuade him to action? She knocked. Nothing. She took a deep breath and turned the knob. If Max were in there she would confront him—no matter what he looked like or what he said.

She called to him, but the room was empty and the private bath was empty. She stood in the middle of the room, looking at her husband's bedroom for the first time. *A large cherry wood bed, smoothly made without a wrinkle. Had the servants already cleaned the room?* Her eyes swept the room. The clothes he had been wearing the night before were crumpled in a heap on the floor. *No maid would leave that... He had not slept in his bed.* She raced downstairs.

Still not a sound or movement. She paused before the closed library door. She knocked and received no summons. She entered. Her heart was pounding. She pulled back the heavy drapes, pale sunlight filling the room, giving it life. Everything seemed as it always did when she saw this room: book-lined walls, athletic trophies, burgundy leather furniture. She sat behind the desk.

"What are you doing Emilie?" she asked herself out loud, startled at the sound of her own voice.

Instinctively she knew Max was not in the house. *He had to have gone to rescue the Muellers! Yet...* A strange, coldness gripped her instead of relief and gladness. *The thing I wanted him to do, he has done, but wouldn't that mean...* Her eyes fell on the bottom drawer that had been hastily closed, yet something was caught. She reached down and opened it: *A scarlet wool cap.* She held it up. *For a child. Why would Max...* The edge was frayed, threads dangling free. She peered into the drawer again and pulled out a drawing pad. *Someone had scrawled a picture of the old German flag...*

● ● ●

Max could feel the weight of marks and gold that he had hurriedly stuffed into his pockets from his personal safe that he kept filled for such a contingency as this. In another pocket, the heavy revolver bumped against his chest also reminding him if money failed... He had left the house as quickly as he could dress, giving quick instructions to Rudi, and slipping away into the darkness. He could catch up to the SS van as it reached the suburbs of Berlin if he pushed his Mercedes to the limit. If he had rightly guessed, and his midnight raid was a success, he would return home, leaving the Muellers to his subordinates. Max drove and tried to form a plan. There was little time to plot this raid. *Spontaneous. Should I seek help from other sympathizers or act out this dangerous plan by myself? If it failed, it would fall on me alone....*

From past experience and contacts he knew where the Muellers would be taken first: SS headquarters. He considered it an advantage that it was very early in the morning. The officers on duty would be too tired to interrogate and be content to let the Muellers wait in a cell until morning for processing. Max parked at the corner watching as they unloaded the van. He turned away as they shoved Heinz to the ground and laughed. He counted them. *Ten. Too many.* He drove quickly to his house. He ran up the stairs to his bedroom and slipped into the smart black uniform of the SS. As he pulled on the officer's hat with the mirror-shiny brim, he knew he was putting on this ruse for a final performance. He was counting on the lethargy of the guards on duty—and the likelihood they had only heard of the high-and-mighty Heydrich and not encountered him personally. He slipped on the personal lapel pin that only the highest SS officer could wear.

He swept into the office in the same way he had seen Heydrich only hours earlier in his home. The four men jumped to attention in a fashion that made Max smile coldly. He snapped his leather gloves against his arm, pulling off his hat to study himself in the brim. Then he looked at them slowly, scathingly.

"The Jews you just brought in, have they been put into a detention cell?"

"Ja, ja, Herr Heydrich."

"Good, because when I called to inform you they were coming, you sounded distinctly . . . sleepy."

The men looked at each other then at the floor.

"It would be the most serious offense if you were lax in respect to your duty. Has Herr Himmler been called?"

"No, sir, we did not think for three Jews—and it being the middle of the night."

"Just be sure you keep thinking!" Max snapped irritably. "That is why I left my home to come here. To make absolutely certain this Jewish filth does not escape. I want them, do you understand?"

"Ja, ja."

"You have heard of these rescues of Jewish lice by someone posing as an SS officer? That will not happen again! It will not happen in my SS. Do you know what would happen to the men who allowed that to happen? Do you?" He was nearly screaming.

"Sir?"

"I will tell you—and you may tell anyone else. If anymore Jews escape those who were on watch shall be treated as Jewish lice. Is that perfectly clear?"

They nodded in unison.

"Now bring them out. Tell them Heydrich will see them!"

Another gamble. I only hope young Maria will not inadvertently give me away, he thought nervously.

They were shoved into the room, squinting in the bright light. Max stood rigid, unsmiling, his hands behind his back.

"Squinting like rats brought from the sewer into the light!" he laughed and the guards joined him.

The Muellers' eyes widened.

"You look so surprised that I, Herr Heydrich, would personally come to see after your comfort. Well . . ." He turned to the guards. "Get a car ready immediately. We are going to move our little rats in the middle of the night. There will be no rescues with Heydrich in charge. Now move!"

They were bound and placed in the backseat of a car. Max took two of the SS guards and rode in the front. He directed them out of town. "Pull over!" he commanded sharply.

"Now," he pulled out his gun, "step out of the car, gentlemen.."

"What?" they exclaimed.

"What is the matter, Herr—you are not Herr Heydrich?"

Max laughed and shook his head. "My finger is already ticklish on this gun, please don't insult me."

He motioned Maria from the car. "Hold the gun on them, young woman, while I tie them up. Shoot if they make one little move."

"You will hang for this, Jew-lover," one of the officers spat.

Max laughed again as he tied him up. "Not before you, sir, not before you."

He stuffed a little scrap of red-tied paper in one officer's mouth.

● ● ●

Emilie burst through the kitchen door, causing Rudi and his wife to look up, their coffee cups held in midair.

Rudi stood slowly. "Frau Farber, are you all right?"

"Where's my husband? Where's Josef?"

"Your uncle took Percy for a walk down by the river. He has not come back," Rudi answered.

"And Max?"

"He went out this morning."

"He never went to bed, Rudi," she continued bluntly.

Rudi looked at his wife, then at the table.

"Ja, he went out very early."

"Where?"

"I do not know, Frau Farber."

"Could I please see you in the library, Rudi? Please excuse us, Magda."

Rudi stood nervously at attention as Emilie closed the door and went to Max's desk.

"I think you know exactly where Max is."

He said nothing.

Her composure was breaking. "I found this." She held up the cap and drawing pad. "Rudi . . ."

She stood before him and he looked away.

"Please, Rudi, tell me."

But he was mute.

"Rudi, you do not need to feel like you are betraying Max's confidence." Her voice was shaking. "He has gone after the Muellers, to try to rescue them . . . out of . . . Heydrich's grasp. He is this . . . man who has been in disguise and rescuing Jews while leaving a paper with the German flag tied in a scarlet thread. He has . . ." she choked. "He has been posing, pretending . . ." She slumped in a nearby chair at the power of her own words.

Rudi stood watching her.

After several moments she looked up at him.

"When they took him the first time, and held him in Munich, it was true—he was trying to pass information to the British."

Rudi's voice was soft. "Ja, it is true. He had contact with Churchill himself. . . . He was trying to save Jews, and he was trying to warn the Allies. He was going between the two, killing himself with exhaustion. I have never seen such a brave man . . . a man who did not have to be brave."

"What can I do?" she whispered. "Heydrich will . . ." she began to cry.

"He told me before he left last night, if I did not hear from him by this afternoon I was to take Magda and try for Holland. And I . . ."

She looked up, searching his face. "He gave you a message for me?"

"He was afraid that if he is caught, Heydrich will suspect all of us and will try to exact revenge. He would . . . Max thought Heydrich would . . . press you to become his mistress in exchange for safety for yourself and the doctor. He has your papers all ready if, as he said, you were willing. He is very afraid for you and the doctor."

"You don't know where he is or how he planned to rescue the Muellers?" she asked hoarsely.

Rudi shook his head. "He would not tell me."

He left her alone then. She closed her eyes a moment before she ran outside, calling for her uncle.

Berlin

Emilie wasn't sure how long her uncle could continue under this strain and tension. The Gestapo never appeared to question her and Heydrich never called. Rudi and Magda went into hiding, but Rudi refused to leave Germany until he knew what had happened to Max. But it seemed as if Max himself had left Germany. There was no word, no news.

Josef had aged in the week since Max had disappeared. He saw no patients. He ate only sparingly. He read or sat in the window seat in the library, hoping to see Max come jauntily down the street, whistling for Percy. So the days passed for Emilie in a dual agony: concern for her uncle and fear for Max.

"How did I . . . How could I have ever doubted him, Emilie? How?" Josef had asked a dozen times. "I've known him since he was a boy! Such a good lad in spite of everything around him. Honorable and decent and kind. How could I think he would really believe in this Nazi madness?" He bowed his head and sobbed. "He always thought those who loved him would betray him . . . and I did! Oh, Max . . ."

"He will come back and we can make him understand how we feel," Emilie soothed.

"But will he forgive us?" Josef cried.

Emilie didn't have an answer for that.

On a rainy morning at the end of the week, the front doorbell shattered their silence. They looked at each other in an alloy of fear and hope. But it wasn't Max who stood there. Wilhelm Mueller waited on the steps.

Emilie smiled tiredly. "The first time you appeared on my steps, you looked much happier and confident, Wilhelm."

"I felt much happier," he admitted.

"Please come in."

He stepped into the foyer, twisting a cloth cap. They looked at each other a moment, then started to speak at the same time. They laughed a little nervously.

"You have heard—I hope I don't have to be the one to tell you about your parents," Emilie said.

He nodded. "Ja, I heard what happened. But they are safe, so—"

"Safe?" She clutched his arm. "What have you heard? We only know they were taken."

"You do not know? They are safely in Switzerland—except... Walther. He was sent to a camp."

"Who told you this, Wilhelm?"

"I went to the Farber estate last night to see my parents again. One of the servants told me what had happened, about the night Heydrich came and what Herr Farber did."

"The servant, what did he look like?" she asked with a pounding heart.

"An older man, dark hair. He was washing the windows. He told me they were safe in Switzerland. I asked him, of course, how he knew all of this and he smiled. He didn't answer but said perhaps their house held some clue. I ran in there and looked. I found this. When I went back to the main house, he was gone. I couldn't find a trace of him."

She knew what he would pull out of his pocket. *A scrap of paper tied with scarlet thread. He was alive...*

"Are you all right, Emilie?"

She told him everything—including why she had married Max Farber the summer before.

"He saved my family," Wilhelm said with wonder.

"Yes, and at least 30 others."

"He is saving the honor of Germany."

She fell to crying again. "We don't know if he is... if they captured him or . . ."

He knelt behind her. "He is safe then, Emilie. He doesn't approach you for fear the Gestapo or SS may be watching the house. I'll watch my tail when I leave."

"Where are you going, Wilhelm?"

"I'm going to Munich to try to find an old friend."

"Something in the way you say that makes me think this old friend is a girl," Emilie smiled through her tears.

"Ja, it is so. I hope I can find her and that she is safe."

"You are in danger yourself—a young man on the street not in a uniform."

"I am very careful."

"You must need money. I will give you some before you leave. What will you do after you find her?"

"I don't know, Emilie. I just know I have to try to help my people however I can. If Herr Farber can risk so much when he is not a Jew, can I do less?"

"Oh, Wilhelm . . ." She reached out to hold him. "Those days in Washington were so long ago, so innocent . . ."

He held her tightly. "And I will treasure them always, Emilie Morgan Farber. Can you forgive me for what I did?"

"Oh, Wilhelm, I forgive you."

He held her a moment more then pulled away.

"Herr Farber is a very fortunate man. You love him deeply?"

She nodded. "I didn't know how much."

"He is a good man."

"The best—everything I treasure."

"I think someday when the madness is over we will see each other again. I look forward to that day, Emilie."

• • •

Eric looked very tired. He stood in Max's library looking out over Tiergarten. Finally he turned, gazing at the old doctor and his brother's young wife in silence a moment. Before he said a word, he noted how Emilie looked pale and sad. He didn't know she had said goodbye to a friend only a few hours earlier. A wet gray fog descended on the city as the street lights blinked to life.

"Max was arrested this afternoon as he tried to leave the city," he said finally.

Emilie felt a sudden hollowness in her stomach. She sank down into a chair. Josef stood beside her.

"It will be all right Emilie, Max is strong," Josef said.

"He's being held at Gestapo headquarters, but he'll be moved to Tegel, outside the city in the morning. For now, Tegel is for political prisoners. That may change of course if Tegel fills up," Eric reported quietly.

"Fills up with innocent men," Emilie whispered.

"Tegel isn't a hotel certainly, but it isn't a camp either. I know the man who is in charge. He is thorough, he likes . . . his work. It won't be comfortable or easy for Max, but he's strong—stronger than Irwin or I." His voice swelled. "Max is stronger than any man I know!" he said with pride.

Emilie wiped her tears. "Eric? You . . . love Max?"

His eyes filled instantly. "It has taken me years to find out just how much . . . I love my brother."

She clutched his hands. "Oh, Eric, if he only knew! If you could tell him it would mean so much. He's locked away not knowing how much two people love him!"

His eyes searched her face. "Two?"

She reddened and looked to her lap. He cleared his throat.

"Emilie, the Gestapo and I have talked, off the record. They had to question me about Max of course. Everyone is suspect. I tried to convince them you knew nothing about what Max what was doing."

"I didn't, really."

"They still want to question you. You must convince them you know nothing. Whole families disappear when one is indicted if they aren't careful. And I don't know how much . . . pull I have if they really suspect you. Very little, most likely."

"She will not have to lie," Josef spoke up. "Neither of us knew what Max was doing. I wish we had."

"Couldn't Irwin help Max?" Emilie pleaded.

"Could or would?"

"Eric, what can I do? How can we help Max?"

He shook his head.

"Eric don't! There has to be something we can do."

"It's a Nazi prison," he said without turning. "There's nothing we can do but hope."

Emilie leaned forward thinking. Suddenly she stood up, her eyes brightened, her voice eager. "Will be sent! He hasn't been moved yet?"

Eric turned slowly.

"Eric, tell me please. You know—"

"Emilie, this isn't easy."

"You have connections."

"Connections?" he smiled sadly.

"Please, Eric, please. I have to see Max. I have to tell him how I feel. He has to know! Please!"

"Emilie, if you show up at the prison and are spotted by the Gestapo, they will pick you up."

"Eric, you said yourself they'll find me sooner or later. If they see me, so be it. I have to see Max. You understand, don't you?"

"Emilie, this is dangerous. This isn't a cheap thriller movie that's over in two hours."

"I know that, Eric. My husband is going to prison! I saw what they did to him last time. Please!"

He sighed. She took his hand, her eyes pleading.

"Be at the prison, the east gate, tomorrow just before 11—not too soon. I'll arrange for you to see Max—"

"I must have the chance to speak to him, Eric."

He smiled. "Max has not apprised me of your stubborn streak, Frau Farber. Well . . . the guards can be bribed if there aren't any high officers around. You'll have only a few moments Emilie, that's all. You won't see me, but I'll have a car waiting. You can speak through the fence. You'll follow my directions completely, right?"

She put her arms around him. "Thank you, Eric, thank you."

● ● ●

Emilie was swept by a wave of weakness that sent her slumping to the bed. She felt chilled, she felt feverish. *What a time to come down with the flu*, she moaned. She knew if Eric Farber or Josef saw her at this moment they'd insist she was too ill to go to the prison to see her husband. She was afraid—the dizziness and nausea had come suddenly after a restless night. *My nerves must be completely shot*, she reasoned. *Get a hold of yourself, Emilie!*' But the self-admonition failed. Her fear did not revolve around the menacing shadow of the Gestapo, she gave them little thought. It was the fear that she would not get to see and speak to Max, that he would be swallowed by Tegel. She didn't trust that the prison director would be benign or accommodating to family members when an enemy had entered the depths of the jail. She spent the morning pacing her small bedroom and being physically sick in the bathroom.

By midmorning a slow, steady rain was falling. Her anxiety increased. Could the rain change the Gestapo plans for transferring prisoners? Only one more hour. She went to the bedroom mirror.

"I look horrible!" she groaned aloud. Dark circles under her eyes accented the stark white of her face. She cringed. *How can I go to Max looking like this!*

She closed her eyes and allowed herself the comfort of remembering that night, remembering the look of surprise and gentleness on his face when she'd told him she didn't want to be alone. *Her husband... Her husband now a prisoner of the dreaded Gestapo.*

Eric had said she'd have no more than two or three minutes. *How can I tell him in such a small time the volume of feeling in my heart? And that I have misjudged him? I must apologize and tell him he is noble, and courageous—and everything I want in a husband!*

So much to say to him... and only three words that mattered most.

• • •

The rain had washed the skies clean; it was now unruffled blue over the German capital. For a time, the war was forgotten as scandal gripped the city. Maximillian Farber had been arrested by the Gestapo for treason! The son of a wealthy German patriot, descendent in a long line of military heroes. What had gone wrong with this young man?

Max felt a calmness that surprised him. The long months of nerve-racking activity, the secret trips, the indifferent posturing, the scorn and disappointment, the pretending. It was finally over, and it had come to this hour. He looked out at the magnificent blue sky from the car and smiled. The Muellers and the others were safe and free. He had done something and only regretted that he hadn't done more.

"How does it feel to be a traitor to the German reich, Herr Farber? You are smiling this morning."

"Ja, it is a beautiful morning," Max replied.

"You will not think it so beautiful from the barred window of Tegel," the Gestapo guard sneered.

"No, it will be more precious to me then," Max returned calmly.

"You and your charades, playing dress up! Did you not think the Gestapo would finally track you down! You had both the SS and Gestapo after you. A hefty price on your head and Herr Beck collects it! I have heard you were a foolish, silly, immature man—an embarrassment to your family. And riding around with a dog for a companion!" He shook his head in disgust.

"Did you say Herr Beck?" Max asked calmly.

But the guard was silently staring out the window.

• • •

Emilie waited in the car that Eric had sent. It was parked in a small area beside the prison where tradesmen and prison staff parked. A high, barred fence would separate her from him—but she would see him. She would see him!

Her stomach knotted as a open army truck pulled up and six men were unloaded and moved toward the prison. Ragged, thin, and searching with their eyes for some hope. Men who only days before had their own life and future and dignity. Max wasn't there. "I'll pray for them as well as Max," she whispered to herself. Emilie found herself crying. *Max* . . . At the appointed moment a car pulled up. She watched. They opened the door and Max stepped out.

She leaned forward. He wore dark pants and a white shirt that was untucked. His hands were shackled in front of him. He stopped a moment and she saw him look up at the sky. Then the guard prodded him toward the entrance with his rifle. Shaking, she stepped from the car and moved toward the fence.

The movement caught his eye and he saw her. His steps slowed only a minute. She could see he was surprised. He was coming closer. *You will have very little time, Emilie. A bruise is coming up on his face*, she noted sadly.

"Herr Farber . . ." she said.

His voice was very low. "Frau Farber . . ."

He wanted to turn away. How could he look at something so lovely, and be denied?

"You should not have come. It is too dangerous," he whispered.

She was looking at the ground, sobbing quietly. This was not the way she had planned for it to go.

"Please, don't cry. Please, he said gently."

"Josef sends you his love . . . and to tell you how proud he is of you. And Eric . . . he . . ."

The guard shouted to him. "Farber! Move along!"

"Danke, Emilie."

The guard came up to him. "I said move along, Farber, that's enough!"

He smiled at her. "Perhaps one day we will dance to your American music. What was it called?"

Her voice was a whisper. "Moonlight Serenade."

"Moonlight Serenade." He looked past her a moment. "I have memorized the sky, ja, but I wish I had more time to memorize your face." He turned away from the fence.

"Max!" Everything was in the word. He whirled around. Pushing past the guard, not caring if he felt the piercing shock of the gun muzzle in his back. Her face appealed to him.

"Max, I came to tell you ... Max, I love you so much!"

His look was incredulous and would stay with her forever.

"What?"

The guard was cursing and pulling Max roughly by the arm.

"I said I love you, Max!"

His fingers touched her through the fence for only a fleeting moment, his voice soft, "Emilie ..."

● ● ●

Emilie was sitting on the river bank. Max loved this land and river now clothed in the drab garments of winter. He'd spent pleasant hours here. She felt close to him here. Even now she couldn't think of him in prison—it would not intrude on her thoughts for these first moments. She knew Max would want her to be reveling in her happiness. An hour later it grew too cold to sit out any longer, the late afternoon shadows were purple and lengthening. She brushed off her skirt and headed back to the house, Percy at her side. Josef had been watching for her.

"Magda has dinner ready," he said linking his arm in hers.

He smiled. "You look so lovely this afternoon, Frau Farber."

"Danke, Herr Morgan."

Rudi joined them on the terrace. The Gestapo and SS had dropped their investigation of the Farber household. Emilie speculated bribes must have been exchanged. They had captured the highest prize when they arrested Max.

"You look so ... bright, Frau Farber. Is there ... good news of Herr Max?"

"No, no—not directly." She laughed suddenly. "Well, yes, directly but nothing of his time in prison."

Rudi stopped walking and peered at her. Clearly he was confused by her words. He looked to the doctor who was smiling and tugging at his chin.

"Don't mind me, Rudi, I'm ... I'm a little giddy." She smiled, then shrugged at something in the distance.

"Giddy?" He pondered the unfamiliar word. "Over the news?"

"Hmm ..." she returned absently.

Now he shrugged. "Magda and I take this as good news, also. Hard for Germany true, but good in the end we believe."

"Yes, Rudi? What news?"

He blinked rapidly. "You spoke of news that made you happy, giddy? I thought . . ." Again he looked to Josef.

"You know? How?" Emilie asked.

"The radio. There has been nothing else all afternoon. Hitler has been screaming about it!"

Emilie started to laugh. "Oh, Rudi, I thought . . . well, never mind. We're talking about two different things, I think. What is your news?"

"You have not heard? Magda and I, thought that it might help Herr Max—"

"We haven't heard, Rudi," Emilie replied hurriedly, suddenly feeling a little frightened. "What has happened?"

"The Japanese bombed the Americans at Pearl Harbor in Hawaii. President Roosevelt has declared war on Germany! Hitler is very angry!"

America joined in the war!

"Frau Farber, are you all right? You are shocked?"

But Frau Emilie Farber was hardly listening to Max's friend and aide. His news was dramatic, but still it paled by the news she hugged to her heart. She smiled, looking to the house where the man she had so suddenly fallen in love with had spent his childhood, even if it hadn't been a happy childhood in many ways.

Her hand went instinctively to her stomach. Their child would love this house. War and shadows . . . still their child would be happy.

Afterword

I'd like to share with you some of what I've felt and thought about during this writing process. It isn't easy reading about the years of Nazi terror. It's like reading the post mortem of a civilization. But it has always been a fascinating story. How could a highly civilized nation regress to such savagery and barbarism? Could it happen again? Are there any parallels between those tragic years and our own times?

From the shadows of evil come the wonderful and inspiring stories of men and women such as Raoul Wallenberg, Oskar Schindler, Corrie ten Boom, Andre Trocme, the Scholl siblings, Dietrich Bonhoeffer, and many others. There were hundreds who resisted Nazism—often to the point of death. Some are remembered, some are forgotten, some remain nameless like the Polish man who, for three years, fed and cared for Jews hiding in the sewer beneath the streets of a German city.

The story of the rise and reign of the Nazi government is so much more than just Hitler and his company of rogues. It is also the story of the impotence of the surrounding European countries, the isolationist-policy of the United States, the apathy of the German people, and the compromises of the Christian church.

In writing fiction, an author sometimes has to exercise a little creative liberty with history. For instance, I know that the beginnings of the Nazi party—the beer hall pusch where Hitler took leadership with one vote—took place in Munich and not Berlin. There may be a few other changes but I have tried to remain true to the facts. If further reading about the Nazi years interests you, the absolute best book of the many I've read is *The Rise and Fall of the Third Reich* by William Shirer. It is well written, easy to understand, and very interesting. (It also could be a great doorstop or weapon in a pinch. Don't be intimidated by its size!)

I hope you enjoyed *Before Night Falls*. The story of Max and Emilie, Wilhelm, and Natalie continues in book two of the Legacy of Honor series.

—MaryAnn Minatra

Harvest House Publishers

For the Best in Inspirational Fiction

Lori Wick

A PLACE CALLED HOME

A Place Called Home
A Song for Silas
The Long Road Home
A Gathering of Memories

THE CALIFORNIANS

Whatever Tomorrow Brings
As Time Goes By
Sean Donovan
Donovan's Daughter

KENSINGTON CHRONICLES

The Hawk and the Jewel
Wings of the Morning
Who Brings Forth the Wind
The Knight and the Dove

ROCKY MOUNTAIN MEMORIES

Where the Wild Rose Blooms
Whispers of Moonlight

CONTEMPORARY FICTION

Sophie's Heart

MaryAnn Minatra

THE ALCOTT LEGACY

The Tapestry
The Masterpiece
The Heirloom

Lisa Samson

THE HIGHLANDERS

The Highlander and His Lady
The Legend of Robin Brodie
The Temptation of Aaron Campbell

THE ABBEY

Conquered Heart

Ellen Gunderson Traylor

BIBLICAL NOVELS

Esther
Joseph
Joshua
Moses
Samson
Jerusalem—the City of God